RAZZMATAZZ

RAZZMATAZZ

A NOVEL BY PHILIP D. WHEATON

EVEREST HOUSE PUBLISHERS

NEW YORK

Library of Congress Cataloging in Publication Data:

Wheaton, Philip D., 1916–
    Razzmatazz: a novel.
    I. Title.
PZ4.W554Raz   [PS3573.H413]   813'.54   80-12978
ISBN: 0-89696-097-8

Published simultaneously in Canada by
Beaverbooks, Pickering, Ontario
Manufactured in the United States of America
Designed by Joyce Cameron Weston
2FG1180

To Amy

RAZZMATAZZ

CHAPTER ONE

··

WHEN I LOOK BACK AT THE SUMMER OF 1938, MORE THAN FORTY years ago, and the unfolding of its extraordinary events, I see it as a turning point in my life, one that arrived at the early age of twelve. It was a turning point for Penny, too. She was my sister, sixteen, and she knew a lot more, but it was not easier.

In June of that year, when our parents were killed in an automobile accident, Penny and I went east to Eastfield in Connecticut to live with Uncle Lambot and Aunt Addie. It took us almost three days on the train from Des Moines, and it was like going from nowhere to nowhere. I remember that I hoped the in-between would last forever. Penny said that three days was not even a hummingbird spit in time. I asked how she knew how long a hummingbird spit was, and she replied, "Willie, dear Willie" and let it go at that.

When I was six or seven and identifying emotions, I had hated my sister. Now that I was twelve, Penny was my whole world, and when she selected a book from her bag of books and transferred herself with a flip of a page into another world, which I could not enter, I cried.

I cried to myself for almost an hour on the train, and wondered how I could go on living. I wanted to tell Penny how I felt, but she would have suggested that a good cry could be a delicious moment in life and that I ought to make the most of it.

To look at Penny you would never have known that our parents had died but a few days ago, and that Granny Winston had passed away two months before. Penny was the same as always, a mite in a navy blue skirt, a white middy blouse, and a book, her all-year costume. A limp, inert mass at the moment, shapeless, with an Iowa cornfield flatness to her body both fore and aft. She had a pudgy, pale face that wore a permanent benign smirk, readying for a smile, but not always making it. She had anybody's brown eyes, a small nose that rabbit-wrinkled, and teeth begging for a brace. Her brown hair was straight, cut short, and had no style at all. She looked twelve, my age. Actually she was sixteen, going on sixty.

I remember that trip east as well as I remember anything else. From that time on I think I remember everything that ever happened to me; what I remember before that time is spotty at best. The first memory I have of almost anything is that of my father sticking a shaving brush full of lather into my mouth because I called Mother a son-of-a-bitch. I didn't know what that meant and I was only repeating what Father had been fond of calling Mother, but he stabbed me with the brush all the same.

The biography of my father is short and blurred. He was a book salesman. That is to say, he traveled, representing publishing houses in New York, Chicago, and Des Moines. He traveled west to Seattle and down to San Francisco. It was neither here nor there with me when he was gone. He was full of loud, smutty blather, red-faced from drinking, and forever with a foul cigar in his mouth. If I had had a choice in the matter, I could have picked a better father with all my senses yet unborn, but I will say this for him, he did know how to make money. He had massive wads of it way up to here. Penny, who always knew ten times as much as I did about anything, said that it came from alcohol in the twenties and heroin in the thirties, that book selling was a cover-up. Be that as it may, if he actually did make his money selling books, you would have thought that everybody on both sides of the Rockies was trying to read everything in print before the advent of the millennium, which was due six hours the day before yesterday.

We never really knew him as a father, or even as a human being for that matter, someone who could give succor or deliverance, someone you could like and dislike, love and hate, obey and disobey. Mother was from Des Moines. Father had met her at college before he flunked out. Father couldn't bring her back to Eastfield to live while he worked at the Winston Mills (someday maybe to become the boss) because he'd flunked out of there several times, before, during, and after he flunked out of college. Just why was a forgotten family secret, one among many family secrets that were arousing curiosities, Penny's more than mine, because she was older and born Miss Curiosity. Mother was an only daughter, and, like Father, forever a spoiled brat. She did not like the East, easterners—with the exception of Granny Winston—or Eastfield. She detested her sister-in-law, Aunt Addie, and thought Uncle Lambot was dull. She had no desire to become part of the Winston family to live in frayed gentility, in togetherness, down on the farm. In no time at all, she went home to her parents in Des Moines, dragging Father along. That was not too difficult to do as Father was *persona non grata* at the mill and thus about town. Besides, Mother's family was well-to-do, and money was always a powerful attraction for Father. Just before Penny was born, Grandpa Winston, who had cancer and business and marital troubles, had taken his life by hanging himself on a beam in the barn on the farm in Eastfield, and Granny Winston went west to take care of the new baby. Granny Winston was supposed to remain there only a few weeks, but she had no desire to return east alone to live forever where her husband had done himself in. And she had no desire to leave her favorite son, unprotected in the wild, wild West, so there she stayed. And if all that was not enough to keep her there, she developed a friendship with Father's father-in-law that was a cause for divorce, deceit, and instability. Penny was born soon after they all moved from Eastfield, and Penny thought there was something fluky about that. She didn't know exactly what it was, as our elders were not inclined to talk about entanglements, but she was intrigued with the notion that she was the real reason the family moved west, a fact covered by a convenient rearrangement of Mother's and Father's wedding date in history. Penny had a spell of using the word *fluky* to explain the unexplainable, and she said our parents were fluky people. I remember once I asked what fluky meant, and she said, Go look it up in a dictionary. I did and found that a fluke was some kind of fish, and I told her. Penny laughed and said that was good, because there was something fishy about the Winston family, always had been, and always would be if somebody didn't do something about it. Penny said the word also meant "accidental," and that's why she used the word to describe our parents, because everything about them was accidental. At least so it seemed.

Father was away for more than half of each year, which was all right with Mother, because when he was home they argued and blessed each other with all sorts of crude insults, usually joining in battle five minutes after Father returned from some tour of duty. These sorties frightened me terribly when I was old enough to know they weren't play, but Penny wondered and marveled, and she watched and smirked at our parents as if the whole show was worth the price of a dozen scalper's tickets. Why they didn't part company, I'll never know. Penny said they grew into an arrangement that let them do things they could not otherwise do. Whatever it was, from my vantage point as a child, adult life seemed horribly complicated, and they could keep it as far as I was concerned.

Our mother traveled, too. The Lord only knew where she went, but she traveled. All her fibbing about being with Father had no more strength of conviction than the whir in the wings of a dying bumblebee. Sometimes she would leave us for a week, or even two. Penny said there were men involved, enough to staff the Minneapolis Symphony, that Mother was a nympho, that the odds were ten to one we had different fathers, that Mother was the main reason Father was so fond of other women, all of which didn't make much sense to me. I will say this for Mother, she didn't just leave us without putting some kind of salve on her conscience. She told the butcher, the baker, and the candlestick maker that Granny Winston was taking care of us. That was, of course, so much barley wash. Granny Winston had a stroke three and a half years before she died. Her left side was paralyzed, and it was a rare occasion when she could speak more than two or three words coherently. But Mother played the game with aces to spare. She had an excuse for every time she played hooky. Penny told me she invented them to protect her present, that she had no mind about our future.

I came along four years after Penny, and if Penny was born some kind of bastard, I wasn't treated too differently, because our mother wasn't the type to hug and cuddle babies. She wasn't that bad to me, but I had that gut feeling that Mother never really cared for me the way everybody says mothers are supposed to care. I felt that I was some kind of hindrance to what she wanted out of life. In a way, that wasn't too bad, because she more or less left me alone. But it wasn't too good either. Now my memory of Mother is nothing more than a collage of nauseating impressions—the smell of whiskey and cigarettes, tight dresses and bleached hair. Opportunism and cold calculations: Life tells me that there was more to her than that, but I can't remember. Not even her face.

At home, Granny Winston was the closest thing that Penny and I had that we could call love. However, I did not feel earth-shaking love for a sickly old woman in bed. I do not remember her as the tall, stalwart woman she must have been. I see in my mind's eye only her white hair, her ghostly pale face on her bed, and the old paisley shawl she constantly fingered with her right hand, like a kid with a security blanket. But she was there, we knew it, and she was doing something for us. And that, I supposed, was giving love.

Granny Winston spent the last year of her life in bed. It was a difficult household at best, and not made easier when our parents were gone and Penny was in command. Penny became the chief nurse and bottle washer for Granny Winston, but her chief chore was reading to the old lady—everything from Aristotle to the mating of zebras. Poetry, philosophy, religion, politics, history, biology— anything under decent cover. When Penny gave the slightest indication she did not understand, Granny Winston insisted upon a second or third reading. Penny talked with her, and for her, taking both ends of the conversation. Even now I remember the reading hours with awe, and sometimes with fascination. Penny would say something. Then she would watch Granny Winston for a reaction—a furrowing of the brow, a twitch of the nose, maybe nothing more than a few tears that limned her eyes. They were the signs through which Penny learned what was in the old lady's mind and heart. Then Penny would reply to her own remarks as if she were Granny Winston talking, saying things beyond her years and even her understanding. Granny Winston, who could have heard a pin drop on the floor of the ocean, reacted to every nuance in every syllable of Penny's words. She frowned when Penny talked stupidly and smiled when Penny talked intelligently. She approved or disapproved with the bat of an eyelash. Knowing that she was soon to die, she acted as if she were transferring life's accumulation of wit and wisdom into Penny's brain for storage and future use. Life with Granny was a trial for Penny, but she was sixty percent ham, and she managed. This kind of tutoring gave Penny an incredible verbal ability beyond her years, a kind that could sometimes startle fitful elders.

Besides taking care of Granny Winston, Penny was chief cook and keeper of the keys. She ran our household, not well, but she ran it, and her first impulse after the accident was to keep it in operation.

Penny did not fight the facts of life, though. She knew there were laws and anxious, worried kin. Penny said we'd live with Aunt Harriet instead of with Aunt Addie, that Aunt Harriet would spoil us rotten, and we bubbled at the prospect. But even that idea died as it was born. Aunt Harriet was not of our blood. She was one of a passle of pseudorelatives we had garnered on our summer trips to Eastfield, which was something we both endured, because calling people Aunt and Uncle, who were not, entitled them to remember us at Christmas and on birthdays when our parents sometimes didn't. There were times when even Penny knew how to strike the proper sentimental pose. But Aunt Addie, who was our real aunt, would not have stood for it. Aunt Harriet was not what Aunt Addie considered due and proper influence, despite her being a member of Aunt Addie's exclusive club of the female powers-that-be, the Friday

Club. Aunt Addie was the law, one that even Penny, with all her worldly ways, yielded to on occasion.

But Penny was firm on a few points. Over the long distance, she told Aunt Addie in polite but certain terms that neither she nor Uncle Lambot were to traipse halfway across the country to go to a silly old funeral for a couple of relatives they didn't give a tinker's dam about except that they were objects of disapproval and scorn, and that we were quite capable of going east without a chaperone. After all, we had been going east each summer by ourselves since Penny was nine. We could do it, and when we were on the train headed east, Uncle Lambot was on another headed west to sell the house, talk with lawyers, and otherwise settle the affairs of a wayward brother. We would have waited for him, except we wanted to go it alone. So Penny told Aunt Addie that we would fluster the poor devil out of hell if we were under foot, and although Uncle Lambot in all his life never got more flustered than a half-dead toad, Aunt Addie relented.

So we up and left. Each of us carried a suitcase full of dirty favorite clothing, and trinkets we didn't need. Penny carried her diary, which she had shared with Granny Winston, but with no one else, not even me. She wrote in it constantly and I suspected it contained fantastic pronouncements, but I never questioned. Life was easier that way. Penny also carried a bag of books. And money.

Neatly folded among the pages of her two dozen or so books were some eight hundred dollars. We found this nest egg stashed away under the guest towels in the linen closet back in Des Moines, and Penny figured we had better not share the goodies. "When they count the rest, we'll be able to buy half of Eastfield, I suspect," she said, "but it is another thing to have pin money you don't have to beg for." So we kept that secret to ourselves.

"What are you reading?" I asked after a while. Not that I cared.

"Candide," Penny said. "By Voltaire."

I grunted.

"French," she said.

I grunted again.

"You ought to read it," Penny replied. "It makes Saturday afternoon at the movies tame. It's about this man who falls in love with a beautiful girl, and from then on all is catastrophe. All the nasty tricks the world ever dreamed of are played on them. But it doesn't matter for all is for the best."

"Ugh," I muttered.

Penny sighed. "Willie, dear Willie, don't you see?"

"See what?"

Penny didn't answer. She sighed again and returned to her reading. I closed my eyes and counted the clickety-clacks.

But it was not long before Penny opened up again. As we left Chicago, she sparred with our immediate past. We had drifted into the dining car, where Penny commanded and got service as if she were the Duchess of Windsor and I were the Duke, and then we ambled into an adjoining car, where we flopped into a couple of lounge chairs. The car was empty except for a young woman with a baby in her arms, and all the time Penny talked I noted her staring at them.

"Willie, dear Willie," Penny began, as she assumed her customary curl in the chair and casually began to emote. "Candide had a teacher by the name of Pangloss, and do you know what he said?"

"Who's Candide?" I asked.

"I just told you!" Penny said. She tapped her book. "Him. The young Frenchman who went to hell before he died. Pangloss said all was for the best in this best of all possible worlds. What do you think?"

I said nothing and waited for Penny to answer her own question, as she so often had with Granny Winston. "Some day when we are old and gray, Father William," she continued, "we shall be living together in the old house in Eastfield, as brother and sister, after we have lived in hell, which is going to commence damn soon. Our visit is not temporary. We are permanent now, and we shall live out our lives just as Uncle Lambot and Aunt Addie are doing. We are going east to take their places. I can feel it in my bones. That is our fate, the fate of our family, and there is nothing we can do about it. It's all for the best. What do you think about that happy prospect?"

"Not bad for you," I said. "As you always say, 'Aunt Addie rules the roost.'"

Penny thought about that for a while and said, "Oh, but she doesn't. She rules in that tiny little island called the house, and that's all. Know why? That's all that's been spared her. The rest of the world belongs to Uncle Lambot and she's given no part of it. That's not the way I want it, Willie."

"I don't get it."

"You get it. I don't. You get the outside. I only get the inside. I want the outside, even in Eastfield, and I have a right to the outside as much as you." Then before I could say "I don't get it" again, Penny put her feet on the edge of her chair, wrapped her arms about her legs, and sighed as if dismissing it all. "You think about it, and it won't be too bad, at least for a while. That peculiar brother-sister combination we have inherited may have advantages."

I thought about that and agreed. Uncle Lambot and his sister, Aunt Addie, living together as though they were husband and wife for all I could see, seemed about a hundred years old to me, not quite of the human race. Aunt Addie could scratch our backs the wrong way on the hour with her do's and don't's, and Uncle Lambot was crackpottish, but we knew them to be dependable, and we knew that we were not taking a trip into the impossible. As a matter of fact, it had dawned on us when we heard of the accident that something worse could have happened to us, and at first the only thing we wondered about was how Mother and Father happened to be going somewhere together. Penny later said that was about as unlikely a happening as Franklin Roosevelt and Herbert Hoover going fishing together on the Rapidan four days prior to the Bank Holiday in 1933. I had not the slightest idea what she was talking about, except that I saw her eavesdropping on Father's lawyer who said that at the funeral. I didn't tell Penny though. She did not take kindly to reminders that her adult originality was sometimes part of someone else's mind.

Luck or not, the closer we got to Eastfield the less we liked the idea.

"We're people, Willie, two out of a hundred and fifty million Americans. Two out of the two billions on earth. Maybe two out of trillions in the universe. What percentage point? I want to be some-body in this world, not one of the nobodies in Eastfield, where women, like kids, are seen but not heard, except at Saturday night church suppers. The best of all possible worlds. Ugh!" She sounded like an old-maid school teacher, positive, and slightly absurd.

Let her talk, I thought, I've heard all this before, but at least she won't be reading. Penny shifted gears in her seat. "Remember Granny's favorite poem?" she asked, then acting as if the parlor car were full of passengers, she recited, " 'My name is Ozymandias, king of kings: Look on my works, ye Mighty, and despair!' Nothing be-side remains." I remembered. I had heard that poem a hundred times. "Kids!" Penny grunted as if she were swearing.

"So?"

"I suppose we'll have to go to that dinky school in Eastfield this fall. The intellectual stimulation and competition there is one tenth of a hummingbird spit," Penny said, and this time I didn't ask how much that was.

"If there was ever a stupid law, that one with the twenty-one years of age jazz before one is labeled an adult is a dilly," she continued. "Why couldn't it be eighteen when one is able to accept full and free responsibility for one's self?"

"Or sixteen."

"Or twelve. I would rather have your vote, your decision on life than that of either of our parents. What a team! They dedicated their lives to foolishness and got a big fat bonus for work beyond the call. Do you think they were happy?"

"Doesn't matter now," I said. "What's happy?"

"I'm not sure I know," Penny said, surprised. "I read once that happy people are never satisfied. But neither are unhappy people. I don't know. 'My name is Ozymandias, king of kings: Look on my works, ye Mighty, and despair. Nothing beside remains.' What was Ozymandias, happy or not? Two days before the accident, I heard the craziest conversation in the locker room at school. You can't imagine."

"I can't imagine," I said, which was gospel truth.

"Seniors, about to graduate. Before long they will be twenty-one, and thus wise men who will run, rule, and ruin the world as men do," Penny said. Then she fumed. "Men!" she scoffed. She could have said, "Bastard," and the word would have sounded the same. "They had to read that sonnet by Shelley, and they didn't have a scintilla of a notion what it was all about."

I didn't ask what a scintilla was, and I didn't care. I looked out the window and tried to get lost in the passing scenery.

"I explained the sonnet to them," Penny said, "and they still couldn't see why it might be good to know about it."

"Neither do I," I said.

"Our parents," Penny replied, linking her arm into mine. "Everything in the world continues to whirl as if they never were, and it isn't going to be long before they aren't even a memory. Now do you see what it means?"

I shook my head negative.

"We could finish our lives in ten seconds by jumping off the rear of this rickety old train. If we did, so what? Know what I mean?"

Penny had this thing going about life and death all the time. I could only take so much of it. I felt a trickle of a sniffle building in my nose. "Forget it," I said.

Penny squeezed my hand. "Sorry, Willie," she said softly, and then she tossed me a sop. "I didn't tell you what else the boys in the locker room said to me when I finished. 'Ozymandias, kiss my razzmatazz.' There's a thought for you. 'Ozymandias, kiss my razzmatazz.' Like that?"

I rather did. I immediately suspected that we might be saying that a lot this summer, like a password that could be our own special link to each other. I only grunted, however, and asked Penny what she was doing in the boys' locker room in the first place.

"I heard them shouting about that poem, and naturally I'm an authority on it," Penny said.

"Naturally," I agreed. "And on everything."

"I know, Willie. Sometimes I want to thumb my nose at the world, stick my tongue out at it, and then kick its ass," Penny said. "When was the last time you really had fun?"

I had no answer. I stared out the window.

"Remember Miss Sprague, my Freshman English teacher? She assigned us two books to read for the whole year. Imagine! But she was magnanimous about it all. She said we could read more for extra credit. Know how many I read?"

"Fifty-two," I answered drearily. I knew that story backwards and forwards and up and down the side of the barn. Penny decided to read a book a week for a year, and make reports on all of them. With Granny Winston to listen to her read, she finished them in half that time.

"Good boy!" Penny said. "I gave Miss Sprague the whole kit and kaboodle of them in a shopping bag and she gave me a lot of lip. She asked what did I take her for? She said she couldn't even read that many books in such a short time, that there were things in some of those books I was too young to know about. I asked her what did she want me to do, cut out some of my brain? Old Smith heard about it, and he said he couldn't wait until I was in his class." Penny paused and sighed, and when she did, she sounded like Uncle Lambot. "Remember when Granny could talk how she used to say everything is connected to everything, the knee bone to the thigh bone to the hip bone? Everything. Remember?"

"I remember."

"Do you know what she meant?"

"Nope."

"Think about it. Did you ever hear of Logan Pearsall Smith?"

"Is he Mr. Smith, the English teacher?"

"No. He's one of Granny's favorite writers. Once he wrote that some people were born in this world to do its work and win its prizes, and some are simply to look and see what happens. And when these people meet each other they are shamed."

"So?"

Penny pounded the window sill. Obviously I should have known.

"Nothing, Willie. I only wonder who is going to feel shamed when our granny meets our parents out in the great beyond. Makes you ponder and think about yourself, and what kind of person you are going to be. That's what about our mother and father. I wonder if the first group were all he's and the second she's?"

I didn't have to strain for comment because Penny decided to visit the other passengers in the parlor car, the young mother and her baby. She returned after a half hour or so, her face flushed with some new discovery.

"She reminds me of Hilda Nason," Penny said. Hilda Nason lived in Eastfield with her crazy parents, her mother occupying the house and her father the barn. Aunt Addie called them in-bred and trashy. Without bothering to explain, that meant, Keep away from them. I more or less did. Penny more or less didn't. She thought the Nason family exciting. I didn't. I thought Hilda and her parents were batty and not at all bright. I didn't know Hilda very well, but well enough to see there was no resemblance between the young mother and Hilda. Hilda *was* trashy, and a pain in the neck to boot.

"Don't look like Hilda to me," I said. "She looks nice."

"Hilda's nice, too," Penny said. "Not bad at all once you get to know her. What I mean is that I could talk with that mother like I can with Hilda. About life, with no holds barred."

"Sex," I said.

"Sex," Penny echoed. "Like what's it like having babies, and does she love her husband, and did they want this baby, and does she like being married, and who runs the show."

"Junk," I said.

"Maybe," Penny said. She sat back, relaxing, with her hands behind her head. "I held the baby in my arms, Willie. Know something? I never held a baby before in all my life."

"So?"

"So I liked it. Warm and cuddly and sweet smelling. That girl is only eighteen, and she has a baby. I envy her. I really do."

"Nuts."

"According to Shelley, I guess it doesn't matter. In the end, there's nothing. But when I was holding her, I wondered if she was born to win the world's prizes, or is she just to look at, and wash dishes and clothes all her life. When I have babies, I wonder which they will be."

"If," I said.

"I can have them now. I want a baby the worst way. I do, I really do."

"Crap."

Penny had a sudden thought. "Know what, Willie? I might just try my luck this summer. See if I can find somebody to help me make a baby. If I had a baby, I would love it as no baby has ever been loved before. Maybe I'll shoot for twins or triplets. What do you think of that?"

I shivered at the notion.

"It's worth thinking about," she said.

"I don't want to think about anything."

"Well, I do. The summer and all the rest of life is going to be dull and dreary if we don't do something about it. Now. Making a baby could change all that. Imagine, Willie! Me, a Winston, sweet sixteen and haven't been kissed, having a baby without a husband in little old Eastfield!"

Penny knew that in Aunt Addie's world—and for us that meant

most of Eastfield—you didn't talk about anything connected with sex. You didn't use the word. You didn't spell it. Not even backwards. Even at twelve, I knew that.

"Not a bad idea when you think of it," Penny said.

"A lousy idea! Double lousy!"

"But Willie, can't you hear all the yakking when word gets around that I'm having a baby! Be a lot more fun than forever playing the game of minding your p's and q's with Aunt Addie. Got to do something this summer, or we'll go dippy."

"Of all the dumb things, that is the dippiest."

"Maybe not. At least I'm going to do some heavy thinking about it. I'm going to find me a baby to hug and hold and love. Making a baby is making a miracle, Willie, did you ever think of that?"

I said nothing. She was only yakking for the sake of yakking, giving vent to her own misgivings about the summer. It was best not to disturb her. Penny and I were an odd couple. I was tall, physically matured beyond my years. Penny had not yet been afflicted with enough adolescent growth to make anyone blink an eyelash, and she looked like anybody's kid sister. Even my kid sister, which a lot of people called her. But she was much older than I, even though she didn't look it, and even though we were separated by only four years. She was ready to move into new worlds. I wasn't. Talk about babies numbed me, and I dared not probe the future as she was doing. I had to make myself believe that everything was going to be all right in Eastfield. I hoped nothing would change.

"I wonder," Penny said.

I was supposed to say, "What?" but I said nothing.

Penny responded as if I had. "I wonder about Aunt Addie," she said.

I waited.

"I wonder what she was like when she was sweet sixteen, my age. I wonder, was she cute and pretty? Did she have boyfriends? Did she ever have a crush, fall in love? I wonder if anyone ever tampered with her heart, broke it maybe, permanently? I wonder if she's still a virgin, and if she isn't, how it happened that she isn't. I wonder how come she never married."

"Nuts," I said. "So Uncle Lambot never married either. Does that make him a virgin, too? Who cares?"

"I do, all of a sudden. Old people never tell you anything, and I want to know. Curiosity. Once it gets growing, it grows and grows."

"Puke," I said. I didn't want to hear. I preferred not to know. "How old are they?" I asked, as if to change the subject.

"Aunt Addie is forty-eight, and Uncle Lambot is only forty-five."

"They look older to me. They always looked old."

"And they always act old," Penny said. "Like their lives were short-circuited, and they were switched from young to old, skipping all the in-between. They missed it all, Willie, and that's not for me. I don't want to be buried as of tomorrow, forever in Eastfield, and I am going to do something about it this summer. You can depend on that."

Of that I had no doubt. The notion did not fill me with anticipation.

CHAPTER TWO

I N NEW YORK, OUR TRAIN WENT UNDERGROUND FOR A SHORT STOP AT Grand Central, so except for the worn and dirty outer fringes, we saw none of that site that Penny called never-never land. Being pulled underneath the city without seeing anything was Penny's idea of giving punishment to the guiltless.

"Let's get off now and never go to Eastfield," Penny suggested.

"And live here forever. I bet you can find forever here in no time at all."

"Fat chance," I said.

"Why not?" Penny knew why not. "Anyway, I mean to come to New York this summer."

"Fat chance. Aunt Addie will never let you."

"I'll come. Eight hundred bucks says I will come," Penny said, patting her books containing the money. "The first time Aunt Addie puts her whammy on me."

"Fat chance. Aunt Addie has her periscope on us twenty-four hours a day. You know that."

"And that is why I will go," Penny said. "We came from parents who were blind to anything we did. And now we go to Aunt Addie. I don't think I can take it."

"You will because you have to," I assured her. "Anyway, if you go, I go, too. I'm not staying alone with Uncle Lambot and Aunt Addie." I thought a bit more and added, "Or with Aunt Harriet, or Aunt Lucretia. I don't like her."

"Aunt Lucretia Woodbury," Penny mused. "She's an interesting bore."

"I don't like Myrtice Bean either. Aunt Myrtice," I said sourly.

"She's a weirdy," Penny said.

"This year, I'm not going to kiss all those old biddies in Aunt Addie's Friday Club. Aunt Emily, Aunt Edith, Aunt Bertha, Aunt Bess, Aunt Sarah, none of them. And I'm not going to call them Aunt, either. I don't care if I ever see them again."

"Not even Aunt Harriet?"

"She's different."

"You can say that again. She lives by herself in a big house in the woods, and we don't even know the why's and wherefore's, except that her mother lived with her until she died. Most of our other aunts don't quite know what to do with her. They would give her the boot, probably, if she didn't have money of sorts, and wasn't related to Auntie Lucretia."

"I didn't know that."

"Of course you did. Aunt Harriet's last name is Stone. Aunt Lucretia was a Stone before she became a Woodbury. I told you that long ago. They are sisters."

"I forgot."

"Remember I told you how I heard that Aunt Harriet used to have a crush on Elisha Woodbury before Auntie Lucretia snared him. Behind that is a lot of story we don't know about. Old people never tell young people much, if you ask me. Not even Aunt Harriet."

"She tells stories."

"But not about herself. Did you ever think of that?" Penny said as if realizing it for the first time.

"Who cares?" I said. I had too much on my mind as it was.

"Sorry. Let's skip it all and get off the train now and hide out in New York," Penny said.

I shuddered and felt sticky-tight all over. "There must be something in Eastfield," I said.

"Holmes Woodbury."

"Puke." Holmes Woodbury was a nephew of the Woodburys'. He lived in South Carolina, went to Harvard, and spoke as if he had swallowed a hot potato. He stayed with Aunt Lucretia part of each summer because she gave him money for Harvard. He was a snot and I couldn't stand him. Suddenly Penny forgot New York, and lost herself, I supposed, fancying romance with Holmes. I remembered her talk about having babies during the coming summer and felt like vomiting.

When the train pulled out of the dreary underground and rumbled past dreary tenements, I decided Penny could go to New York alone. "I wonder if Uncle Lambot painted the house this year," I said.

"Not unless they can find a paint that will paint it dirty gray and half-peeled. They like it that way."

"I wonder who will be first to find a speck of dust on the inside," I said.

"You could find it at the North Pole faster," Penny said.

"Penny, tell me one of Aunt Harriet's stories," I blurted. "We've hardly mentioned her since we left Des Moines."

"Aunt Harriet is for children. We're no longer kids, Willie. Put it all in the memory book," Penny advised, and with that returned to her reading.

Penny or no, I could daydream Aunt Harriet, and I did. Aunt Harriet was all sourdough, rough and tumble. She had gobs of comfortable fat and she didn't care where it was, or whether it was there or not. She had a big, round face that was always filled with fun talk and haloed in sinful cigarette smoke. And when Aunt Addie and other members of the Friday Club dared to criticize, she told them, "I like to smoke, and if I die five years before my time, who would care?" and kept on smoking.

I would care, even if her stories were one part truth and nine parts fabrication. She talked about things nice old ladies in Eastfield didn't talk about and children were not supposed to hear. That her stories would not have received the seal of decency of Aunt Addie's Friday Club was recommendation enough for them. She spoke indecent thoughts as calmly as if she were reading a recipe for gingerbread cookies over the telephone. Penny noted deception about Aunt Harriet, for she never talked about certain matters in front of Aunt Addie, and that was too bad, because Aunt Addie sure missed a lot.

Penny said that Aunt Addie had been cast into a leaden mold soon after puberty and in it she remained. Aunt Addie had a soft, almost flawless complexion, and if I didn't know better, I would have thought she spent half her life covering her face with gunk and stuff. And yet she looked tired and distraught. There was a soft wave of graying hair that rolled along her forehead. It was rather nice and it was always there. Even in the morning, which was Aunt

Addie's special time of life. She was forever scrubbed in a sturdy, starchy sort of way. She forever acted as if she were deathly afraid that some day the President and his wife—Franklin and Eleanor, God forbid!—might drop in unexpectedly and she would be caught the one time in her life, unpinned and unprimmed, a condition that could only cause her instant demise.

Aunt Addie was a cold tablet, and Aunt Harriet was its sugar coating. With Aunt Harriet about, we could endure life, even in Eastfield, even anticipate it, and in my childish way, I was positive Penny would prove to be wrong about Aunt Harriet being only for children. Aunt Harriet made life easier to take. Without her about, Aunt Addie would be a rugged test to endure. As Penny said, Aunt Addie ruled the roost, there was no doubt about that. She ruled with the strength of meekness. She would tell you to do something, and if you did not do exactly what she expected you to do, and when she expected you to do it, she took it as a personal insult. Then she would lower her eyes and not glance at you again until you gave in. If you double-crossed, fibbed, or gave her the slightest bit of lip, you were in real trouble. She would fix your meals and otherwise wait on you hand and foot, and she would admonish, "Don't slam the screen door," or "Wash your face real good. It's got half the grime of Eastfield on it," or "Keep your elbows off the table." She'd say these things as she always did, but in a flat, hurt voice that sounded as if it were coming out of the horn on the old Victor phonograph in the parlor, but she would never really talk to you, and that was gruesome. Even Uncle Lambot, who believed as he did in the Gospels that talk was cheap, was no match for her. Uncle Lambot did all his thinking and talking in slow motion, and if you wanted a conversation with him, you had to have a bushel of time to spare. With Aunt Addie, when she hit you with a whammy, you could feel her thinking ninety miles a minute.

Only once did I remember Uncle Lambot ever really bucking Aunt Addie's hypersensitive control mechanisms, and that occurred in Uncle Lambot's clubroom in the old red barn that sat high on the knoll behind the house. The barn wasn't used for farming any more. Uncle Lambot kept a few hens in the coop behind the barn and that was all. The barn contained Uncle Lambot's private clubroom made over from the milkroom, right and front. Uncle Lambot had put a Franklin stove in it, and a lot of ratty furniture for which there was no longer house room. It was his domain, the way he wanted it, a place in which his cronies could gather of a summer evening or a rainy Saturday afternoon. Uncle Lambot was exceedingly tolerant of its undisturbed dirt, and despite all of Aunt Addie's mumblings, he was not of a mind to have her go chasing it.

For Aunt Addie, cleanliness was next to godliness, as she was fond of stating, and I had to admit that God was on her side when it came to the clubroom, with its smells of stale cigar smoke, dried manure deposited there from various assorted heels, and all compounded with the smell of Adam, the hit-or-miss hired hand, who snoozed away his afternoons there. One summer the mess was more than Aunt Addie could take, and when Uncle Lambot went to town one day to do some errands, she made a frontal attack with a mop, a broom, a carpet-sweeper, and tons of pent-up fury. It would have gone all well and good, only Uncle Lambot forgot his wallet and returned when Aunt Addie was smack in the midst of her misdeed. Penny and I were playing in the hayloft at the time, and we heard everything. It was the only time I ever heard Uncle Lambot speak harshly to Aunt Addie. I remembered at the time it sounded mildly like home, like a husband-wife feud, not a brother-sister spat.

"Addie, this is *my* place, dammit," Uncle Lambot said. "I keep it the way I want it. You keep the house the way *you* damn well please and no other way. The only time I enter *your* parlor is when the church pledge committee comes every November. I keep out of *your* space. You keep the *hell* out of mine." With that Uncle Lambot climbed into his Packard and drove to town, forgetting what he returned for. I was real proud of him that day. It was the longest speech I ever heard him make. He swore, too, and *nobody* dared a cuss word in front of Aunt Addie. Penny said there was a lot more at stake than a mere swear word or two, which I supposed could be.

But it was obvious that Uncle Lambot wasn't going to get by with a tough approach to life's problems. Aunt Addie took herself and her paraphernalia back into the kitchen. For two hours she swabbed the decks, which she had already done that morning. By noon, when Uncle Lambot returned for lunch, she had worked up a twenty-four-carat whammy. She pouted her lips, and she lowered her eyes, I swear, nearly to the floor. You couldn't get her to look at you no matter how you tried. Aunt Addie acted as if she had just consummated the greatest sin since the eating of the apple, and had been caught in the act by the entire civilized world. Oh, she kept on doing. She cooked and she ironed and she cleaned the living daylight out of the house, not once missing a cue in her performance.

For a whole month, Aunt Addie played it stage front. Uncle Lambot was as tough a codger as any ride-the-range cavalry sergeant, but she finally broke him. We never knew how it all happened, but one day there was Aunt Addie out in the club room, sweeping it as if she were performing a final rite before dying. After that, she swept the place once a month, and otherwise never stepped foot in it. I was relieved when it was all over. It was a horrible month that made me moody, homesick for a home I didn't want to return to, and scared of life. Penny thought it marvelous drama. She said it was a good way of working out frustrations, and as effective for them as shouting matches were for our mother and father. Only it was more subtle and it took longer. I thought it a form of cruelty.

I looked at Penny. She was miles away in the middle of a book, so I closed my eyes and dreamed one of Aunt Harriet's stories, the one about the operations, the time when Uncle Lambot and Adam, the hired hand, who was dirty-clothed, dirty-tongued sometimes, and not at all bright, used to indulge in a bit of surgery. This was long ago when Uncle Lambot thought he was going to be the chicken czar in the county, and Adam was a young squirt who had come from nowhere, and had built himself a cabin in the woods between the farm and Aunt Harriet's place. Aunt Harriet used to tell how they borrowed the instruments from Dr. Townsend, a crusty, old-fashioned dentist—the pliers, the wires, and so on—to manufacture capons out of the latest brood of young roosters. Aunt Harriet said they used hard cider for an antiseptic, and for thirst as well. As the afternoon wore on, their skills wore off. Sometimes they would disengage or mutilate the wrong glands altogether, and there you would have some young he-hen going without a kidney, a half a liver, or an adrenal. Sometimes they missed one of the gonads, and thus the poor things were left betwixt and between on matters of sex. Aunt Harriet, taken with her own story and forgetting her audience, ran ahead of us with it, and said that some years there were more fairies running and prissing about the farmyard than you could find in all of London and Paris together. I remember asking did Aunt Harriet believe in fairies, and later that night Penny told me all about them.

Penny sensed that I had been reminiscing. She put her book down and said, "Aunt Harriet drinks. I think she mostly told her stories when she had been drinking."

The remark was heresy. "She doesn't," I said.

"Willie, she does. She has a reputation. She has what Aunt Addie calls a problem. That means she's an alcoholic."

"Crap!"

"She smokes. No reason to suppose she doesn't drink."

No reason at all, except as far as I was concerned, Aunt Harriet had no bad habits. I did remember empty bottles hidden here and there, but now I wanted no further discussion of the matter. "Wonder if Adam is still about," I said, changing the subject.

"Forever," Penny said. "He'll last longer than the remembrance of Ozymandias."

"I wonder if he still carries his satchel," I said. Adam always carried a briefcase, like a business man or a diplomat, except that it was worn, scratched, and tattered. "I wonder what's in it."

"What Adam said was in it—money."

"Baloney," I said.

"Maybe that, too, but money. He's got money."

"Baloney," I repeated, and dismissed the matter by asking, "How about the cats?"

"Adam's cats. They will be a race unto themselves when mankind is no longer around."

To us, watching Adam's cats was like watching monkeys in a zoo. Adam was a bachelor. He was as thin as a cornstalk, wore the stale odor of the abandoned cowshed behind the barn, and lived in a cabin that every child should have, except for its mantle of filth. It was part tin, part slab wood and split rails. It was splashed with paints of many colors. It was decorated with gewgaws, horseshoes, scraps of brass, and wood whittlings. Over the front of the cabin he had built a steeple, painted it dirty purple, and stuck the Confederate colors over it—the largest flag I had ever seen. At the rear he had erected two long poles, and had strung an old-fashioned, sway-backed swing between them fifteen or so feet above the ground. So far as anyone knew, Adam never used it, except that one night when Penny and I were walking from Aunt Harriet's through the woods, we saw Adam tossing his cats up into it, and marking on a slate which of them came down one pole and which came down the other. What Adam expected to prove for posterity he could not explain.

Adam loved his cats, and there were always a dozen or more about his cabin. They liked him, too, and they followed him pied-piper fashion hither and yon. The queen of the yard was Sheba, a wheezy calico, who, according to Adam's statistics, had produced one hundred and nineteen kittens in a decade. Once Sheba gave birth to eleven kittens at a lick, and when they were beyond the creeping stage, Adam had a pot of stew at his table, letting it cool.

While waiting, he made a short visit to his air-conditioned water closet in a clump of bushes at the side of his cabin, and he was gone just long enough for all eleven kittens to climb the table, line the pot, and start slurping the stew. We got this scoop of information straight from Aunt Harriet, who claimed that she had just happened on Adam's cabin when he returned from the bushes, and she saw the whole proceedings. Adam caught his kittens demolishing his dinner and was extremely perturbed. He grabbed the iron ladle in the pot and konked each of the kittens on the head, saying, as he did, "Goodness gracious God, you little bastards, don't you know I'm hungry?" Eleven words, one for each tap on each head, and Aunt Harriet said it was the fanciest figuring that Adam ever did. Aunt Harriet claimed that those taps were powerful enough to knock all those kittens straight off their rockers, and that every last one of them and half their offspring became mentally deranged, and on certain days when the heat of the sun baked and parched the earth, you'd think they were in the middle of a feline snake pit. To hear Aunt Harriet tell it, even though Penny said it was apocryphal, you suspected that all of this mental derangement in the cats had some parallel with the human race. Penny gave credence to the idea when she named the cats after some famous nuts in history, and she said she had a lot more names for future batches of Sheba's offspring.

Now Penny said, "How would you like to live with Adam?"

"Crazy," I replied.

"But interesting. I wonder how old he is. I wonder if he ever fell in love."

"You got love on the brain."

"I bet he was good looking when he was sixteen."

"Impossible."

"Adam may not be that bright, but I bet he *was* good looking. I wonder if he ever was a father."

"Crazy," I repeated.

"I think I'll find out this summer. Find out what he's like, I mean. I wonder if he is as important as any other human being who ever lived."

"Like Abraham Lincoln maybe? Junk."

"Maybe. But if everybody is important in God's world, then Adam is important, and so are you and me. And Mother and Father, too, don't you see?"

"Everybody don't have to be important," I said.

"Doesn't," Penny corrected.

"You keep away from Adam."

"What do you mean by that?"

"You don't watch it, you'll get into real trouble."

"You mean having a baby?" Penny cocked her head mischievously. "I wonder if Adam ever sired a child. I wonder if he is a father."

"Damn it, shut up. You got men on the brain, too. Pooey!"

"Adam might be an interesting partner for my summer project," Penny said.

"I said, shut up!" I knew what she was talking about and I didn't want to hear.

Penny decided she had gone far enough for the moment. "Willie, dear Willie. Something beside Adam, then. How about the boat? Do you suppose it is still there?"

"Maybe," I said, surprised that mention of the boat didn't excite me more. Between the farm and Aunt Harriet's lay a large hayfield and a stand of pine. Down the hill and south of Aunt Harriet's, the Wampanaug River lazily wended its way to Long Island Sound. Years ago, before most folks' memory, the Wampanaug had a day of fury and flooded the lowlands. The field behind the barn became a lake, and when the waters receded, one of the mementos left behind was an old wooden scow, big enough to hold a cabin atop it. Nobody ever claimed the boat, and it remained in the field year after year, fifty feet or so beyond the barn. Slowly it became buried in muck and mire, and a patch of bramble bushes almost covered it in the summer. Yet somehow it withstood the onslaught of time, a weather-beaten reminder of the past unpredictable history of the Wampanaug.

When we first came to Eastfield, the boat was our ark, our castle. With Penny as pilot, we traveled into all sorts of worlds for hours on end, braving all kinds of evil. When we first discovered the boat, it was enormous, but each year as we returned to it, it appeared smaller and smaller. Each year we spent less time on it, though never quite wanting to desert the ship entirely. I thought about it now, not caring whether it was there or not. I sensed this year was going to be different. A lot different.

Penny asked, "I wonder who built it? Ozymandias maybe?"

"Him again."

"Maybe Adam's father. Maybe Adam came with the boat. They both look in the same condition. Do you believe in God, Willie?" Penny asked, but before I could answer she said, "If you do, then you must believe there is a reason for everything. I wonder what the reason is for our boat."

"To travel on water," I said. I thought it a stupid question.

"I mean why did God put it to rest where he did? How long will it last before it disappears completely." When she asked that, I got a faint glimmer of what that Ozymandias business was all about, but search for reason was hardly appealing so soon after three deaths in the family and I wanted none of it. "I don't know and I don't care," I said. "I hope it's gone. I hope we don't ever have to see it again."

"Shall we talk about places and things and people we no longer want to see? You're only twelve, Willie."

"I don't want to go to Eastfield. I want to stay on this train forever," I said.

"And keep on seeing what we'll never have to see again." Penny sighed. "Fate has decreed otherwise, and you know what I bet fate has decreed for us this afternoon? I bet a dollar Aunt Addie will be at the station to meet us no matter how late the train arrives, that

Adam will be there with her, sober for the first time this summer, to drive us home in Uncle Lambot's Packard, and that the Reverend James will be at trackside to give us solace and prayers. Know what? I think I'll offer a prayer and a wish of my own. Maybe a couple of wishes, about going to New York, and having babies."

I caught a glimpse of Penny's face. She was wearing a smile that stretched halfway to China.

"Penny, you've got to stop that," I said. "Aunt Addie won't like . . ."

Penny shut me off with a groan. "Willie, dear Willie, what do you remember about Ozymandias?"

"Kiss my razzmatazz," I said. It was the only way I knew how to say then and there, "Penny, dear Penny, I love you with all my heart and soul." I guess she understood, because I could tell by the way she changed her smile that I couldn't have said a nicer thing.

CHAPTER THREE

THE TRAIN PIDDLED ABOUT THE STATION AT BRIDGEPORT FOR OVER an hour. Both of us were getting edgy. Penny said, "Now, about God . . ."

"Not now. You told me you didn't believe."

"As the man in the book said, 'It's the best of all possible worlds. Everything is for the best.' That's what God is supposed to say. Somebody had to create the heaven and earth, and want everything for the best. Somebody had to create me, and want me for the best. So today I want to believe in God."

"So?"

Penny shrugged as if giving up on me. "Say something funny," she asked.

"Something funny," I replied.

"Funnee."

"Eastfield."

"You are a clown."

"Clown is funny," I said, "Eastfield's not. I don't want to go there."

"No choice. You are a condemned man. But it's for the best. See what I mean? Lots of good things in Eastfield. Adam's shack. Hilda. Holmes Woodbury."

"Crummy."

"Would I make a good Eve for Adam? What do you think?"

"Puke," I responded.

"Wonder if Holmes Woodbury is a virgin."

"Double puke. If he is, let him stay that way."

"Maybe, maybe not," Penny said. "How about Stan Wynewski?"

Stan Wynewski was older, and married. He drove trucks in Eastfield and did all sorts of odd jobs. He had a booming voice and he liked to yak. I liked him, but I didn't feel like talking about him now.

"How about Sam Brown at the mill?" Penny asked.

"Maybe," I said. Sam Brown was the boss at the Winston Mills. He had points in his favor. He was a half dozen of our pseudoaunts all rolled up into one lovable pseudouncle. He took us to the movies, gave us money for candy, bought us huge banana splits, and slipped quarters and half dollars into our pockets. He never said no about this or that without making us feel grown-up. "Aunt Addie hardly ever lets us go to the mill, so it doesn't matter much. I hope she doesn't keep us from going to Aunt Harriet's."

"We'll go once a week at least. Aunt Addie may not approve of Aunt Harriet, but she is relieved to the point of sinning to shift the burden of our care off her shoulders even temporarily. Aunt Addie worries huge burdens onto herself, and we are two of them, now,

more than ever. We are no burden to Aunt Harriet because she is
not responsible for us. Have no fear, Aunt Addie will let us have
our day with Aunt Harriet, even if corruption sets in."

I prayed Penny was right, because life was a trip to Aunt Harriet's
when you lived in Eastfield and that's all there was mostly.

For one thing, Aunt Harriet didn't order us to bed at eight o'clock,
which Aunt Addie insisted was the perfect time for all people under
twenty-one and over forty to retire. Aunt Harriet let us stay up and
play games, dominoes, friendly blackjack, and sometimes Monopoly
far into the night. She let us fill our faces with all kinds of gunk, not
once warning us that some kind of green sickness would overtake
us. And when we finally did bed down, it was never just prayers
and good night. There were those tales that Aunt Harriet told while
we lay on her four-poster and listened in the dark.

"How about a story?" I asked again.

"No, Willie," Penny said softly. "And no more bedding down
with Aunt Harriet, cuddling under patchwork quilts. No more eat
what you like and stay up half the night. No more never-never land.
I sense it in my psyche."

"Aunt Harriet's different," I persisted.

"That she is. She is different from what she appeared to be to us
when we were kids, and I suspect the older we get, her differences
will be more noticeable even though she will remain the same. Know
what I mean?"

No, I didn't know what she meant, but I wasn't about to tell her.
"We were never kids," I said.

"Yesterday we were, let's say for the sake of argument." Penny
patted my knee. "But then it has always been different with us, too.
We wander in and out of our childhood as if we were going through
a thousand revolving doors. It's not easy but that's the way it is.
Maybe you are right, Willie. Maybe we never had a childhood."

"We were never kids," I said again.

"Maybe we just pretended. That's why we believed Aunt Harriet, and let a lot of old ladies we called Aunts think we were children. We were just messing around until we became adults."

"What do we do if Aunt Addie isn't there? Maybe we could call Aunt Harriet and she could come and get us," I said hopefully.

"If Aunt Addie is not there, we'll take a taxi," Penny replied. "But she won't miss. We could be six years late and coming from Mars without a wireless hookup and she'd be there to meet us. You know her. She's got a brain that was made in a Swiss watch factory." Penny sighed. "Remember, Willie, no tears. And don't go asking about Aunt Harriet first thing. Sort of make Aunt Addie feel we want to be with her. For our own sakes."

"I can't feel what I don't feel," I said.

"Find a day you don't do that and I'll give you my inheritance. Tell her you can't wait to eat her corned beef, her hamburg and potatoes. Something. Even I'll give it a try, but you know something? If I were a mean little runt, do you know what I would do?"

"What?"

"I'd give Aunt Addie my own little whammy so that in three days she'd beg us to pitch our tents in somebody else's pastures. But I'm too nice."

I scoffed at that. "You weren't nice last year," I reminded her. "You whammied Aunt Addie a hundred times. You ought not to do it. You know it upsets her for days."

"I would like to throw a dash of sand into her clockworks," Penny said, ignoring what I said. "Do you realize what we are in for from today until we fly the coop? Get up at seven, on the nose. Breakfast at seven-fifteen sharp, even in the summer when there's no school. Make beds at seven-thirty, dust at nine, and on and on and on. For another five years, it says here, unless we do something about it. We had a hard year, Willie, and we're different this year, you and I. Old. Not older, old. And somehow we've got to get that message across to our aunt and uncle."

"How old is Aunt Addie?" I asked. "I bet she's old."

"I told you, forty-eight."

"Ancient."

"Too young to die, Willie," Penny said coldly. "Not much older than Mother."

That didn't tell me much, and I quieted myself by thinking how it might not be bad. As Penny said, Aunt Addie was a good cook. She baked cakes and cookies and bread and pies, and there was always plenty of food on the table for three squares a day, which had not always been the case at home. "She's a good cook," I said.

"The best in Eastfield," Penny agreed sarcastically, and then she added, "And every day with all the fine food, we shall also have, 'Willie, take your elbows off the table.'" Penny roiled her face. "Razzmatazz," she added for good measure.

"You told me to think of good things, and then you make them bad," I said.

"Sorry," Penny said, giving me a kiss on the cheek.

"Won't be long now."

"Forever," Penny said. "From this moment on, forever."

"I wish Aunt Harriet would be at the station, I really do."

"Dear Willie, our lives are not inhabited by miracles."

"All the same I wish she would be there."

The train was slowing, and the conductor announced, "Westfield."

"Willie, Eastfield is next, and reality is Aunt Addie and Uncle Lambot who are unreal," Penny said. "We can do nothing now, but when we get there . . . maybe I will find a boyfriend. And maybe I will have a baby! And go to New York by hook or crook. Maybe find out a few things about this and that."

"Nuts," I grumbled.

"Time for dreams to end," Penny said as we pulled out of West-field. We looked out the window and it wasn't long before we could see Uncle Lambot's farm sitting on the edge of the hayfield across the valley. The big white house was there with its rambling veranda, and behind the house, on high land, the barn with its silo and sheds. I looked for the old boat, but I couldn't find it. Beyond the fields and in the woods separating the field from Aunt Harriet's, we could see the tip of Adam's purple steeple, with the Confederate flag flying. Except that the trees seem to have grown, nothing had changed. Last summer we craned our necks to see everything. Today we took it all in with a brief glance, hardly moving a muscle.

"Home sweet home," Penny said.

"Seems different," I said.

"When we are in bed tonight and the window is open, I wonder if we'll hear the nine o'clock freight train pass on this track, with its wheels rattling, with its whistle tooting at the crossing."

"I hope so," I said. I know how Penny felt about that. No matter what time Aunt Addie sent us packing off to bed—it was rarely later than eight—we never went to sleep until we heard the train pass, and then we knew we could go to sleep if we wanted to. Or dream of faraway places. It was that small part of our world that spelled out to us that we had lived another day, and I prayed the freight train would still be making its appointed round at nine.

Then, on the edge of the town and by the river, we saw the mill. The Winston Mills. We had all but forgotten it.

"The mill," I noted.

"The mill," Penny said. It was a hodgepodge of stone, brick, and dirty windows, and we had always supposed it had been there since the earth was formed.

"I presume it more or less belongs to us, now, except for what Aunt Harriet and Uncle Lambot own," Penny said. "Ride the elevator, man the machines, fire the foreman. Burn it, Willie, and we can collapse Eastfield. Some day when you are a man you can have my share and then become Sam Brown when he retires. How would you like that? Or we could switch roles and I could run the mill and you could run the house. That I would like!"

I made no comment. Penny had told me that Father's share of the mill would go to us, but I had only a vague notion as to what that meant. I remember Father and Mother arguing about the mill after Granny Winston died, but I paid no attention. I was about to ask

Penny some questions when I saw the people. There was a long line of people milling about the gate and fence. On the opposite side of the street there was a small crowd watching. "Look!" I exclaimed. "A parade."

"Not a parade, Willie. A strike, I think. I remember Father telling about it. I remember him saying they were selling the mill and it was moving South. Not enough money left to run it. We've got money, Willie, and we don't have to worry much. Just living with Uncle Lambot and Aunt Addie and keeping from going stir crazy is all we have to worry about."

We passed over the trestle above the Wampanaug River, and Penny said, "We're crossing our Rubicon."

I knew what that was and I said, "Except we didn't have to make any decision. It was made for us."

Penny liked that and squeezed my hand. She was pleased that I remembered. "I still have you, don't I, Willie?" she said. "Had I tried, I couldn't have selected a better brother." I let a flushed face make a response for me. Penny could not have said a nicer thing at that moment.

"We arrive at the shank of the evening," Penny said. "Five minutes from now we become children again, because that is what Aunt Addie thinks we are and that is what we shall be as long as we live in her kingdom." Penny closed her eyes. "I wished to hell I knew how to pray," she said. "Really pray."

My sister, I remembered, was full of hell and unhappiness and you never could tell one from the other. A scrawny, wide-eyed, pasty-faced runt. Her voice was a flat drone, with hardly a ripple in it. Gladness sounded like anger and vice versa. So, too, with sadness and joy. After three days alone with Penny on the train, she was all I knew. Every blasted bit of that thing called Life was Penny. I suppose what I felt then was something akin to love, but then it had no name. Just a sensation, one I felt all the more when the train pulled into the depot and we looked out and saw Aunt Addie standing all by herself, stiffly, like a statue. There was no Reverend James, nor could we see Adam. Aunt Addie waited as if she were the only person on earth.

CHAPTER FOUR

At the corner of the old, dilapidated brick station, I saw Uncle Lambot's 1928 Packard. Beside it stood Adam, the hired man, looking for all the world as if he expected royalty. He was dressed in a dark suit and tie and white shirt. I had never known him to wear anything but soiled overalls before. I wondered if he was driving for Aunt Addie. I couldn't quite believe that, for legend held that only Uncle Lambot ever sat behind the wheel of that ark. It was Uncle Lambot's pride and joy. Fore and aft were separated by a glass partition. Aft was Aunt Addie's domain. Big enough for pitching a tent, it was all decked out with polished walnut and grained leather. When they went riding Sunday afternoons, Uncle Lambot sat at the wheel and Aunt Addie sat behind him. It was quite a sight and it caused more talk than a town meeting. People used to say it was obvious that Uncle Lambot had money and didn't care what people thought, or he'd get a new car every couple of years or so just like the other rich folk did. They said Uncle Lambot was a smart coot, and don't you forget it, and the reason he had money was because he was stubborn and knew how to hang on to it. I personally thought it was crazy to keep that ancient chariot when they made new autos every year, but Uncle Lambot said it was as comfortable as any Pullman, and he'd be damned before he parted with it. I wished he would get a convertible just as long and just as big.

"There's Adam," I said.

"Don't forget the kissing," Penny said.

"Kiss my razz," I said. You always had to kiss Aunt Addie twice, once when you arrived and once when you departed. Aunt Addie gave no indication of liking it, and kissing her was no better than kissing the cold nose of a sick cow, except that Aunt Addie always smelled scrubbed with Ivory soap. Custom, however, demanded strict attention to this ritual. There could be no other reason.

"Give her your best yearling smile and keep your upper lip at the ready," Penny advised.

I groaned again and picked up the valises to follow her out of the car.

On the steps, Penny tripped. She landed in a heap in front of Aunt Addie. That was typical Penny. She'd walk into the side of a barn door if she had anything on her mind. I thought now, however, that she was already giving Aunt Addie a whammy, and I got all tensed up. Then I saw blood oozing from her knee, and her face squeezed into a painful grimace.

But when she looked up at Aunt Addie, she pulled a fast smile. "Somebody pushed me," she said, and she jumped up and brushed herself off. It was nothing at all.

I looked at Aunt Addie and saw what Penny saw. Aunt Addie was trembling, and she never trembled. Her cheeks were pale and her eyes watery. Aunt Addie never cried. She could get the craziest look in those narrow eyes of hers when you did something she didn't like, but she never cried. Penny was not about to let her develop a crisis over her tripping and falling.

"Nothing, Aunt Addie, nothing," Penny said, dabbing her knee with her handkerchief. "Eager to see you, that's all. Willie, don't just stand there, pick up my books." There was relief on her face when she saw no money had spilled. "Adam, come help us with our goods and chattel. And for heaven's sake, look like you're glad to see us." She turned to Aunt Addie. "You haven't kissed us yet. Of course, you needn't if you don't want to." Penny was making a lot of quick chatter. I presumed she didn't want mention made of Mother and Father and Granny Winston and was trying to forestall talk about that, and that was all right with me.

Aunt Addie stopped whimpering long enough to let us both kiss her, and I wondered when we would go away again and have to give her another. Not for a long time, I guessed.

"Don't worry about my knee," Penny told her. "I've had worse, and I'll have worse again, and you are not to fret every time my body fails to follow my feet." With that, Aunt Addie started all over again. "You poor dears, you poor, poor dears," she moaned as she led us by the hands, like children, to the Packard. It was going to be gruesome.

I asked, "You got a license, Adam?" I didn't think so, because you had to read and write to get one, and Adam wasn't good at either. "Uncle Lambot know you're driving his Packard?" Adam didn't answer either question. I asked to sit in front with him, but Aunt Addie said no, and we had hardly got seated in her territory but what she came all to pieces with sobbing. I looked to Penny for rescue.

"Aunt Addie, it's not that bad, and you know it," Penny said. "To be perfectly frank, you never did set much store in for your brother, and as for our mother! . . ."

Aunt Addie gasped, sounding as though she were trying to breathe in and out simultaneously. It was getting sticky already.

Penny did not relent. "If you knew what the two of them had done in the past two years, you would forever damn them." Aunt Addie gasped again. She wanted to call Penny on swearing, if nothing else, but she couldn't find words.

"The funeral was two weeks ago," Penny said. "It's all over. It was all for the best."

Aunt Addie took a lace handkerchief from inside her dress and dabbed her eyes. Penny sweetened a bit. She entwined her arm about Aunt Addie's, and said, "There, there now. Willie and I would rather be here with you and Uncle Lambot. If you want to be honest about it, we consider it a lucky break, don't we, Willie?"

Aunt Addie sobbed some more, and so I didn't have to answer.

"Aren't you glad to see us?" Penny persisted.

Aunt Addie saved herself a reply by rapping on the window to Adam. "What are you waiting for?" she scolded. Aunt Addie had no love for Adam, and she sounded like herself again for a trifle, much to my relief. Adam started the car and got us moving—jerkily at first, but he did all right. "We won't go by the mill," Aunt Addie ordered. It was the usual way to the farm and Penny asked, "Why?" knowing just as well as I did that Aunt Addie didn't want us to see the fuss.

"The other way is prettier," Aunt Addie said. It wasn't. It was down along the railroad tracks where the unpainted, smoke-charred houses looked as though they didn't have a shred of kindness in them.

"What's happening?" Penny asked. "We saw everything from the train. What are they striking for?"

"Nothing, child. Adam, not so fast. There's a sharp corner ahead." The respite had been short. You could feel Aunt Addie fighting tears again.

"There must be something. People just don't Sunday parade in the middle of the week for nothing. Our father didn't decide to sell his part of the mill before he died, did he?" Penny asked. "I heard him talking about that over the phone with somebody."

"Child, child," Aunt Addie whispered.

"Is there a union? Are we hiring scabs?"

"We won't talk about it now!" Aunt Addie snapped as she fluttered her handkerchief about her face.

"Is that it, Aunt Addie?" Penny persisted. "Did Father decide to sell to some New York people? I wouldn't be surprised. Mother nagged Father about the mill never paying dividends any more. Is the mill sold? Are they going to close it out here and move it South? That's what Father said ought to be done. Or was it Mother?"

"Child, child," Aunt Addie admonished. She was acting really weird.

"It's only four o'clock, Aunt Addie. There's plenty of time before dinner. It is probably the most exciting thing that has ever happened in Eastfield. I never saw a strike before. I'd like to see if I know any of the strikers. I can't see why you object. Maybe Aunt Harriet will be there. After all, she owns a good slice of the mill, too," Penny said.

"If we can't go by the mill, can we drive around by Aunt Harriet's and have Adam toot the horn? Just to let her know we're here. We don't have to go in," I said, mindful of Penny's admonition to me.

It didn't help. Aunt Addie's face became ashen. We thought she was going into shock. Penny took Aunt Addie's hand, just as she did mine on the train, and asked, softly, "Aunt Addie, what's the matter? What's happened?"

There was no reply.

"After all, we're family, and what is family for if not to share?" which was a rare thing for Penny to say, as she was not one to make much ado over the ties that bind. "What is it?"

There was still no reply.

"You'll have to tell us sometime, Aunt Addie," Penny said, sounding slightly like Aunt Addie when normal. "Is something wrong with Uncle Lambot?"

Oddly, that moved her. She straightened up. She assumed a pose, holding her head back, looking strong and indomitable again, looking for all the world as if that was the only positive way to face life's horrible problems. Like a mountain, and just as impersonal.

You sensed that she was holding her breath, that she was praying, or waiting for a crisis to pass. But when it didn't she leaned forward and tapped the window again. "Drive by Hattie's place."

"Oh boy!" I exclaimed. "Can we stop?"

But Aunt Addie gave no response, and I didn't feel the silence to be ominous. Penny seemed to, though, as she sat tensely, silently trying to figure out what it was all about.

Adam was through town now, and soon we were going over the Wampanaug bridge, where, on the other side, the roads diverged, the right one leading to the Winston farm a half mile away, and the left one leading up the hill past the old Nason farm and to Aunt Harriet's. The rickety bridge creaked more than usual as we drove over it, and I wondered how it held the Packard, let alone trucks, but I didn't even think about hunting for crawfish among the rocks underneath the bridge, which Penny and I did every summer. I guess I was really beginning to get a feeling that something had changed.

The road to Aunt Harriet's continued past her home in a wide arc, curving through woodland and reconnecting with the main road down on the other side of the farm. Whenever Penny and I went to Aunt Harriet's we preferred traveling over the field and through the woods, past Adam's shack and beyond. If Aunt Harriet knew we were coming, by the time we got to the old apple tree at the other side of the pathway, she would often be on the porch waving to us. If not, we waited at the apple tree and whistled, and she came flying out of the house as if she expected the pony express. I thought, let's skip Aunt Harriet now, and once we got home and changed our clothes, we could sneak over to the apple tree and whistle. And then last year would return, same as always.

But when we turned the last corner to where you were supposed to see the white house of Aunt Harriet's, with its white fences and the big stone steps leading to the porch, there was nothing but a charred chimney standing, the stone steps, and a mass of black rubble. A few wisps of smoke twirled about.

Adam stopped the car at the side of the road, and we looked at the mess as if we were paying homage to some monument, but only for a second or two. My mind went numb, and it stayed at dead center, concentrating on nothing.

Penny broke the spell by asking what we both knew. "Was Aunt Harriet home at the time?"

Aunt Addie managed a nod. A slight toss of that old-maidenish head, and we knew what we had guessed, that Aunt Harriet was no more. She had left our world, just as Granny Winston and our parents had, and there was nothing left of her but her stories. But Penny had told me on the train that those were vanishing already.

Aunt Addie, struggling with her voice, ordered Adam to drive to the cemetery. As we rode away, I looked back at the house, and I saw a grey squirrel munching an acorn on the stone steps. Except for the squirrel, there was nothing there but death. You could see it and you could hear it, even though there was utter silence.

At the cemetery, we saw where Aunt Harriet was because of the flowers. There were lots of flowers, and I supposed she might be underneath them, though I didn't care to argue that fact with Penny.

"When?" Penny asked.

"Four days ago. She was buried yesterday," Aunt Addie mumbled.

"How did it catch on fire?"

Aunt Addie twisted her shoulders. She otherwise ignored the question.

"Was she smoking in bed?"

Aunt Addie sobbed.

"Was she drunk?"

Aunt Addie caught her breath. "Hush!" she admonished.

"Did someone set it?"

"Penny," I said. Clearly Penny ignored feelings when she wanted to know something.

"Did someone set it?" she asked again.

For answer, Aunt Addie lowered her head and found refuge in the Lord's Prayer. We all chimed in, even Adam. After, Aunt Addie recited from the Psalms, "I will lift mine eyes unto the hills, from whence cometh my help." It wasn't, I thought, a prayer for Aunt Harriet; rather it was for Aunt Addie herself. Rigid discipline was about to take over again. You could almost feel Aunt Addie telling the powers that be that she had wasted enough time on sympathy, that it was time to return to the Lord's work. At least when she had finished, she resorted to old Aunt Addie, and that was a relief.

"We won't talk about it. Not now. Not ever. Aunt Harriet passed away, and we must be thankful that we're the fortunate ones to have known her. Talking about the way it happened will only add to the ugliness of our memory of her." Her voice returned to normal. It wasn't loud, but the message was clear. She not only let us know how she felt about Aunt Harriet, but how she would react. She had issued a command, and you took a terrible risk with both the devil and Aunt Addie if you ignored it; of the two, it was a toss-up as to which risk was worse. I didn't ignore it, and neither did Penny, at least for an hour or two. We didn't get a chance.

"I suppose you'll want your same bedrooms. At least that's the way I've planned it," Aunt Addie said. "Put all your dirty clothes in the hamper in the bathroom. I put your last summer's clothes on your beds. Maybe a bit short for you, William, but you're a boy and it won't matter. I don't want you to go running off, Penny. Supper is early because I know how tired you are and will want to go to bed early. We have a new minister, Reverend James. I've invited him to dinner."

Our rooms were on the second floor, mine being at the far end of the hallway, and separated from Penny's by our bathroom. Uncle Lambot's room was opposite mine, and Aunt Addie's room was opposite Penny's. It was a cozy arrangement that induced in us certain habits of stealthiness each summer.

I put on a pair of khaki shorts and a white shirt with the sleeves lopped off. Penny changed one navy blue skirt for another, and her blouse for one of my shirts. Aunt Addie was not given to frilly clothes; she only insisted on cleanliness. Penny agreed on the former, but not always on the latter. When she was dressed, she came to my room. I hoped she wouldn't talk about Aunt Harriet, and she didn't.

But her mind had not been idle, for the first thing she asked was, "Did you ever think about old people, Willie, and how they got to be in that condition?"

"What condition?" I asked dumbly. I thought it a dumb question.

"Did you ever think that once upon a time Uncle Lambot and Aunt Addie were little tykes wearing diapers, and there was a time they couldn't even talk?"

"Uncle Lambot hardly ever talks now."

"I know they must have been born as all babies are born, but I can't find any in-between in them."

"You already said that. So who cares? Sometimes I think you were born old. So what?" I said. "I think I'll play sick so I won't have to go to supper. I ain't hungry anyway."

"Do that and you'll have to be sick three or four days," Penny warned. "You know your old auntie when it comes to sickness. Now getting back to basics, would you like to know what I think about older people?"

"Not if it means talking about death," I said. I had had enough of that.

"All the time with Granny I thought about it," Penny said. "Age, I mean. Couldn't help it. You're young, you think the world will last forever, and then before you know it, poof, the forever has disappeared, and you have nothing left but a few habits you've picked up along the way. That's what Aunt Addie's got plenty of, habits. Uncle Lambot, too. Habits are the only thing they've got left from living."

"So?"

"So who wants it? Who wants to be dead in a live world? When you die, the world dies, too. The whole world."

"And the universe, too," I said sarcastically.

"Good, Willie. A philosopher yet you'll be."

I could care less. "Why do you keep thinking dumb things?"

Penny sighed, exaggerating her despair of my density. "Granny, our parents, and now Aunt Harriet. So everybody is going to feel sorry for us all summer. Like it was the first time all this ever happened to anybody since the world began, and it could happen again, that's all I'm saying. We all have to die when our time comes, so why should we be dead before that time?"

"I don't want to talk about death," I said.

"Remember what I said on the train. Someday you'll be Uncle Lambot and I'll be Aunt Addie. It makes no difference whether or not our parents lived or died, because we wouldn't be them, but someday we'll be Uncle Lambot and Aunt Addie if we don't watch it, because that's the way it can happen. When they die, we'll take their places. I have a premonition about that and it scares me."

"They ain't going to die. They'll never die. Damn it, Penny."

"Maybe not," Penny said patiently. "I said it once and I'll say it again, I'm going to kick in the walls a bit this summer and fight for our future. If we don't do it, nobody is going to do it for us."

Penny kept on talking until in a vague sort of way I got the drift of what she was saying, but there was only so much I could take. I didn't want the past or the future, only the present. "Let's go to the barn and jump in the hay. I wonder if the rope is still hanging from the bat's belfry?" The cupola on the barn roof was known as the bat's belfry, although it was inhabited mostly by barn swallows. There was a beam across its bottom, and from it Uncle Lambot had slung a block and tackle he used to hoist old pieces of farm machinery he occasionally tinkered with. We could swing side by side on the rope, from one hay loft to another. I started down the front stairs and Penny followed.

"Let's sneak out before she can tell us not to play too hard and get all sweaty," I said.

But Aunt Addie spotted us and said exactly that, adding, "Don't forget, the Reverend James is coming to supper, and I want you all washed and cleaned."

We kept on going.

"I knew it," Penny said.

"What?"

"In the car, she referred to us as children, did you hear?"

"Nope."

"Well, she did, and already she's giving orders. Already she's using her favorite word, don't. Damn it all." Three or four of Adam's cats came from nowhere and Penny picked one of them up, a fluffy orange and white one. "And did you note how she won't talk about Aunt Harriet and how it happened? Cat's got her tongue worse than last year."

"So what? Didn't she say the Reverend James was the new minister?" I said, changing the subject. "He was here last year."

"She forgot. She's getting old, as I said. But then she's always been that way for centuries," Penny said.

"What's that got to do with it?" I wondered.

"Oh, what the hell," Penny said, and she dropped her cat unceremoniously. "So the Reverend James is coming to supper. He will talk and we will have conversation! Something besides a flock of don't's. I think I'll sneak into the parlor said the spider and do a bit of reading in the family Bible before supper."

"We're not supposed to go into the parlor," I said.

"To get caught reading the Bible," Penny said impishly, "will never produce punishment, only a reward."

When she left, I went to the chicken coop behind the barn to look for hens, but there were none. They were gone and I would miss them, for I used to watch them and feed them when there was nothing else to do. I thought I would play on the old boat, but it was dirty and weedy, and without Penny it would not have been fun.

I returned to my room in the house. I went to the window and remained there until Aunt Addie called me for supper. All the time I looked across the fields and through the woods to where Aunt Harriet lived. I don't remember seeing a thing, but I remember crying. I tried to stop but the tears and sobs kept on coming. Put it all together and I guess there was a lot to cry for. But I was glad Penny wasn't there to see me do it.

CHAPTER FIVE

SUPPER WAS AT A QUARTER TO SIX. THE REVEREND JAMES ARRIVED A few minutes before. His mission was to give us aid and comfort and otherwise keep Penny off Aunt Addie's back. The Reverend James looked younger than last year, but maybe it only seemed so because I was older. He thought Penny had grown. I could tell by the way he ogled her. He arrived in an old Ford coupe. He was thin, had thick lips, a long nose, and floppy brown hair, yet he was not ugly, as we had intimated on the train. He smiled a big friendly smile and he looked as if he could be fun if he were not a minister. When he greeted us, his face tried hard to create wrinkles of sadness and solicitude, and he spoke in a deep-throated voice that was not his at all. At first, he acted his role just as if he had found out what to do on such occasions on page twenty-two of his ministerial guide-book.

I plugged for crackers and milk and blueberries on the veranda, because it was hotter than bath water inside. The veranda rambled halfway around the house and was screened. It was real comfortable, with a mish-mash of old folks' furniture and all kinds of potted plants. Outside the screen were bushes, and sometimes there were birds in them, and you could make out you were interested in them and then you wouldn't have to talk. Besides, when we ate outside, Aunt Addie would say it was like a picnic, and she would excuse us from the after dinner chores. That night I only wanted to eat and run—until I flopped.

But Aunt Addie said no, this was a sad, solemn night. And so the four of us sat at the big table in the dining room, each at a side, and far enough apart so that one had to speak out to be heard. Uncle Lambot was still away and I missed him. I never liked the room. It had oak beams in the ceiling, and a long buffet that Aunt Addie claimed had been Winston property even before the Revolution. On it was a ton of heavy silverware, kept spotless and tarnishfree by a good portion of Aunt Addie's time. The dining room, like the parlor, represented money and class. You looked at them and you said to yourself the Winstons had both. Long ago, Penny said, they lived a different life from Aunt Addie's and Uncle Lambot's. Maybe so, but to me the room was stuffy and dreary. It gave me an inferiority complex.

Not so, Penny. She liked the atmosphere and reacted accordingly. It was quite correct for formal and informal and any other kind of conversation, and as far as she was concerned, there would be conversation that evening that would take us far beyond Aunt Addie's usual fare of trivia.

Aunt Addie served scalding chicken soup from a large, white tureen. Aunt Addie always said soup was for winter to help stay colds, and serving it on a hot summer evening was indicative of her inner turmoil, no matter how hard she might try to conceal it. She forgot to mention that it didn't taste just right, or that maybe she added too much salt. She was oblivious of elbows on the table, or that Penny dawdled her spoon in her soup. She even forgot to ask for the saying of Grace, and we had to pause while the Reverend James gave thanks to God at this time of sadness.

There was an awkward moment when he finished, but it didn't last long. Penny asked, "Where do you suppose Aunt Harriet is now?"

"Penny!" Aunt Addie said, sotto voce.

Penny acted hurt. "It's not improper to wonder, is it, Reverend James? Dying is a natural phenomenon. It's going to happen to all of us."

Aunt Addie turned white, but the Reverend James spread out a relaxed smile. He was pleased. Penny's question was quite proper.

"Now don't you fret, Miss Winston. I don't mind if we talk about Aunt Harriet. After all, that is what I'm here for. Penny, your Aunt Harriet is in heaven, God rest her soul."

Penny nodded. She shifted gears. Not much, just a cog or two. "How do you know that?" she asked. "How do you know she's not in hell?"

"Penny!" Aunt Addie was louder this time. She dropped her spoon. It clanked the corner of her dish and flipped off the table to the floor. It was probably the only thing she had dropped in the past twenty years.

"I'm not being irreverent, Aunt Addie," Penny said, taking note of Aunt Addie's state, but pressing on regardless. "I'm curious and I wonder how we know that. Did someone get a message from Aunt Harriet already? Maybe she is no more than a body even now, and after a few spotted moments of time, she'll be nothing but dust again."

"Her body was given to the earth from whence it came. Her soul was returned to God, who is in heaven," the Reverend James said.

"Yes, but how do we *know* that?" Penny asked.

"It's in the Bible," Aunt Addie blurted. Then she looked as if someone might ask her to cite the exact passage, and she lowered her eyes so that you couldn't talk to her.

The Reverend James played it cool. "Don't you believe that Aunt Harriet was a good woman? Don't you believe that God would want her?"

"Yes, I believe that Aunt Harriet was a good woman, but I'm not everybody. There may have been some who had good reason not to like her, even to hate her. After all, she did live a life that was cause for some to disapprove. Isn't that right, Aunt Addie?"

Aunt Addie was horrified. Clearly, in her frame of reference, events in the nether world invited no public speculation, especially from children. For answer, she took the soup and our dishes to the kitchen, mumbling something about it going to be a hot, steamy summer and there would be no escaping it.

But Penny's question intrigued the Reverend James.

"You can place Aunt Harriet where you want to place her by what you believe. If you believe she was a good woman, you can place her in heaven. If you continue to believe, you can keep her there. If you do that, if you keep on believing, then the goodness that was hers keeps on living in you, making your own life fuller and richer. And this process can continue from person to person from generation to generation unto eternity."

Penny was impressed. "It's a matter of faith," she said.

"Yes," the Reverend James said.

"O.K., but how about other people?" Penny countered. "Suppose somebody else believes Aunt Harriet was bad and keeps on believing, does that belief put her in hell, and how can she live in both places at once, except"—Penny winked at me—"except if she lives on earth?"

The Reverend James liked that. Aunt Addie didn't. She swept back into the picture with a huge platter of sliced ham and potato salad, and a tart response. "Aunt Harriet was a good woman! She *is* in heaven!" Aunt Addie proclaimed, saying it in such a way as to warn that the conversation about Aunt Harriet had better end then and there. To make certain, she told us that the ham was dry, that she forgot to salt and pepper the potato salad, and "Penny, I hope I don't have to go through another summer telling you to take your elbows off the table every mealtime."

It didn't work. "You don't have to, Aunt Addie, if you don't want to. We could talk of other things," Penny said, honing the edge of her flat voice. Then she ignored Aunt Addie. "Granting that Aunt Harriet is in heaven, where in heaven's name is heaven, Reverend James?"

"It's where God is," Reverend James said, stating the obvious.

"And where is God?"

"Where you find Him."

"A riddle," Penny said, pleased. "But suppose you do not believe in God, and then you can not find Him. Then where is heaven?" The questions continued. I had heard some of them a dozen times in one or more of Penny's monologues with Granny Winston, and now she asked them with the confidence that comes with practice. "Suppose you die without believing, and are dead, and that's it. Have you read 'Ozymandias'?"

The Reverend James could not recollect. Penny didn't bother to help him. "I wonder if our parents will see Aunt Harriet, heaven forbid, when her name is added to the roll. And if that occurs in that place called heaven, what kind of place would it be with them there? Would heaven then be hell?" Penny took a quick detour. "I read somewhere that there were millions, maybe trillions of stars in the sky. In our galaxy alone, there might be a hundred million stars, and that beyond our galaxies, there might be a hundred million more galaxies just as big, all on an endless traveling spree through space. Maybe souls go to one of those stars, and maybe to all. Maybe there are millions of heavens. Maybe at this precise moment, Aunt Harriet's soul is winging its way through space to one of them. Her own private star. Maybe her soul might take a million years to get there. Do you think this is possible?"

The Reverend James nodded. "The concepts of religion were formed when the world did not know much about stars, nor how many there were, but does it matter? There could be as many conceptions as the number of people. Or stars."

"How interesting," Penny replied. "If that is the case, if there are heaven stars, then there must be hell stars, and all kinds of in-between stars. Except for one thing."

The smile was no longer on the Reverend James's face. "And what is that?" he asked as if he didn't want to know.

"What if you don't believe, or don't care? Then what happens to the soul? And another thing, who decides for whom where the soul goes? And who decides for those who do not believe in the decider? Can you believe, really, that Granny Winston, our parents, and Aunt Harriet will all land in the same place to live happily into eternity?"

"Penny!" Aunt Addie croaked. She turned to the Reverend James. "You haven't eaten a thing," she noted.

"So I haven't," he agreed, ready now for respite. At least the beads of perspiration forming on his forehead suggested that. He ate some ham and managed to recover some equilibrium, and I thought he shifted his gears rather well. "If you make room on your agenda for a bit of church this summer, it is possible that I might find answers to your questions and deliver them in my sermons," and before Penny could toss a rejoinder, he turned to Aunt Addie and told her, "Miss Winston, at last I'm going to have your famous potato salad!" He turned to me. "William, at potluck suppers at church, everybody always asks which table holds your aunt's potato salad. By the time I'm ready to sit, it's all gone."

"I'm afraid this weather has made it soggy already," Aunt Addie said. "I declare it's going to be an odd summer. Feel it in my bones. Don't know when it's been cold and dreary one day and hot and sultry the next. William, elbows."

It was a nice try but it didn't work. Penny was not about to surrender this early in the game. The Reverend James gobbled some salad and proclaimed it manna from heaven, which was not exactly an appropriate response at that particular meal. Penny took her fork and brazenly speared a piece of ham on her plate. "This once was a hog. When this animal was killed that we might eat it, and thank the Lord for His bounty, where did its soul go? Are there good pigs and evil pigs? And such things as pig heavens and pig hells, Reverend James?"

I had to admit that they were interesting questions even though I didn't care to hear them. Clearly the Reverend James had not thought of them, and suddenly he looked startled and embarrassed, and turned to Aunt Addie as if for help. She gave it quickly. "That will be enough! Penny, leave the table and go to your room!" Then, fearing Penny would disobey, she countermanded her order with a finesse. "But not before you eat," she said. "You haven't touched a thing. I hope I'm not going to have to beg you to eat all summer." She resorted swiftly to her own familiarity. She asked the Reverend James if his salad needed salt, and she told me to take my elbows off the table again. Then she told Penny and me we could have our dessert of cake and milk on the veranda, and she added that we must be tuckered out from our trip and all, that we need not help with the dishes. She said everything in one breath. Not once did she look at anyone. She was stonewalling and even Penny realized that.

Penny retreated temporarily. She ate some food, and made small talk with the Reverend James, asking about the church and the congregation. But when matters had relaxed again, she returned to Aunt Harriet, talking about her past, now, instead of her possible future.

"Was it a nice funeral? Were there many there?" Penny asked. The questions were directed to Aunt Addie. They were quite harmless.

"Very proper. Everybody that knew her was there."

"Even the Nasons? Did Mr. Nason come with Mrs. Nason?"

"They were not there," Aunt Addie said, in a way to suggest that the Nasons were nobodies.

"Was the funeral at the church? Was Aunt Harriet a member of our church? She never went to church, did she?"

"In the winter," Aunt Addie said quickly.

"It was at the church. She was a member," the Reverend James said.

"Did she have relatives? Were they there?" Penny asked. "We never knew much about them, did we, Willie? Aunt Harriet was a world to herself. She never bothered to talk family. Did she have many relatives, Aunt Addie, besides the Woodburys?"

"Goodness, child, so many questions all the time. I get flustered.

I hope this is not what I'm going to get all summer," Aunt Addie said, once again evading.

"It's more than all summer now, Aunt Addie," Penny said. "Before you know it, you can put a tag on us saying 'Made in Eastfield.' If I don't ask, I'll never know anything around here, that's for sure."

"You won't find out much by being fresh, young lady. There's ways of asking and there's ways of not asking. And you are getting old enough to know the difference."

"Thanks for the compliment, Aunt Addie. I'm a young lady and old enough. I'm glad you have taken notice," Penny said snottily.

"That's enough, Penny." Aunt Addie moved about nervously again, clearing the dishes from the table. "Out on the veranda, both of you, and remember we go to bed early here."

That was that. Out on the veranda, I said, "So much crap. You're even worse than last year."

"You told me that last year."

"Well, razzmatazz. It was a lot of junk."

"So is, 'Take your elbows off the table,'" Penny said. "That's all it will be all summer, and it will get worse when Uncle Lambot returns. She'll drive me daffy if I don't do something about it."

"And if you do, you'll drive her daffy," I said. "Maybe Aunt Harriet didn't talk about relatives because she didn't have many."

"Everybody has relatives."

"Even Adam? He was the first man."

Penny raised her eyebrows. "I hadn't thought about it. You're right. Maybe Adam didn't have any. Except for her sister, Auntie Lucretia, maybe Aunt Harriet didn't have any either. Come to think of it, I like to think of her having none, except maybe us. Maybe that's how she wanted it, Willie, and so she didn't talk. But getting back to Aunt Addie, she never tells us anything. You mention the past, and she clams up, and why I can't help but wonder." She thought about that for a while and then she giggled. "You know what Aunt Addie is, Willie? She's a clam, that one. Whenever I ask her anything, she shuts up. Like a clam. Old Aunt Clammie! God, that fits!" Then she dismissed the matter. "Aw, what the hell. The Reverend James is nice. I like him. I think he likes me."

"If he does, he's crazy."

"Thank you, Willie. Well, he does. I think he wished Aunt Addie wasn't there and there were only two of us and then we could have opened up."

"Junk," I said, sensing that I was not to be one of the two.

"Maybe. There's all kinds of junk," Penny said. "Know something? Maybe the Reverend James could help me make a baby! Wouldn't that be something! Whee! He's not married, you know, and just supposing he got me fixed before marriage. This summer. Having him father my child would cause more shock than having Adam or Holmes do it."

"Puke!" I said. She was beginning to sound as if her having a baby was an established fact and all she had to do was go push a button somewhere. The idea curdled my insides.

"At least I can have fun thinking about it, having a baby, I mean, and holding it and keeping it. That's all I'm doing, Willie, thinking about it, so let's not go bongo about what's not going to happen. Still, the summer offers intriguing opportunities. One must make of them what one will."

"Puke!"

" 'There is a tide in the affairs of men.' Shakespeare," Penny said. "There is also a tide in the affairs of women."

"Puke!"

"There must be more to the English language than that word," Penny said, dropping the subject. She decided she didn't want her cake. She took it outside, crumbled it, and tossed it into the bushes. You didn't leave cake or anything else on your plate—Aunt Addie talked for hours about waste if you did. I scooped up mine and followed her.

"I was polite to Aunt Addie," Penny said. "I could have asked the Reverend James where he thought Aunt Addie might go. *If* she ever died. I'm old enough to know a few things, and so I asked a few questions, all legitimate. Aunt Addie gets upset over nothing and if you ask me I think she does it as a convenience to get out of answering embarrassing questions should they arise. Well, I'll tell you one thing, Willie, I'm going to find out a few things this summer, you can bet your inheritance on that."

"Like what?"

"Lots of things about our parents, for instance. We hardly bothered with them, if you want to know, and they up and died before we could find out things."

"You'll get us into real trouble this summer, I can feel it."

"I've got a haunting fear we're already in trouble," Penny said.

I found a stalk of rhubarb and peeled it. I bit into it and its sourness made me squirm. "You've never shown fear of anything. Nothing."

"Not true, but thank you, Willie."

"You don't care about anything. I don't see how you could talk to Aunt Addie like that. Like, like . . ."

"Like I didn't care? Oh, Willie, I care. If only we could have seen Aunt Harriet once more. Somehow. I have to tell you something."

Penny paused, as if she were about to change her mind. "Yes, I will tell you. If I don't I shall soon be like Aunt Addie. Not talking."

"What?"

She told me then, measuring her words carefully. "Last summer, the day before we went back home, I sneaked over to Aunt Harriet's to say one more goodbye. I thought I would surprise her, so I didn't yell or whistle or anything. I just opened the door and walked in, and when I didn't see or hear her, I thought she might be sleeping, so I peeked into her bedroom. She was there, Willie, sleeping. At her bedside, on the floor, was a whiskey bottle, and she wasn't alone, Willie. That's how I knew this year would be different all on its own without our parents or Granny dying. But I wanted to see her the worst way just the same, to see her just the same as always, and then maybe . . ."

She didn't finish. I was numbed. "How come you didn't tell me?"

"Willie," Penny whispered.

"All the same."

"I couldn't. You were so young last year. Sorry."

"Who?"

"Does it matter? All I know is she wasn't sleeping with a stuffed teddy bear."

I chomped on the rhubarb. Its sourness caused me to make a face. It kept tears away. I knew Penny recognized the man, but she wasn't going to tell me. Not now. Not ever.

A cat had been following us, one of Adam's. It brushed Penny's leg and she reached down and stroked it.

"The Reverend James liked what I said," Penny said.

"He would."

"I think he's developing a crush. On me."

I had no hankering for more discussion, least of all that. "You said that already. If he is, he is a nut," I said.

"I think I'll go back and tell him that he's cute, too cute to be a minister," Penny said. "And see what he does with that."

But she had no chance. Aunt Addie had already manned the defenses and she beat Penny to the punch. She told us how tired we were and it was time for bed. But not before we had prayers and sent the Reverend James rolling off in his Model T. In a trice, he was gone.

Upstairs Penny undressed to a cotton shirt and her shorts and came to my room. We moved an old blanket box to the window and sat on it. We looked out, our eyes taking in things together in the waning twilight. We saw the old boat. There was not much of it left now, and Penny said the grass around it reminded her of sea waves, and the grass growing, because of all the rain, would submerge it all this summer. A bird landed on the prow and we listened to its song. I guessed it was a red-winged blackbird, but Penny said they mostly sang in the morning. Our eyes took us across the field, to the setting sun that silhouetted Adam's steeple in the pines. Neither mentioned Adam, because we both knew we were thinking beyond Adam's cabin, through the woods, and beyond the apple tree that was a home for bluebirds. "Aunt Harriet?" Penny said. I nodded.

We both cried. I wasn't ashamed and neither was Penny. We had to cry it all out. Penny almost never cried in front of anyone, even me, and I tried to comfort her.

We heard Aunt Addie slam the front door, and we knew she was locking up for the night and was on her way to bed. Penny kissed me and took quick leave. At the door, she paused. "Guess what I discovered, Willie?"

"What?"

"The family Bible in the parlor is not a Bible. That old leather covers nothing but an empty box."

CHAPTER SIX

THE KITCHEN WAS LARGE, OLD, AND OLD-FASHIONED. ITS SINK WAS slate, and the faucet was a water pump, its handle protruding into the room. The cast-iron stove burned gas at one side and coal on the other. Near it was Uncle Lambot's enclave, with his comfortable wicker rocker, his reading stand, and his Atwater Kent radio. Here he read his newspapers, snoozed, and listened to his favorite radio programs, Lowell Thomas, Amos 'n' Andy, Fibber McGee and Molly, and Fred Allen on Sunday nights. Aunt Addie listened too, sitting in her rocker sewing, seldom saying anything to Uncle Lambot.

Beyond, by the windows, was the breakfast table with its spotless oilcloth covering decorated with roses. The window sills were filled with potted plants. Off at the side was the pantry where the cookie jar was always filled, though Aunt Addie's rules and regulations often kept us from it. Except for the radio and the electric lights, the kitchen was a prop out of the past. It had charm, and at times even I was aware of it.

But alas, the kitchen was the seat of government, the place where decisions were made, and the place where the daily routine began. After meals, Aunt Addie washed the dishes and pots and pans, Penny wiped, and I put all away. We hated kitchen chores, and we crabbed daily, but Aunt Addie insisted. Training, she called it. Routine, Penny said, routine, routine, routine. The way of life for millions upon millions of God's creatures, Aunt Addie said. Maybe so, but Penny did not exactly consider herself one of them, especially if that was what He meted out to them.

The following evening, when we were doing the dinner dishes, Penny said, "Willie, do you remember Freda O'Halloran, the girl with the nice un-midwestern name?"

. I did. Freda lived three streets down from us in Des Moines. She was a frumpy mean thing of sixteen or seventeen. Once she pushed me out of a swing at the school playground during recess and stole it from me. I never forgot her.

"She's got the whole recording of *Fidelio,* the Beethoven opera, and she told me the story," Penny said to me, but in such a way as to stretch Aunt Addie's ears. Penny was fabricating. I saw her that very afternoon reading out of *The Victor Book of the Opera,* a book she got from Aunt Addie's parlor. She had only become acquainted with *Fidelio* but a few hours ago, and in typical Penny fashion, she was going to make the most of her new findings. Something about love, I could tell. The mere thought of what she might say made me want to douse her head in the dishwater.

"It's a lovely, romantic story, Aunt Addie. Do you know it?"

It was a question rudely put. Penny knew very well that Aunt

Addie didn't know it. Aunt Addie's face twitched. A promise of embarrassment always did that to her.

"I wonder if I shall ever have a love like Fidelio's. To have a man imprisoned because of you, and then die a slow death a thousand meters underground. Imagine! Making the supreme sacrifice for love. And then to rescue that love with the breath of song in the great magnificence of Beethoven's music. When I can't dream of anything else, I dream I am an opera singer on a great stage framed in gold curtains, singing before the cream of the world's humanity. I should like to sing *Fidelio*."

That was hogwash. Penny, like Aunt Addie, was a monotone. She made no pretense of carrying a tune. Aunt Addie was quickly aware of this and she parried Penny in her own way. Suddenly she yipped. She had cut her finger on a knife in the dishpan, she said, and she had never been that careless. And, goodness, she didn't know how she could have dirtied so many dishes, considering she only baked a macaroni casserole for supper, and Penny should get a clean towel. One thing she prided herself on was having plenty of clean towels for dish-wiping. She made sure of that.

When she had finished her mini-monologue, Aunt Addie sighed, and held her breath. The gambit didn't work. Waiting with patience, and unperturbed, Penny said, "Do you suppose I shall have a similar love affair, and if so, how soon? A really noble experience that fires every cell in my body? Do you suppose I shall have that, Aunt Addie? I'm old enough of course. This morning I awoke dreaming of Aunt Harriet. Did she ever have a love affair? Did she ever marry? Hilda told me she had male friends. She was a lovable old doll if ever there was one. I know that if I were a man . . ."

Aunt Addie tightened her lips and pursued her own defense. "Wait until I pour hot water over the silverware before you wipe. Makes it shine better. If you need a new dish towel, there are plenty in the drawer."

"I know, I know," Penny said, losing her own patience. "You're a good teacher, Aunt Addie, give credit where credit is due. Good teachers repeat. And repeat and repeat and repeat. Last summer you told me how to shine silver a hundred times. The lesson took. May it rest in peace. As I was saying . . ."

"Mind your manners, Penny. There's no place for sauciness in this household. When I don't keep telling you to do things, you either don't do them, or you do them wrong," Aunt Addie retorted with vigor. "Now we've had enough of useless chatter. We'll finish the dishes, and then go out on the veranda. I have something to say."

Penny twisted her lips into a pout. Clearly she had lost the encounter and normally she would have clumped off. But she was curious.

Aunt Addie discovered that she had forgotten to wash the pans, which she always did first, and wiped them herself because we could never do them to suit her. So she decided that she could talk to us in the kitchen while she did the pans. She hemmed and hawed, then blurted, "I suppose I might as well tell all I know. Uncle Lambot should be the one to tell you, but he won't. It's like pulling teeth to get him to talk about anything, let alone business. Besides, you'll hear it sooner or later. They are going to sell the mill, and the new owners are going to move it South. So the mill hands are striking. They don't want the mill to move because they will have no work, and there isn't much else to do in Eastfied. We aren't at all popular about town these days."

Penny dropped her dishtowel and folded herself neatly upon the kitchen stool. There was plenty in that mammoth speech of Aunt Addie's for Penny to dissect. She was delighted with the prospects of a family conference. Suddenly *Fidelio* had vanished.

"I'm all ears," Penny said.

"It's not wise for either of you to go into town. You can play right here on the farm. There is plenty for you to do," Aunt Addie stated.

"Another don't. I suspected as much," Penny said quickly and angrily. "Little snots, and we own a mill, Willie, and we can't see it," Penny said. "Who are *they* who are going to sell the mill we own? Who is doing the selling without our permission?"

"It's being arranged, that's all I know. I don't suppose we could stop it. It's a very sad thing. The mill has been part of the family and this town for generations. Started in 1802. Right on the same spot. Last week somebody tossed a rock through the kitchen window. Right in broad daylight when I was putting a cake in the oven." Aunt Addie pointed to the center window. "Right there. Liked to have stopped my heart from beating. It's best that you don't go to town, Penny. I want you to stay right here for the time being. Is that clear?"

I wanted to know more about the rock tossing, but Penny would have none of it. "I understand what we have to do," she said, and loosely interpreted that meant we would sneak into town at the first opportunity. "Suppose *we* don't want to sell it, Aunt Addie?" Penny asked. "Suppose Willie and I want to keep it?"

"Lord, child, I don't know about such things."

"Aunt Addie, I'm not a child!"

"Goodness! All I know is that there are creditors who want to be paid and your Uncle Lambot did what he thought had to be done. But everything is all mixed up somehow because of your father's sudden death. I'm telling you now, because when Uncle Lambot returns, it will be best not to talk and argue. But I guess you know that."

"I know that. Best not to discuss. Right or wrong, men are always right," Penny said, and you could almost feel her preparing a brief. Penny said she saw no reason why she couldn't talk her concerns out of her system, clear her conscience, and maybe come up with some idea of her own. "Who is to argue with Uncle Lambot?" Penny asked. "It's a simple matter of having to sell, I guess. That's what I heard Mother say to Father. If we don't, and the mill keeps losing money, it will close completely and then there will be no jobs North or South. I don't see why we can't talk about it. What has to be done has to be done. How much did we sell it for?"

"Child, how would I know!" Aunt Addie said despairingly, and then she attempted to close the conference. She wanted to know what we wanted to eat tomorrow. She even asked about Granny Winston and her funeral, which she hadn't been able to bring herself to talk about before. Penny bided her time and asked again, but if she knew, Aunt Addie wouldn't part with the information.

"According to Father, a quarter of a million might be our share. Mother thought more," Penny said.

"So what? I bet we don't see it," I said. I didn't think it would much matter whether or not we did. I never thought much about money the way Penny did. I didn't have to. It was always there when you needed it, in Father's or Uncle Lambot's trouser pockets. It never occurred to me how it got there, but I didn't care. Besides, we had eight hundred dollars, more or less, stashed away in Penny's room. That was enough to last for years. "Was the Winston family always rich?" Penny asked.

"We've talked enough," Aunt Addie said.

"They call us 'those rich Winston kids.' Did Uncle Lambot ever spend much, or does he just keep it? Did he ever buy anything he wanted other than his Packard?"

"It's not proper to talk about money," Aunt Addie said. "Penny, pick up your towel and help William finish drying."

Penny didn't move from her perch. "Willie, what are you going to do with your share?"

"Buy a bicycle," I said.

"It's not proper to talk money," Aunt Addie insisted.

"Why not?" Penny asked. "Father and Mother talked and argued money all the time. Father used to say it was stupid to let it bother your conscience as long as it was yours, no matter how you got it. Was Aunt Harriet in on the deal to sell?" Penny asked.

For the second time that evening, Aunt Addie yipped. She didn't cut herself again. This time she dropped something. The something was the soup tureen that I had finished wiping and she was putting on a high shelf herself because it was too valuable for me to handle. It bobbled and then crashed into the stone sink. It broke into a thousand pieces, and there was a big to-do about finding each piece because the soup tureen was Aunt Addie's oldest and most precious possession. "Damn! Damn! Damn!" she exploded. For a moment even Penny was speechless. The tureen was china, pure bone china, snow-white still after all these years, priceless. Worth more than all the family silver in the dining room. Penny asked what bone china was, but Aunt Addie didn't stop. She hadn't the slightest notion what was possessing her to be so careless these days, and the Lord only knew how she was going to manage the summer.

At last she ran out of words, sounding like the Victrola running down for lack of cranking. She sighed, scrubbed extra hard at an invisible spot of grease on the frying pan, and held her breath.

Penny waited until Aunt Addie started breathing again and said, "Last summer Hilda Nason told me Sam Brown and Aunt Harriet were lovers. Were they, Aunt Addie?"

Give Aunt Addie credit. This time she didn't flinch. She simply acted as if Penny said nothing. "William, this can be your project the first rainy day," she said as she put the pieces of the soup tureen into a large baking bowl. "Gluing all the pieces together. Been in the family for generations. Hate to part with it. Uncle Lambot and I have had soup in it all our lives. I don't know what he would say if he ever found it missing."

"Won't say a thing. Never does. He won't even notice if you don't tell him," I said.

"I'll ask Sam Brown about the mill," Penny said.

"No, you won't. Mr. Brown has all kinds of problems with the strike and all. You are not to go to the mill," Aunt Addie warned again.

Another warning would not stop Penny from talking with Sam Brown somehow. I rather thought she would bombard him with a couple of hundred questions when he came out on a Saturday afternoon to join Uncle Lambot and his cronies. "Aunt Harriet used to tell us a lot about Sam Brown, an awful lot," Penny said.

That was a bold-faced lie, but it got to Aunt Addie. "That old fool . . ." she said. She didn't finish her sentence, and we didn't know who she thought was an old fool, Aunt Harriet or Sam Brown. She took off her apron and wheezed a sigh. "Am I going to have this all summer?"

"Not if you tell us what we ought to know," Penny said.

Aunt Addie fluttered her hands above her head, as if waving a flag of surrender. "All right," she said. "Your Uncle Lambot sold his share of the mill to Aunt Harriet just after the Depression started. He sold it because money was needed to keep the mill going. It then belonged to Aunt Harriet and," Aunt Addie hesitated, and then she added, "and your father. He would have no part in helping out. Your Uncle Lambot had the responsibility of the mill for years, and instead of helping, your father pulled the rug out from under him. Uncle Lambot would have sold everything he had, even his Packard, before he would have closed the mill. He did everything he could to save it, and for that, somebody threw a rock at us. It could have been a bomb. I declare I don't know what the world is coming to."

"Even his Packard." That amused Penny. I guessed it was because Uncle Lambot didn't have much else to sell.

"Even his Packard," Aunt Addie said. "This town was founded on the mill and has more or less lived on it ever since. Uncle Lambot loves Eastfield and its people, despite what they're saying about him. Your father didn't. He didn't care about anything here. The Lord only knew what he cared for. Now I hope you're satisfied."

Penny wasn't.

"You hardly ever mention our father. When you do, you sound bitter. Did you hate him, your own brother?" Penny asked.

If nothing else, the question clearly suggested lack of Christian love, and Aunt Addie wanted no part of it. For answer, she flopped her hands about and groaned.

"Nobody ever talks about anybody in this family and I don't know why. You never even talk about *your* father or *your* mother, our Granny. I wonder why."

"That's the way I was brought up," Aunt Addie said. "When you're older . . ."

"I'm old enough now. When you get to my age, you can't help but wonder."

"Talk, talk, talk, nothing but talk," Aunt Addie replied evasively.

"If Uncle Lambot felt that way about the mill, why did he sell his share to Aunt Harriet in the first place?" Penny asked.

"Selling to Aunt Harriet was one thing, and selling to unknowns is quite another thing. Goodness, child . . ."

"I'm *not* a child."

"Sometimes you act like one. Is that all I'm going to have this summer? Questions, questions, questions," Aunt Addie complained. "In families such as ours, menfolk don't talk business matters with womenfolk. It's not proper, and your Uncle Lambot has not given me the slightest hint that he wants to change. I *don't* know. All I know is that money was needed. If I recollect, it was soon after the stock market crash that he sold to Aunt Harriet."

"What was that?" I asked.

"That was when the country went berserk," Penny said. "Including this family."

"Penny!"

"Well, it seems that way. There are some things I know. Other people tell me things. If I wait for you to tell, I'll be ancient before I know."

"Young lady, you are being saucy. That is not nice at all."

"Neither is not knowing," Penny said. "Was Uncle Lambot ever poor? Does he have money now?"

"Your Uncle Lambot is a faithful provider," Aunt Addie said. "Always was and always will be. That's all that matters. Goodness, no more questions!"

"Does Uncle Lambot work?" Penny asked.

I wondered about that. Uncle Lambot puttered from morning until night, and sometimes beyond, but as far as we knew, he never really had a job any more than Adam had.

"There's not a lazy bone in his body," Aunt Addie affirmed.

"Do you have money, Aunt Addie?" Penny asked abruptly. Penny was certain she did. We talked about it on the train coming east. Penny told me that Aunt Addie had a peck of money all her own. Little piles of it here and there and all over. She said Aunt Harriet had told her how near and distant relatives and old maid friends died every so often and added to her kitty. Aunt Harriet said that Aunt Addie had the kind of money most people don't have, that kind that accumulates through thick and thin. She told Penny that if we lived long enough, Aunt Addie's booty would someday be ours, because Aunt Addie was old New England stock, the kind that left the bulk of possessions to younger members of the family, after making a proper donation to the church to assure a place in heaven. If Penny knew this, I wondered why she bothered to ask the question in the first place.

"We don't talk about money in this family," Aunt Addie said, and the way she said it you could tell that was a fact.

"When I get some, I'm going to talk about it," Penny said.

"How about the eight hundred . . ." Penny kicked me and gave me a dirty look.

"Do you own any of the mill, Aunt Addie?" she asked quickly, cutting me off.

"No."

"Why not?"

"Your grandfather left it to the boys."

"And none to you and your mother."

"Your grandfather had his peculiarities," Aunt Addie said.

"Which he willed to his children."

"That is nasty."

"Who owns Aunt Harriet's share of the mill now she's dead?" Penny wanted to know.

"O good Lord, child, *you* do! Aunt Harriet left her shares to you and Willie!" Aunt Addie exploded. "Questions, questions, you'll be the death of me yet!" Then Aunt Addie told us once and for all she had had enough of finance talk, it made her head swim, and if Uncle Lambot chose to tell us what she had told us, we were to make out as if we had not heard before. We weren't to lie about it, though, because lies never live long and the teller always suffers, no matter how small the lie. Then she told us we were awfully tired and it was time to go to bed. We didn't think so. It was frightfully hot, and the old school clock on the kitchen wall said it was only seven-thirty.

"Did she really leave it to us?" Penny asked.

"That's what I said. I don't want to talk about it."

Neither did I. "Can we go out to the barn and the old boat?" I asked.

"They'll be there tomorrow and the next day and the next," Aunt Addie said.

"I presume we get Father's shares, and now Aunt Harriet's. Did anyone else own shares?" Penny asked.

Aunt Addie groaned again. "Mr. Woodbury owns some shares. The bank owns some. Who else, I don't know."

"But it is mostly ours."

"It's being sold."

"Still mostly ours. What a playpen!" Penny exclaimed. "Willie, let's go outside and look at the flowers." Obviously Penny had heard enough for the time being and she wanted to do a bit of thinking.

"They are betwixt and between," Aunt Addie said. "Spring has gone, and summer hasn't quite caught up with it, despite the spate of heat," Aunt Addie said. It was mid-June and we were having a heat wave. We persisted and she relented. We guessed she wanted no further test of her authority.

Aunt Addie was right about the flowers. There wasn't much left of spring but some old peonies and some faded iris, and the roses had not yet broken their buds. But the lawn was clean-shaven, a cool-looking green, and Penny and I took off our shoes, and curled our toes in the grass. Everything looked about the same as last year, except maybe the trees looked bigger and the house smaller. There was a swarm of chimney swifts whirlpooling about the stone chimney, and the barn swallows were zooming in and out of the barn. A big mosquito with legs an inch long landed on my arm, and I let it stay there and bite me.

Aunt Addie corraled us at eight, but it was so hot I couldn't sleep. I sat by the window and looked out, watching the slow descent of a hazy summer night. At nine, I heard the clatter of the train, and then the toot of its whistle, the same double toot as last year. It sounded lonely and tired.

I wondered if Penny had heard and decided I had to find out. I waited until I heard Aunt Addie snoring before I sneaked down the hall to Penny's room. She had pulled the night table lamp underneath her bedspread and was reading. I told her Aunt Addie was taking a trip into another world and she could come out of her hole.

"Did you hear it?" I asked.

"Yes. Nice."

"Yeah." That was that. I had nothing else to say about it, and neither did Penny.

"You make Aunt Addie real upset with all your nit-wit talk," I said suddenly.

"I'm getting quite good at it," Penny said. "Knocking Aunt Addie off her rocker, I mean."

"Why?"

"You're a boy so she doesn't bother you like she does me. Figure that out."

I didn't pursue the matter. "Why doesn't she ever talk about Granny Winston? After all, it's her mother," I said.

"It has something to do with minding p's and q's, something to do with protecting our innocence. And being a New Englander from way back when. If you are a New Englander, true blue, you talk as little as possible about important things. Life is easier that way. It's possible that Granny Winston was driven out by all the no-talking signs all over the place," Penny said.

"Already, I am forgetting what she was like. Was she really Aunt Addie's and Uncle Lambot's mother, and Father's?"

"That's what they say."

"Granny Winston never talked about them much."

"Maybe she did when we were too young to remember. But there are skeletons in the closet, Willie, and our dear relatives never told us where the closet is."

"Like what?"

"Like who? Like Grandfather Winston, for instance."

"He was rich," I said.

"*Was,*" Penny said. "He was not yankee shrewd at all. He made some bad investments around 1920, and he borrowed money from the mill to cover them and it didn't work out the way he hoped. Our grandfather extended himself in more ways than one before he strung himself up. Granny told me all this before she had her stroke. Along the way I got the notion that Grandfather was not much taken with our dear old Granny, and vice versa. I think sometimes that Granny did not talk much about him because she couldn't stand being near to him, if you know what I mean."

"B.O.?" I wondered. "They talked a lot about that on the radio."

Penny laughed. "And halitosis. I think it was more than that. Remember how Granny used to mutter about life being a prison even though you had everything you needed?"

I didn't remember.

"In any case, apparently our family is not something that anybody wants to talk about. And if you can't talk about some things, then there are still more things you can't talk about. The thigh bone is connected to the shin bone. Remember what Granny used to say?"

What Penny told me hardly registered, and what did, caused a blur in my head. "You shouldn't talk to Aunt Addie the way you did. And say things. All that opera junk," I said.

Penny patted my hand. "Merely testing. But don't worry. Aunt Addie doesn't mind that much. Gives her something to think about."

"Why did you kick me?"

"What Aunt Addie doesn't know about our money won't hurt us." Penny hardly got the words out of her mouth before she realized what she had said. "I know what you're thinking, Willie. Secrets. Some are necessary, but some aren't."

"Yeah, sure. Sounds like something Aunt Addie would say."

"Caught," Penny admitted. "You got a point."

"I want to go home," I said.

"Willie, dear Willie, this *is* home," Penny said softly. "For better or worse, home sweet home, 'till death do us part.' "

"Don't say that."

"Until we are twenty-one, then, or earlier if we can find a way to fly the coop. Is that better? In the meantime we'll discover new things to do. Tomorrow you can join the scouts if you like. You could join up with the girls and I could join up with the boys. I'd like to see how the boys discover the world belongs to them."

"Knock it off."

"You ought to read more, Willie. Makes life bearable. If I had not read so much, I probably, at my age, would not be mature enough to say, 'I love you, my brother,' without either of us blushing." Penny leaned on my shoulder and let me ponder that. I didn't mind. She felt soft and comfortable.

"Willie?"

"What?"

"Did you ever think that if you learn one new thing a day for the next three months, you'll learn ninety new things? If you learn ten new things each day, you'll learn nine hundred? Did you ever think of that?"

"No."

"One new thing a day. A name of a tree or a flower. Anything. About people and work. About God. Strikes. Family secrets. About snakes and frogs and toads. And do you know what I'm going to do as soon as possible, Aunt Addie notwithstanding? I'm going to visit the mill. And we'll see Sam Brown and wheedle some ice cream money out of him. And some information about the mill, and how Aunt Harriet died. We can go swimming tomorrow. And visit Adam's shack, and see how many cats he has this year. And we can walk through the woods to visit the bluebirds in the apple tree, and . . ." Penny stopped. Walking through the woods to the apple tree was walking to Aunt Harriet's.

I left her then, to return to my room. Outside the door, I paused, thinking I didn't want to go to bed yet, and I heard her say, "Razz-matazz," as if she were swearing. I didn't reenter because I heard a couple of sobs. My kid sister was crying.

CHAPTER SEVEN

PENNY DID NOT SKIP OFF TO SEE SAM BROWN AT THE MILL. SHE called instead. The next morning Aunt Addie was more explicit about our traveling outside of our playpen, and she glued a couple of extra all-seeing eyes onto her head just to play it safe. There was no way we could escape her. Penny decided on the telephone. The phone was in the kitchen by Uncle Lambot's chair, and Penny sat there reading and listening to the radio, waiting for Aunt Addie to go chasing dirt elsewhere in the house. Penny had whispered to me what she was up to, so naturally I hung around.

So did Aunt Addie. She was no dodo and she suspected scheming. We were about to give up when suddenly she left to go upstairs to the bathroom. "On guard," Penny ordered, pointing to the stairwell, and in no time at all she had Sam Brown on the phone. One thing we liked about Sam Brown—we didn't have to call him Mister, and we didn't have to call him Uncle. Even Aunt Addie thought that a bit too cute. We called him Sam, and he didn't mind at all. So when Penny said, "Hi, Sam" she got instant recognition and she wasted no time. "Willie and I want to come to the mill to see you," she said. Sam's response was obviously negative, for there was a pause and Penny's lips sputtered an aside, a cuss word. "Then how about coming to see us?" she invited. "Willie and I want to see you in the worst way, please, please." There was another pause, a couple of monosyllabic responses, and Penny hung up. "Aunt Addie beat me to him, I could tell," she said. "I don't know how she did it, but he sure got the message."

"Maybe he *is* busy," I said.

"That's what he said. I didn't even get a chance to tell him we only wanted a peek at him."

"Even I wouldn't fall for that," I said. "Did he say he would come?"

"Maybe."

"I bet he comes."

"Apparently he has to check in with Aunt Addie first. That's how much he thinks of us."

"Who thinks what?" It was Aunt Addie. She had returned unawares. Penny tried to cover. "Freda O'Halloran, our friend back home. She lived next door, and didn't even bother to say goodbye. That's how much she thought of us."

Aunt Addie was not taken in. "Sam Brown is the busiest man in town these days. Awfully tired, I expect. You are not to bother him for the time being. I thought I told you that."

"We only want to say hello," Penny said.

"In due time. He's got too much to handle right now."

"I don't see why we can't go to the mill by ourselves. We came all the way from Des Moines without a chaperone. We are old enough to do that, but apparently we are not old enough to go a mile and a half into Eastfield. Why don't we all go? Why don't you come with us, Aunt Addie?"

"No!"

"Tell us about the mill, Aunt Addie. Tell us about it. Did you play in it when you were a child? Did you ever work there? Do people like to work there?"

"Goodness, child, I have work to do, and so do you. Your room," Aunt Addie said. "You've hardly been in it and already it is one colossal mess. I don't know how you do it."

"I've had a lot of practice. As you say, practice makes perfect."

"Don't be saucy, young lady. Before you step one foot outside this house, you are to clean and straighten out your room. You, too, Willie, you go along and help."

Aunt Addie was right about Penny's room. All Penny had to do was to look at her room and it would rearrange itself into a junk heap, and if the past summers were any judge, it would remain that way this summer no matter what Aunt Addie said about it. But room or not, clearly we had got another brush-off. Aunt Addie could not or did not want to talk about the mill. Or Sam Brown. "It's only a hunch, but I've got this sputtering in my brain that tells me that Sam is not one of her favorites," Penny surmised. "And I have another hunch that if Aunt Addie goes to prayer meeting tonight, and we stay home . . ."

"Doubt it."

"We'll see."

Sam Brown came. Penny managed to flash a bulletin to him about Aunt Addie's plans. Aunt Addie did go to the Thursday night prayer meeting at the church. There would be prayers for the mill, for the strikers, for the decision makers, for the whole community, and she would do her bit. We pleaded exhaustion, nerves, and a half dozen other things and so, against Aunt Addie's better judgment, we remained at the farm. Myrtice Bean, one of our pseudo-aunts, a yakkity-yak spinster, dropped by to take Aunt Addie to church. We had to go out to the car and get kissed and hear a lot of dumb talk about deaths in the family, and we collected a whole new batch of don't's from Aunt Addie.

Ten minutes after she was gone, Sam Brown drove into the yard in his Chevvie. "Just happened to be passing, and I thought I'd stop to see if your uncle had returned from the West."

"Of course," Penny said.

"You haven't heard from him?"

"You know Uncle Lambot."

"Do you know when he is returning?"

"You know Uncle Lambot."

Even to me, Sam looked tired. Worried and distraught. He was a tall, broomstick-skinny man, with bony hands that dangled at the end of long arms. His legs were lanky, and when he sat, he kept crossing them to keep his big feet from twitching, but they twitched all the same. The hair on his head was thinning, and it looked moldy, as if it needed a heavy sprinkling of fertilizer. His skin was bleached and his eyes were bloodshot. He slouched as he walked up the stairs onto the veranda. He didn't look as I had remembered him. Hardly at all.

Penny once said that Sam wasn't the brightest man God ever created, but that skinny face of his could win prizes all over the globe for the warm, friendly smile it could concoct. When we came bounding out of the house to greet him, he gave us one of his very best. He brought along a ton of ice cream, and in no time at all, I was shoving gobs of strawberry and vanilla down my throat. Penny only dabbed at hers. She preferred talk.

"Aunt Harriet. What happened?" Penny asked bluntly, not even waiting for Sam to do with amenities about our parents. The question startled him.

"She's gone, Penny," he said. "We'll miss her. You will miss her, won't you?"

Penny managed a touching response. "More than I shall ever know how to say," she said soberly. "There's much to remember."

"Lots," Sam said.

"For how long? How long will she last?" Penny asked. She didn't mention Ozymandias.

"A long, long, long time," Sam said as if talking to himself.

"What happened?"

"The house burned. What she was doing and how it happened, no one really knows. She was found in bed."

"Alone?"

"Penny! Shame!" But the remark brought color to his face.

"Did you love her?" Penny asked, taking a sympathetic tone, yet asking with her customary boldness and curiosity.

"Penny, Penny, Penny, you haven't changed," was the answer Sam gave.

"We talked about her all the way across the country. We wanted to see her more than anybody," I said. "We couldn't wait to see her."

"I understand," Sam said.

"Did she talk about us?" Penny wanted to know.

"Always said you were something special. Really special. Both of you."

"Did you see much of her before she died?"

Sam was evasive. "But then I can't imagine anyone not talking about you. She missed you. We all missed you. I guess we won't have that problem any more, will we? It's too bad the way things are. In normal times, I would be working for you. What do you think of that?" Sam put his dish on a table and stood to go. "Sure glad to see you kids here, despite all that's happened. I would like to stay longer, but there's a meeting at the mill and I have to be there. I'm late as it is."

"Tell us about the mill," Penny said quickly. "What's the strike all about? Is it bad?"

Sam sat again. "It's a long, involved story. The Winston Mills was a solid piece of property, but not big enough to withstand years of depression, and we ran out of money and business to keep it going. The Winston Mills is small potatoes in the business world, and . . ." Sam paused, not certain what to say. "It's a long and complicated story. These have not been easy years for your aunt and uncle, and I trust, young lady, that you will act toward them with your customary concern for people and their problems, and do all you can to help. The coming days are not going to be easy."

"Ugh," I muttered. That compliment was so much malarkey, but Penny liked it, and she fluttered her eyelids to show it. "I suspect you are trying to tell me more than you are saying," Penny said.

"It's difficult to tell you anything, young lady, and you are growing up. Into a nice lady, I hope."

"A woman," Penny shot back. "One who can have babies, and hold her own in a man's world. Were you ever a father, Sam?"

"You're sweet," Sam Brown replied. He stood again to leave.

"Sorry," Penny said quickly. "About the mill."

Sam Brown sighed. "I wish I knew the answer. Right now it's closed, and unless your uncle can discover how miracles are made, and makes one in a hurry, I think it will stay closed."

"Will the prayer meeting help?" I asked.

"You never can tell what God does with what he hears," Sam said, inching toward the exit.

"Do you believe in God?" Penny asked.

"Quite a lot lately," Sam said, and then added quickly, "but don't ask why, young lady, because I've not time to give you an answer tonight. The trouble with you, Penny, is that one question always leads to another."

Penny ignored that. "Are you the boss, Sam?" she asked. She knew, of course, that he was.

"Kids, I love you, but I really got to go. Tell you what. Next week, when things calm down a bit, I'll bring you to my place and we'll bake a cake. Whatever you want."

"Were you ever married, Sam?" Penny asked abruptly.

Sam paused at the top of the veranda steps. I thought he looked angry, and was going to tell Penny off. But he managed a good smile, the kind that erased tired marks. "I was not that fortunate to have lived any place where there was someone like you around to marry, my pet, and I was never one to settle for second best."

"I'm old enough now. I'm sixteen," Penny said.

Sam Brown flicked a frown onto his forehead. "And I'm too old," he said.

"How old is that?" and when Penny saw that he was going to hedge, she kept on going. "I'd say you're about forty-five. I bet you're Uncle Lambot's age, or Aunt Addie's, even though we think they are older. How long have you been working at the mill?"

Sam sat on the steps. "Long enough to know the name of every brick and stone in the walls. Long enough to know it's part of me, and I am part of it. Long enough to know that it has been my life. Most all of it. Long enough to make mistakes." Penny raised eyebrows on that. Obviously she wanted to hear more. "Mistakes, Penny. Maybe someday I'll tell you. It's not been easy."

Penny made a pointed remark. "If the mill goes, then you will have to find a new one. A new life, I mean."

He gave Penny a queer look of surprise, as if she had peeked into his mind, and he stared away from her, into the bushes outside the screened veranda until Penny brought him back with more questions. "How old were you, Sam, when you came to work at the mill? Did you grow up on a farm where you raised sheep and that's why you came to work at a woolen mill? When you came were you boss right away? What will you do if the mill closes for good? Will you go away? There's an extra bedroom here that nobody ever uses."

That seemed to bring him around and he managed another smile. "Young lady, someday you'll make a great lawyer," he said. "You ask as many questions now as you did when you were a kid. This year your questions seem to have aged a bit, and I'm not certain they are as polite as they ought to be. Still, if you really want to find out about things, you have to go in there slinging. If not a lawyer, maybe a reporter, or a scientist. Mostly, I guess a lawyer, and that's what you ought to be thinking about. There aren't many women lawyers in the world, but there are a few, and so you know it's possible."

"It's a man's world," Penny said.

"It's a man's world," Sam agreed.

"And you didn't answer one of my questions."

"And you haven't given me opportunity to ask any of my own. About your parents. Nor have you given me opportunity to extend sympathy."

"We don't need any," Penny said.

"Everybody does," Sam said. He looked into the bushes again, dreamily. "O.K., an answer or two, but no more. I came to this mill when I was a kid. I was an orphan, Penny, just like you and Willie are now. I lived with foster parents. I ran away when I was sixteen. I hitched on a freight train and got booted off in Eastfield in a rain storm. I discovered the mill. I went inside and fell asleep. A shop foreman, Tom Mulligan, long gone, found me, and got me work as a twenty-four-hour weekend watchman, which gave me a place in the mill to live and sleep. Mr. Mulligan worked the shirt off me, and my pants, as the saying goes, and in the process made me one and the same with the mill. And when my judgment day comes, Penny, that's what you have to remember about me. The mill became part of my life. That's why I'm single and never married. Now don't say, Penny, that I never tell you anything."

"What's judgment day?" I asked.

"The day of reckoning, the day when you go to one place or another. After it is decided," Penny said. "Sam's is a long way off."

"Maybe I've already had it," Sam said.

"That's an interesting thought," Penny mused.

"You kids clean up the dishes and spoons," Sam said, and this time he moved off the porch to his car. But Penny was not ready to call a halt to the proceedings, and she scrambled along side him and slipped an arm around one of his. "I figured out a couple of things already," she said.

"I dare not ask," Sam Brown said as he climbed into his Chevvie. Penny held onto the door. She would tell him anyway. "You came to Eastfield on a train as we did. You were an orphan, same as us. You were sixteen, that's my age, and you made it on your own.

You were independent. If you could do it, so can I. If that's not food for thought, I don't know what is."

"That's food for thought," Sam agreed.

"And if you came to work at sixteen, you must have known Aunt Addie when she was my age or thereabouts. Was she ever sixteen, Sam, or was she always old as she is now?"

"Penny. That's negative."

"I only meant did she do things like kids do at sixteen."

"Like asking a million questions."

"Like thinking about boys. Like dating. Like . . . Did you ever date Aunt Addie?"

"Aw geez, Penny," I said.

"Did you, Sam?" Penny asked.

Sam was not pleased with the question, and he evaded a direct answer. "Your aunt and I were born on different sides of the track, kiddo, and that's a fact of life," he said.

"I bet you were handsome, really, when you were sixteen, Sam, because you're still good looking. Know what I bet. I bet Aunt Addie had a crush on you. I bet you went to high school when she did, and I bet you sat 'side of each other, in geometry maybe, and you helped her. I bet she really had a crush on you. I know I would have. She did, didn't she? Just like Aunt Harriet had a crush on you. *She* did, didn't she? And in case you think I forgot, you didn't really say much about how Aunt Harriet's house burned."

Sam shook his head as if to shake off the onslaught of questions. He started his car and managed a smile. "You're too much, Penny, much too much. I have to go. I'm already late."

"Can we come to the mill tomorrow?" Penny asked.

"Ask your Aunt Addie," Sam said as he drove off.

"He looked sick to me," I said. "Did you see his eye twitching? And he couldn't keep his hands still."

"A bundle of nerves. I saw," Penny said. "He didn't enjoy us like he used to."

"Don't blame him."

"I didn't handcuff him, Willie. He could have gone as soon as he got here. He didn't have to come."

"Baloney."

"Maybe he felt duty-bound. Maybe. You have to admit that I asked some tricky questions. Like my question about dating Aunt Addie."

"You got a tricky answer."

"Tricky. He didn't say no, Willie. And he could have said that. That is a very easy word to say. Aunt Addie says it all the time. It has only one syllable and it hardly twists the tongue."

"You know what you are this year? A smart ass."

"Yes, Willie," Penny said. "So maybe he did answer. They were of the same age. They must have known each other. If he hadn't dated her, he could have said no."

"Yes is an easy word, too."

"You make my point, but it would have been more difficult if it's the truth," Penny said. "It apparently is as difficult for Sam to talk about Aunt Addie as it is for her to talk about Sam. Or to talk about Aunt Harriet. Old people have difficulty talking about some things with young people. It's silly, if you ask me. All in all, he disappointed me, if you want to know."

"Don't blame him."

"He twitched. Something's wrong."

"The mill, dummy," I said.

"Something else, too. He was nice to us, same as ever, but yet he wasn't. Something's different."

"I think I'll get some more ice cream," I said. I had had enough of talk. Penny hadn't.

"I care, Willie, I really do. There are empty spaces in our lives, and I aim to fill some of them. If I don't know, I get this sick feeling deep inside of me, and the only way I can get rid of it is by finding out. I want to know. Besides, it's fun to find out what makes people tick, don't you think?"

"Bunk," I said. "You know what Uncle Lambot says?"

" 'What you don't know won't hurt you.' I know. He doesn't mean that. He means he doesn't like to tell us things that might embarrass him. Just like Aunt Addie saying, 'Children should be seen and not heard.' It's a put-off."

"Know what else Uncle Lambot says?"

" 'Talk is cheap.' *Funnnee.*"

"I'm tired of talking," I said. "Let's do something. We've got a chance to do something with Aunt Addie gone, and we stay right here and do nothing but talk. Let's go find Adam."

"You go, Willie. I want to think. You know what I was thinking last night in bed? I was thinking about what the Reverend James said at supper, about how what people do keeps on living. Now you take the Reverend James, he's smarter than he looks."

"You take him. Are you coming?"

"I think I will go to the attic."

"We're not supposed to go there. What for?"

"To find a diary. I bet Aunt Addie kept a diary when she was a girl. She looks like the type."

"Just like you."

"*Funnee,*" Penny said, not at all pleased that she had stumbled over herself again. "Love letters, then. I'll bet there are a peck or two of them in a trunk or two."

"Trunks are locked," I said. "If Aunt Addie's got something hidden, you'll never find it. She can hide things better than anybody. If she wants, she can hide fudge under your pillow, and you'd never find it. Besides, you searched the attic last year."

"I wasn't looking for letters then."

"You were looking for anything you could find that you knew Aunt Addie didn't want you to find."

"She would keep us forever in ignorance if I didn't."

"She's not the only one," I said. "You keep your diary secret. You haven't even shown it to me, not that I want to see it. Would you show it to Aunt Addie?"

That got to Penny. "Willie, dear Willie," she sighed. "What a wonderful brother to have. What do you want to do?"

"Let's go to Aunt Harriet's. Have we got time? I want to go."

"We could run. Let's. I want to go, too."

CHAPTER EIGHT

WE DIDN'T SNEAK OVER TO AUNT HARRIET'S THAT NIGHT. WE dawdled until Aunt Addie came home and it was too late. Neither of us would admit it, but we didn't go because we couldn't bring ourselves to face what we didn't want to believe. We still had the notion that come next Wednesday we would be going for the night, the same as last year.

We cleaned up everything, almost. Somebody had spilled a dab of ice cream on the kitchen counter and we missed it. Aunt Addie spotted it, put two and two together, and did some more leaning on us about not leaving the compound.

The first time we got out was on Sunday, and that was to go to church. After church, Charity Chase came calling. She was new, having moved to Eastfield from Hartford during the winter. She brought along a book, *Lorna Doone,* and that was for Penny. A book to Penny was a key to eternal and everlasting friendship. Charity Chase soon became Aunt Charity. I minded. Penny didn't.

Charity Chase was a big lady, with mixed-up puffs of gray and black hair, on which she wore a red hat which she changed each week by adding or subtracting ribbons and artificial flowers. She wore horn-rimmed glasses on a large nose. Her face was rather bony, and she wore rouge on her lips, and in round spots on her cheeks.

She was a talker. She talked about everything and she talked as if she knew all about everything she talked about. Penny was enthralled.

That first afternoon they talked politics, and Charity Chase said some nice things about President Roosevelt and Mrs. Roosevelt, which was almost sacrilege. She said she had voted for Alf Landon because it was still proper to be Republican, even though most people were Democrats, but her vote had been a mistake. She enjoyed the President's fireside chats. He had a sense of humor, used fine language and correct grammar, and he never mispronounced a word. She said that all the common people who did not know how to use fine language and correct grammar voted for him, whereas most of them that could, did not. There were more common people, as Abraham Lincoln had stated, than uncommon people, and therefore Roosevelt could act with all the dignity and freedom of a man bound to succeed. Aunt Addie glued her eyes to the floor. I thought she would faint a dozen times.

Charity Chase talked about Mussolini taking Ethiopia, and all about world morality. She talked about communism in Russia, about the Japanese invading China, the war in Spain, and Hitler. She said the world was one big mess, and no wonder it was filling up with schizophrenics, both rich and poor. She said someday those schizos would be parents, and they would mess up their children so that they didn't know which end was up, and the children would mess up the world even more. It was heady stuff that the old gal dished out.

She sparred with Penny on literature. Penny asked if she knew Ozymandias, and Charity Chase recited that poem as if she were saying, "Now I lay me down to sleep, I pray the Lord my soul to keep." She talked of Byron, and Keats and Shelley, and how she had once been to Rome and had visited Keats's home there. She told

how Keats had died at the age of twenty-five, and how Shelley died
when he was thirty, and they must have been remarkable men to
have known so much about life so early. They both could have lived
to be a hundred, Charity Chase averred, and they could not have
known much more. Education and wisdom were peculiar com-
modities, one does not always beget the other, and not many people
knew one from the other. It wasn't hard to tell that she used to be a
school teacher.

Aunt Charity invited us to a tea party on the following Wednesday. Unless I pleaded sickness, I knew I was hooked. I chose to go.

Aunt Charity lived in a rambling, brown gingerbread of a house
that was decorated with lots of white frosting in the eaves and over
the doors and windows. I thought the insides were musty and dull.
To Penny it was a house of wonder because there were books
strewn everywhere—on the living room sofa, in the dining room, by
the kitchen sink, in the bathroom—and most were open and care-
worn. At the first "tea," they latched onto Shakespeare. Penny impressed by reciting a sonnet she had learned only that morning, and
Aunt Charity countered with Portia and the quality of mercy.

To say that I was bored was to put it mildly. I sat most of the
time on a footstool covered with needlepoint and looked at pictures
through the stereopticon and scratched the cat's back, a black angora,
as big as a pregnant skunk.

Except at odd moments when she pushed a batch of stale oatmeal
cookies my way, the lady of the house ignored me. When we left,
she gave Penny a volume of Shakespeare to borrow until next week,
and she filled my fist with cookies. On the way home I scaled them
into the trees for the birds. As far as I was concerned this new Aunt
Charity was for the birds as well. Wednesday afternoon with Aunt
Charity was not a decent substitute for Wednesday evenings with
Aunt Harriet.

It didn't take long to discover a number of other items that were
going to be different that summer. Aunt Addie was stricter for one

thing, and her nerves were more collapsible. Penny said it was because she was completely responsible for us now, and she would not be able to relinquish that responsibility in September, and that made a lot of difference. Be that as it may, you certainly felt the change. Last year, Aunt Addie had the "druthers." "I'd rather not have you do so and so or such and such," she would say. It was never quite an order, and it was neat, because if you wanted, you could do things without really disobeying. Now she ordered. She told us repeatedly that we were to stay put, with no and's, if's, or but's, and not to wander out of sight or sound. We were in mourning, she said, and it would be indecent to be gallivanting about. She watched our every move from every window in the house. Penny argued and crabbed. At first, she got nowhere.

Aunt Addie didn't mind our being outside when the skies were clear. She said we should soak up loads of sunshine to fight off colds in winter. Naturally we preferred the out-of-doors, sunshine or no sunshine. We dawdled about and poked our faces here and there. One day we hunted for birds' nests. We found a blue jay family high in a pine behind the house. We could hear the chirpings of the fledgelings and we climbed the tree to see them. In the nest were four chicks, wearing iridescent pinfeathers, and each with two enormous eyes, unafraid and curious. Penny waved her finger over them, and they opened their beaks until you could see down to their toenails.

"Quadruplets," Penny said. "Adorable. I wonder what it would be like to have four babies to hug and cuddle at once."

I didn't have time to respond because the baby birds all began to chirp, and in an instant, half the blue jays in the country descended upon us.

Aunt Addie heard the ruckus and came rushing out of the house. She added to the melee by shrieking, "Penny! Get down out of that tree before you break your neck! Penny, do you hear me!"

We heard. We were coming down anyway, as we had no intention of being maimed by pecking jays. Penny said, "Did you notice she called only me and not you? 'Tis the way the wind will blow all summer, I bet, I bet."

With that, she fell, knocking me to the ground along with her.

Aunt Addie screamed, and I yelled, "Damn it, get off my back." Penny groaned. She had hit her knee again, and had scraped the skin on the bark. But that was not enough to stop her. "Help me up, Willie, and make out as if nothing happened. If Aunt Addie thinks I'm hurt, she'll haul me off to bed. Aunt Addie likes sick kids. She knows exactly where they are. In bed."

But there was no cause for worry. Aunt Addie made for the veranda and collapsed into a wicker chair, palpitating the air about her with her bamboo fan. We headed for the barn.

"Let's jump rope," Penny said.

"Your knee."

"If she sees me jumping, she'll never suspect. It doesn't hurt anyway," Penny said. So we got some rope and tied it to a clothesline behind the house and took turns twirling and jumping. Penny did well, and I guessed the knee didn't hurt much. After a while it got hot, and I took off my shirt.

"Lucky," Penny said. I knew what she meant. In the house, by ourselves, we still paraded in front of each other with this or that off as we pleased. Last year we did outside, at the swimming hole at least. But now Penny was sixteen, and we were Aunt Addie's charges. I could see that Penny was tempted, indecisive, then she decided not to do likewise. But as she was jumping, she looked toward the house, and saw Aunt Addie peeking and fretting at the kitchen window. "She's got out her periscope," Penny said.

"So what?"

"So watch." With that she wiggled out of her middy blouse and kept on jumping. She reached the count of thirty before Aunt Addie bellowed, henny-penny, the sky is falling. She banged on the kitchen window, then flew out the kitchen door. "Penny! Put your clothes on this instant!"

I stopped twirling the rope. "Why?" Penny asked, as if she didn't know.

"Do as I say."

Penny gave Aunt Addie a long unladylike stare that was a sign of battle, but she obeyed. As Penny pulled her blouse over her head, her arms stretching a bit, I suddenly realized that Aunt Addie had a special reason for yelping. Penny had grown. Not much, but there was more up front than there had been last year. Then I saw Adam. He was hovering by the open door of the barn. I saw him because Aunt Addie gave him a blast, and he jumped. Then he faded, abracadabra, he was gone, and Aunt Addie went chasing her own heat wave back into the house.

"Let's go swimming," Penny said.

I demurred. "Aunt Addie."

"Do you want to go swimming or don't you?"

"Let's ask. She might let us."

"Of such stuff are dreams made," Penny said as she headed out into the field. So I went along.

Beyond where the field and forest met, through which was the path to Aunt Harriet's, was our favorite swimming hole. It was as round as a silver dollar, and not much bigger. It was spring-fed, and the bubbly water was crystal clear. About it, marsh grass harbored schools of tiny black polliwogs, and there were snails and an occasional crawfish to be found under the stones. Sometimes we found minnows and were amazed because we never saw any grown-up fish. Last year Adam told us they came down with the rain from the clouds, and Penny asked him how it was that fish coming from nowhere could navigate precisely to our pool without splattering themselves to death on the land. Adam told her they did it the same way birds flew north and south every year, and he said the raindrops acted like parachutes.

There were bushes at one end of the pool, and the way they were located, you could go swimming and nobody could see you from the house, not even from the attic windows. We skirted the edge of the field and stalked our way among the trees to lose ourselves from the sight of the spy in the house. Penny said even if Aunt Addie did see us, her voice couldn't possibly carry that far, and if we didn't hear, we would have no compulsion to obey.

At first we explored. I caught a bullfrog that must have weighed a pound, and Penny said keep it, because we could dope him later, cut him open, and watch his heart beat. It might beat for days if we dabbed it with salt, then when it stopped we could fry him and each have a leg. I said Aunt Addie wouldn't let us, and Penny said, "We'll cook him in the woods, silly, along with some potatoes."

But I let him go. "No bathing suits," I said.

"So what?" Penny said. "I know what you look like and you know what I look like."

"Aunt Addie said . . ."

"Aunt Addie is scratching away in the kitchen. You've seen me naked, Willie. Just as naked as any cow in the field. Do you turn your head when you look at a cow?"

"Suppose she catches you again?"

"At least our shirts," Penny said, pulling hers off. "I want to be free, Willie, free. Last one in is a pighead," she yipped. I jumped in after her, and suddenly we sensed we were having fun, and we made the most of it, as if to grab it and hold it forever. I had a sense of belonging to something I hadn't experienced before, something familiar and foolish. It was good to be in Eastfield and swimming without a care, and before we knew it, as we splashed and ducked each other, and hardly thinking about it, we took off all our clothes and tossed them on the bank to dry. I even had a notion that Aunt Addie wouldn't have minded a whit if she could see how we were enjoying ourselves, and minding our own business.

Then I noticed Adam. Adam's shack was but a couple of dozen yards into the woods. The swimming pool was Adam's private bath in the summer. Other years we would wash ourselves with Adam. He would bring along soap and we would lather up, and it was more fun than bathing at home in Aunt Addie's ancient tub, which had a faucet that emitted water by the drop.

I noticed him staring at Penny, not me, and decided then and there I didn't like that, or him. I was about to tell Penny to get her clothes, but decided to poke her instead, and let her handle the matter.

I was too late.

"Penny!" The command rolled over the field like thunder. You would have thought that Aunt Addie had piped herself into Uncle Lambot's Atwater Kent in the kitchen.

I jumped out of the water and made for my soggy clothes. Adam jumped, too, and in an instant there was no Adam. And then I saw why Aunt Addie's voice came in loud and clear. She had carried it to us in person. There she stood, in the stance of Moses, on the mound just beyond the pool.

"Penny, get out of there this instant! Shame! When you go swimming, you go with my permission and you wear your bathing suit! Always!" she thundered, her bellow curling my nerves. Penny stood immobile, and I could not tell whether it was in shock or in defiance. In the end, she succumbed and climbed onto dry land as if nothing happened and gradually slipped into her wet clothing while Aunt Addie slid into a dither about how decent people wouldn't do that sort of thing. I was not included and I realized that it was something serious, not just another don't, and it had something to do with Adam.

"Lunch in a half hour and I don't want to call either of you! Now finish dressing and march home!" And oddly—perhaps because she couldn't take it any longer, or because she couldn't trust herself—she wheeled and marched herself alone back across the field, fading out in a torrent of mumble.

"Told you so," I said.

"I told you. You want to act like a ten year old and you'll not have trouble. I'm not going to do it."

"You are acting like a ten year old. You do dumb things like a spoiled kid."

"That's debatable," Penny said. "You know what I think. I think somebody pays her to make life miserable for us. Willie, you have to join me in the good fight this summer. Fight the good fight, I always say. 'Onward Christian soldiers, marching as to war!' Or is it 'on to war.'" Penny sat on a rock and squeezed some water out of her clothes.

"It's not easy on Aunt Addie," I said. "All that talk about death and all that opera love stuff. It gets *me* all screwed up inside, too. I don't want to run my life as fast as yours."

Penny became serious. "Willie, I do feel sorry for her. She's got more complex angles in her than there are in all the problems in geometry, but her chapters are completed, if you know what I mean. Ours aren't. So are you with me or not?"

"For what?"

Penny gave up on me. "Willie, dear Willie. We've got a half hour," she said. "So I say let's take a look at Adam's place."

"Let's not."

"To see the cats," Penny said, getting up and walking on. "And maybe to eat some strawberries."

I followed, but less like a pet poodle than a bodyguard. I remembered what she had said about Adam and having babies, and I saw how Adam had leered at her, and I didn't want to leave her alone with him. If I went home by myself, Aunt Addie would ask where Penny was, and I would have to face her fretting, even if I lied. At the age of twelve, I was beginning to realize that moments of happiness were short-lived. Memories of our innocent splashings of yesteryear in the pool, were going, going, soon to be gone forever.

CHAPTER NINE

ADAM WAS SITTING OUTSIDE, HONING UNCLE LAMBOT'S SCYTHE. Beside him was his ratty, leather briefcase, which was always with him. Adam said the only reason he had it was for us to ask why, which we did, and got an Uncle Lambot grunt for reply.

Adam drawled and he shuffled, and the muted word to describe him was "retarded." Penny said he was one of God's favored, for he never worked much, and neither of us thought that was exactly dumb. He did minor jobs here and there when the spirit moved him. He washed and polished the Packard. He kept Aunt Addie's flower gardens. He and Uncle Lambot shared the weeding of the vegetable garden aside the barn, Uncle Lambot working mostly in the spring and early summer, and Adam taking over when Uncle Lambot and the garden were getting tired. You hardly ever saw Adam, because he did most of his work before breakfast, had wine at siesta time, and slept in between here and there. Adam was a good gardener, I'll say that for him. His vegetables grew wildly and even Aunt Addie said he must have a handful of green thumbs. Uncle Lambot, in a rare venture into humor, said it was Adam's tobacco juice that did the trick. Adam chewed while he worked, and he could work up some of the dirtiest spittle ever concocted. Aunt Addie was appalled at the idea, and she countered Uncle Lambot by saying that Adam's juice killed everything it touched, that it was the scrapings from the poultry house that made the flowers and vegetables grow the way they did.

We looked for the cats, first. We found only eight, including Sheba, and Penny said that she must be in her seventh or eighth life and at the petering-out end of producing kittens, and that her ninth life could well be virginal and in that condition she would go to her final rest. We petted the cats out of politeness, but neither Penny nor I were smitten with the scrawny creatures. Last year we had a thing about trying to decide which cats were related and how. And one day we pulled two dead mice about on strings and played the pied piper in reverse with them. That was the day we named them after dictators near and far, from Attila the Hun to Hitler, Togo, and Mussolini. But we didn't play with them much. Cats were cats to us, and we thought the only thing, sometimes, they might be good for was to toss them into Adam's cradle behind the house. But that was his pleasure, not ours.

We squatted at Adam's side.

"How many cats you got this year?" I asked.

"Fourteen, so far as I know."

"What have you been doing all morning?" Penny asked. So much for cats.

Adam's answer came slowly. "I polished the car. I went over to Ranse Sherman's lumberyard to get some pieces of wood to make some birdhouses. Still summer enough to catch second nestings of tree swallows and bluebirds. Stan Wynewski drove me home in his truck, and I fed the cats. Too hot to work," he said. In the winter, it was often too cold, he had told us. "You going to help me do the lawn this year, Willie? It's not bad, once you shape your mind to the job. You kids hungry? Ain't much in the garden yet. There's a new batch of radishes, and there's some strawberries left."

"Radishes," Penny said. "Strawberries," I said.

"There's salt on the table for radishes and some sugar and cream for strawberries," Adam said. He acted as if he hadn't seen us that morning. He looked at Penny mostly. I was aware of that.

In the radish patch, I whispered, "He gives me the creeps."

"Adam?" Penny laughed. "Every home should have an Adam.

Let him alone and he does lots of things and he doesn't cost much. Just look at that garden!"

It was a patch the size of a parlor rug, spring-green and leafy, fresh-washed, the whole looking as though it was nursed in a large terrarium.

"As pretty as a painting," Penny said. "And Adam did it."

"With the help of God," I added.

"Maybe so, but still a work of art. There is Adam's soul."

I could care less about Adam's soul. I noticed the blossoms on the pea vines. "Looks like we'll have peas by the Fourth," I said. A row of peas was already in blossom. Uncle Lambot always said you could tell a good growing season if you had peas by the Fourth of July.

We picked some radishes. We wiped them clean on our pants and ate them, a half dozen or so apiece. Then we picked some strawberries, which were as big as plums. We filled our handkerchiefs with them, and inside we put them in tin cups, showered them with sugar, and drowned them in cream.

"Yummy!" Penny exclaimed. "Kings can't find better."

Maybe so, but the shack was hardly a palace. Last year I had hardly noticed the place; this year I did. It was cruddy. Uncle Lambot's private room in the barn was a surgical room by comparison. Adam's chair was ratty and the springs were dragging on the floor. A moth-eaten mattress on a rusted iron bed was only half-covered by a couple of moth-eaten blankets. Odds and ends of broken chairs, obviously purloined from some dump, stood forlornly about a dirty stained table. A wood stove, encrusted with soot, stood shamefully in the corner.

"Picturesque," Penny said.

"A flea bag," I said.

"Comfortable," Penny said. "And there is no one here to proclaim the don't's. Quiet and cool on a hot night and you can hear the crickets and peepers. And I bet the train toots louder here. This place is a lot easier to care for than our big house. There's time for other things."

"Like what does Adam do with his free time?" I wondered.

"He enjoys life. That's the whole point of living. I believe Adam has found time to do that."

Finding time was one of Penny's pet hobbies, so I didn't argue the point. All I said was that with a place like Adam's all she'd ever do would be to sit on her fanny and read books, and she said that was not a bad idea. She would talk to Adam about renting the place for the summer so that she could do just that. Not with my money, I told her.

We heard the cowbell in the distance. We had forgotten the bell. Aunt Addie used it to beckon us from field and forest.

"Can't be twelve yet," I said. "We just got here."

"Aunt Addie always rings a fifteen-minute warning."

"Let's go, else we get a lot of yakking."

"I'm not hungry."

I wasn't either. In fact, I could already feel the radishes and strawberries fighting it out in my stomach. But I said, "Makes no never mind. You know Aunt Addie. Come on, Penny. We're already in the doghouse because of the swimming."

Penny was not moved. She asked Adam if he ever lived in a better place.

"Bigger, but not better. Have everything here," Adam said.

"See," Penny said, looking at me. "Adam, do you ever read?" Penny asked that of everybody.

"Sometimes. Don't have much call to read in my occupation. If I did read, what would I do with what I read? Might get some foolish notions. Besides, my eyes are bad."

I thought, baloney to that. The way I saw him ogling Penny that morning, he could have read a page of the Bible on the far side of hell if he had had a mind. I thought it funny that Adam didn't read because it might suggest things for him to do. Penny read to keep from doing.

Penny asked what he considered his occupation.

Adam plopped himself into his chair. He thought about it. Time was running out. I wanted to leave, but this was too good to miss.

"Keeping alive," Adam said.

"Great!" Penny exclaimed. Clearly Adam could not have responded more intelligently. "Did you ever go to school?"

Adam wiped some dark saliva from his lips on his sleeve. At the moment he had no answer.

"Did you come on the boat in the field?" Penny asked.

"Did it belong to your father?" I asked.

"I don't reckon I had a father," Adam drawled, and when he said that, I reckoned he'd been drinking already that morning.

"Everybody has a father," I said.

"Not everybody has a human father," Penny reminded me. "Remember Jesus? If it happened before that men could be born without human parents, it could happen again. What about that! Adam, born of a virgin! Willie, just supposing!"

"Puke!"

"Of course, it would be better if the first Adam were an Eve. The second time around it ought to be a girl, a woman instead of a man. How about that!"

I made a face.

"Just a passing thought that I might just grab and keep," Penny said, pleased with it.

"I reckon I go to school every day," Adam said, finally answering Penny's question. "All the world is a school."

"Why, Adam!" Penny's eyes twinkled with pleasure. "And what did you learn in school today?"

"Nothing I didn't already know."

"Then you didn't try. I try to learn something new every day. Like about Aunt Harriet's fire. Did you see it, Adam? Were you there?" Penny asked.

Adam shifted his position slightly. "Couldn't live this close without knowing something was going on," he drawled.

"How did it happen? Who set it?"

Adam shifted again. He was slow in answering. "Maybe it wasn't set. Maybe it just happened. Nobody knows. It doesn't matter one way or other," he said. "Ask your aunt, if you want to know. She knows everything."

"Aunt Clammie, who knows all and tells nothing," Penny said. "Not a chance, so you tell us. Tell us about Aunt Harriet, Adam. What was she really like? Did you know her, really know her? She used to talk about you a lot."

Aunt Addie clanged the cowbell again. It sounded angry.

"Come on, Penny," I urged, and when she didn't move, even though I wanted to hear if Adam had anything to say, and even though I didn't want to leave Penny with him, I moved without her. I arrived hot and sweaty, and I washed with a frenzy at the kitchen sink to forestall a scolding. But Aunt Addie only said, "Is Penny coming?"

"She said it was too hot to run," I fibbed. I noted the waffle iron on the table, and scowled. Another day I could have eaten waffles until the cows came home. Today my stomach said no. But I ate, hoping that Aunt Addie wouldn't mention swimming.

When Penny came, she came running, despite what I had told Aunt Addie. She was full of chatter. She told Aunt Addie a lot of baloney about how she had been discussing logarithms with Adam, and she said she had had lunch, radishes, strawberries, and stuff, and she was not about to cram waffles on top of all that, thank you just the same. That didn't stop Aunt Addie. As usual she had mixed a large bowl of batter, and she kept making waffles and stuffing them into me, lest the batter go to waste.

Penny dabbed at her waffle, studied her plate, and pinged it with her fingers. "These are pretty dishes," she said. "How long have you had them?"

The plates were thin and plain white. The broken soup tureen belonged to them. I smelled a rat.

Aunt Addie didn't. "They belonged to your great-great-grandmother. They came with her from England. They are bone china. They are my most precious possessions."

"I remember. You told us when you broke the tureen. Bone china is the whitest china of all. I read about it the other night in the encyclopedia in the parlor. Do you know why it is called bone china, Aunt Addie?"

Now Aunt Addie smelled the rat. "Child, eat your food and hush up," she admonished.

"This *child* has discovered that bleached ground bone has been mixed into the clay. English bone china contains bone from the black angus. But the whitest china of all is made with human bones, and maybe these dishes . . ."

"That will be enough of that!"

"I wonder how many people have eaten off this plate," Penny said, forging ahead. "I wonder how many of them knew they were eating off a plate made of congealed bones, possibly human bones. If so, I wonder if they came from a man or a woman."

"What did I just say?"

"O.K., Aunt Addie, something else then," Penny said, not ready for a squelching. "Willie, do you know that window in the church, the one with Jesus and the children? I think it's beautiful. I love the extravagant crimson color of his robe. Did you ever see a picture of Jesus wearing anything but white?"

I hadn't.

"The children look like today's children," Penny said, and even I knew that was meant to suggest that *we* were no longer children. " 'Suffer little children and come unto me.' That's written beneath that window. I can't remember the rest."

"Matthew 19, verse 14. 'Suffer little children, and forbid them not, to come unto me: for of such is the kingdom of heaven.' " Aunt Addie couldn't resist that response, and she spoke it as if she were ticking off the beat of her heart. For a second or so, she was pleased, and so was Penny.

"Thank you, Aunt Addie," Penny said, smiling sweetly. She

paused and reflected, a bit longer than was necessary. " 'Forbid them not,' " she said, lifting a phrase out of context. "I like that. What a wonderful idea. 'Forbid them not.' "

Aunt Addie's moment of contentment disappeared. "Penny, you haven't eaten a thing," she said.

"Strawberries and radishes, remember?" Penny said. "What do you think of that, Willie?"

"What?" I asked.

" 'Forbid them not,' " Penny repeated.

Suddenly Aunt Addie had had enough. "All right, all right!" she snapped. "There are do's and don't's, and you have to learn the difference. One of the things you don't do is to parade in the nude in public. If that's a don't, so be it." She turned to me. "Willie, you are not to go swimming without a bathing suit, either. Especially with Penny. What on earth were you thinking of?"

"Another subject, then," Penny said.

"Eat your food," Aunt Addie said.

But Penny didn't want to eat. She wanted to talk. "Do you think Adam is happy, living alone in his shack? Willie and I were discussing that."

"We were not," I said.

"He doesn't have to live there," Aunt Addie said.

"Then where could he live?" Penny asked. "Could he live here, Aunt Addie? We have plenty of room. Three quarters of the house goes begging for people."

Penny touched a sensitive spot, one that made Aunt Addie squirm. Apparently she had thought about the house before, and of Eastfield people living in unheated mill tenements, but it was a feeling she preferred to let remain dormant.

"Penny invited Sam Brown to live here, too," I said.

That hardly helped matters. Aunt Addie shuddered, and got flustery. She told me to take my elbows off the table, and she plopped yet another waffle on my plate, and said I had enough syrup on it for a dozen more waffles.

"If Adam had a bigger place, would he like it better?" Penny asked. "And suppose he had a new home, would it some day become as dirty as his shack? I admit it is *filthy*, Aunt Addie."

"I know, I know! Goodness! One look at Adam and you know that. You are not to go there!"

"Don't, don't, don't! I wish I had counted them this summer!"

"That is enough of that!" Aunt Addie said, a couple of decibels higher.

"Enough. O.K.," Penny said. "Just the same, you know what I'd like to do? I'd like to paint it inside and out and clean it. Mend the furniture and Adam's clothing. See if he would like living better. See if it would change him. I'd like to clean his place like you clean this house, Aunt Addie."

The idea did not appeal to Aunt Addie. "You'll do nothing of the kind. You are not to go to Adam's. Is that clear? And while I'm about it, lest you get some foolish notion, you are to stay away from the Nason farm this summer. There's trouble there."

"Trouble? What kind of trouble?" Penny asked.

"Trouble. They are not fit people for you. You stay clear of Adam, and you stay clear of the Nasons. Is that clear?"

"Who said anything about the Nasons?" Penny wanted to know.

"I did," Aunt Addie stressed.

"You let us go last year. You let us go swimming with Adam last year," Penny said.

"Last year you did lots of things despite my wishes. This year is different, and you are different. I mean it, Penny."

"And if I disobey?"

"Don't press your luck, young lady."

Penny sighed. " 'Forbid them not.' The world has gone negative. Aunt Addie, you have filled my world with don't's."

"Someday you'll learn you can be as content with your don't's as with your do's," Aunt Addie said. "But if you want a do, you can clean your bathroom. It's six inches deep in your dirty clothes. As for don't's, you've done nothing since you've been here."

I thought that funny and clever, but Penny didn't. She gave up the battle and marched outside, clomping her feet and slamming the screen as she went.

Filled to the brim with waffles, and anxious to get moving, I followed after Penny. I said, "Aunt Addie bested you," and she didn't like it. "Well, kiss my razz," I said and told her she was getting too damn fresh and that she was heading us both for a peck of trouble.

"No worse than what we got," she said. "Suppose I had said nothing this noon, but had clamped my tongue. Stared at my food as if I were a prisoner. What then? What would life be like at the table? Answer me that. Aunt Addie wouldn't know what to make of it, except to believe that I must be sick and about to die. If she's afraid of me, that's her problem, not mine."

"Dumb," I said. "Aunt Addie talks a lot. She'd talk more if you'd give her a chance and not say all those dumb things."

"She talks all right. To herself, all the time. You know what they say that's a sign of? Money in the bank. The way Aunt Clammie mumble-jumbles while she's working must mean she's got more money in the bank than the Woodburys and Aunt Charity combined, and if you want to know, it is my secret opinion that the Woodburys and Aunt Charity are loaded."

"Who cares? What's that got to do with Aunt Addie?"

"Aunt Addie. Ho hum. If you think about it, I do her a favor. And us. I make her forget. I make her forget a don't or two. Do you know what she forgot this summer? She forgot to tell us what a nice idea afternoon naps are. How about that? If I can make her forget naps for a few more days, it will be too late to have them."

"Then think of another way than saying dumb things. All that jazz about bones in the plate and that Jesus talk was driving me nuts, never mind Aunt Addie."

"I wanted to know what bone china was, so I found out. The church window popped into my mind. Both were interesting subjects for conversation."

"Not the way you did it," I said.

"Willie, dear Willie. We seem to be quarreling a lot this year."

"Let's do something besides talk," I said, tiring of it all.

"I already know what I'm going to do."

"What?"

"Read, Willie. To find something new to talk about."

"Crap."

"From *Lorna Doone*. I shall venture into Glen Doone with John Ridd and help him rescue his lovely Lorna. And then I shall tell Aunt Charity all about it. It impresses her! I like to impress people. Want to come along? I'll read to you."

"Nuts. The more you read the more dumb things you do."

"And stupid. You've intimated I am just that quite a lot this summer. Maybe so. But wait until you see what I have in mind for the summer."

"Do me a favor?"

"What?"

"Don't tell me. Don't bother."

CHAPTER TEN

"**W**HERE ARE YOU GOING TO READ?" I ASKED.

"*Where* will be some place private and out of Aunt Addie's sight line. I would not want her to fret and stew at the sight of me contentedly curled up with a book, and worry about what such a sedentary occupation would do to my health and sanity. Besides, when I am hidden from view, she is less likely to think up silly games for me to play, such as dusting the parlor or polishing the dining room furniture. Now let me see. Where?" Penny pondered the question. "If you would have freedom, go where Miss Killjoy doesn't. The barn."

So we went to the barn. Along both sides were stalls used in other days for horses and cows. Now they were clean with whitewash and draped with cobwebs. At the right of the front barn doors was the milkroom that had long ago become Uncle Lambot's hideout. The barn itself contained various pieces of machinery, a tractor, a mower, a hay rake, and so on, all of which Uncle Lambot rented out from time to time to farmers here and about. Uncle Lambot was a machinery bug. He was forever cleaning and oiling parts, taking machines apart and putting them back together again. It was as much of a hobby as he had. Penny tagged it "Keeping out of Aunt Addie's hair." In the barn he was not likely to be disturbed, and thus his tinkering was slow and thorough.

Hanging from the cupola in the center of the barn was the block and tackle that Uncle Lambot used to lift various mechanical pieces from the floor to his workbench, which was located in the center of the barn. We used to swing from hayloft to hayloft with the rope, and sometimes we could cut quite an arc from side to side.

Sometimes we just liked to romp in the hay. Above, on each side of the barn, above the horse and cow stalls, were the haylofts, still with hay in them because Uncle Lambot stored hay for Seely Jones, who had the farm down the road and owned lots of cows. New hay was already in the barn and it smelled sweet and fresh. "Let's," I said to Penny.

"Tomorrow," Penny said. I didn't complain. My stomach felt as though I had swallowed a glob of molten lead.

"Where to read," Penny pondered. She scanned the barn. I thought she would settle for the hay, but she said that could get hot and stuffy. "Uncle Lambot's room," I suggested. That smelled, she said, and besides Aunt Addie could sneak up on her there unawares. Then she noted a platform, a quarter the size of a boxing ring, jutting out from the wall halfway up its side. "Up there," Penny said pointing. "She'll never find me there. That platform will be all mine. I shall call it Mine."

"How are you going to get there?" I asked. "Fly?"

Penny surveyed the situation, then said, "Fly. Watch me." She pointed to two similar platforms, one above the other, on the other side opposite to the one she named Mine. She commandeered Uncle Lambot's rope on the block and tackle, then climbed to the first platform by way of a rickety ladder. There were pegs, leading to the platform above, sticking out from the wall, and she climbed them, carrying along the rope. "A swing from here to Mine. And when I return, from Mine to down there," she explained, pointing to the platform below her. "Easy."

I climbed to the first platform. The other side of the barn where Mine was seemed miles away. So did the floor below. I looked at the farm implements there, the rake, a binder, and a tractor. If you fell, plop, you'd land smack in the midst. I shook my head.

Penny noted my concern and said, "Never fear, Willie. I have to go. Take chances. That's what I have to do."

"Dumb."

"It will be like stepping out into the world, and I have to go." Penny studied the platform on the other side, and considered how she would swing to it. "I have to do it," Penny said again for reassurance. "And Willie, I shall call my new hideaway, not Mine, but Olympus, and I shall go calling on Zeus. He'll see to my safety."

She stepped back and poised for flight. "The good die young!" she shouted, as she charged off the platform into space. I doubted she could make it, but she did. "Excelsior!" she cried. "Want to try it?"

"No," I mumbled. I was getting sicker by the minute from the gunk in my stomach. Besides, I would have to listen to her reading *Lorna Doone*. Penny protested, but only slightly. Now she had her privacy, even from me. She tied down her rope, scraped together bits of hay left on the platform and flung herself into it.

Another time I would have pouted at the exclusion. Not now. I was bilious, feeling as I had when I tried my first cigarette at the age of seven. I was afraid I would faint, but somehow I managed to climb back to the barn floor. I headed for Uncle Lambot's clubhouse, flopped into his old leather chair, and passed out.

But not for long, nor was I completely cold. Otherwise I would not have heard Aunt Addie and company moving in on our fortress for the day.

"Penny! Penny!" It was hardly the cry of the meek. Penny must have heard, but there was no response. Apparently she was determined to remain atop her cloud nine to the point of starvation if need be. I was in no shape to move, but I knew that Aunt Addie would soon come snooping my way, and I did not want her to see me sick. Evading the penalty for illness was worth the suffering of a martyr. I decided to make a run for it, hoping I would have enough strength to sneak out behind the barn before she could find me.

But she was nearer to me than I had realized, and I bumped smack into her as I stumbled out of Uncle Lambot's den.

"Where is your sister?" Aunt Addie demanded to know.

For an answer, I made the sacrifice for Penny. I put an end to the search by vomiting. A cascade of radishes and strawberries and syrupy glue poured out of me accompanied by the painful sounds of retching.

Aunt Addie shooed me to bed and kept me there that day and beyond. Now if only she could find Penny sick, she would have it made.

As I lay in bed, I thought of the summer ahead. Although I couldn't understand why, I could not help but be aware that Penny and Aunt Addie were running on a collision course. I even sensed that Penny was actively seeking confrontation, that she wanted to bump Aunt Addie out of her way, and I was frightened. I was beginning to have a vague, panicky feeling that Penny and I were not, after all, one and the same. The Penny ensconced in my head was less and less the Penny I saw with my eyes and heard with my ears. She was running far ahead of me in the matter of knowing her what's and why's. A separation was occurring that was filling me with dread. She looked the same, a scrawny, flat-bodied kid. She acted the same, her actions expressing no more excitement for one thing than another. She talked the same, incessantly it seemed, her voice all too often a flat monotone. When she talked, more and more I wished she wouldn't. When she wasn't talking, I wished she would. She was the same, yet not. Penny was a carnival joy ride, spinning and churning, snapping and breaking, endlessly. She was forever shattering windmills, huffing and puffing and blowing houses down. Kicking in walls, as she had said she would. She was restless, urgent, blindly competitive. Every moment of life had to have its own special excitement. She acted as if she were in complete control of everything she said or did, yet even I knew otherwise. I could never be certain that she had any real care for anything or anybody, except me, and even of that I was becoming less and less sure.

And there was Aunt Addie, a bundle of chewed nerves. Last year and the years before, she nagged, but that wasn't much more than her way of living, and it really didn't bother us too much. It was different this year. Before, you at least had the feeling she knew what she was doing, that she was in control of herself. This year you couldn't tell if she wanted to hug and love Penny with all her might or push her in the face and close her mouth forever. Talk about living on pins and needles. It wasn't easy. And the summer was far from over.

CHAPTER ELEVEN

IT RAINED ALL THE NEXT DAY AND THE NEXT. AUNT ADDIE KEPT ME mostly in bed, watched me like a hawk, and babied me as if I were newly born. With the rain and her usual strictures, I couldn't have gone anywhere, so I didn't much care.

Penny read. And wrote in her diary. And argued with Aunt Addie. Sometimes she helped her. The day following the rain, Penny was dusting the hallway stairs, and I had a conversation with her. This was easy to do as Penny was not involved in a difficult task. In Aunt Addie's house, nothing ever needed dusting in the first place.

"Never collect anything, Willie," Penny said. "Every time you collect something, even an old shoe, you have to care for it somehow, and each little care can only add to life's burdens. Jesus was smart. He had no possessions. No cares in that respect."

"I'd like to collect a bicycle," I said.

"Take this place. The parlor is filled with bric-a-brac and clutter that almost nobody sees year in and year out except Aunt Addie. I can't imagine the amount of time she has used just in cleaning in the past twenty years. Better to live in the barn. Never collect property. It kills time. Know something? I don't think Aunt Addie's been farther than Hartford since she was a kid, and do you know why? Her possessions possess her. Aunt Addie lives in prison here. Go away for a day and the dust would collect and that would drive even Aunt Addie to drink."

"You collect a headful of junk," I said. "Yesterday she yelled and yelled for you. Where were you?"

"When she was yelling, I was at Olympus. I'm getting to be quite an expert with that rope. Only trouble with Olympus, the roof above it leaks. I have appealed to Zeus about the rain, but to no avail."

"Remember what our grandfather did to himself in the barn. Maybe he used the same rope."

"What a ghoulish thought."

"You'll break your neck yet."

"It's my neck."

"I think I'll tell Aunt Addie. She'll put a stop to it."

"You wouldn't! You wouldn't kill that beautiful sight I have of looking down on her and seeing her peering into the abyss of the barn, knowing I'm there, but finding nothing." Penny sighed and put down her dust rag. "You don't think I'm a jerk, Willie? A really first-class jerk?"

"Why don't you leave her alone?"

Penny leaned against me and nudged her nose on my chin. "It's revolt, Willie, and I don't know exactly why. Aunt Addie's the salt of the earth, I know that. She's got character that is worthy of emulation."

"What does that mean?"

"It means she's got a lot on the ball," Penny said. "But it doesn't go anywhere, and that's why I don't want to be an Aunt Addie, and I'm not going to let her trap me into being one. Aunt Addie's got more don't's in her body than she has corpuscles. In her book you have to learn the don't's before you learn the do's. Only trouble is you can end up running your life to the end on don't's before you get a chance to do the do's. Aunt Addie's negative, and I'm positive. She's past and I'm future. We're bound to clash. One must put up with it."

"What am I?"

"Doesn't matter. She provides me with the don't's, not you," Penny said. She thought about it a bit, and added, "You're neutral. You are both to be envied and pitied. Sometimes I think you lean negative. Do you?"

"Who cares?"

"Happiness is positive," Penny said.

I had had enough of talk. I got up and dusted the bannister with my pants by sliding down it. We heard a car in the yard. It was Uncle Lambot.

He came from the station in the town taxi, because Aunt Addie thought it unwise to send Adam in the Packard. Uncle Lambot was tired and drawn. I guess maybe that was the first time I ever really looked at him. I used to think of him as a "thing" that was there whenever we needed him, just like the kitchen table. That was always there, too, but I never really noticed what kind it was, how it was made, what was on it, what new flowers, or whether or not the oilcloth had been cleaned.

Uncle Lambot was a big man with a head that looked, Penny said, like Daniel Webster's must have looked, and she said she read once that Daniel Webster was considered by many to look like God himself. Penny said that Uncle Lambot must have been handsome in his youth, because when the light was right, he was handsome still, even if he did pout his thick lips and sometimes assume the expression of the meanest man in town. Maybe so. To me he was powerful, afraid of nothing. Except possibly, on rare occasions, his sister. I felt better with Uncle Lambot back at his post. The world seemed saner with him about.

Uncle Lambot was not one given to showing emotions, but you could tell he liked Penny. Penny knew how to take the edge off his dour disposition. She knew how to crawl onto his lap and sit there, like a contented cat. It didn't bother her a whit to play the child when she wanted something. After lunch she did just that.

"Did you have a nice trip?"

"Uh-huh."

"How was the train ride? Did you get tired?"

"Uh-uh."

"Did you talk with lawyers?"

"Uh-huh." The first grunt was yes, the second, no, and the third was neither here nor there.

"Are we going to sell the house in Des Moines?"

Uncle Lambot said nothing. Penny got up from his lap, went behind the chair, and massaged his forehead. Uncle Lambot always liked that. Today she worked especially hard at it. "For how much?" Penny asked.

"Fifteen thousand, if we are lucky. Not a good time for selling houses."

"How about the insurance money?" We already knew about that. Father's policy with our names on it had a face value of fifty thousand dollars.

"Won't believe it 'til I see it. When it comes to what my brother did with money . . ."

Uncle Lambot let his thought dangle. It didn't bother me. "I want a bicycle," I said. "Penny wants a doll."

"I have a list," Penny said. "How much can we spend?"

Uncle Lambot didn't even bother to grunt, and that meant the conversation was finished. Penny didn't press him. Uncle Lambot required patience. Another time she would squeeze a bit more out of him.

With Uncle Lambot home, Aunt Addie didn't fret or watch quite as much. A few days later, she was hostess at the church, for an all-day mission for the ladies, and had to leave home at ten. She gave us a list of don't's ten miles long, one do for Penny—straighten up her room—told Adam to watch us, and went off with Uncle Lambot. Adam wasn't up to his assignment. He had been sipping wine that morning and slipped into Uncle Lambot's enclave in the barn for a snooze. Suddenly we had freedom.

"Aunt Harriet's. Maybe we can find out a thing or two," Penny said. Reluctantly I agreed, and we headed past the old boat and the swimming pool and up through the woods to Aunt Harriet's.

There were no clouds in the sky and everything looked freshly washed. The fields were green, except for some late dandelions, and some new black-eyed susans and red clover. We heard a brown thrasher warbling and stopped to listen. We saw a chewink hopping in and about the underbrush. Penny chewinked and the chewink chewinked back. Birds'-foot violets were growing in splotches along the path in the woods, and we stopped and picked some. Penny made a nosegay of them. The violets gave off some soft, fragrant perfume that was pleasantly familiar.

And then we saw the old apple tree at the edge of the woods. It was mostly trunk and a few scrawny branches. There were several holes in the trunk, one special one where a branch had rotted off. "I wonder if the bluebirds are still there," I said. We approached the tree slowly. Soon we saw a pair fly in and out.

"I wonder if they are the same ones as last year."

"They have to be," Penny said.

We inched quietly closer and we could hear the chirpings of young ones inside, but we didn't get so close to the tree that we had to look beyond to Aunt Harriet's. We both still believed that she might still be there, and that what we knew was only a bad dream.

Penny said, "You want to hear a miracle. Listen." I was already listening. The warble of the male bluebird was clear silver, and we remained entranced with its song until it flew away. Finally, we had to look beyond to Aunt Harriet's place.

There was nothing left but charred embers. I didn't believe a place could ever look dead, but Aunt Harriet's place looked dead. We both walked to the edge of the charcoaled mess in silence. My mind was numb. Even Penny didn't talk. We didn't hear a bird. Not even a cricket.

We stood and stared for some time before Penny broke the silence. "By the time we'd get to the apple tree, no matter what time of day, Aunt Harriet would see us and she'd come out here on these steps," she said as she climbed onto the stone slabs, "and she would wave to us as if we were celebrities. Each time as if she were seeing us for the first time. No matter how you felt before . . ." Penny didn't finish. Her voice choked and tears came to her eyes. Mine, too.

Penny took the nosegay of violets and placed them on the top stair. "Peace," she whispered. That was all.

CHAPTER TWELVE

I NSTEAD OF RETURNING TO THE PATH, WE WALKED DOWN THE ROAD toward town. It was cool and fresh under the maples that lined the road and arched it with their branches. There was a stone wall on each side, and at the left a pasture with some of Seely Jones's cows.

"I wonder how long we'll remember," Penny said.

"A long time," I said.

"Death happens to everybody. You shouted I could die from swinging on the rope in the barn. The sky could fall on us this instant, said Henny Penny. One time or another, it really doesn't matter. We'll remember until that moment."

"Don't talk that stuff."

"O.K., Willie. It's only sometimes I feel like a tiny piece of nothing."

"How can you be a piece of nothing?" I said. But I felt what she meant.

"Let's talk about Aunt Harriet," Penny said.

"Let's not."

"We have to talk about her sometime."

"Let's not now."

"I saw a newspaper, Willie."

Immediately I knew what she meant. "What newspaper?"

"The *Eastfield Observer*. You know how Uncle Lambot saves all the old newspapers out in the barn, except for those used to wrap garbage. I was up in Olympus dreaming, when it occurred to me to go look. You want to know what it said?"

I didn't answer. I did and I didn't.

"Not much. It said the fire was started sometime after midnight, and by the time it was discovered and the fire department arrived on the scene, that the house was completely enveloped in flame, and the Westfield fire department came, too, but the house couldn't be saved. It didn't know how it got started, except it suggested that it may have burned too fast for it to have happened accidentally."

"Not much," I said.

"I was thinking that if it wasn't an accident, then somebody wanted it to happen. Funny thing about that."

"It's not funny."

"Fluky, then," Penny said. "Well, she's gone, Willie. I wonder if it mattered to anything in this world if Aunt Harriet . . ."

"I don't want to talk about it."

"I know, but she's gone, and that's a fact. The paper said her body was burned beyond recognition."

I started to cry. "All you ever do is talk about death," I said.

"I do, don't I?" Penny said, as if she hadn't realized it before. She thought about it, then said as if making a discovery, "Life, Willie, that is what life is all about. There are mysteries, and when I find them I want to eliminate them. Like scientists do, know what I mean?" I shrugged. "Of course you know." She did not pursue the subject, but dismissed it by saying, "And speaking of mysteries, we are almost to the Nasons'."

"Aunt Addie said no." But I was curious, too. Adam's shack paled by comparison with the Nason set-up. At one time, the house, a large, frame colonial, must have been one of the better houses in Eastfield. Now it was ramshackle, looking as though it had lost its life long ago. Its paint was mostly gone and it was tinged with moss and lichen. Its roof wore patches of tar paper where there had once been shingles. An ell of the house had burned and the charred beams were left protruding and rotting. A half dozen hollyhocks growing spindly by the dilapidated steps at the side of the house added a touch of color, but even they looked tired. Behind the house was a gray, weatherbeaten barn, sitting ugly and discontented, sulking as if ashamed of its plight.

It might well have been sulking because of the Nasons. The Lem Nasons were old New England. "Once a fine family," lamented Aunt Addie. Now they looked like squatters on their own property. Lem Nason lived in the barn, and his wife, Pearl, lived in the house with their daughter, Hilda. Aunt Harriet claimed that they had been living that way for more than ten years, not once uttering one word to another. Penny said Hilda told her that wasn't exactly so, but most people believed that, and it made the Nasons more interesting. Once Penny asked Aunt Addie how come about the Nasons, and she opened up a wee bit. She admitted she knew the family for a long time, but you couldn't put your finger on anything other than inbreeding, and that the times and luck had finally run out on the Nason bloodline. When Penny asked about inbreeding, she clammed up.

Aunt Harriet had said the arrangement was not as crazy as it appeared, that some marriages would be better off with the same kind of arrangement, that a lot of people lived worse lives than did the Nasons, that some people who lived together and slept together were further apart than the Nasons. Aunt Harriet said they put spice into their lives by being different, and if you couldn't find anything else to talk about in Eastfield, which was usually the case, you could always talk about the Nasons. She said that being the way they were made them somebodies, and that was more than most people were. Maybe so, but as far as I was concerned, they were spooks, except that I remember once Lem Nason whittled me a willow whistle, and Mrs. Nason always had soda pop for a hot day. I was hoping she would have some now.

We ambled into the yard. We saw Hilda first, sitting on the

broken steps. At first I did not recognize her. Last year her hair was dark; this year it was cheapie blonde. Her face was blotched with lipstick and rouge. She wore eyeshadow. She was sunning herself in a faded and tattered pink bathing suit. She looked coarse, vulgar, and in her twenties, yet she was hardly older than Penny.

She was pleasant enough, though. She greeted us in a voice that had got old before its time. "You kids back again? How the hell you doing? That old maid Addie still after you? How many times has she told you to stay the hell away from here this year?" Her smile didn't last long, but what showed was warm and friendly.

"Hello, Hilda. How is your mother?" Penny greeted.

"Same as ever. Hey, Ma, those Winston kids are here again," Hilda yelled into the house.

"How's your father?"

"Same as ever. Sick most of the time, and he's up in the barn."

"Still not speaking?"

"They talk to each other. Not much." Hilda shrugged. "Lots of people don't talk to each other, and when they do, they don't say no more than my folks do. Addie's old man ever tell her much?"

"He's her brother," I said.

"Yeah. I forget. Everybody forgets around here. Do they sleep together?"

"He's her brother," I said again, and Hilda gave me an odd look.

Penny sat down on the steps beside Hilda. I found a desiccated rubber ball and bounced it against the house. I stayed within hearing distance.

"They have separate rooms, Hilda," Penny said.

"Just like my folks. Ha!"

"Not much difference," Penny admitted to be nice. "Do they love each other?" Penny asked.

"As they said in the movie the other night, 'Tell me what love is and I'll give you an answer, maybe.'" Hilda sounded as though she were trying to imitate Bette Davis. It was funny the way she said it, but it was sad, too. Hilda had already lost all her dreams. She looked twice Penny's age.

Age was on Penny's mind, and she asked, "How old are your parents, Hilda?"

"Who knows? Who cares?"

"How old?"

"I told you I don't know."

"Sorry. Did you go to the fire?" Penny asked.

"Yeah. Everybody in Eastfield went."

"What time was it?"

"Maybe around midnight."

"Who set it, Hilda? Who didn't like Aunt Harriet?"

Her answer came slowly, as if she were exercising caution. "Who knows? A lot of people said it had to do with the strike. She your aunt, too?" Hilda sounded envious.

"Who do you think set it?" Penny asked with persistence.

"Who knows? Probably herself. Probably she boozed up, lit a cigarette, and that was it."

"How about Adam?"

"Pa said he was up there that night. Don't mean much. Adam is a snail, but it's surprising how he gets around."

"Did she drink much?"

"A lotta talk. I never seen her. Ask your friend, Mr. Wynewski. He picked up her trash every week—he'd know. I wouldn't. All I know is he'd go up every Monday afternoon to pick up her garbage and sometimes stay an hour or two. It ain't hard to figure where he's been when there ain't no other house on the road except ours."

"You didn't see anyone heading up that way the night it happened?"

"Wasn't looking. Got enough problems."

I heard that and wondered if they were the problems Aunt Addie talked about. Penny wasn't satisfied yet. "Haven't you got any idea how it started?"

"Pa might know. He knows a lot, but it don't do him much good," Hilda said. "He can't remember what he knows, and when he does, he can't always put it together in one piece. I figure that's why he dreams so much."

"Interesting," Penny said.

Mrs. Nason poked her head out from the broken screen door. She was wearing a frowsy blue dress, and her blondish hair was frizzly. She had bags under her eyes and she was smoking a cigarette. Aunt Harriet said she had a loathsome reputation all over the county, but she said the facts didn't live up to the reputation. Sometimes I wondered if Mrs. Nason was anything like our mother, who also had quite a reputation.

"Heard your folks got killed," Mrs. Nason said. "And your grandmother died." Her voice was harsh, as if her throat was scraped with a file. But like Hilda's, it was not unfriendly or unsympathetic. If there hadn't been a lot of talk about her, I'd think she was nice.

"Yes," Penny said, and she told all about Granny Winston dying, and the accident. Penny said we could have cried an awful lot if we were the crying kind, but we didn't cry over spilled milk.

"Got to go sometime," Mrs. Nason said. "You kids got rich folks so it don't matter. You kids are lucky. Never have to worry. Can grow up decent. But Hilda—she ain't got nothing. You ain't changed much, Penny. You get older, you don't go putting all that junk over your face like Hilda does, and don't go bleaching your hair. Won't give you nothing but trouble, and there's trouble enough without borrowing. I'd get you a soda only we ain't got none."

"Ma, Penny wants to know how old you are," Hilda said.

"The next time I have a birthday party, I'll invite you. Ha!" Mrs. Nason said, and when she laughed she didn't look bad at all.

"Old as Aunt Addie?" Penny asked.

"That old?" Mrs. Nason asked as if she didn't believe the question. "Guess so, more or less. We went to school together. Same class."

"You did? What was she like as a girl?"

Mrs. Nason looked at Penny queerly. "You take good care of yourself, kiddo. Don't get into no trouble," she said, and with that she disappeared into the house.

Penny said, "Another time I'll find out a few things. If your Mother and Aunt Addie went to school together, then they must have gone with Aunt Harriet, and even with Uncle Lambot more or less."

"So what do you want to know for?" Hilda asked.

"Just like to know things. Don't you?"

"No. The less I know about some things, the better," Hilda said. "Got enough damn problems."

"What was your mother saying about trouble?" Penny asked.

"You ever been in love?" Hilda replied.

" 'Tell me what love is, and I'll give you an answer,' " Penny said, mimicking Hilda.

"Nothing much you can do about love once you let it start. I reckon that's what Ma means by trouble. Pa had to go to the hospital last month, and he needed money. He's stubborn, that one. Won't take from nobody. You know how I got it? By fixing myself up and being with a man."

"So?"

"One thing led to another. So what the hell," Hilda said.

"What would you like, Hilda, if you could wish for something nice and get it this very day?" Penny asked.

"A new dress. A nice, red, grown-up dress. If I had that, I'd run away."

"Why don't you do that now? What else would you like?"

"You like to ask questions."

I was still bouncing the ball, nearby. "You can say that again," I shouted.

Hilda shrugged. "I'd like to have my father and mother where yours are. But I got them and I'm stuck with them. As long as I live. Don't ask me how I know. I know. So I bleach my hair. I think it's pretty. Ma's right, kid, don't do it."

"You can do it. I can't. You're lucky."

"Yeah. Three cheers for the red, white, and blue."

"I'm sorry," Penny said. She stood. "Willie and I are walking to town. Got to hurry before Aunt Addie gets back from church. Say hello to your father. We'll come again. I want to talk with him. You really don't have any idea who set fire to Aunt Harriet's house?"

"Nope. Maybe nobody. If I knew, maybe I'd tell and maybe I wouldn't."

"How about your father? He didn't just happen . . ."

"That would be his business, not mine," Hilda said sharply, as if to take offense.

It was time to leave and we left, walking down the hill toward town, just as if we had planned to do so. "Suppose we meet Uncle Lambot?" I asked.

"He'll live through the day," Penny said, dismissing him. "Guess?"

"About the fire? Maybe it just happened."

"Nope. Hilda's going to have a baby."

"Who says?" I didn't believe it. I had known all about babies and how they got started since I was seven or eight. But mothers were older people and they were accompanied by fathers. Hilda didn't fit the scheme. "She got a husband?"

"Hilda is sixteen or seventeen, Willie. At that age, you can have babies according to the law of nature, but you can't have a husband according to the law of man."

"How do you know?" I asked. "She didn't look big in the belly to me. I didn't hear her say so."

"Well, she practically did. Anyway, time will tell," Penny said. "She's lucky. She can have a baby and nobody screams."

"She ain't lucky."

Penny paused, thinking. "Guess you're right," she said. "You want to know how lucky you are, Willie, think of Hilda. She's got nothing but trouble ahead of her. Before long she'll grow mean and nasty. Not a bad kid, either. You know something, Willie? Her unborn child could someday become the President of the United States. He could become a general someday and order your son into battle. If it's a he. Did you ever think of that?"

"Don't think I'll get married," I answered.

"You could marry Hilda some day and then if her son is President, so shall your son be."

"Razzmatazz," I said.

"In a few months, Hilda's going to make the whole town forget the Depression and Franklin D. Roosevelt."

"How?"

"When her belly gets big."

"You just said nobody screams when that happens to people like Hilda."

"I guess maybe I talked too soon," Penny said. "Makes you wonder though."

"What?"

"How about me? Suppose I were to have a baby? How about when my belly gets big, maybe this summer? What do you think of that, my dear brother?"

I had a notion to klunk her with a rock to stop that kind of talk once and for all. She was laughing, but I didn't think it was funny at all. "You do that and you can count me out."

"Willie." She sounded hurt.

"That's dumb talk. You gotta be kidding. If it is, I don't like it," I said.

"Maybe, maybe not. I think I want to help Hilda. She sounds tough and she looks tough, but she's not. She's nice and she's not dumb. She got money for her father. When she told me that, I felt goose pimples grow on my neck, and I wanted to hug and kiss her. I'd like to do something like that, help someone like she did. If I can help Hilda, I'm going to help her. I guess you can say I'm serious about that."

"How?"

"I'll find a way."

"Maybe she's not pregnant," I said.

"Maybe, but if she's not now, she will soon be at the rate she's going. I wish Granny Winston was here. Or Aunt Harriet. They would take Hilda's side. Not many others around here will. Aunt Addie is already against her. Maybe our new Aunt Charity will help. I'll have to discuss the matter with her and see how she ticks."

"Like a run-down clock," I said.

That pleased Penny. "Then I'll rewind her," she said. "Willie, when we get to town, I'm going to Sadie's dress shop and buy Hilda a dress. That's whose side I'm going to take."

"You got money? Enough for chocolate malteds?"

Penny smacked her lips. "Enough. What a delight to anticipate. How nice to be out of prison! Razzmatazz!"

"Suppose we get caught?"

"Never happen. And Willie, after the malteds, maybe we'll just happen to stop by the mill on our way home, and maybe we'll just happen to bump into Sam Brown, and maybe I'll just happen to say that Mr. Nason told me that he saw Sam Brown going to Aunt Harriet's the night of the fire."

"That's a lie."

"Or maybe coming. Or coming and going. See what he says. And then I'll ask a few questions. In any case, maybe we'll find out why he was walking on so many pins and needles when he came to see us the other night."

"What you don't know won't hurt," I said, thinking of Hilda.

I reminded Penny of someone else. "Yes, Uncle Lambot," she said. "And speaking of the devil, here he comes. Hide! Quick, Willie!"

I didn't bother to look. I jumped the stone wall and landed smack in some cow manure. Penny peered over the wall. She laughed at me, hard. When I saw no car coming and there was no Uncle Lambot, I didn't mind too much. It was fun seeing her laugh the way she did.

CHAPTER THIRTEEN

....

P ENNY HELPED SCRAPE THE MANURE FROM MY PANTS. IT WAS STALE stuff and so not too difficult to get off. "Reminds me of your favorite word," she said.

"Puke?"

"I forgot that one."

"Oh, the other? So what?" I said. "What do we do now?"

Penny jumped the wall and commenced to run. "Last one to the bridge is a dink," she yelled.

At the bridge, she stopped to catch her breath, and I caught up with her. "So I'm a dink," I said.

"And your first name is Rinky," Penny said, giving me a big carefree smile that made me feel good.

We leaned over the rickety, wooden rail of the bridge and saw our images in the lethargic waters below.

"I wonder how come we don't go under the bridge with the water and everything else in it," Penny pondered.

"It's only our reflection," I said.

"Are you sure? It may be you down there. Maybe your soul, and it remains there when your body walks away."

I stepped backward. "Am I still there?"

"Gotcha," Penny said. "Makes you think."

I returned to her side and looked down into the water again. "Dirty, isn't it? I wonder if any fish are there."

"None, except fish that eat dye and chemicals coming out of the mill. The dye is what makes the water rusty looking. They dump all the gunk from the mill into the water, and the water takes it out to sea. It's been doing that for over a hundred years. Junk from our mill has been pouring into the ocean all that time. I bet some of it has made its way to the North Pole. Made in Eastfield, U.S.A., at the Winston Mills. What do you think of that?"

I didn't. "Water's higher than last year," I said.

"Uncle Lambot said it was going to be a rainy summer. He said it was a good thing, as last summer was a dry summer. He said rain is like money in the bank. Uncle Lambot said a lot for Uncle Lambot. He's saying even less this year than last, I think, like he's got something locked up in his brain, and he wants to keep it there."

"Uh-huh," I murmured.

"He's nice to me, though."

"Always was. You're his pet."

"Uncle Lambot's nice. Even to you."

"You're still his pet."

"And you are Aunt Addie's," Penny said. "But it's different now and I don't know why."

I didn't care to talk about it. "I think it's too deep to go hunting under the bridge for crawfish this year," I said.

"I am pleased that it is too deep," Penny said.

"Suppose we get so much rain, it floods," I said. "Maybe another boat will land out behind the barn. Be fun to see that field flooded. I bet a nickel this bridge wouldn't last long if there was a flood. How would we get into town without it?"

"You could swim, or walk to one of the bridges farther north or south. Maybe you could cross on that boat you said would come floating along. Maybe on our boat. Too much rain, then, would not be money in the bank, would it? This bridge looks as though it is waiting to be taken away. I don't think it would last long. It would be fun to watch it disappear, wouldn't it?"

"Maybe it would land up at the North Pole with all the other junk," I said.

"With Ozymandias as the captain," Penny said. "Ready to go?"

"What if we get caught?"

"We'll naturally get horsewhipped," Penny said, "and otherwise be told we can't go to town, which we have already been told."

On the other side of the bridge, the road curved back a hundred feet or so, paralleling the river and the road to Aunt Harriet's on the opposite side. On its bank was an ancient oak, looking as if, like the bridge, it was ready to topple. From one of its branches that reached over the river was strung a heavy piece of rope, fifty or so feet long. Its bottom end was lashed to the trunk of the tree.

"Look, Willie. A rope swing. Just like the one in the barn. I bet the guys who put this up had a lot of fun."

"Maybe girls did it," I said.

"Girls then," Penny said. "Look, Willie, it takes you from *here* to *there.*"

"*There* is in the middle of the drink," I said.

"That's the fun of it. But with a good swing, you can make the other side! Let's try it!"

"And be all wet going into town? Not me."

The decision to swing or not to swing was soon sealed, for down the road, we could see a truck coming toward us, and right away we knew it was Stan Wynewski and that he would stop and pick us up. Stan was self-educated and rough and tumble. He had a big round face, a mop of red hair, and a mustache to match. He was six feet tall, all muscle, as thick as the trunk of an old oak. Except that he had a temper, I used to think he'd be a nice father to have. When he was sober, he mostly listened, and when he had been drinking, he mostly talked. Generally he was in a state of in-between on both drinking and talking. He was a member of Uncle Lambot's group that came to the barn on rainy Saturdays, and that's where we mostly saw him. There he did a lot of talking. He was not held in high favor by Aunt Addie.

Stan stopped his pickup and opened the door. He greeted us

jovially. "Each year you grow bigger," he said. "Next year, I won't know you, except you're going to be here from now on, and I won't have to wait all year. Sorry about your folks. Real sorry."

"A lot of people aren't," Penny said.

"That's not nice. There was something good about them, or they could not have grown good kids like you and your brother."

"Maybe we aren't good," Penny said.

"You've grown, but not older, smarty," Stan said.

"Maybe it was somebody else that made us grow into good kids," Penny replied. "Maybe it was our grandmother. Maybe Aunt Addie and Uncle Lambot."

"Maybe," Stan said. We climbed into the truck.

"How's your family?" Penny asked.

"The same."

"You still fight all the time with Mrs. Wynewski?"

Stan laughed. He didn't mind Penny saying that. "Yeah."

"You ever going to stop?"

Stan laughed some more. "Never thought about that, but I reckon not. We done it so long we wouldn't know what to do if we didn't. Kind of like playing a game. We got another girl this April. Named her April. You should come by and see. We got nine kids now."

"You must have the biggest family in Eastfield," I said.

"Yep, it was all written up in the paper. Picture and everything. You want a ride home?"

"I'd like to have a baby to hold. What's it like getting a baby?" Penny asked.

The question surprised Stan and shot his eyebrows up to his hairline. "You mean *having* a baby. Ask my wife."

"I want a baby, Stan, I really do. The sooner the better."

"Whoa!" Stand said. "You have to get married first, and before that, college, and before that high school, and . . ." He didn't finish. "Where you kids going?"

"In town," Penny said, and in typical fashion, she changed directions by popping a question. "What happened to Aunt Harriet?"

I didn't look but you could sense embarrassment. Stan took it cautiously. "Maybe an accident. They said it must have been. I guess you kids liked her a lot."

"Didn't everybody?" Penny asked. "Who didn't like her?"

"I only said you kids liked her," Stan said.

"Did Sam Brown like her?" Penny asked.

"Sam Brown," Stan said. "Everybody."

"I don't know about that," Penny persisted.

"So who knows? Everybody didn't like Jesus Christ. Some people don't like me. Some people don't like your Uncle Lambot. And if you go on talking like that, some people won't like you."

"Did her death have something to do with the strike?"

"Questions, questions. You haven't changed, have you? Go ask your Uncle Lambot," Stan said, and we all laughed at that. Finding out things from Uncle Lambot was like fishing for halibut in the Dead Sea.

"I suppose that somehow Aunt Harriet and Uncle Lambot are responsible for the Depression," Penny said. "Eastfield isn't a hummingbird peck on the face of the globe, but we are responsible for the Depression. At least that's what Aunt Addie thinks. Somebody klunked a stone through her window. Did you know that?"

"You're kidding."

"Nope. Maybe somebody took a match to Aunt Harriet's."

Stan whistled. "Kid, you're too smart for your age. Too damn smart, and that's a fact."

"Did you like Aunt Harriet?"

Stan started the truck and drove slowly toward town. "Yup. She always paid when I picked up her trash. Some months, she was about the only person who did."

"Was she good looking?"

Stan smiled. "Don't you remember?"

"I mean did men think she was good looking?"

"With some people you never bother to think," she said. "She was interesting. Yeah, she was good looking."

"Was she older or younger than you? Did you go to school with her?"

"I'm hurt," Stan joked. "What's that gotta do with the price of putty?"

"Who hated her?"

Stan whistled. "Who said? Maybe no one. Penny, last year you talked as much, only somehow it was different. I think I liked you better last year."

"I'm not the only one who's changed. Have you seen Hilda Nason lately?"

Stan blushed. "You ask too many questions. One of these days one of them is going to jump up and bite you."

"I'm a question mark. I was born that way," Penny said impertinently. "Are they still striking at the mill? We are going to the mill if you are going that way."

"You keep away. There's lotsa trouble brewing there," Stan said. "Anything can happen."

"We can take care of ourselves. If you don't take us, we'll go on our own."

We were into town and almost to the street that one took to the mill. Stan slowed the truck, undecided as to which way to go. Then he figured we'd go anyway, so he drove us to the mill.

Soon we could see the strikers parading outside the gate in front of the main building. There were maybe fifty, and they didn't look too friendly.

"We only want to go in and say hello to Sam Brown. We always do it first thing, only this year Aunt Addie wouldn't let us," Penny said.

"She know you were coming here?"

"No," I said.

"Your Uncle Lambot's at the mill, I think. I saw his car at the side gate this morning. I don't think he'd like your being there," Stan said.

"We won't tell him you brought us."

"The crowd could get rough today. You stay away from it."

"We'll keep out of trouble. Just want to see Sam Brown. He's one of our special friends."

Stan gave us another warning, and let us go. We walked gingerly toward the strikers. "See anybody we know?" I asked.

"Not yet," Penny replied, "and I thought I knew everybody in Eastfield." We watched the strikers parade down the sidewalk to the end of the fence, and return. Some of them carried signs. One, directed to Uncle Lambot, asked how he'd like to starve, and another told him to go to hell. They didn't make much sense to me.

As we got closer, we recognized some of the men, and Penny said Hello to them, but none replied, not even a couple of men from our church. It was not a happy group, and I was scared.

"Let's go inside," I said. I thought the sooner the better, but I didn't say it.

We walked inside the gate and up the walk to the front doors of the mill office. Inside was a circular room about the size of the parlor at the farm. Its walls had been painted and repainted some more, leaving a mottled effect of dirty tan. There was a Franklin stove in the corner, and against a wall was a large settee covered with cracked brown leather. In the center of the room was a large, scarred flat-top desk, and there was a girl behind it wearing glasses. That's all I remember about her. That, and how surprised she looked when she saw two kids wandering into the office. It was easy to guess she hadn't been there long.

"Can I help you?"

"We want to see Sam Brown," Penny said.

"He's busy," said the girl.

"We're relatives. He's expecting us."

"Relatives?" The girl was suspicious.

"Practically. We are Winstons. We live with Mr. Winston, the man with the Packard," Penny said.

"He's our uncle," I said.

"He's not here," the girl said. "He left ten or fifteen minutes ago. Mr. Brown is in conference and does not want to be disturbed."

"Are you new?" Penny asked as she brashly marched past the girl to the door that had Sam Brown's name on it.

"He said he was not to be disturbed," the girl said, getting up from her desk.

"If my uncle just left, who is he having a conference with?" Penny asked.

The girl hesitated. "All I know is that is what he said. He is in conference and does not want to be disturbed," she insisted. We knew, then, he was alone, and Penny headed for the door. But we were too late. We heard a shot, then a groan and a gasp. Then silence.

Penny and I looked at each other and we both knew in an instant that we indeed would never disturb Sam Brown again. It seemed we didn't move for a long time. Penny started first, toward the outside door. Then she stopped and said the dumbest thing. "I guess Aunt Addie's not going to have much trouble discovering where we've been today, will she, Willie?"

CHAPTER FOURTEEN

THE NEXT THING PENNY SAID WAS, "I KNEW SOMETHING WAS wrong when he visited us. I knew it."

At the door, we met the strikers. Someone had heard the shot. "Sam Brown killed himself," Penny managed to say, and when everybody crowded in, we ran outside.

We went down the street away from the mill. I was shaking. So was Penny.

After a while, Penny mumbled. "How many?"

"How many what?" I asked.

"Granny Winston, our parents, Aunt Harriet, Sam Brown," she said. "Five in a month."

I cried. Penny put her arm around me. "Remember last year that hotel fire in Des Moines when twelve people died at once? They all had reason to go when they did. Or no reason. Five people or twelve people, it doesn't much matter, except the shock."

Penny was trying to make it easy for me by suggesting anything could happen, that it could be worse, but I cried just the same, and so did she. Then we leaned against the fence and fell into silence.

After a while, Penny said, "Why?"

I couldn't answer.

"The girl said Uncle Lambot was with him minutes before. They must have had a fight."

"Uncle Lambot never fights," I said. "Let's go home."

Penny didn't move. She was thinking.

"Let's go home."

"And do what, Willie? We're here. We might as well stay. Aunt Addie will know sooner or later, Besides, it will be easier to walk to the railroad station and take the taxi home."

I guessed we'd get home sooner in the taxi, so I agreed. We watched people coming and going. Some didn't know which way to turn. Someone in the crowd gave Penny a shove and knocked her sprawling into the gutter.

"You hurt?" I asked. Penny's knee was bleeding again.

We sat down on the curb. "It's nothing," she said.

"We hardly saw Sam this summer. I wish we could have seen him one more time."

"Maybe if we had, he wouldn't have done it. I didn't think he would. I thought he belonged to the race of happy people. Maybe it only seemed that way. What's happy?"

"What?"

My mind blurred, as did hers. We lapsed into quietude again, sitting on the curb like lost waifs. Through watery eyes, we watched the commotion down the street at the front gate. The town's two policemen came in the town's only cruiser. The ambulance arrived. Uncle Lambot came zooming down the street in his Packard and slammed the brakes when he saw us. There was a big dent on the side of his car, and the back window was cracked. We guessed right away it had something to do with the strikers. "William, take your sister home, and when Addie comes, tell her I'll be here for some time. This is no place to be." Uncle Lambot was stern but not angry. We got up and walked away.

"I don't reckon Uncle Lambot is going to have much to say for the rest of the summer," Penny said. "He's got problems way up to here, and when he's got problems, he doesn't talk."

"Let's go home. Uncle Lambot said we had to."

"We'll get a taxi," Penny said again as we headed for town. "Won't ever get there otherwise. How about a chocolate malted? As stated, money I have." Penny pulled some bills from her skirt pocket. "Found them in a book. Just goes to show, it pays to read," she added, trying to sound like good old Penny. "It's fun to carry money, Willie. Makes you feel grown-up."

"Where do you hide it?" I asked, trying to go along.

"In the empty Bible in the parlor. Any time you need some, help yourself."

"She'll find it."

"Never," Penny shot back. "But if she does, it will shake her marbles so much it will be worth losing it all just for that. If she does find it, it will take months for her to decide whether or not to mention it, and then if she does, I'll tell her that it is God's reward for her good works."

"Funnee," I commented. "Lose it and then what do we do? Uncle Lambot hasn't bothered with an allowance for us yet."

"Uncle Lambot thinks I'm special, Willie, and when the time

comes, I'll work on him," Penny said. "Maybe we should be thinking about giving Uncle Lambot an allowance instead. We probably have more money than he has, what with the insurance, the house, and if the mill is sold. We may even have more than Aunt Addie has, and that's plenty."

"I wonder if Sam had much money," I said.

"Maybe, but I don't think so. He liked to read, and readers don't usually have much unless it has been left to them, as in the case of Aunt Charity."

"It doesn't matter any more."

"Guess not," Penny said. "I wonder what he thought when he pulled the trigger."

"Stop it."

"Sorry. We'll think about things to remember. Good things, I hope."

The first thing I thought of was work. Sam liked work, and he was not modest when talking about it. Sam lived in a small apartment over the Butler drugstore in the center of town. He had a lot of old furniture that wasn't much better than Uncle Lambot's, but it was kept spic and span, fussy clean. The other things you remembered were books everywhere, and the fish tanks. Sam raised guppies, hundreds of them, tiny fish you could hardly see, and all they did was swim and chase one another. Except for the mill, I couldn't see much else in life for him.

But he loved the mill, we thought. It was his real home. He was there all the time, working mostly. He liked to talk work in a preachy sort of way. He believed it a man's duty to give two dollar's worth of value in his work for one dollar's worth of pay. That was to allow for slippages and occasional lapses. Only in so doing, he said, could one have a truly clear conscience about work, and without a clear conscience, life wasn't worth the crumb of a fig newton. I wondered about that, and wondered if conscience had something to do with his taking his life.

"The mill was his monument, and he saw it toppling," Penny

said. "He spent his life keeping it and building it and fighting for its survival. And he failed. So he killed himself. Know what?"

I didn't respond.

"I think he died before the bullet hit him. I think he'd been thinking about it a long time. And you know something else? If we hadn't taken our time at the bridge, he might still be alive. If he had seen us, I bet he would still be alive."

"We weren't supposed to come to town in the first place," I said.

"Still, I wonder," Penny said. "I wonder if Sam and Aunt Harriet will meet in another world and get married finally? I think they were in love. Maybe he did it so he could be with her."

We were in town now, and I was relieved because we could talk about something besides what just happened. "Looks the same," Penny said.

You could believe that. Despite electric light poles and wires, some electric signs, and macadam on the roads, Eastfield did not look like a place that liked change.

Its main feature was its central, circular park. On one side was a cluster of stores, and on the other, the brick and stone town hall, and the white wooden church—Aunt Addie's and Uncle Lambot's church. There were tall elms in the park, and you could cross streets almost anywhere without worrying about traffic. Eastfield was something like Uncle Lambot and Aunt Addie. It wasn't all that exciting, but it was predictable and dependable. You knew that it would always be there and not ever change much.

"A pretty church," Penny said. We paused and looked at it, with its simple white spire reaching into the sky. "It *is* pretty!" she exclaimed. "*And* it needs painting," she added, sounding as if God should have noticed that detail long ago and taken care of it. Without thinking that we were doing it, we went inside and sat in one of the pews. We sat silently for a few moments and bowed our heads. Then we both looked up at the window in the apse, with its portrait of Jesus draped with a red robe, with the children at his feet. Penny had always liked it. Now she walked to it, scanned it closely,

and read the verse that Aunt Addie had recited. Then we walked
away and out of the church.

"Did you pray?" I asked.

"Yes," Penny said. "I wonder if my prayer was heard this time."
But she didn't tell me what she prayed. "Now let's go to Sadie's."
That was the end of that.

Sadie's dress shop was next to the five-and-dime. It was not much
more than a hole in the wall, and inside, Sadie's goods looked like
leftovers from a rummage sale. Sadie was a squat, fleshy woman,
and she sat all day on a stool inside the front door. The only time
she moved was when a customer came, which was not often.

"Penny and Willie, I declare!" Sadie exclaimed. "Growin' like
chickweed, Willie. Growin' bigger'n your sister. Soon you will be a
man, and older." Sadie's voice was loud, but she softened it nicely
with a lazy slurring of words. Sadie said just enough about our parents, a bit more about Granny Winston, and a bit more about Aunt
Harriet. Still more about us, and what we were going to do. Penny
thought she might find something out about Aunt Harriet, but
Sadie killed that idea by affirming, "How she died is somebody
else's secret, not mine."

"And if it's Sam Brown's secret, we'll never know," Penny said.
"He's dead, Sadie."

"The hell you say!"

"True," Penny said, and told Sadie all we knew about what had
happened.

When she had finished, Sadie said, "I guess that means the end
of the mill for certain now. As long as he was about, you could still
hope."

"They are not going to sell the mill," Penny said.

"Who said?" Sadie asked, disbelieving.

"I heard," Penny said.

"Did not," I said.

Penny heeled my toe, hard. "They are going to start the wheels
rolling again. You wait and see."

"Believe that when I see it," Sadie said, shaking her head. "If they don't start up soon, I'm going to shut the store. Haven't sold a thing all week."

"You're going to sell something now," Penny said. She pointed to a reddish-orange dress hanging on the wall. "That."

Sadie didn't move. "You don't want that."

"That's exactly what I want."

Sadie turned her head back and forth. "Your aunt know you're buying clothes? She ain't gonna like that one at all." That was putting it mildly. Never mind the color, it was sleeveless and it had a skimpy neckline fore and aft.

"How much is it, Sadie?"

"It's not for sale."

Penny took some money from her pocket. "How much?"

Sadie weakened a bit. "Nine ninety-five. But it's not for sale."

"I'll take it."

"You want it for play, you take it. For nothing. But you don't wear it in front of your aunt. If she knew I ever let you have that, she'd march me out of town. You don't want that dress, Penny."

Penny pressed a ten dollar bill in Sadie's hand. "Put it in a bag, and I'll tell Aunt Addie it's a mackerel from the Wampanaug, if she asks."

"No. Every year your aunt comes here and buys a whole mess of clothes. Every Christmas. Then she leaves them for me to give away. Makes out a lit of names and I see that people get their clothes and they never know who paid. Addie's my best customer and she does it to help me as well as other people. A mighty nice woman, and she'd run me out of town if I told anyone about her giving. You kids are lucky, and don't you never forget it."

"We won't never forget it," Penny said. "I want to give this dress to somebody. It's not for me. I won't tell Aunt Addie anything about it."

"Not for you?"

"Not for me."

"Ah!" Sadie was relieved. "Just like your aunt, you are. Giving is living, Penny. Do that and you ain't never got to worry when you get up in the morning," Sadie said, pouring the dress into a paper bag.

"Just like Aunt Addie," Penny said, not exactly pleased with the conversation. Outside, she said, "What did I tell you, Willie? 'You're just like her, you're just like her,'" Penny mimicked. "That's what I told you. I have to watch it, Willie. Every second of every day. Even through tragedy and death."

"She meant it nice."

"I know, and all of our aunts talk about our Aunt Addie flying with the angels. Even Aunt Charity. Just the same, I've got to watch it."

By now we had crossed the street to Butler's drugstore. Located in a white-framed, two-story building, Butler's Drug was known as the Times Square of Eastfield. Most everybody that could reported in there once a day or so. Mr. Butler looked old enough to us to be one of the town's founding fathers. His marble-top counter was a good place for chocolate malteds, and you could gather your rating about town and with him by the thickness of the malted. You not only got prescriptions filled here, but you got free advice on almost anything whether or not you needed it. Penny and I usually got thick malteds, and "be nice to Aunt Addie and Uncle Lambot, they are what makes the world go around" advice.

The place was in a dither. Mr. Butler was beside himself, and every time he decided to close out of respect to his upstairs tenant, someone else walked in. He treated Penny and me with great solemnity, as if Sam Brown were kith and kin. Mr. Butler whispered words we couldn't hear about Granny, our parents, and Aunt Harriet. While he commiserated, he mixed us our malteds without our asking, adding ice cream until they were as thick as gruel.

Holmes Woodbury entered the store then and transformed it for Penny, in a trice, into a new and different world.

"Penny," Holmes said. He overdid his casualness, and I turned my head so I wouldn't have to say hello to him. Holmes had smooth skin and precise facial features. Tall and heavy-shouldered, he wore dark glasses, gray flannels, a white shirt, and brown loafers. I later told Penny I didn't think he looked much like Harvard, and she said he did indeed.

Penny told him all about Sam Brown.

"You're kidding! When? Why?" Holmes asked.

"Remember Richard Cory?" Penny asked. "There was a man in our town and he was a very good man who had everything, yet one calm, summer night, he went home and put a bullet in his head."

"Edward Arlington Robinson," Holmes said.

"Yes," Penny said, obviously pleased. I didn't know who he was, or Richard Cory, and I wished Holmes hadn't known either. Knowing drew Penny toward him. I didn't like it, and I liked it less when he said he was going to be around most of the summer.

They could not discuss the matter further, because Mr. Butler informed Holmes that his Aunt Lucretia had phoned from the church, and he was to come over immediately and drive her home.

"So soon?"

"Because of Sam," Mr. Butler said, and then in a kind of absent mumble, he added, "He was in here for his mid-morning coffee. He said it was a beautiful day, created by God to make one forget all the problems he ever had."

"Once he had the world on a string," Penny said.

"Come on," Holmes said.

I hoped Penny would balk, but she didn't. "Aunt Addie," I reminded her.

"We'll cross that bridge when we come to it," Penny said.

As it turned out, there wasn't much of a bridge to cross. At the church, when we all got into Holmes's sedan, all Aunt Addie kept saying to Lucretia Woodbury was how awful it was, and she didn't know what the world was coming to, that it was changing so fast she didn't know if she could keep herself in it much longer, especially with that gang down in Washington getting bigger and bigger and ever more greedy, and the mill would be in operation if they were not there. Even Aunt Lucretia was shaken, and hardly anything ever shook that battle-worn harpy. She, too, hardly noticed us, even though this was the first time we had seen her that summer.

Holmes swung around the square, and we passed the town's only piece of public art, a weather-worn statue of a soldier of the Civil War, standing high on a podium of granite. In front of him was a cannon and a pyramid of iron cannon balls.

Penny said, "I wonder who posed for that. Ozymandias?"

"Eastfield's unknown soldier," Holmes said.

"The mightiest of the mightiest," Penny said.

"The lowliest of the lowliest," Holmes said.

He didn't know that Ozymandias bit, but it didn't matter. What mattered was the way their gears meshed, the way they sneaked looks at each other. "Who's Ozymandias?" I asked, as if I didn't know. I thought Penny would bop me, but she kept on talking as if I were not there. "Kiss my razz," I told Holmes, but not so he could hear.

That night, when I heard both Uncle Lambot and Aunt Addie snoring in their respective rooms, and I could stand being alone no longer, I sneaked down to Penny's room. Her light was on. She was sitting on her bed. She wasn't reading.

"I was thinking about Sam. We never really saw much of him. Add all the times we saw him, and maybe it comes down to forty or sixty hours. A couple of days out of our lives and his, that's all."

"We knew him," I said. I began to cry.

Penny leaned against me. "Crying is because of the past," she said. "Everyone lives and dies. So maybe I won't cry anymore for anybody."

"We didn't even get any money from him this summer," and I added, "or a story from Aunt Harriet."

"Yes," Penny said dreamily. "I wonder a lot about her. I have this odd notion that others did not feel the same way about Aunt Harriet as we did. Did you notice how Aunt Addie and Uncle Lambot never talk about her unless I make them, and then they usually get up and go somewhere else? Like to the bathroom where I can't follow."

"I don't care what anybody thinks about Aunt Harriet, except me."

"Good, Willie, good. I feel the same. Bless you. You are the best," Penny said. "Let's get something to eat."

We headed down the back stairs to the kitchen and fixed ourselves peanut butter sandwiches and milk. I felt better after eating and I asked Penny, "How do you know they are not going to sell the mill?"

"A nifty idea of mine," Penny said. "All of a sudden it dawned on me. I asked Uncle Lambot about the mill, and he said because of things happening when our father died, the deal on the mill wasn't completed, and they have to deal some more. Or not to deal, too, he said."

"So?"

"So we don't have to sign anything, and then we don't sell."

"But Uncle Lambot is in charge and we don't sign anything anyway. Besides, you know him when he decides to do something," I said.

Penny smiled coyly. "And you know Uncle Lambot if he doesn't want to do something," she said. "You heard Aunt Addie say he would give up his Packard rather than sell the mill. I think I'll test my powers of persuasion on him. If he doesn't want to sell the mill and if we don't want to sell, then he won't have to sign papers and the mill won't be sold."

"Won't matter. The mill's broke," I said.

"We've got money and we'll get more. I'll go to work on Uncle Lambot, and then if we haven't enough, I'll go to work on Holmes Woodbury who can go to work on his Uncle Elisha."

I didn't respond and Penny quickly noted my silence. "Do you like Holmes? I don't think you do."

I didn't hide my feelings. "Big deal. A snot," I said.

"I suppose," Penny said. "But I like him. I intrigued him today and I'm going to do some more of it. I wonder how much he knows. Know what I would like to know, Willie?"

"You've always got to know something."

"How much does one learn in two years of college, and going on into the junior year? Especially if it's Harvard? How much? This summer, I think I'll find out."

"How can you talk like nothing happened today? Like nothing matters? Like there was never a Sam Brown or anybody else?" I meant Aunt Harriet and Penny knew that.

Penny kissed me. "I have to talk with somebody. You, Willie, you're the one. Always. I don't know always where I'm at, except when I'm with you," Penny said.

We finished our food and started up the stairs. At the top, Penny said, "I don't want to go to my room. I don't want to be alone."

"Neither do I," I said. So Penny came to my room, and climbed into bed with me, and snuggled. I must have slept real good. The next morning, when I awoke, Penny was back in her own bed.

CHAPTER FIFTEEN

IT FELL TO UNCLE LAMBOT TO MAKE ALL THE ARRANGEMENTS FOR SAM'S funeral, and he did himself proud. The church was filled with people and flowers, the biggest funeral in years, they said, and everybody was properly important and somber about it.

Sam was sent to his final rest mostly with some readings from the Old Testament by the Reverend James. At home, Aunt Addie said to Uncle Lambot, "You'd have thought that . . ." but he cut her off. "I had a talk with him before the funeral. He did all right," Uncle Lambot said. "No matter what you do, you have to die some-time." We were all ears, but that was all to the conversation. Penny said later that it was good to know arithmetic when living with Uncle Lambot and Aunt Addie because you had to do a lot more than put two and two together just to see what anything was about.

Holmes Woodbury was at the funeral, and after the prayers at graveside, he and Penny sneaked off for a few minutes. I tagged along until it dawned on me that I was as popular as ants at a pic-nic. But I watched them from afar, and Holmes put his arm around Penny as if he owned her. If I were closer, I would have thrown a stone at him.

There was not much doing in Eastfield, and Holmes found all kinds of excuses to come to the farm. As the summer drifted from one day to another, I noticed changes in Penny. She decided she liked dresses, and even got Aunt Addie to make a couple for her. She experimented with lipstick, which Aunt Addie didn't like, and neither did she. She combed her hair, not only differently but often, and that Aunt Addie liked. There were times when she looked real pretty, but I didn't bother to tell her. She smiled, too, and laughed with our elders, although you could never tell she was not doing it from stage front. She changed her voice. She dropped her flat mono-tone, her drone, and gave her words more emphasis. I didn't like it. Neither did Aunt Addie. She told Penny not to sound so high fa-lutin' every time Holmes came, and I was secretly pleased. On oc-casion she was even nice to Aunt Addie, but she acted as if she had pressed some button on her that ordered her to be nice.

Holmes never came on Wednesday evenings, and that's because Penny visited with Aunt Charity Chase. I suspected where he might be but never asked. Those were black nights for me, and I sat by the window until the wee hours.

In no time at all, Penny sneaked Hilda's dress to her, and she sneaked over quite often after that. I was on Aunt Addie's side on those visits in my mind, but I made excuses for Penny, saying she had gone off to write a poem, or she was taking a nap. Once she told me about Hilda and sex and that made the visits worse.

"Hilda still does it," she said. "She told me every cent she gets she saves for her baby."

"Does what?" I said.

"Willie, she said it was easier than I could imagine."

"What?" I asked again.

"Having sex," Penny said. I told her she sounded worse than Freda O'Halloran back home, and she didn't like that at all.

Every so often Penny would sneak over to Adam's and clean with a passion that would have done justice to all of Aunt Addie's wildest desires. She always said she was going for wildflowers and she always came back with a bunch, but no one was fooled. "You are not to go there, Penny," Aunt Addie ordered again and again. "Adam's not a good influence. You are not to go there, hear?" But she never got a promise signed in blood, and everybody knew Penny would sneak out to Adam's whenever she wished. And after she told me what Hilda told her about men, I worried more than ever.

Once I followed her to Adam's place and spied. She wasn't cleaning. The place looked as dirty as ever. She was sitting on the bed, leaning against the wall, and reading. Adam was sitting next to her, and he looked to me as if he were interested in something else besides what she was reading. I wanted to throw a stone through the window and run, but I couldn't bring myself to do it.

That night I went to her bedroom and told her I saw her. She was not pleased.

"How come you want to clean there, and you don't want to clean here?"

"Nobody makes me do it there," Penny said.

"I thought you said only Aunt Addie says 'don't.'"

"Funnee," Penny said, but she didn't think it was. "You don't like it here, do you? I don't like it here. It's routine, all it is is routine."

"You'll get in trouble."

"You mean trouble like having a baby?" She decided to be serious with me and she talked like the Reverend James when he was trying to make a point. "Hilda's having a baby, Willie, and it's not going to be easy around here when that is known. And I have this feeling for Hilda. Some nights I'm in bed and I think I want a baby the worst way. Other times, no. If I have a baby I'll have it for a good reason. Something about fighting the good fight."

"All the same, you better watch it," I warned.

"Willie, dear Willie. How nice to have a big brother watching over me, and I thank you," Penny said, giving me a kiss. "I was thinking about Adam when you came in. Know what?"

"What?"

"I was trying to answer his riddle. How come, if Adam is not bright, he can know so much?"

"Can't prove it by me."

"He tells me things by bits and pieces. Did you know he's forty-eight, the same age as Aunt Addie?"

I didn't. It never occurred to me that Adam had an age.

"He was born in 1890, and that makes him forty-eight. He came to Eastfield in 1910 when he was twenty. He built his shack in 1930 when he was forty. Adam's good on figuring," Penny said.

"So what?"

"So. Aunt Harriet's stories about Adam. He's been living in the woods for only eight years. Some of Aunt Harriet's stories made out he was living here a lot longer. So do you want to know where he lived before that? He lived at Aunt Harriet's. They lived in the same house for twenty years."

"We knew he was Aunt Harriet's handyman," I said. When we were growing up, there was no reason to know more, no reason to be told more.

"Handier, maybe, in more ways than one," Penny said. "Imagine! There must be something in the air that comes from the river that affects people here. There's the Nasons, married and not living to-gether. There's Uncle Lambot and Aunt Addie. They're not married and they live together. And there was Adam and Aunt Harriet, and we didn't know about it. Now that would make for a spicy story if you didn't know that Aunt Harriet's mother also lived there until she died, and from what they say, Aunt Harriet's mother was a tyrant."

I was confused. Penny was telling me too much. It crossed my mind that I had never really thought much about Aunt Harriet ever having a mother. Or a father. Or anybody else. Except Penny and me. Aunt Harriet was our Aunt Harriet and that was that.

"Something else. Aunt Harriet pushed him out so Sam Brown could move in. That is, move in and move out whenever he wanted to. It was a nice, convenient arrangement, what do you think of that? That's why Adam built his shack. At least that's what Hilda's father told me. He tells me lots, only sometimes I'm not sure he's telling me what's really what. You ought to talk to him, Willie. He's interesting. He's lonely, and he likes to talk."

"Some days you come home from Adam's you smell of smoke," I said, changing the subject. "You been smoking his crazy cigarettes?" Adam rolled his own.

"I've been smoking."

"Big deal. Aunt Addie knows."

"That's why I smoke."

"That's nutty mean. Besides, you used to tell me people who smoked were insane."

"I'm discovering passion, Willie, and when you discover it, you begin to discover life," Penny said.

"What has that got to do with smoking?"

"You'll see. When you do it with somebody."

I couldn't stand it. Penny was getting dumber by the minute, and I got up and left. Out in the hallway I heard creaking, as if a door was being shut. I could have sworn I saw Aunt Addie's door move. I listened for a couple of seconds, and I thought I heard movement in Aunt Addie's room. I guessed she might have been listening, and if so, she would have good reason to worry about Penny.

I didn't tell Penny, though. When I told her things, she got me all mixed up. She did that more and more even when I didn't tell her things.

Sam left no will, and when Penny asked Uncle Lambot if Sam had had any money, all he would say was, "It remains to be seen." And Aunt Addie, who was nearby, made motions with her hands that said, "Don't press the matter," and when Penny asked why, she could only say, "It's not nice to talk about money."

The Reverend James, who, like Holmes, was a frequent visitor, came to dinner one Sunday. That morning in church he read in the Bible about it being easier for a camel to go through the eye of a needle than for a rich man to enter into the kingdom of God, and Penny was ready with a hatful of questions. She wanted to know did the same apply to rich women? If the quotation from the Bible had merit, why did not the church set out with more zeal to make the rich people poor? Would Mr. Nason, when he died, have an easier time of getting into heaven, than, say, Elisha Woodbury? If the meek inherited the earth, was it only after they were dead and it didn't matter much? In light of the fact that she was now quite wealthy, would Penny's very own struggle to enter the kingdom of God be worth it? And if she had to give up her wealth, did she have to do it now, or could she wait until the last possible moment before dying? And was it not possible to buy our own kingdom on earth, which might be more enjoyable than the sweet, quiet, and rather dull place that heaven was pictured to be? The minister and Penny enjoyed their discussions, and they got too cute about it at times, not sounding at all religious. The Reverend James looked at Penny the way Holmes did sometimes, acting as if she were twenty or so, which she certainly tried to act. It was disquieting, and as the summer kept going along, I felt a sense of abandonment that would not go away.

One hot and muggy afternoon, when you couldn't tell whether or not we were going to have our second thunderstorm within an hour, Aunt Lucretia and her husband, Elisha Woodbury, came calling. Aunt Addie corralled Aunt Lucretia for tea and cakes in the parlor, and Uncle Lambot and Elisha went for a walk around the barn. When they came around front, they sat on the old slate watering trough and did some fancy talking. Penny and I were playing in the barn at the time, and we did not find it at all difficult to eavesdrop.

Elisha Woodbury was not much bigger than a toad, and he reminded me of one, squat and puffy. But everybody said that because he owned the bank, he was a figure to be reckoned with in Eastfield, and so you didn't bother to think about his size. He got right to the point that afternoon.

"He was a bastard, Lambot, a bastard, I've been telling you that a long time," Elisha said. His voice was unpretentious, yet powerful, as if it were coming from a much bigger man.

Uncle Lambot merely grunted.

"I'll tell you what I'd have done. I'd have fired the bastard fifteen years ago. If he hadn't been around, maybe . . ."

"Can't blame the Depression on him. Guess things would be about the same if someone else was in charge. Those fools down in Washington . . ."

"And there are fools in Eastfield. You're down to your last dollar because of him and that's a fact."

"Maybe, maybe not," Uncle Lambot, and you could not tell what was maybe, maybe not.

"Oh, sure. Let me remind you again, Lambot, that he landed that contract three years ago to run the mill at a loss, with you begging, borrowing, and practically stealing money to keep the mill going until it broke you. Now I'm going to tell you something, Lambot, because it's you. It's not the kind of thing I ought to tell, and I'm embarrassed because it has to do with one of our customers at the bank and his private business, but he's dead now, you have to handle his affairs, and I've decided to tell you what you will discover eventually. I think Sam Brown got paid on the other end for that contract, that's what I'm thinking, paid for getting you to accept such a low bid. And the reason I believe that is because of the lump sums he put in his bank account from time to time. Two thousand here, five thousand there, and one time ten thousand. You certainly weren't foolish enough to pay him bonuses, were you?"

Uncle Lambot grunted.

"Where the hell do you think it came from?"

This time we heard nothing.

"Tell you something else. I had a talk with my sister-in-law, Hattie, a week or so before she died. Did you know she had a falling out with Sam? She came down to the bank and told me she wanted to withdraw all her money from her account and put it in a safety deposit box, and she wanted it fixed so that nobody could touch it, not even herself, without my knowing it. I asked did she want to talk about it, and she said, no, but she did anyway. You know women."

Uncle Lambot grunted. He was back among the living.

"Sam told Hattie he needed some money in a hurry, and when Hattie fudged—you know her and money—he told her that he had made a deal with the new owners, they were going to pay him good for the way he handled things, but all he needed was a little cash to cover a gambling debt. And when he wasn't getting anywhere he asked Hattie to go South with him. When she didn't move on that, Sam got blustery, said he needed the money, she had some, and if he didn't get it, he might just say a few things about town to make her change her mind."

There was a long pause, and Uncle Lambot said, "Guess she didn't change her mind."

"I'll say she didn't. She kicked Sam out and told him she wouldn't invite him to hell because he was already there. From the looks of her that afternoon, she ought to know what it was like. When I saw her I said to myself that's what is called the wrath of God. Talk about a woman's scorn, Hattie had a bushel of it that day. You should have married her way back when, Lambot, when she was after you. That's what you should have done. Things would be a lot different if you had."

Uncle Lambot merely grunted. Penny jabbed my ribs. "Shhh," I admonished.

"What are you going to do about the mill, Lambot?" Elisha wanted to know.

"Guess I'll have to do what I have to do."

"Now you're getting sensible. I don't know, sometimes, about you Winstons. You got a streak of something," Elisha said. "You are going ahead, then, and sell."

"Might just set on it for a while and see what develops," Uncle Lambot said.

"You're a fool, Lambot. You can't do that unless you got a lot of money I don't know about. I hate to press an old friend, but the bank is overextended and we can't let those loans go down the drain, period. The bank can't stand any more pressure. The men from New York are coming by again next week, and I expect they will want to dicker with you. When they come, I'll expect you to go along."

"We'll cross that bridge when we come to it," Uncle Lambot said.

"Lambot, you came to it a long time ago," Elisha replied. "And you better get over it while the going's good."

We knew the meeting was over then because we could hear them shuffling about, and lest we be caught, we beat a hasty retreat out the rear door of the barn.

"Golly," I said.

"What do I think?" Penny said, interpreting my remark. "I think we got a lot of thinking to do, that's what I think."

"Uncle Lambot's got no money," I said.

"Uncle Lambot's a bachelor and he didn't have to be one," Penny said. "Aunt Harriet's dead and so is Sam." And she wandered off by herself.

We had a supper of crackers and milk and blueberries out on the veranda because that's what everybody wanted because of the weather. When Uncle Lambot had finished eating, Penny climbed a wooden footstool behind Uncle Lambot's chair, and massaged his temples. He had just picked up the Eastfield weekly newspaper to read, but he put it aside, laid his head back, and closed his eyes. For a moment he had sheer contentment.

Penny said, ever so casually, "What are we going to do about the mill?"

Another time, Uncle Lambot would not have heard. We knew he did this time, because he cleared his throat, and we knew he was going to say something. He would take the longest time doing it, but he would say something. I watched Aunt Addie. She was knitting, and it could have been done by an automatic machine for all the attention she was paying it.

Finally a reply came. "Sell, I guess. Won't get much. Got a lot of bills to pay."

"Who is going to buy it?" Penny wanted to know.

"A company in New York that owns some mills in South Carolina."

"Everybody says they were planning to close the mill permanently and move the machinery South because everything is cheaper there."

"Something like that," Uncle Lambot admitted.

"Did Aunt Harriet want to sell out?" Penny asked, as if she didn't know.

Uncle Lambot chafed a bit. "Wasn't making money. Owes a lot. Costs to keep it open. Something had to give. The men are coming back next week. It's take it or leave it."

Penny paused long enough to make certain Uncle Lambot would be listening. Then she said, "Of course it's only a child talking, but I say let them leave it here and not take it South. Willie and I held an owner's meeting this afternoon and we decided not to sell." Penny stopped rubbing Uncle Lambot's head. She pushed the footstool by his feet and sat on it. She looked directly at Uncle Lambot.

"We just think we have to take it through thick and thin. It's not good business without your having an obligation to people as well as property."

Aunt Addie almost stabbed herself with her knitting needles on that. But I knew where Penny got that idea. Uncle Lambot had said something like that to Ranse Sherman, the man who owned the Eastfield Lumberyard, outside of church a couple of weeks back. I remember because I wondered what they were so serious about, and then Ranse laughed and told Uncle Lambot he was sounding more and more like a New Dealer, and later I asked Penny whether Uncle Lambot played poker.

Uncle Lambot shifted uneasily in his chair. "Ain't much I can do. You can't ever tell what those fools down in Washington will do next. Can't plan a thing any more."

It was then that Aunt Addie decided she would make points with her brother by making her one contribution to the conversation. "If they would just let things alone, everything would right itself. If only they wouldn't disturb the swing of the pendulum."

Penny shot me a knowing glance on that. Hardly a week passed but what Uncle Lambot didn't say, "The pendulum swings one way, and then it swings back. Always has and always will, if you don't mess with it. We'd be out of trouble long ago, if they would only mind their business."

"Where is the pendulum now, Uncle Lambot?" Penny asked. Aunt Addie took that as a swipe at her, and told Penny she didn't know everything. Uncle Lambot only added another grunt to the evening's collection.

"Have you got much money, Uncle Lambot?" Penny asked, as if we had heard nothing that afternoon. "Everybody thinks you have."

Asking Uncle Lambot about money was like tossing a lighted cherry bomb in the midst of a church prayer meeting; it just was not done. Aunt Addie gasped. Her face was saying again that decent people most certainly did not talk about such money. Uncle

Lambot puffed his lips into a pout, a sign of impatience. "What do you want to know for?" he grumbled.

That was all Penny needed and a torrent of words spilled from her. "To solve a problem. Willie and I have the insurance money coming, and lots of other money. More than we need. You could give each of us five dollars a week spending money and that will be enough," she said. She paused, and maybe mindful of Hilda's sacrifice for her father, she added, "We don't even need that. Maybe Willie and I could go to work. We could raise vegetables, or get some hens to make eggs. We could have an egg factory going right here in no time."

"I declare! Really, child!" Aunt Addie didn't like hens.

"Eastfield would not be Eastfield without the Winston Mills, Uncle Lambot. I've heard you say that dozens of times, and I agree. I say keep the mills. But if we sell then I say we ought to move out of town. To New York, and out of harm's way. New York is certainly a more interesting place to live than Eastfield with or without the Winston Mills. Wouldn't you like to live in New York, Aunt Addie? Do something different for a change?" Penny didn't wait for an answer. She got up from the stool and gave Uncle Lambot a hug and a kiss, which he didn't mind at all. "Let's gamble. If we have to go down the drain, let's go whole hog. Given the kind of people we are, I don't see any other choice." She gave Uncle Lambot another kiss. "My favorite uncle, I'd sell that beautiful old Packard before I ever sold the mill. No matter how much I loved it, I'd sell it."

Penny realized she had said enough for one sitting, and when she spotted Adam out in the yard fixing to clean the Packard, she said, "There's Adam. I think I'll go help him." At the door she paused. "Know something? Adam's not so dumb as you might think, and I bet he was good looking when he was younger, wasn't he, Aunt Addie? I asked him if he had any girlfriends when he was younger, was he ever really and truly in love, and he said there was love in everybody at one time or another. What do you think of that?"

Penny bounded down the steps without waiting for an answer and I thought that was a good thing, because that wasn't the kind of a question that made for brilliant repartee with either Uncle Lambot or Aunt Addie.

Later, outside, I said, "What did you have to say that for?"

"About Adam? I don't know. The devil in me, I guess," Penny said, laughing.

"Smart ass. She's real upset. I watched her while you worked Uncle Lambot over. I'd watch it if I were you," I said. "Besides, I don't get it."

"About the mill?"

"What do you know about business anyway?"

"That's like saying, 'Mind your own business,'" Penny replied. "It is our business." She forgot about helping Adam and walked toward the barn. I followed. "What have I got to lose? I don't know. I honestly don't know. Something about what we mostly don't have. Living in a tomb, Willie, is what we mostly have. Not just this house. Eastfield. You tell me all I talk about is dying. If I do, I'm sorry, but something is dying, something . . . I don't know."

"I don't care," I said. I didn't know what else to say.

"Suppose I didn't say anything, and we watched Uncle Lambot fall asleep over his newspaper as usual, and Aunt Addie would dream up a new batch of don't's, all the while knitting." She started up the ladder to swing over to Olympus. I followed to the first platform. "So what's dumb about wanting to know something about the Winston Mills?" Penny asked. They both act like it's a sex matter, and therefore you don't mention it, ever, ever. We are sixteen and going on seventeen, at least I am. I've been sixteen for a half dozen years, if you want to know, and it's time I learned about dollars and cents as well as about the birds and the bees. Cripes!"

"Aunt Addie's about to whammy you. I could feel it."

"Razzmatazz." Penny scoffed. "Around men, she's Madame Caspar Milquetoast, and I'm not going to be that way. What a no-getter she is. Every day she sets a record. What a thing to be remembered for after you die."

"I thought you said everybody forgets everything about everybody sooner or later after they die, so what does it matter."

"That I did," Penny said, unruffled. "So what does it matter what I do? Right now I'm going to swing over to Olympus. Coming?"

I had no opportunity to decide. Aunt Addie interrupted with one of her clarion calls. "Penny! Come down here this instant!" We looked below and there she stood. She had discovered Olympus.

I climbed down, and Penny, undecided at first, followed. "When I say you are not to do something, you are not to do it. Don't think for one moment you are the only one around here that knows all there is to know," Aunt Addie began. She was talking to Penny, not to me.

"You told me that," Penny said brashly.

"Don't be fresh, young lady," Aunt Addie said. "You are not to talk money to Uncle Lambot. We don't do that in this household. We don't talk about his money, because he has none."

We, of course, had got the word from Elisha Woodbury that afternoon, but it didn't really sink in. Aunt Addie's pronouncement exploded like a bomb. Even Penny looked at Aunt Addie in disbelief. "That's not what everybody thinks."

"Well, it's so. Uncle Lambot is very sensitive about the mill, and that's a fact, too."

"I don't see why," Penny said.

"Well, I'll tell you then, and you listen carefully because I don't want to repeat," Aunt Addie said, sounding at last as if she had made up her mind to tell us a few things with no and's, if's or but's. "When Lambot sold his part of the mill to Aunt Harriet, he did so to get more money for the mill. And now that's gone, and more besides. Your grandfather was not much of a businessman, and when he died, he left one big mess at the mill, a mess of bills, a mess of trouble, and Lambot had to take over all the responsibility. His brother wanted no part of it," Aunt Addie said, making a point of not calling him our father. "Your Uncle Lambot has had the whole responsibility for the mill since the beginning of the Depression, and almost the whole responsibility for the welfare of this town because of the mill. If he decides to sell the mill for whatever he can get, he has a right to make whatever decision he thinks he has to make, and you are to say nothing. One more thing, you will have to know some time, and that's about Sam Brown. The mill would have been better off without him. Nothing but a four-flusher. He thought charm could forever take the place of work, but it never does. He was an embezzler, and do you know what that means? It means he took what didn't belong to him from the mill. Slipped goods out of the mill and sold them for his own benefit. Taking money for repairs never made. Been doing that for years. Finally, your uncle caught him."

Aunt Addie had said almost more than she could handle, and she decided to end it all by saying, "Remember you are to say nothing about this. Especially you are not to mention this to Uncle Lambot. Never. Is that clear?"

Penny never let anything go if she could help it. "Why didn't Uncle Lambot have Sam arrested?" she asked. I thought it a good question.

Aunt Addie shook her head and fluttered her arms. "He was too late. Uncle Lambot finally had it out with Sam that morning. He was on his way to get help to have him arrested when somebody banged the Packard with a club, and that delayed him. Why he didn't do it before, I don't know. There's no accounting for what my brother does or does not do. He's the stubbornest man God ever created, bar none. Part like his mother, and part like his father, and the parts never seem to get along with each other. Sam Brown said he would make restitution and Lambot agreed. I told Lambot the time was long past for trusting Sam, but I couldn't budge him.

When Lambot was out west and going through his brother's papers, he found out a thing or two. He found out Sam and his very own brother were wheeling and dealing together to cut Lambot out entirely, and when he returned home he had it out with Sam. But it was too late."

"Was that when Sam killed himself?" Penny asked. "Why didn't he just run off? He didn't seem like the kind of person to do what he did."

"Goodness, child, I don't know about that. One thing I know is that more and more people do things you don't think they are going to do. Everyday something different. Never used to be that way. You grew up, you knew what you had to do, and you did it."

"Our father didn't," Penny said.

Aunt Addie turned. Her eyes gimlet-sized themselves and shot tiny bullets into the air. You couldn't tell whether she was aiming at Penny, or at space, perhaps hoping to land the shot into her departed brother. She started toward the house again. "Nothing about this to your uncle. Is that clear?"

She should have known better. "No. It isn't," Penny said. "If Uncle Lambot has no money, then how about using your money, Aunt Addie?"

Aunt Addie whiplashed about, her face drained of color. "That is *none* of your *business!*" she fumed, and before Penny could ask, "Why?" she wheeled away. "And I don't want you playing with that rope any more. That is an order!"

Aunt Addie went inside, and we walked around the house and sat under a maple. "Well, razzmatazz, Willie!" Penny exclaimed. "Uncle Lambot has told a few things. And now Aunt Addie. They can talk! They said enough to last for years. Can you believe it!"

"Aunt Addie says Uncle Lambot is as honest as the day is long," I said, not sure what Penny was talking about. "I believe both of them."

"What do you think?" Penny asked.

"What?"

"Remember Pangloss in *Candide*?" I didn't, but it didn't matter. "Remember how he said everything that ever happened was all for the best? It makes you begin to wonder. I wonder what God had in mind when he made people the way they are."

I didn't care too much about that. "What do we do now?" I asked. "Give Uncle Lambot the money we got hidden in the Bible?"

The question surprised Penny but she recovered nicely. "Willie, dear Willie, you are a joy forever!" she said. "We'll do what Uncle Lambot does, naturally."

"What's that?"

"Cross that bridge when we come to it."

CHAPTER SIXTEEN

THE DECISION ON THE MILL WAS DELAYED BY ONE OF UNCLE LAM-bot's favorite gambits. He played his disappearance act and become a missing person. When Elisha Woodbury brought along the prospective buyers from New York to talk business, Uncle Lambot drove off to Providence for the day. Aunt Addie didn't even offer them a cup of tea. She told them the mill was Uncle Lambot's business, she didn't know a thing about it, and that was that. "Wouldn't you think he'd know better?" Aunt Addie complained, but not too much.

Out in the yard, Penny told the men that we owned the mill and weren't about to sell at any old price, and we doubted if we would ever do business with anyone who had dealings with Sam Brown. The men were not at all pleased, and they left sputtering unpleasant things about Uncle Lambot and all of Eastfield. For a month they sent telegrams to Uncle Lambot. He tinkered with machinery in the barn, wrestled with his conscience, avoided the Woodburys, and otherwise did nothing.

What little I knew and understood was very unsettling. With Penny, one never knew. She had other important matters to consider.

One night I came into her room and discovered her reading Plato from a book on loan from Charity Chase. She read a passage to me, something about a conversation with Socrates. "What do you think?" she asked when she had finished it.

"Nothing. What do you think?"

"For one thing, I was wondering whether or not Socrates had a high I.Q., or just a great big warm heart."

"Who cares?" I asked. "Who in Eastfield besides *your* Aunt Charity will ever know or care?"

"It is possible that Eastfield may not be the only place I will have lived in before dying," Penny said. "In the second place, Holmes. He thinks I'm incredibly intelligent, and I seek to preserve my reputation. Holmes says to know Greek civilization is to know all there is to know."

"Puke," I said.

"In the third place . . ."

"The Reverend James. Puke."

"Neither Holmes nor the Reverend James have a high opinion of each other's intellect," Penny said.

"Neither do I," I said sourly.

"Willie, dear Willie," Penny said tenderly. "You worry too much, almost as much as Aunt Addie, and you shouldn't. That's not living."

"Aunt Addie manages."

"That she does. She manages and manages. Know something? There's one thing she never worries about."

"Money," I guessed.

"I was thinking something else, but you're right on that, Willie. When it comes to using it, she just plain doesn't."

"Not what Sadie said at the dress shop," I reminded her.

"That's peanuts."

"How do you know she's got money? Just because Aunt Harriet said so? Aunt Harriet said lots of things," I said. "Besides, you never see it."

"That's how I know. When you don't see it and you don't talk about it, you've got it."

"What else were you thinking about that she hasn't got?"

"Happiness, Willie. She never even thinks whether she is happy or not. Maybe that's the way. Maybe happiness doesn't have to be. Did you ever think that? Maybe you are better off without trying to find it, or even wanting it. Most people never seem to have it, and if that's the case, why bother? One less thing to worry about."

"You're never satisfied with anything."

"I am with reading."

"Do you really like reading in that cruddy place in the barn?"

"I like to read anywhere."

"You really like to read?" I tried not to betray my jealousy of her books. "Well, you ought not to go swinging on that rope. You could break your neck if you don't watch it. There's been enough dying, if you really want to know. If you have to read, you ought to find a better place. In the cellar, maybe. Aunt Addie never goes there in the summer and at least it's cool there."

Penny ruffled my hair. "Worry, worry, worry," she said. "Worrying is minding other people's business. A bad habit."

"O.K., go ahead and kill yourself, I don't care."

"Thank you, Willie. Had I a thousand brothers, you would still be my favorite," Penny said. "Aunt Addie told Uncle Lambot to take down the rope, but he hasn't got around to it yet. I don't think he will. He likes to put things off."

"Just like you."

"Just like me."

"You can find a better place."

"I'm not really disobeying the rules of the establishment, because there are no rules to cover my little world up yonder. So I go there. It does little harm. If she doesn't actually see me go to Olympus, she never can be certain I am there. And if I keep quiet, I have privacy, and freedom from don't's."

"If you did more do's, you would have less don't's," I said.

"That's good, Willie, really good. You're quite a thinker."

"Aunt Addie said you could read in the parlor. She said it was not right for a young girl to be in that dirty, filthy barn. She talks about it on the phone to somebody all the time. She told somebody this morning she gets a headache every time you go there. You could go to the parlor."

Penny was pleased with the revelation. "So I am right. She doesn't dare tell me that, and she's using you to tell me and persuade me. As for the parlor, no. If she saw me reading there, she wouldn't give me a moment's peace. She'd find something for me to do. She would fret about my not reading in the correct light, or the way I sat in the chair. Something. No, thank you. And when I'm at Olympus, what do you tell her, Willie?"

"Once I told her you swallowed a bookworm and you had to keep feeding it. And I told her she was lucky not to have you under foot all day."

"That's my Willie!" Penny said. "If I had *ten* thousand brothers, you would still be my favorite."

"Then don't go up there any more. Aunt Addie doesn't talk to you because you talk back, and so she talks to me. It's a pain in the neck way up to here, if you want to know."

Penny looked at me with a new concern. "You really think I won't make it some day?"

"You're not that good," I said.

"O.K. For you, my dear brother, I shall find another spot," Penny promised. "But I have to read, Willie. If I didn't read, I would have to be doing something else. I could be thinking about getting pregnant, like Hilda, and if I did, you would become an uncle before you were old enough to be a father. What do you think of that?"

"Crap."

Penny mulled the idea over. "What an interesting topic for speculation and consideration!" she said gleefully. "Talk about the mill made me forget it temporarily. Imagine the consternation here and about if your little sister were to announce she was creating a baby?"

"Fat chance," I scoffed, but I found myself wondering for the first time if she had ever been with a man.

"I could," Penny said.

I didn't argue that point. When Penny came of age, she had had no hesitation in telling me all about menstruation. I went over to the window. Penny followed.

"I sometimes wonder what makes you tick," I said.

"I'm really no freak of nature, beloved brother of mine," Penny said. "Sometimes I think I'm a bit backward, a slow starter. Did you ever hear of Joan of Arc? She saved a country when she was my age. I've done nothing. And then there's Romeo's girlfriend, Juliet. She gave her life for love when she was younger than I am. I'm a nothing."

"Forget it," I said. I looked out the window into the moonlight. "Nice."

Penny agreed. "You don't see many nights like this one."

The moon was full and it flooded the field with its cool, silvery light. Wisps of fog told where the river lay. Fog patches hung over the field, like ghost clothes on a ghostly clothesline. Fireflies twinkled. The forest beyond was a translucent shadow. In Adam's shack, we could see a lonely light. The train came along at nine, and gave us a toot.

"Life can be worth living, can't it, Willie?" Penny asked. " 'Beauty is truth, truth beauty.' I can never remember who wrote that, Keats or Shelley? Keats, I guess."

"You can't prove it by me," I said dumbly.

"I learned a poem today. Would you like to hear it?"

I didn't reply. I knew she would recite it anyway, and I waited. She whispered:

> *The white mares of the moon rush along the sky*
> *Beating their golden hoofs upon the glass Heavens.*
> *The white mares of the moon are all standing on their*
>   *hindlegs,*
> *Pawing at the green porcelain doors of the remote*
>   *Heavens.*
> *Fly, mares!*
> *Strain your utmost,*
> *Scatter the milky dust of stars,*
> *Or the tiger sun will leap upon you and destroy you,*
> *With one lick of his vermilion tongue.*

"Like it?" Penny asked.

"Uh-huh," I said. I didn't hear the words, but it was soft and soothing the way Penny said it. "Did you make that up?"

Penny squeezed my hand. "If I thought for one moment you really thought that I was capable of writing that, I would be tempted to lie and tell you I did. However, an extraordinary lady, Amy Lowell, wrote it. She smoked a pipe in her garden, and she did some other things a lot of people thought she ought not to do. Tomorrow night, I shall recite it to Aunt Charity. Do you think she'll like it?"

"Uh-huh."

Penny looked out the window and said, "Amy Lowell would have liked this night." She savored the scene for a while, then asked, "Willie, did you know that some of the best poetry was written by women?"

"No, I didn't," I said.

"Neither did Holmes," Penny replied. "But he does now."

CHAPTER SEVENTEEN

•••

O N THE LAST SATURDAY IN JULY, PENNY LIT A FUSE AND TOSSED A
bomb. Aunt Addie was hosting a special meeting of the
Friday Club that afternoon to decide whether or not the
club should admit a new member to take the place of Aunt Harriet.
Charity Chase was the candidate. She hadn't been admitted before
because, according to the unwritten constitution of the Friday Club,
there could be no more than twelve members, and so openings occurred only when a member moved, died, or otherwise disappeared.
It was a foregone conclusion that Charity Chase would make her
membership, but before they voted, the ladies would solemnly dissect her credentials. That the club was exclusive there could be no
doubt; certainly it was more difficult to get into Aunt Addie's inner
circle than into Uncle Lambot's. Uncle Lambot's regulars even admitted Adam.

Low-hanging clouds spilled an inch or so of rain that Saturday,
but rain would not stop the members from turning out. Aunt Addie
was the best cook of the lot, and they always expected and got something special when she was hostess.

The kitchen was Saturday-morning busy. Huge gobs of meringues
had to be made for the gobs of vanilla ice cream, strawberries and
cream that made the special dessert. Besides, Aunt Addie performed
the usual Saturday chores. Saturday was pie day and Aunt Addie
always baked a half dozen pies, sometimes more when she cooked
for a church supper. Today, it was apple, cherry, and coconut
cream, the latter in case some of the girls didn't want the specialty of
the house.

The Saturday beans, which had been soaking overnight, had to be potted and baked. The brown bread had to be made. The Sunday roast had to be prepared for the Sunday morning oven. Aunt Addie would not hear of any suggestion to reduce her workload because of this special day.

Most Saturdays I stayed near the kitchen, because there were frosting pans to lick. This Saturday I was there, hoping for a spare meringue. Penny was there, too, and I had the foolish notion that she might have been there to help Aunt Addie because there was so much to do.

At first it seemed that way. Penny had made the beds and dusted the front hallway and parlor without prodding. Then she washed the breakfast dishes. She tried a bit hard to make it seem that she did this every Saturday, I thought, but Aunt Addie was given no cause to yap.

Penny even said nice things. When she told Aunt Addie that the girls in the Friday Club wouldn't get a better dessert at Buckingham Palace, Aunt Addie was greatly pleased.

Aunt Addie had taken the coconut cream pie from the pantry and was moving it toward the oven. She had opened the oven door, and was about to slip the pie inside, when Penny asked, as if she were only eight, "Aunt Addie, where do babies come from?"

Penny said it casually, as if she might be asking what day it was. In fact, I hardly heard her. But Aunt Addie did, and especially because I was present, the words must have exploded like a torpedo in her ears. She posed, as if for a still life, but only for a moment. Then she rocked and wove, and she dropped the gooey mess of the coconut cream pie, splattering it all over the stove and floor. Aunt Addie verged on panic, but she did not drop that pie accidentally. She knew what she was doing—she dropped it deliberately. Aunt Addie knew a few of the tricks of life.

It was incredible, of course, that Penny should have asked that question in the first place. There was ample evidence to prove beyond all shadow of doubt that Penny knew the answer to that question. I had only to remember that it was but a few weeks ago she told me all about Hilda Nason. Penny not knowing where babies came from? I was as astounded as Aunt Addie.

In a sudden flurry of energy, Aunt Addie first scraped at the oven and then cleaned the floor. If she could have scooped up the pie and replaced it in the pan, she would have done so. "Wouldn't you know I'd do a thing like that on a day like today?" she said with vehemence. I tried to help, but she said no. "Too many hands in the kitchen. Both of you go out and play."

"It's raining," I said.

"Go somewhere. I can do better myself. Go on, now," she urged. "Penny, the parlor, it needs dusting."

"I've done that already today, and yesterday and the day before."

"Your room, then. It is worse than ever. Why you can't put clothes in drawers and cupboards and books on shelves, I'll never know."

In the end we went to the barn. "Smart," I said. "She talked her way out of answering that stupid question."

Sheba, the queen cat of Adam's domain, had found her way out of the rain and into the barn. She rubbed against Penny's leg and Penny picked her up and stroked her. "I wonder if she's pregnant," Penny said.

"That was mean. How can you be like that to Aunt Addie?"

Penny examined the cat, conspicuously. "Aunt Addie was talking about Hilda on the phone this morning. The word is out. This afternoon, they will forget Aunt Charity and talk about Hilda, you mark my words. Aunt Addie can't answer a simple question, but they can discuss the answer all over God's green acres. That is what is mean, unfair, and cruel."

"So what has that got to do with the question?"

"Suppose it was somebody besides Hilda? Me, Willie? Then what would you think of the gossip? It could be me. I'm old enough."

"Maybe it only seems that way," I said.

"Maybe I'm already pregnant."

"Like hell you are," I said.

Penny tossed Sheba to me. "I think she is pregnant, but maybe it only seems that way," she said. With that, she climbed the ladder to swing over to Olympus.

"You promised you wouldn't go there any more."

"I left my book. I have to go after it."

"If you're pregnant, you ought not to go there." When she didn't come down, I shouted, "I thought you were only going for a book."

There was no answer.

"You promised." Still no answer. I went to the cellar and pounded some nails into a piece of wood.

Penny returned before lunch. She was not about to miss the Friday Club meeting. The day before she had given me the scoop on the club. Years ago it had been established as a literary and do-gooder club, but through the years it had become something else. She told me that Charity Chase was lukewarm about becoming a member, that she loved the ladies dearly, except when they got together. She said they were the old guard of a passing era. She said they knew they were old guard and on their way out, but just the same they held to their position with a passion because they didn't have much else. They had been the windmills in Eastfield, the big wheels that kept things moving, not that there was much to move in Eastfield. They were upper structure, and they equated themselves with upper crust in large cities. They ruled the world. They could not afford to let just anybody into their group.

"I thought you said men ruled the world," I said, but Penny took no note. She said Charity Chase told her you had to be a whole lot of things and believe a whole lot of things to belong. You had to be old yankee stock. You had to have an ancestor who came over on the *Mayflower,* or darn soon after. It was helpful to be D.A.R., the Daughters of the American Revolution, and if you had a patriot general lurking in the background, it was a point in your favor, even if he was a woman-chaser and a boozer. You had to be Protestant, and in Eastfield, being a Congregationalist was preferred. You were Republican, and that was beyond question. Your candidacy was strengthened in accordance with your dislike of the Roosevelts. You could never quite forgive the President for ending Prohibition. You had to be apoplectic about communism. You didn't really have to have money, but you had to live in a colonial home, and not spend money just as if you had it. You didn't have to be married; in fact, it was appropriate to be an old maid, and if you were not, you acted like one during meeting time. Your manners and morals had to be above reproach. I asked how come Aunt Harriet was made a member of the group if she smoked and drank. Penny said that her smoking and drinking put her on the outer fringes, but they couldn't kick anybody out once in. She belonged, and that was that. Besides Lucretia Woodbury was her sister.

You had to measure the mark, and you only knew that you made the grade when Aunt Lucretia invited you to tea. Aunt Lucretia claimed relationship through her husband to the Woodburys of New Hampshire, and the fact that they had once been Democrats and supported Andrew Jackson made little difference now. There were, after all, skeletons in everybody's closet. Aunt Lucretia lived in a white colonial surrounded by elms and oaks on the upper end of Maple Avenue, which was *the* street in Eastfield. Since her husband was president of the Eastfield National Bank, the only bank in Eastfield, Lucretia Woodbury's credentials were miles long. She was the court arbiter, the publisher of the lists, and don't you forget it. Penny said she was not that bright, but it didn't matter, because she knew her position.

Charity Chase said it was sad in a way that their influence was on the wane. Times were changing and people like Stan Wynewski, and Conrad Gilman, a carpenter by trade and French by birth, didn't give two hoots and a holler about all the biddies in the Friday Club, and neither did their wives. Besides, there were more Democrats and Catholics in town than anything else, and most people weren't interested in anything any more, except being baseball fans of either the Boston Braves or the Red Sox.

The women came as they always did. Emily Winters, spindly and meek and full of jitters, arrived first. She came in the town taxi and the ride cost seventy-five cents. She could have ridden with someone else, but it was worth the taxi fare to be there first. Bertha Spaulding and Lottie Trowbridge came together. So did Edith Dean and Beth Sherman. And Alice Rich and Myrtle Strahan. They all came, all of them our more-or-less aunts, and I went to my post in Uncle Lambot's room early, to get out of the kissing business. Holmes Woodbury brought Aunt Lucretia in his green Plymouth.

Penny spotted Holmes, and she bounded out of the house into the rain and sat in the car with Holmes, just as big, horsey Myrtice Bean arrived and duly noted the two together. I watched from the window and wondered if they would stay there all afternoon. But it wasn't long before they headed for the barn. I decided to join them, and I scooted down the back stairs and out the kitchen door. When I got to the barn, they had already taken flight to Olympus. I sulked. And then I slinked alongside a wall until I was underneath them. I listened.

There was talking and laughter. I couldn't tell what they were saying, but Penny obviously was enjoying it all, and my insides curled and contracted. Then they were still. I waited, wondering.

At last they came down, swinging on the rope together. I wished it would snap, or they would slip. But the rope didn't snap, and Holmes, if nothing else, had broad, strong shoulders.

They made the opposite side of the barn clear and easy. They dropped the rope. Then I saw Holmes take Penny in his arms and kiss her. Not just an Aunt Addie peck, either.

"I saw you," I told Penny later, when she joined me in Uncle Lambot's room which was over the parlor, and had a heat register in the floor so we could hear everything below. "I saw you and Holmes in the barn. Puke."

Penny was not displeased. "Well, razzmatazz, Willie," she said. "You saw me."

"It was dumb."

"It was human. I am learning how to live. I don't want to live to Aunt Addie's age without having been kissed, if you know what I mean. To change the subject, let's listen."

I think I knew what she meant, and I wanted to know, did they or didn't they, but I was afraid of the answer I might get, so I grunted, which meant we would listen. Penny whispered, "We shouldn't be here, eavesdropping. But then again, this can be considered educational. We can compare what the women talk about today with what the men talk about the next time they meet in the barn."

"Shhh," I said. Below they were yakking away, on to bad times in no time at all, Hitler, and communism. And Hedy somebody or other.

"Hedy Lamarr. A movie star. She swam nude in a movie, the way we do in the pool."

"Did." I said. "Naked? Really?"

"Guess so, but I read you could hardly see her," Penny said. Then somebody mentioned the Lambeth Waltz, and Penny told me about that, and did a few steps. "Everybody's doing it," she told me. "Except people by the name of Winston. Maybe if I changed my name . . ."

To Woodbury, I thought. Puke. I guessed I was right when she said, "Know what I want, Willie? Someone to love me. I want to love and be loved, sometime before I die. That's all I want."

"Nuts."

"Me. As I am, and as I want to be." She put her hand on my shoulder. I brushed it off and returned to listening. So did Penny.

"How do you know that?" Charity Chase was asking.

"By presuming."

"I presumed most people presumed it had to do with smoking in bed, and too much drink. It was accidental," Charity Chase countered.

"That did it!" Penny whispered. "She mentioned the unmentionable."

"Not so. They talk about Aunt Harriet all the time on the phone. Even Aunt Addie. I heard her."

"That's different. Aunt Charity is not speaking the language of the group," Penny said. "She's on a different wavelength. If I had a golf ball I could change that."

"A golf ball. What's that got to do with it?"

"I'd push it through the register and let it bounce all over the floor. Better still, let's drip some water. Wait till Aunt Myrtice is directly below us and let it ping her pate. Come to think of it, the ball would be better. We could klunk the old bean with it. That would change the subject of the discussion in a hurry."

"Nutty."

"Oh, Willie, you never want to have fun."

We returned to the listening as they were talking about the mill. Again Charity Chase talked against the fold. "I do not think it proper for us to be deciding the disposition of someone else's property. Is not that the process of communism?"

That should have shaken them but it didn't. "Elisha has shares, my dear, and the mill is deep in debt to the bank. The mill is an Eastfield institution whose fate concerns us all," Aunt Lucretia said.

"Especially Addie and her family," Charity Chase said. "To all extents and purposes, the children own the mill, don't they, Addie? That's what Penny told me."

"Oh?" Aunt Lucretia said, taking due note.

"Penny said Lambot doesn't intend selling," Charity Chase countered.

"Indeed. Penny is an unusual girl," Aunt Lucretia said. "Don't you find her so?"

Charity Chase understood, I think, the relationship of the question to hers, but she didn't flinch. "Indeed. In all my years of teaching I have never had a student quite like Penny," she said proudly.

"Oh? Is she a student of yours?"

Charity Chase laughed gustily at that. "More often than not it is the other way around," she said.

That pleased Penny. "If she doesn't get admitted downstairs, I'll form a new club with her. The Wednesday Night Club," she said. "And I would invite Holmes and the Reverend James, Stan Wynewski, and Adam, and all the Nasons. What a marvelous group we'd make!"

"Count me out," I said.

But we didn't continue because the discussion downstairs was getting heated. We sensed that when we heard Aunt Addie excuse herself to go to the kitchen, for refreshment time was a long way off.

Myrtice Bean posed a question. "Do you suppose that when Sam walked up the hill and then back down again that he . . ." but she didn't say it directly. "Well, he did have to pass the Nason farm!"

"I told you," Penny snapped. "I knew they would talk about her."

"Who?"

"Hilda!" Penny was not pleased. I sensed her readying for battle even though she had no adversary.

When no one stopped her, Myrtice Bean took a deep breath and plunged onward. "Where do you suppose he got his liquor during Prohibition? Where everybody else did that drank—from the Nason still, that's where. Of course he went there. And I bet he kept going even after the still dried up. If you know what I mean."

"We are on the subject of Mr. Sam Brown and the Nason girl," Charity Chase snapped, "and it is quite obvious to me that it is not proper that we should be there."

"It may not be proper, but it sure is interesting. I never did trust that moth-eaten old bachelor," Myrtice Bean said. "The fact of the matter is that Hilda *is* pregnant, and it takes two to tango, as they say."

"Don't wonder," Emily Winters said, "when you think of her folks. They never bothered with that girl. Never had control. Just yesterday I saw her walking up the main street dressed like a streetwalker, her face covered with make-up, and wearing a hideous red dress in the heat of the day. Nothing more than a trollop, that's what she is."

Penny said, "That's the dress I gave her."

I looked about and was stunned to discover Penny was not at my side. I couldn't believe that she could have moved downstairs so quickly and so quietly. But she had. Aunt Addie had returned from the kitchen at the precise moment that Penny made her utterance. She gasped and sputtered incoherently in a diversionary maneuver, as she did that morning when she dropped the pie, but to no avail. When Aunt Addie subsided, there was stillness, and Penny explained.

"Hilda doesn't have much, and so I gave the dress to her. I asked her what she wanted more than anything else in the world, and she said, a red dress. So I bought her one at Sadie's. When I gave it to her, she said she couldn't remember the last nice thing anyone in this world had ever done for her. She said she would remember all her life. She cried. So she's wearing a red dress. So what's wrong with that?"

This was no little girl act. Penny didn't say much but she whacked hard. The ladies were embarrassed, not only because of what Penny said, but because there was some defiance of authority somewhere, Aunt Addie's, and you could almost sense a locking of doors, lest Penny puff a bit harder and blow the house down.

Someone said, "It's not the dress but what she uses it for." Charity Chase took exception to that and said to Penny, "Bless your heart!" It occurred to me that Penny must have told her about the dress; certainly she did not appear to have been caught off guard as had the others. I thought she said the right thing, but possibly at the wrong time. The buzz that followed crescendoed until it was incomprehensible, and it was not difficult to discern lack of rapport with Charity Chase's thinking. Suffice it to say she wrote herself out of the club that afternoon. It was all handled with finesse. The women didn't get around to voting. Penny told me later that her Aunt Charity was not at all shaken out about that.

When the party ended, Uncle Lambot, who had been hiding out at Seely Jones's farm down the road, appeared as if by magic, driving his big Packard into the yard. And routine took over as if nothing had happened that day, my sister excepted.

Penny did not act according to expectations. She cleared and cleaned the dining room. She helped wash the party dishes without prodding. She told Aunt Addie how delicious the desserts were, that she was full and couldn't possibly eat another thing all summer, and if she were a bear, she would have eaten enough for next winter's hibernation. But Aunt Addie said the beans and brown bread were already in the oven, and so we had supper as usual. Nobody said anything, except once Aunt Addie told me I wasn't eating and added, "I declare I don't know what's happening to your appetite this summer." Tensions kept us all on edge.

Later, when the locomotive had given its toot at nine, I sneaked down to Penny's room. She was writing in her diary. She told me that Aunt Addie had come into the room, caught her reading, and didn't say "It's time for bed" or anything like that. She said it was a nice thing for Penny to give a dress to Hilda, but that it would be best not to go there. And when Penny asked, "Why?" Aunt Addie dared to tell her that Hilda was pregnant. Then, before Penny could respond, Aunt Addie backed out of the room. Penny was writing in her diary, she said, because she simply had to put that conversation, word for word, into the record.

Impulsively, she read, for the first time ever, an excerpt from her diary to me. She had written that she hoped she would never grow old in a small town, that old women in small towns never grow, except older, after a certain point, and if they didn't grow, life stood still, and if it stood still, so did living. She wrote that the world was out of whack, even in Eastfield. You couldn't always see it, but the world was changing, and everybody felt it even if they didn't know it, and it made them feel lonely, frustrated, and unwanted. Penny had her smarts about some matters, there was no doubt about that.

She closed her diary. "So that's what I don't want to be, lonely and unwanted. I want to be wanted, wanted. Not needed, just plain I want someone to want me."

"Holmes," I said. "I don't like him. He's a snot."

"I do," Penny said.

"He kissed you, that's why. Puke," I said. "He can get you into trouble."

"He kissed me once, he missed me twice, and he kissed me once again," Penny sang.

"You're just a kid," I said, sounding like an older brother. "You've got no business doing . . ."

"I've never been a kid, Willie," Penny interrupted. "And neither have you. Only when we forget."

"Or when you don't want to be," I said. Which was getting to be less and less, but I didn't add that.

Penny studied my mood. "Willie?"

"What?" I grumbled.

"I'm not lonely when you're around. You have to understand that. I'm never lonely when you're around, but there has to be someone else. Even for you some day," Penny said.

I looked out the window and listened to the rain on the roof. When it didn't rain quite so much, it was nice. With all the rain that summer, it was sounding dreary. After a while, I got up to go to my room.

"Angry?" Penny asked.

"Night," I replied.

"Willie?"

I paused.

"Know something? Guess what's for dinner next Saturday night? And the next and the next? Served at quarter to six exactly. I wonder how many beans I'll eat in the next five years. I think I'll count how many I eat next Saturday, and then multiply that by all the Saturdays in the next five years."

I started to leave again.

"Willie? Aunt Addie."

"What about her?"

"She's a riddle. I can't figure her out. She's, she's . . . I don't know. Know what I noticed? All those women like her. They really like Aunt Addie. I think I should be that way too, but she doesn't give me a chance."

"Leave her alone."

"She acts like she's afraid of me, no matter what I say. I don't know what to make of her. And Uncle Lambot, he's getting as skittish as his sister. I know he's got problems, lots of them. And responsibilities. All the same, I can't figure out what's going on."

"Nothing's going on, except you pick on them. Leave them alone."

"I'm mean, aren't I? Penny replied. "Know what I was thinking?"

"Who cares?" But I tarried.

Her answer was slow in coming. I could tell she wasn't thinking about anything, and so she had to find something in a hurry. Suddenly a smile grew on her face. She looked like a happy gnome. "I was thinking how can horses manage to keep eating nothing but hay year after year every day of their lives!"

With that, there was nothing I could do but grab a pillow off her bed and whack her with it. Just to let her know I was still her favorite brother.

CHAPTER EIGHTEEN

WE FIGURED IT WOULD RAIN NEXT SATURDAY BECAUSE IT WAS A rainy Saturday summer. I didn't figure that Penny would pull another trick. It rained, and Penny pulled a trick. A beauty.

Penny and I guessed that the rain would bring the boys to Uncle

Lambot's clubhouse, and it did. We guessed they would come because they were absent last Saturday, and because quite by accident,
we came across Uncle Lambot pushing a broom in his bailiwick.

That was the evening I discovered Hilda Nason and Holmes
Woodbury giving the old green Plymouth a moment to remember
whether it wanted one or not. Penny got a Friday permission to
spend the evening with Charity Chase to toil with the literary muses.
Lonely, I walked across the fields and through the woods, wandering
aimlessly about Aunt Harriet's place.

I was returning home and was almost to the apple tree when I
saw the green Plymouth careen into Aunt Harriet's drive and stop
in front of the stone steps. It was still light and so I could see that it
was Hilda with Holmes. They stayed there for almost a half hour,
and so did I. I sat down, hidden by a clump of bushes, and waited.
I don't remember anything else except waiting.

I decided that Holmes couldn't start another baby in Hilda because there was already one on the way. I even thought there
couldn't be another baby because of Holmes. My opinion of him was
not high. In any case I thought that Hilda and Holmes weren't true
blue, loyal friends, and I didn't like that.

When they left, I left. That night Penny didn't sleep at Charity
Chase's. When she returned home and poked her head into my
room, I feigned sleep. I didn't want to hurt her by telling her about
her friends.

But the next day, Penny wormed my discovery from me. She knew
something was wrong because of the way I squirmed at breakfast,
and afterward she bugged me until I told her.

At first, Penny took it calmly, and she shared a bit of her private
world with me. She told me one of the reasons she liked visiting
with Charity Chase was because Holmes came there to see her, that
Aunt Charity, like Aunt Harriet, was not a snooper, and she didn't
fret about Penny's bedtime, and a lot of other things. Penny said
she came home early last night because Holmes didn't show, and

quite frankly, Aunt Charity was not all that interesting when Holmes was not there.

Then she whacked the palm of her hand real hard on the hood of Uncle Lambot's Packard, shouted that Holmes was a snotty, crazy, son-of-a-bitch, the hell with Harvard, Adam was smarter than he was, and more interesting. With that, she hied herself off to Olympus, despite her promise not to go there any more.

Penny showed for lunch. She was unusually preoccupied with whatever she was thinking and hardly said a thing. I suspected she was all to pieces because of Holmes, that she had a case on this, and sensing she wanted to be alone, after lunch, I went down to the cellar and put a steering wheel on a gig I was making.

In short order I got tired of that and went searching for Penny, but I couldn't find her. I didn't think too much about it because I assumed she would not want to miss Uncle Lambot's meeting.

There were a couple of outside windows in Uncle Lambot's clubroom, and there was also an inside window through which, except for the dust, you could look out into the hay in the barn. In the hay just outside the window was our listening post. The light in the barn being the way it was, you could look in without being seen, and the hay nicely absorbed sound. That day I went there alone and I hoped something special would happen before Penny got there and I could punish her by not telling her.

Ranse Sherman came first, in his lumber and hardware truck. He never came without an excuse. This time it was paint. Uncle Lambot had ordered paint for the veranda floor that Aunt Addie had been nagging him for, so that Ranse would have to bring it. I liked Ranse Sherman. Big-shouldered and ramrod straight, wearing a burly, bulldog face, he gave the impression of being indestructible—safe, solid, protective. He was also a kind man, and he made people feel at ease.

Stan Wynewski came next in an old Dodge truck. I heard him say he was just passing by, saw Ranse's truck, and thought he would stop to see what the old bastard was up to. I guessed that was the way he would tell his wife, if he had to tell her anything. Conrad Gilman happened to be riding with Stan, and he could say he was there because Stan was. Conrad Gilman was a French carpenter and builder from the east part of Eastfield, which was mostly French. He spoke English with a French accent, and of course he spoke French. Penny said that most of the people on the other side of the river could speak two languages, and that was quite an accomplishment as most had not gone beyond the eighth grade, including Conrad Gilman. She told me that Holmes Woodbury had studied German and French at Harvard, but could speak no more than a dozen words in either language, and then one could not always tell which was which.

Seely Jones comes next. He had the farm down the road, and it was so situated that he could see our yard from his. He always waited until he saw activity before he came flying up in his flivver. Seely Jones traded in cattle. To look at him, you wouldn't think he owned a Connecticut yankee wooden nickel. He hated barbers and razor blades, and seedy overalls were his favorite suit, for parties or any other time. Seely Jones also wore the odor of the cow barn wherever he went. Sometimes he had over five hundred head of cattle for trading, and Elisha Woodbury said he never borrowed a cent from the bank for business. And they all said—never tiring of their own corn—that what Seely Jones had was not all hay.

Elisha Woodbury came, too, without any excuse. He merely said he was damn glad to get out from under foot, and he hoped it would rain every Saturday as long as he lived. He always dressed in clean clothes, a suit, shirt, and necktie, and I thought, when I was young, that he was out of place in the club. As I got older I guessed it was only his clothes. Out of place or not, he came, I thought maybe for some other reason than to merely chew the fat. Penny said the kind of security he offered was different than Uncle Lambot's or Ranse Sherman's, yet you could put the three men together, and you could cuss all you wanted about them, but they were indeed pillars of the community. As long as they were about, the world was safe from cheats, liars, and bandits, whether they were of the two-bit variety spawned in the boredom of Eastfield or those born in the turmoil of the city.

Last summer, Penny had learned from Aunt Harriet how Mr. Woodbury had come a long way in Eastfield, which actually wasn't very far unless you considered Eastfield the center of the world. Mr. Woodbury had been a clerk in Ned Petersen's general store back in the twenties, and from that humble beginning he had become the richest man in town. He was proud of the fact that he saved two-thirds of every dollar he ever earned, even when he was earning but a few a week. Penny said it was helpful to marry a woman with money, too. Elisha Woodbury had had an off-and-on-again relationship with Lucretia Stone, whose family owned most of Eastfield's only bank. The relationship lasted for years, and when everybody was convinced that neither Lucretia or her family would ever say yes, it happened, and on the day that President Roosevelt was inaugurated, Lucretia and Elisha, middle-aged now, were married. On the day after, President Roosevelt declared a bank holiday, and Elisha Woodbury decided that was as good a time as any to buy all the bank stock he could, even much owned by the Stone family, thus insuring a prosperous and everlasting life for himself in Eastfield.

Last there was Adam. He ambled in more or less unnoticed, carrying his briefcase, as if he were a lawyer entering a courtroom, yet entering like some stray cur. He sat down on an inverted wooden nail keg next to Stan Wynewski, who sat in a sway-back wicker chair with its seat almost touching the floor. Uncle Lambot took a bottle of liquor from a wooden cabinet hanging on the wall, kept locked and thus away from the all-seeing eyes of Aunt Addie on her once-a-month dirt-chasing sprees. Uncle Lambot put some glasses on the table and invited his pals to help themselves, and Elisha Woodbury said it was better than spending that afternoon with Lucretia, and they all agreed to that. Stan Wynewski had his own bottle, and I noted when he took a swig from it, he would put it down on the floor by the side of his chair. Adam spotted it, and whenever he thought anyone was not paying any notice, he would maneuver the bottle to his lips and take a good hard swig for himself. I couldn't wait to tell Penny about that. Then I thought the hell with her. She still hadn't appeared.

I had a sneaky feeling that she had skipped off somewhere with Holmes Woodbury. I didn't like the idea, but there wasn't much that I could do about it.

The men's talk, except for the cussing, wasn't much different than the women's meeting, but it seemed as if it were. Somehow it was more haphazard, more casual, and yet at times more direct and to the point. The men joshed and yet there was an undertone of seriousness and concern. They talked about the weather and all the rain and the soggy ground, and they talked about the Boston baseball teams and the New York Yankees. Even Uncle Lambot talked, not much, except it seemed like an awful lot for him, and he swore some, too. Penny once said it was too bad he didn't drink in the house and thus loosen his tongue. She said life would be far more interesting if he did, and maybe it would have been.

Mostly the men talked of money, who made it and who lost it, and how. I learned a lot. I learned that nobody ever made any money any more but everybody there was always losing it. People not there were the ones who had barrels of it. Sometimes, as today, when they tired of talking about money, they talked sex. After money, came sex. Not much different from what the women talked about when you got right down to it.

They turned to Uncle Lambot then and badgered him about the mill, their favorite subject. Uncle Lambot was evasive, and he started swinging his economic pendulum again, but Stan Wynewski stopped it. Elisha Woodbury said Uncle Lambot ought to sell the mill. Stan Wynewski said that was only because the mill owes the bank a hell of a lot of money. Elisha Woodbury retorted that was a damn good reason for selling, Uncle Lambot had to sell and that was that. That's when I began to listen hard.

Uncle Lambot said, "Ain't got no right to sell it. Doesn't belong to me. Belongs to the kids, Penny and William, lock, stock, and barrel. Don't feel right about selling if they don't want to."

"You better feel right about it," Elisha said, "or you'll not only lose the mill, but the farm as well."

"Penny wants to keep it," Uncle Lambot insisted, and the men understood that Uncle Lambot was really expressing his own personal desire.

"Reminds me. Almost forgot," Elisha Woodbury said. "I saw Penny catch the one-thirty train for New York. You ain't sending that kid to the big city to dicker about the mill, are you, Lambot? Not that she couldn't. Two to one she'd get double the price offered."

I was stunned when I heard that, but it didn't appear to bother Uncle Lambot. "Probably just going to Westfield. Probably hatched something up with Addie. The womenfolk don't always let me in on their plans, and I figure the less I know the better." And that ended further discussion about Penny's whereabouts.

My mind buzzed. Penny was most certainly not going to Westfield, not with Aunt Addie's blessing on a rainy or any other day. She was headed for New York. I knew that immediately, and I knew that just as well as I knew that Aunt Addie was not going to believe my complete ignorance about Penny's taking French leave.

I was hurt, deeply hurt, because I was not included in her plans, jealous because Penny would have an experience that I could only share vicariously, if at all, and angry because she showed no appreciation about leaving me alone, without explanation, to settle with Uncle Lambot and Aunt Addie. When she returned, if ever, I thought, I would whammy her. If Aunt Addie could do it, so could I.

Meanwhile, inside, the men had been sidetracked, as had been the Friday Club, and they were talking about Hilda. They wondered who knocked her up. They said it could have been anybody, even Uncle Lambot. They laughed at that. I didn't.

Then they got going on Sam Brown.

"Let's not kid ourselves," Stan Wynewski said. "We all knew what he'd been up to at Harriet's. Been doing it for years. Can't tell me they did nothing but play tiddly-winks all that time."

"Know damn well they didn't," Conrad Gilman said. "Remember the time five or six years ago, I did some fixin' in her kitchen. Supposed to get there in the morning, but didn't make it till afternoon and I guessed she figured I wasn't coming. Rang the bell, but it was busted, so I walked in. And I caught Sam Brown naked to the skin. He knew he was caught and he didn't say a damn thing. Neither did I. I figured a man worked like he did was entitled to his pleasure. I never told anybody, and he knew I didn't and wouldn't. He liked me a lot for that."

"He didn't work that hard," Ranse Sherman said. "Not that day, anyway."

"Be damned!" Seely Jones said. "Didn't think he had it in him. Come to think of it I never thought about it at all. All I ever thought was they were like two old maids. Or like a brother and sister, Lambot. Lucky smart people. No wife or no husband to make life miserable." The men knew that was personal. Mrs. Jones was forever sickly. She didn't like living on a farm. She was no farmer's helper.

"They're no different than anybody else when it comes to wanting it or not wanting it. Those silent dogs, like Sam, get as much as any of us. And variation, too, because they ain't married. And they got no need to feel guilty like you, Stan, because they ain't cheating on anybody. Smart, when you think about it," Conrad Gilman said.

"How about that, Lambot?" Stan Wynewski said, laughing at the dig. "They tell me you used to be Harriet's sweetheart in the old days. You ever get into her pants?"

"The question is whether he ever got into her pants *since* the good old days. Wasn't far back through the woods to her place," Conrad Gilman said. "I hear tell you beat a path to her door right up to the day she died. Talk about the silent types."

"How come you never married her, Lambot?" Stan asked.

"Too cheap," Conrad Gilman said.

"Too smart," Ranse Sherman said.

"Just like on the mill," Seely Jones said. "Then again, maybe it was Addie that was the smart one. She derailed that match, and that's a fact. Ask my wife. She sits and mopes all day long, but she knows everything about everybody."

Elisha Woodbury spoke finally. "If Lambot hadn't been so all-fired stubborn, and married Hattie, he would have saved us all a peck of trouble. Including Hattie. Sam was the cheapest, tightest man that ever walked the face of the earth."

"And if Lambot married Hattie, he'd be related to you, and the two of you would own Eastfield, and you'd be the tightest, cheapest *men* that ever walked the face of Eastfield, and that's a fact," Stan Wynewski said.

It was all good-natured joshing, but Elisha Woodbury didn't like it. You could tell by the way he twitched in his seat. I didn't know what to think about what I was hearing. If Penny were there, she'd have plenty to say later. But she wasn't.

Once they stopped their talking and looked toward where I was. I thought they must surely hear my breathing, and I thought to run, but I stayed, and they went back to their yakking.

"Lambot had it all to himself until Sam came along," Stan Wynewski said. "And Elisha had Pearl Nason before she married Lem, or was it after?"

Elisha Woodbury stood abruptly. He said he had some work at the bank, and he left. He was gone before you could blink your eyes.

Seely Jones said, "Elisha's high up in the world and he can't stand his past. He and Pearl Nason used to work together in Ned Petersen's store way back when, and he is real sensitive if you get too close to his good old days."

"Forgot all about him and Pearl," Conrad Gilman said. "That was hot stuff then."

"Wonder what it would be like if Elisha had married Pearl instead of Lucretia," Seely Jones said with a sneer.

"Different," Uncle Lambot said.

"Ever know why Lem Nason hasn't talked to Pearl for so long?" Seely Jones asked.

"Just happened," Uncle Lambot said. "Lem was a loner from the day he was born."

"Like you, Lambot," Conrad Gilman said. "If that's the way he wants to live, what the hell. But you can't tell me he doesn't sneak into the house for his rights. I bet it's all a gag. He wants it from time to time same as your bulls, Seely."

Uncle Lambot poured some more whiskey into his cup and peddled his old routine again. He said there was enough money in Eastfield to start the mill wheels turning again. If only the people in Washington wouldn't tinker so damn much with the gears of the economy and scare money into hiding. Uncle Lambot got to swinging the pendulum far right, and all the shouting of Stan Wynewski and Conrad Gilman couldn't budge it.

Suddenly Adam burped. He was sitting quite by himself, left out of these important matters of discussion. I noted Stan Wynewski's bottle was almost empty now, and I couldn't tell who had drunk the most, Stan or Adam. Adam burped again, and they all stopped swinging the pendulum. Seely Jones said, "Guess you get left out of this money talk, Adam. One thing you don't worry about is money. You ain't got any, and you don't worry about other people having more than you ain't got."

"Adam's Mr. Lucky. You ain't got money, you ain't got no responsibilities, and if you ain't got responsibilities, you ain't got worries," Stan Wynewski said. "I got six drivers and I kill myself working to get work for them. Six drivers got six families and they got to live, and right now they think I'm God, so I got to worry even when I'm not worrying. When's the last time you worked, Adam? Steady, I mean, on a forty-hour hitch."

Conrad Gilman tapped Adam's satchel with his toe. "Bet he's got money," he said. "Bet his bag is full of it. You ever been on relief? If you have, I've been supporting you and didn't know it."

This got to Adam. "Don't believe in it," he said. His voice was wobbly; otherwise his short answer reminded me of Uncle Lambot talking.

"I'll be damned!" Stan Wynewski said, saying it for all of them. "A Republican yet."

"I live different," Adam said. With that he reached for his brief-case. Just as it occurred to me that it might be full of money after all, he pulled out a loaf of bread. "See this?" Adam said. "It's day-old bread, and it cost me eight cents less than a fresh loaf, but it's bread, and it's good, you don't mind it being a bit crisp." He reached again into his bag and retrieved a tired piece of Swiss cheese. "See this? It will make twelve sandwiches with the bread. Maybe cost me twenty cents a day to eat. In the summer less, because I have a garden. Man don't need much, only fools know that. I keep healthy. You don't need much to keep healthy. I'm as healthy as you be. Ain't had a cold since I can remember. Ain't never been to see a doctor. I got enough, and I got time to enjoy. I got no depression. Lots of people got depression because they got too much. Ever think of that?"

Adam was real smug about it all, sounding as if he had won a Nobel prize in economics. It wasn't often that anybody listened to him—except Penny—and he began to feel his oats and kept on talking.

"Don't reckon this country would grow much if there was too many like me not working and buying things," Adam continued. "But it might be food for a spell. Might be real good."

"Amen to that!" Seely Jones said. "Adam, I have to have you talk to my wife. Don't mind her spending. But she buys more damn pieces of nothing that only get in the way."

Adam paid no attention to Seely Jones. "I do some work," he said to Stan Wynewski. "Last month I did some painting for Miss Chase."

"I know. She bought a whole gallon of paint," Ranse Sherman said. "Takes a lot of time to paint a whole gallon. How much did she pay you for all that?"

Stan reached for his bottle and discovered it empty. "I'll be damned!" he said, and he poured himself some whiskey from Uncle Lambot's bottle, all the while signaling to the others to let them know where most of his own liquor went. They began to realize then that Adam was coming around a curve on a fast bender and decided to have some fun with him.

"Did you ever work there for nothing, Adam?" Conrad Gilman asked.

"Sometimes she cooked me a meal. Depended on what I did," Adam said. "She paid me."

"There's some hidden wealth we forgot about," Ranse Sherman observed. "She owns property in West Hartford, and one of these days her land is going to be more valuable than if it had oil under it. Don't know where her money comes from, but she's got it. Born to it, I expect."

Conrad Gilman was more interested in Adam. "Anything else besides money, Adam?" he wanted to know. "You ever get laid? You ever get poon-tang? Man's got to have it, even you."

Adam giggled. He wasn't used to that kind of attention, but he liked it. "Woman's got to have it, too," he proclaimed.

"Hear that!" Seely Jones said. "What do you think of your hired man, Lambot?"

Uncle Lambot grunted. The grunt said anything you wanted it to say.

"I bet you know a lot about what happens in these parts, Adam," Conrad Gilman said.

Seely Jones laughed. "Nothing much. Most nights it's deader than the inside of church the Monday after Easter."

"Maybe so, maybe not. There's the Nasons just down the road from Harriet's, and Adam's hideaway is nearby in a bramble patch.

I got a suspicion you know a lot of what's going on," Conrad Gilman said.

Adam snickered. "A few things."

"You ever go up to the Nason house? I know you do because I seen you there," Conrad Gilman said. "You ever get laid there, Adam? By Pearl, or Hilda, or both of them? Somebody's doing it. How much do you pay? I heard tell you and Pearl were sweethearts way back when before Lem knocked her up."

It was difficult to tell if Adam heard it all. He was weaving on his nail keg, a silly grin on his face and spittle drooling from the corner of his lips. "I play chess with Lem in the barn, and sometimes I sleep there," he said.

"You get that girl pregnant?" Conrad Gilman persisted. "Did you, Adam?"

"I ain't never did that to anybody," Adam said.

"Who did?"

"I thought about that. I reckon you did, too, or you wouldn't ask," Adam said.

"How about that!" Seely Jones exclaimed. "Adam, did you ever see action up there those nights you stayed in the barn with Lem?"

"You mean at Hattie's or the Nasons'?" Stan Wynewski asked. "Elisha's been up to both places a time or two this summer."

"Hattie was his sister-in-law," Ranse Sherman said.

"Yeah. Well, he had something going up there somewhere. He sure left in a hurry. I wonder how come?" Stan asked.

"You know Elisha," Ranse Sherman said.

"Reckon I did," Adam said. He was responding to Seely Jones' questions about seeing action at Aunt Harriet's while he was staying at the Nasons', and it took the men a few seconds to remember. "Who?" Uncle Lambot wanted to know.

Adam sobered a bit. He stopped grinning. "Don't remember," he said, his usual drawl slower than ever. "Don't remember." Clearly he was confused.

"You don't remember?" Stan Wynewski asked. "You don't remember who? It wasn't you that you don't remember, was it?"

"I didn't do nothing to Hilda. You ask Lem. He knows. He knows everybody what goes there," Adam said.

"Baloney," Stan Wynewski said, but he changed the subject in one fast hurry. "Adam, where were you the night of the fire?"

"The fire?" Adam asked, as if his brain was smothered in smoke.

"*The* fire, Adam. The fire."

"I went to the fire. Come to think of it, I don't remember seeing Adam," Conrad Gilman said.

"A lot of people were there," Ranse Sherman said. "Most of Eastfied."

"But how about Adam? He'd know if he was there or not, wouldn't he? Were you, Adam?"

"Can't remember."

"You can't remember what!" Stan Wynewski shouted. "You live a quarter of a mile away, and you can't remember. I don't believe it."

"You didn't stop at the Nason place and then go live it up at Harriet's? For old time's sake?" Conrad Gilman wanted to know.

"Did you know what Lem Nason did that night, Adam? He didn't go see Hattie, did he?" Ranse Sherman asked.

"I never thought about Lem," Conrad Gilman said. "He's not right in the head. He coulda gone and done it."

"I don't remember," Adam said.

"If he did, I guess he'd remember," Uncle Lambot said.

"Remember some things, though. I don't remember what I did, but I remember some things I saw you might not want me to remember," Adam said. He arose from the nail keg then and started uncertainly for the door. I noted he didn't pick up his satchel, which always went with him. I could only think that Adam was drunk, and was headed for a whiff of fresh air before the drink flopped him.

"Gotta take a leak," he mumbled. I wasn't surprised at that and I thought I had a lot of talking to do with Penny, if and when I ever got over the stinky trick she played on me.

Sometimes when they had to go, the men went behind the barn. On rainy days, inside the barn was the rule, so I was not at all sure that Adam knew what he was doing when he headed for the outside door. I figured he needed some fresh air in a hurry, the same as I had when I got sick from eating radishes and strawberries and waffles. The clubhouse door to the outside was at the corner. The wood of the door was warped and it hung in a slant on its hinges. The dog-day humidity made it more difficult to open than usual. Adam kicked the door, and when it didn't open, he heaved his shoulder against it. Suddenly it gave. Adam lost his footing, tripped, and fell in the mud outside.

It was over almost in an instant. The rain had mixed with the cow dung that had long ago matted the dirt, and now it was a slippery slop. When Adam stumbled and slipped, he toppled onto the stone watering trough just outside the door. He yelped, loud enough to be heard inside. The men rushed out, and I scrambled out of the hay to see what happened.

Adam lay in the mud, a deep, bloody gash in his head. Fifteen minutes later he was dead.

CHAPTER NINETEEN

P ENNY RETURNED THE FOLLOWING TUESDAY. WE DIDN'T ALERT THE police, the F.B.I., or anybody. We decided to wait it out. The shock and the confusion on Saturday afternoon were such that Uncle Lambot didn't tell Aunt Addie until just before supper when Aunt Addie was yelling all over the place for Penny. Aunt Addie cried. Uncle Lambot said, "There, there, Addie," but he wasn't much comfort. I told Aunt Addie not to worry one whit because Penny was used to going off by herself. I told her about the time Penny skipped off to San Francisco when she was thirteen and had a ball. If she got in trouble, I said, then we'd hear about it! I sounded a bit like Penny.

Uncle Lambot agreed, and he even provided cover. "Anyone wants to know where she is, she's visiting down state with friends," he said.

Aunt Addie fretted and whimpered. She stayed away from the phone, and we all stayed away from church Sunday. She fumed and sputtered all day Monday and said if Penny didn't come by Tuesday that she was going to call the police. "I'll wait until after Adam's funeral," she said, "and that's all."

Uncle Lambot was responsible for Adam's final rest, as he had been for Sam Brown's, and he arranged well. Half the town was there, and that was quite an accomplishment for a nobody who came out of nowhere without even one relative that we knew of. Aunt Addie said it was out of respect for Uncle Lambot and let it go at that. She stayed home, and Uncle Lambot and I drove to the cemetery. We watched the burial, the other side of a hill from Aunt Harriet, and a stone's toss from Sam Brown. In a way I was relieved that Penny wasn't there. She'd be talking about life after death and wondering if the three were having a rendezvous up or down yonder.

The train for New York came daily at three-fifty, and after the burial, we headed for the station to continue our vigil at trackside.

My first prayer was for Penny to be on the train, and the second, that it be on time. Being alone with Uncle Lambot had a peculiar pain of its own, because he didn't talk. When somebody else was about I didn't mind his not talking. When I .was alone, it was painful. Penny said Uncle Lambot knew what he was doing by not talking because a lot of people thought him smart when they couldn't discover that about which he was ignorant. One thing, he didn't say a lot of foolish things that people who talk a lot do, and another thing, when he did talk, slowly and haltingly, people listened.

Today he talked a mouthful. "They found some money of Adam's," he said. I recognized immediately that there must be something special about the money. I waited patiently.

"In his briefcase, there was a wad of bills. Almost five hundred dollars."

"Whew!"

"When I got his suit for burial, I found more. All told, two thousand dollars," Uncle Lambot said. "Adam made a will. Made it a month ago, with a Norwich lawyer. Must have taken the bus. Left everything to Penny. William, do you reckon Penny knew anything about that?"

"Can't tell what Penny knew," I said. "All I know is she said Adam would live forever, that he was as important as anybody else, that Adam's shack was his monument, which was more than most people on this earth ever had or would have, that his real monument was the way he lived, which was better than the way most people lived, and a lot of other crazy things."

Uncle Lambot capped my monologue with a grunt, and he was relieved when he heard the train whistle. We both looked down the track to watch the cow catcher of the engine emerge, like the prow of a small ship, from the hills at the edge of the horizon.

"Pretty sight, William," Uncle Lambot commented. "When I was a boy, they used to come to Eastfield on the hour. Now they only come twice a day. Times change."

"Uh-huh," I said.

"Penny's got to spend everything in two months. Adam put that in his will."

"If she's on the train, I'll tell her," I said. I knew that was what Uncle Lambot wanted me to do. That is why he told me.

Luck was with us. Penny was on the train. She didn't have a speck of baggage, nothing except a couple of books she carried under her arm. She was wearing the simple navy-blue dress that she was wearing last Saturday.

Uncle Lambot pouted his lips, but said nothing, not even "Hello." All I said was "Hi," and we climbed into the back seat of the Packard. Our coolness did not bother Penny at all, and she treated us to a lengthy monologue, talking as if she had gone nowhere.

"I sat with a most interesting man coming home. You know what he's doing? He's riding all the way to Katahdin Mountain in Maine, because that's the point where the sun first hits the United States each morning, and he wants to be the first American one day in his life to do something before anyone else can, and seeing the sun rise is as good as anything. He came all the way from Little Rock. He's an authority on snakes. Started learning about them when he was yay-high, and he hasn't stopped learning. He's almost sixty. He told me an awful lot. He told me that boa constrictors, snakes charmed by Indian fakirs playing their flutes, are deaf. No ears. The snakes are not dancing to the music, but are dodging possible blows by the snake charmer. Do you know why snakes have to swallow whole? They have no teeth for chewing. They have fangs for other purposes. I asked him why he studied snakes, and he asked me why did man want to climb the highest mountain. I told him all about Eastfield, and he said it must take a heap of imagination to live in Eastfield, unless you were satisfied with merely existing. He thought that most people were satisfied, whereas he believed we would all be better off being dissatisfied. He asked if there was any culture in Eastfield. I told him we had books, and if we put them all together, there was probably enough for a lifetime of good reading, which he thought was a good answer.

"On the way to New York, I sat with a woman, maybe thirty-five, and no matter what I said to her, she didn't utter a word. I followed her off the train at Grand Central, and she ran into the arms of a man and talked and talked and talked. What do you think of that?"

Uncle Lambot, and even I, realized the cascade of words was to forestall questions and condemnation, and we were not impressed, but we said nothing, so Penny continued her soliloquy. "I read the Bible on the train. A Gideon Bible somebody left on the seat. I took it to the hotel and left it in the room, and now someone will wonder why there are two Bibles there. I wonder why other books are not put into hotel rooms. I suppose you want to know what I did. Because of the rain, I spent most of the time in the library. I told the man on the train that. He was a Negro. What do you think of that?"

Uncle Lambot grunted. So did I.

"I told him I thought it odd that I should go to New York to read books, when there are books in our parlor that have never been opened. Know what he said? Perhaps it would take less imagination than he had supposed to enjoy living in Eastfield, even though nothing ever happened. Except life beginning and ending, and all that goes on everywhere. He said that if man could ever find out what life was all about, there would be peace in the world. He said that man couldn't do that in a hurry though, because it took millions of years to create the physical world, and it might take at least that long to create the world of spirit in the physical world. So there would be more wars, and there was going to be one soon. Anyone who could see beyond his nose could see that. He said every once in a while, man catches up with his sins and tries to destroy himself, and that was about to happen. That's why he wanted to see the sun rise before anyone else did. Uncle Lambot, do you think there is going to be another war soon?"

I answered for Uncle Lambot. "Yes," I said, but I wasn't thinking of the war she was thinking of. Uncle Lambot said nothing then, but as we drove into the yard and stopped, he looked at Penny through the rear-view mirror. His brows knotted and his lips pouted, and there was a strained, cutting moment of silence. Then Uncle Lambot said, "Before supper you apologize to your Aunt Addie. If you don't I shall thrash you." He said each word as if he were measuring it with a ruler, and I was proud of him. Penny might be his favorite, but even she could go only so far.

Penny got the message. Yet she waited until the last possible moment before telling Aunt Addie, putting to the test as best she could the force behind Uncle Lambot's brazen pronouncement. Penny set the kitchen table just as she always did, haphazardly, forgetting something, this time the spoons. Aunt Addie had a ham in the oven, and Penny whiffed the aroma and marveled. She told Aunt Addie that the first roasted pig must have smelled like rotting leather compared to the aroma coming from Aunt Addie's oven. She said she read a story about the first pig and did Aunt Addie know it? Aunt Addie didn't. Penny wondered how combining clove, brown sugar, and pineapple on ham ever happened at all. Then she said, "I wonder if city imagination or country imagination discovered such a delectable treat. One thing I know, no one in the city could cook ham better than you cook it, Aunt Addie. Is baking a ham a difficult task?"

"Nothing is too hard if you put your mind to it," Aunt Addie puffed.

"You have to be cut out for it," Penny said. "A cook, I mean, or anything. I would be the worst singer or painter, and I don't think I could ever be a good cook."

"You can say that again," I said.

"Could if you tried, could if you tried," Aunt Addie said, fighting furiously to control all kinds of emotions.

"I'm not that much interested in food. I had enough money with me, some I brought from Des Moines, but all I had to eat in New York was a hamburger and some pea soup, three times at the Automat. And some spaghetti. Even then I hardly knew what I was eating because of all the people. I thought I might never see so many again, so I watched them. I had the spaghetti in an Italian restaurant where I went to escape a thundershower. The sign said the place was famous for Italian food, but the spaghetti was not nearly as good as you cooked last week, and you don't even think of spaghetti as being one of your specials. I am sorry, Aunt Addie. I am sorry about going away and not telling you. I had to get it out of my system. You can ask Willie. If I told you, I wouldn't have gone. So I couldn't tell you, could I? I was about to bust if I didn't go."

The apology came finally. I didn't think she would make it.

"It wasn't a nice thing to do. I've not slept a wink for three days. Like to have gone out of my mind with worry."

"I said I was sorry."

"Punishment doesn't work," Aunt Addie said. "I declare I don't know what to do with you. And, by the way, you left your room in its usual jumble. I wish to high heaven that you would work that out of your system!"

"You don't understand."

"What don't I understand?"

"I had to get by myself and think. So much has happened this summer. I had to go where there were lots of people. There was no way you could have stopped me. I was moving to go and I couldn't even stop myself, and I would guess you had relief to have me out from under."

"You're too young to go traipsing off by yourself. It's dangerous. Lord knows what could happen to you. It's not decent," Aunt Addie replied sharply.

"I can take care of myself," Penny said.

"Much too young to go off by yourself," Aunt Addie repeated. She didn't dare say more, and so she reverted to old Aunt Addie. "Look at those potatoes. Water's most boiled out of them. Means rain tomorrow, and the Lord knows we've had enough this summer. Penny, you mash the potatoes. Plenty of milk, but not too much butter. No matter how much butter I put in anything, your Uncle Lambot always adds more. Why men like so much butter . . ."

She didn't finish and Penny sighed. She wanted to tell Aunt Addie everything, but routine had returned. Eating dinner was the same that evening as any other. Neither Uncle Lambot nor Aunt Addie brought up the subject of Adam. Neither did I. Not once did Penny ask what happened at home, and I was still mad as hell at her. So I guess were our aunt and uncle. It was a sticky time, with poker faces out in force.

After dinner, Aunt Addie said, "It's been a long day. You must be tired. It's time both of you went to bed."

But we didn't go. Penny asked if we could go for a walk first, and Aunt Addie relented almost eagerly. "Go now," she said. "I'll do the dishes. If you wait much longer it will be dark. Days are already getting shorter." So she got out of facing Penny and finding out things she didn't want to find out.

We walked about the house first to seek what the weekend rains had done to the flowers. Zinnias and marigolds were leafing extravagantly, but the flowers were few. The asters wore a blight. "Summer's just arrived and already it looks as though it's on its way out," Penny said. "Before you know, we'll be saying the same thing next year. And every year until we die."

"Why did you go?" I asked abruptly.

"Well, let's see," Penny said, dawdling. "I saw a play Saturday night on Broadway. *Tobacco Road*. On stage was a Georgia cabin, exactly as you might see it in Georgia, but it wasn't much different from Adam's place, except for his decorations. And Jeeter Lester and his woman, they were just like the Nasons. You don't have to go to Georgia to find Tobacco Road. You can find it anywhere. Right here in Eastfield, and even in Des Moines, come to think of it. Not much difference between Jeeter Lester and Father, except Father had money in his pocket and a car for the open road."

I didn't know who Jeeter Lester was from a hole in the ground, and I didn't care to know. She didn't fool me with all the talking. "You coulda told me. You know damn well they'd ask me, and I either had to lie or cover for you, and no matter what I said, they'd think I was lying."

"What did you do? Did you lie for me, Willie? Really?"

"I didn't do a damn thing," I admitted. "Uncle Lambot did some fibbing, and we kept away from people. But it was rotten. Don't you ever bother to think of anybody else except your own stupid self?"

"Willie." Penny was hurt.

"Just once in a while think of somebody else."

"Sorry."

"Sorry in a pig's neck. What a dumb, stupid thing to do."

We found ourselves walking across the fields toward the swimming pool. All my repressed anger was emerging. Penny sensed it and entwined her arm in mine, saying nothing for a while. Then she said, "Know something?"

"What?" I grunted, sounding a bit like Uncle Lambot.

"I heard something beautiful in New York."

"So?"

"I went walking Sunday morning. You can walk forever in New York and still be in New York. I walked block after block on wonderful streets lined with scrumptiously dirty buildings where people live. A girl was sitting in a window, singing. I stopped to listen, and so did everybody else. You couldn't hear a sound other than her singing. When an elevated train passed, you couldn't even hear it. She wasn't older than I am, Willie, but she was creating a miracle. That's what I want to do. I wanted to go to New York, and I had to go the way I went or I wouldn't have got there. You know that."

"A dumb reason," I groused. "Why did you really go?"

"Just to go. Didn't I tell you I would?"

"Baloney." I guessed maybe that was so, but I didn't know what else to say.

Penny sighed. "All right, I'll tell you. To undo a miracle. Promise not to tell."

So there was a reason after all. "What?" I hardly dared ask.

"I don't know if you can understand."

"I can believe that. What?"

Penny took her time answering. Finally she said, "I went for

Hilda's sake. And you have to bear with me, Willie, because I may go again, one more time."

"Crap. You do and I'll tell, so help me I'll tell."

"Hilda's having a baby. Everybody in this town knows it by now, and that spells nothing but trouble for her for the rest of her life. I found a way to help her."

"Like what?" I asked suspiciously.

"Sam Brown was going to help Hilda, Willie. She told me. Now he can't. I want to help."

"Did he do it?" I asked.

"I don't know, Willie. Hilda's locked her jaw on that. Maybe it's another immaculate conception."

"What's that?" I asked, and Penny explained, and when she had finished, I asked what all that had to do with New York.

"O.K., I'll tell you. Hilda is alive and what's done is done. A living being is adding legs and arms already within her, and already it is being branded with miserable words of shame up and down its spine. You don't need a ouija board, Willie, or much savvy to figure out its future, or Hilda's."

"They are going to have a future, and that's a fact," I said.

"Shhhh, Willie. Quiet."

Without realizing it, we had come to our swimming pool. The sun had dipped behind the trees and there wasn't a breath of wind. This was a good time to spot turtles and frogs.

We moved forward by inches. We knew how to do this well. Nothing splashed. On the rock jutting out from the pool were two turtles, still savoring the lingering warmth of the day. They would slip into the water when it got cool, but not yet, if we didn't move.

Penny elbowed my side. "Over there," she whispered. It wasn't much, but the turtles got the message, and flipped out of sight. There was no more need to whisper.

"Where?" I asked.

"Over there," Penny said, pointing to the water's edge about ten feet from us. There I saw a black water snake, maybe a yard long, sucking in a bullfrog, headfirst, the frog's legs being kept to the last as if they were a specialty of the house.

"I'm talking about snakes today, and now we see one doing what the man described." We walked closer. The snake went on alert.

"The man said snakes have disconnected jaws," Penny whispered. "I bet that one could stretch his mouth all the way over a baseball if it wanted to. Let's catch it."

I was not a snake fancier. "Let's hit it with a rock," I said.

"No, let's catch it, and then we can see what is left of the frog."

"Puke!" I said, but I helped her. We found a half-dead branch from a bush, snuck up on the snake, and then I pinned the snake to the earth with a sudden sweep of the branch. The snake wriggled like a startled shimmy dancer, but the twig held it firm.

"Hold it hard," Penny advised. She bent down, and when the snake stopped moving for a second, she grabbed its neck.

"Now we shall see what we shall see," Penny said. She grabbed the frog's feet that still had not been swallowed, and patiently and evenly pulled the frog out of the mouth of the snake. Penny put it down and tickled it. It blinked a couple of times and then leaped into the water as if nothing had happened to it.

"The man said that maybe a frog could live a day and a half in the stomach of a snake and still come out kicking. He said some snakes swallow snakes because snakes are the best size and shape for snakes to swallow. And some snakes are big enough to catch and swallow humans. How would you like to be slowly sucked into the jaws of a snake, Willie?"

"Never happen," I said.

"You think so. That's what's happening to Hilda. She's being sucked into the jaws of a snake, and I'm going to try and pull her out. Let the snake go, Willie."

"Let's squash its head," I said.

"It's harmless, let it go. Maybe that snake will eat many harmful insects before it dies," Penny said. "It is a symbol of evil, not the real thing." She thought about that and added, "I like that. It could fit Hilda."

I let the snake go and it wriggled its way into the tall grass. "The man said he timed snakes to see how fast they would go," Penny said. "The fastest one he ever had traveled only eight miles an hour."

"They look as though they go faster than that," I said. "Want to go for a swim?"

"We haven't our suits. Aunt Addie wouldn't like it," Penny said, and laughed because she had said that, not me. She sat on a rock, and I sat beside her. "Know something?"

"I know a lot," I said, thinking of Adam, but I had no hankering to tell her. After all, she didn't tell me about going to New York. "Hilda. What about her?"

"You really want to know? Then I'll tell you. To pull the snake out of Hilda is why I went to New York, and thus Hilda out of the snake. How's that for a riddle?"

"Dumb," I mumbled.

"Know what an abortion is?" Penny asked.

I did. "You told me what it was when Mother was going to have another baby, and didn't," I told her.

"So I went to New York to find a doctor. I gave a bellhop ten dollars, told him I was pregnant, and that I would give him ten more if he would help me."

"Baloney." I said. But I didn't put it past her.

"Did, and I found a doctor who would," Penny said.

"Didn't."

"Did."

I had all kinds of reactions, not the least of which was fright. "Remember what you said about Mother not keeping a baby once it got growing?"

"My memory was never as good as yours, Willie, no," Penny said, dismissing the matter. "I had a very interesting session with a Doctor Smith, which I didn't believe was his name. I told him all about an older sister named Hilda and about her problems. I gave him a hundred reasons why he would be doing civilization a favor. He was impressed. We talked about lots of things. He treated me to some beer. Wasn't bad, but not particularly good, either. Then he told me he wouldn't."

"Wouldn't what?" I asked.

"Help me with Hilda. He indicated he thought I might be Hilda, Willie, and I said no, but I wished maybe I was. I suggested that he ought to reconsider because I had learned a lot about him and I might have a tale to tell."

"You didn't."

"I did. Surprised even myself with my boldness. I indicated that I had had a bit of training dealing with elders," Penny said. "He began to think differently of me, that maybe I am not as naive as I sometimes look."

"Don't believe it, and all the rest of the junk you told me."

"I wouldn't lie to you, Willie," Penny said, taken aback.

"Oh no? You already told me you went to New York for no reason at all," I said. "I believed that, but now you are telling me junk."

"Junk then," Penny said, pouting.

"And just in case you don't remember what you said about Mother, I'll refresh your memory. You said maybe Mother might be doing in a future president. Of a bank or a country. Or an artist, maybe. You said that should not happen. You said the house needed a baby to give us something to love."

"I said that," Penny admitted.

"Then why?"

"I told you why. Hilda will be murdered if she has a baby. Maybe crucified is a better word. I am going to go through with this, going to New York with Hilda. And when it's over, just for you, I'll be so nice to Aunt Addie you will shout to me to stop. I'll give her so much attention that she'll beg me to go to New York and live there happily ever after. That would be scrumptious."

"Don't believe you. You go and it's not fair."

"Life is never fair."

"I have to live here, too."

"I'll make amends. I'll atone my sins, and I shall love you forever after. I am going to do this, and you will have to help, Willie. Maybe if Hilda and I take the early milk train to New York, we can return on the afternoon train the same day, and nobody will be the wiser."

"That's what you think."

"Come on, Willie, don't worry so much," Penny said. "Wouldn't you like to be around to see what happens when the baby Hilda is supposed to have several months from now doesn't arrive? That should certainly make for an interesting chapter in these parts."

I began to believe. "Are you fibbing? About finding a doctor? Did you fib about the girl singing and all that crap?"

"I saw that girl, Willie. She sang beautifully. I asked a man what she was singing, and he said she was singing magic. He asked me what I was doing, and would I like to go to his flat and listen to some opera records. I asked was that all? And he gave me a funny look. He was English. Maybe it's all imagination. A lie. About the doctor, even. You wouldn't know it, but I'm getting tired of life already. What's a lie? I don't know."

"That's another lie. About the man."

"I guess not. He had a beard and an English accent."

"Did you go?"

"He carried a cane."

"Did you?"

"He had a dog. A Scotty."

"Oh, crap."

"Doesn't matter if I went. All I know is you weren't there," Penny said, not caring to answer.

"And you weren't here, and I don't want to go through that again. Especially if you go with Hilda and it is discovered."

"Sorry, Willie, but we are going."

"What if you're caught? What if something happens to Hilda?"

"Nothing worse than what is happening now."

"Jesus!" I uttered, and felt a sudden, cold chill. Last year we were kids, bumping each other and sliding all over the place. Swimming together in the nude. Now all that was gone, and we were disposing of an unborn baby. There wasn't a speck of childhood left in either of us. We had jumped from that into something else and neither of us knew what that was, not even Penny. "Let's go home," I said.

"It's early. Let's go see Adam," Penny said. "We've got time."

All mixed up in my mind because of Hilda, I had forgotten Adam. I gave her a funny look and I am sure she noted it, but I couldn't bring myself to tell her. "Aunt Addie said be home before sundown. Let's be on time for once," I pleaded. I started toward home, but Penny grabbed my arm.

"It'll only take ten minutes. Then we can race back and make up for lost time. We haven't raced all summer, Willie. I'm growing faster than you. I bet I can beat you this year. Come on. Maybe we'll catch Adam tossing his cats."

There was nothing to do then but blurt it all out. I thought I would choke, but I managed. "Adam's dead. He got drunk and fell against the water trough outside the barn. He cracked his head. He died quick. They buried him this afternoon before we picked you up at the station. And you had to be smart and sneak off to New York. No wonder Aunt Addie and Uncle Lambot are . . ." I couldn't finish. I commenced to cry. "Let's go home."

"Adam dead?" Penny could not believe it. "He was supposed to live forever!"

"Let's go home."

"Home? Where's home?" Penny asked vaguely. After that, we walked together, without saying a word, yet feeling that we were one, through the field of grass, to Aunt Addie's and Uncle Lambot's.

CHAPTER TWENTY

A UNT ADDIE WAS A SIX O'CLOCK RISER DURING THE WINTER, AND a five-thirtier during the summer. Uncle Lambot always phased out of sleep and bed a half hour earlier. It made no difference what they had done the night before, what the crisis that might have enmeshed brains and body in a trap of sheer exhaustion. Clock time was ritual at the commencement of any day, and disturbance of it made Aunt Addie fret and fume all morning. Penny said it was foolishness bordering on stupidity, for life needed variety. It was fun getting up early, and it was also fun sleeping late. But Penny also admitted that people like Uncle Lambot and Aunt Addie were the heartbeat of the world, and that they ticked their lives to the absolute rhythm of the earth's motion. She admitted, too, that there were times when she was envious of those gifted with the art of creating routine and living with it.

The next morning, Uncle Lambot was up at five, and Aunt Addie tiptoed down the back stairs at her appointed hour. I awoke earlier than my calling time of seven. I had slept in and out of the night until I finally remained awake. When I got up I discovered Penny's door open. She was not in her bedroom or the bathroom, and I had that odd feeling that she had vacated the premises some time ago, perhaps to take the milk train to New York. I shivered at the thought and the horror that would grip the house when Aunt Addie discovered Penny missing again.

"Did you wake Penny?" Aunt Addie greeted me.

Uncle Lambot was at the breakfast table. He cocked his eye at me, hardly moving a muscle. I knew what he wanted to know.

"I didn't tell her everything yet," I said, evading Aunt Addie's question. "I told her about Adam's dying and the funeral, but I didn't tell her about the will. She didn't give me a chance."

Aunt Addie took all that to mean I did not call Penny, and she went to the head of the stairs to do it herself. She sounded as she did any old day, monotonous and mechanical, and I thought that if Penny had thumbed her nose at Aunt Addie the night before and called her an old bitch, Aunt Addie would have called Penny the same way.

We were having pancakes that morning, and Aunt Addie called again in a moment, as she ladled batter onto the iron skillet. Getting no response, she told me to waken Penny.

I started up the stairs for a dry run, when Penny burst into the kitchen from outside. She was sweaty and panting, and her hands and face were smudged, but I was so relieved to see her that for a split second I thought her beautiful. Before anybody could question her about anything, she cried, "What happened to Adam's cats?" We knew then, without asking, where she had been.

"What are you talking about?" I asked. I supposed they had scattered, and she ought to have guessed that.

"Adam's cats. They are gone. Every blessed one of them. Did you give them to somebody, or did someone steal them? Maybe they were buried with Adam," Penny said suspiciously.

"Penny!" Aunt Addie registered her first shock of the day on her seismograph.

"I took 'em," Uncle Lambot confessed. We waited for an explanation. Uncle Lambot was in no hurry, and he created a fearful, suspenseful moment. Finally he said, "I put 'em into a sack and dropped 'em into the river." That was all he said, and he lathered his pancakes again with butter. To Uncle Lambot, his action was a kindness to the animals, but not a matter of great importance. I no longer felt like eating, and idly I wondered if some cats would end up at the North Pole and some at the South Pole.

"Sheba, too?" Penny asked. "She was pregnant."

"Penny!" The needle wavered, and poor Aunt Addie registered another shock. Aunt Addie, I am certain, was remembering that it was less than two weeks ago that Penny had asked about the origin of babies as if she had never heard about pregnancies, even in cats.

"Maybe I should have brought them all over here for you to take care of," Uncle Lambot mumbled.

"She couldn't be bothered," I said. Aunt Addie nodded.

"You killed cats not even born," Penny said.

Uncle Lambot grumbled and let it go at that.

"I certainly couldn't take care of them. Lord knows I have enough to do as it is picking up after you," Aunt Addie said. "Cats drop hair with every step."

"They could live in the barn," Penny said.

"Somebody would have to feed them. Every day. Last weekend they would have died if they had had to depend on you," Aunt Addie shot back.

That quieted Penny for a moment or two. Points had been scored against her and she was smart enough to know it. She shifted her sails temporarily to the windward. She poured syrup over her pancake and dabbed it with butter. She ate it and asked for more. She reminisced fondly about the cats. "We named them after all the dictators, remember, Willie? Hitler, Mussolini, Stalin, Ivan the Terrible, and just think, Uncle Lambot, you rid the world of them all at once!"

"Penny, not so much syrup!" Aunt Addie did not want to think about dictators, dead or otherwise.

"Sheba is gone, and with her, unborn babies," Penny continued. "Maybe another tyrant. Maybe a new breed of cat would have been among her offspring. Someday I am going to write a book about Adam and his cats. As a matter of fact I think I'll commence today."

I was flustered, as was Aunt Addie, and it's a wonder I didn't blurt out that it was like an abortion, killing Sheba with her babies, and Sheba dying as well, and maybe Penny would get the point. I retreated, however, and tried to reduce the charge in the atmosphere. "Adam left you all of his money," I stammered.

"Me!" Penny stated. It sounded more like a statement of fact than a question.

"You," I said.

Penny smiled. "Enough to buy Hilda another dress? Enough for another trip to New York?" she asked sarcastically. "Adam left me his money. How nice."

"Two thousand dollars," I said. "Uncle Lambot says it's legal. You have to spend it as soon as you get it. That's what Adam wrote in his will."

Penny took it calmly. "He said he would do it, and I told him I would be proud to be named in his will, but I doubted that I would outlive him, because he was living a life that had no beginning and would have no end. One day I found him counting money, and I said, 'Adam, why do you keep it? Why don't you spend it?' He said, 'What for?' and asked did I want it. I told him no, and he said I should have it someday to travel with it to Paris. I asked, 'Why Paris?' and he said he heard it was special and I was special. I was touched, and I said, 'Adam, would you really like me to have that money?' He said, 'Yes,' and so I kissed him, and I bet half of my inheritance that he had not been kissed since he was a baby. Maybe not even then. Know what he did? He cried, and rubbed his cheek where I kissed him. I kissed him again, and I hugged him, and gave him my love. At least enough to let him know he was a human being. Remember what Granny Winston said about love, Willie?"

Granny Winston had said a lot of things about love. At the moment I could remember none of them. I only remembered what Penny said about having babies, even with Adam, and I felt like vomiting. I looked at Aunt Addie. She looked as if she could do the same.

"She said love is the difference between what you do for yourself and what you do for others. She said that was the chart, the map, upon which you measure all humanity. Remember?"

I didn't remember, but I don't think Granny Winston had had Adam in mind if she had ever said that.

"Ozymandias?" Penny asked as if she were talking to him. "How long will Adam last without a monument?"

"You haven't eaten a thing," Aunt Addie said.

"You told me his shack was his monument," I offered.

"Something better," Penny said.

"Even monuments turn to dust. Like in the poem," I said.

Penny ignored that. "Yes, I will do something special with Adam's money. Something for others. For the love he gave me, and do you know what I think it will be, Aunt Addie?"

"It will go in the bank for your education," Aunt Addie said.

"It has to be spent now," Penny said. "What kind of a monument for Adam? Anyone care to guess?"

No one dared, but we were curious.

"The church. Last Sunday in church, know what I noticed? Dirt and grime on the walls. Yes, I did, and I thought what fun to paint the church and spruce it up. You look at the church and it makes you feel good it's so pretty, but it hasn't been painted in years. So I shall give the money to the church to have it painted. In remembrance of Adam. And I'll put a sign up that says, 'Painted by Adam.' What do you think of that?"

Nobody said a thing. Uncle Lambot grunted, and one guess was as good as another as to what that meant. Aunt Addie wheezed a bit, and otherwise held her breath. Penny was bumping up and down all over the place and we wondered why.

"And the Reverend James and I can have a long conference or two or three about the work. What do you think of that?"

Nobody thought anything about that.

"How much time have you and Uncle Lambot spent at the church?" Penny asked. "How much time of your life? Did you ever think of that?"

That we were all experiencing an emotion-laden scene there could be no doubt. Still, it was difficult to believe, later, that we could not have heard the commotion outside at first.

The whistle of sirens, the town firetruck racing across the field below Adam's shack, the cars and trucks and people that followed, we didn't notice. Nor did we hear the cracking of the dry wood of Adam's shack as it succumbed to flames. Not until a switch of wind brought a balloon of black smoke swirling toward the house. I saw it first and pointed. Aunt Addie rushed to the window. Uncle Lambot moved to the door, faster than I had ever seen him move. Penny remained in her seat. I suspected then, in an instant, where Penny had been that morning and what she might have been doing.

I darted out the door. Aunt Addie shouted for me to come back, but a fire didn't come to Eastfield every day, and I ignored the call. I ran across the field, and for the first time in my muddled mind I began to wonder about Penny's sanity. She would do as she pleased. Nobody could stop her, in any way.

Adam's creation all but disappeared in twenty minutes. It seemed like half the town got to the fire, and there was a lot of talk. Somebody said there was a firebug about, possibly the same one that had set fire to Aunt Harriet's house. I panicked when I heard that until I remembered we had not been in Eastfield when Aunt Harriet's house burned. Somebody even suggested that Adam, whom most people considered mental, had set fire to Aunt Harriet's place, and God, or somebody, took vengeance on him by burning his place. Someone else said it might have been set by someone who didn't know Adam was dead but wanted him dead. Another bet the secret of Aunt Harriet's fire disappeared when Adam died. Stan Wynewski was there and he said he drove by early that morning and thought he saw Penny in the hayfield headed for Adam's place. I lied through my teeth, and said that she overslept that morning because she was sick last night because she had skipped off to New York, got poisoned with some food, that she wasn't even dressed yet, and that's why she wasn't here now, and you could just bet

Penny would be there if she wasn't sick and weak and had cramps and stuff. I don't think Stan Wynewski believed me, but he let it go at that. On the way back home that morning, I vomited.

I couldn't find Penny. At first I didn't care, but after a while I went searching for her because I couldn't stand not knowing. She was at Olympus. I shouted until she surrendered. She swung down on the rope, Uncle Lambot not having yet removed it.

"The pendulum swings back and forth. If only they'd let the damn thing alone!" Penny sang out as she sallied forth. She acted as if nothing had happened in a year or two, as if she had not a care in the world.

"I sneaked a book out of the Nason barn. Did you know Mr. Nason has stacks of books?" she asked when she reached ground level. She showed me a tattered copy of *An American Tragedy*. "This was one of the famous fifty-two that I read for Miss Sprague back in Des Moines. I made a book report on it, and she told me I was too young to read it. Perhaps she was right. I can see now I didn't know much about life when I read it. I wish I had kept that book report to see what I did write when I was young and ever so innocent. Do you know what the American tragedy was, Willie? And is?"

"Puke. You don't fool me one bit. Don't pull any more of that crap stuff on me," I warned.

"All right, so I went to New York. So now you want me to serve a sentence for breaking an unwritten law. Give it to me, and let's be done with it, Willie," Penny said.

"What did Aunt Addie say?" I wanted to know.

"About what?"

"About what? About the junk you spouted this morning! About the fire, dummy! All that sputtering with Adam's shack burning. As if you didn't know."

"Oh, that," Penny replied, as if that were nothing at all. "Don't worry about the old folks, Father William. Aunt Addie didn't say a thing, because she's a smart old codger, I told you that, and she knew she couldn't say anything. If she had asked me, and I told her yes about the fire, she would have been duty-bound to report me to the authorities, or wrestle forever after with a guilty conscience. On the other hand, if I said no, and she believed I was lying, she would be in agony, not only for my sin, but for hers for failing to develop me properly. The first lesson in life is to think what others may be thinking, it says here. The second is to keep them from thinking what you may be thinking." She paused, then added, "I just thought that out for the first time. Intriguing, isn't it?"

"Smart ass. You know all the answers. You got everything all thought out. Big deal."

"Big deal. That's what life is, Willie, a deal. Up for grabs. A bargain. A puzzle. Fit the pieces together and move forward. Or stay forever as you are. Willie, Willie, strong and able, take your damned elbows off the table. How hard do you bargain to be yourself, Willie?"

"You're a devil," I lashed out. "A real devil."

"I'm sure Aunt Addie would agree, for I am certain she sees horns growing out of my head."

"Did you?"

"Did I what?"

"Set the fire in Adam's shack?"

"Willie, dear Willie."

"Damn it, did you?"

Penny sighed. "This morning, I lugged my diary over to Adam's, all of it. I was going to possess Adam's shack and use it for reading and writing. It was to be my new Olympus. I was going to write a novel about Adam there. But then, with no decision at all, I put the diary into the stove and set it on fire. I went to the john in the bushes, and then came home. What do you think of that, Willie? I left the house this morning carrying sixteen years of my life with me. Now it is gone."

"You're screwy."

"All gone. Razzmatazz!"

"Penny!" I exclaimed. "You make me sick. Really, really sick."

"Willie, dear Willie," she said tenderly. She put her arms around me. I wanted them to be there, but I pulled away. She teased. "How about a piggy-back, Willie? You haven't tested your strength this year. Your shoulders look stronger than ever."

"Damn it, tell it to me straight. Just once in your life."

"You don't believe me."

"You can say that again."

"Does it matter? Will you feel better if you know, or will it be better not to know and to therefore presume nothing? Soon it will be noon, and we'll be eating whether or not we are hungry. Same as ever. You don't say anything, and I won't. If you don't know, there is nothing you can say, is there, Willie? And Aunt Addie can tell you once more to stop slurping your soup, and eat the crusts on your sandwiches because that's where all the goodness is. Whatever."

"Why did you do it?"

Penny fluttered her hands. A sign of partial surrender. "I don't know, Willie. I honest to God don't know. I awoke this morning, and I had to get out and go for a walk, that's all. I told you why I took my diary. Maybe I burned it because it was nasty and mean and bitchy. That's mostly what I wrote about, all that was bad. Except maybe about Aunt Harriet and our dear old Granny. They were shining stars, and already they are getting dim. Know what I mean? Adam told me things about Aunt Harriet, and I guess some people thought she was no great shakes. And then we heard those things about Sam Brown when old man Woodbury was trying to get Uncle Lambot to sell the mill."

I knew what she was saying, but I didn't want to hear. "Then you did it," I said.

"What?" Penny said.

"Set Adam's shack on fire, dummy," I said, exasperated completely.

Penny sighed and tossed her hands into the air. "I don't know even that. I don't know what I did this morning. I burned the damn diary, yes. Deliberately. Life was phoney, and I want to start over. What else I meant to burn, if anything, I don't know. Maybe nothing. It could have been the result of carelessness, but I was thinking of other things and I don't know. This morning, if you want honesty, I felt like smashing things. Could be. Willie, if I set fire to Adam's shack, I did not know that I did it. Even if my hand held the match, I cannot be certain. So I did not tell Aunt Addie I did or I did not. Do you understand that? If I don't tell, nothing will happen, nothing, you wait and see. If I do tell, think about what will happen then, Willie. Think about that."

"Damn it, Penny!"

"Damn it, what?"

"I'm too damn young to keep thinking all the time!" I blurted out.

Penny thought that was funny, and she laughed. I thought she was laughing at me.

"Go to hell," I told her.

She laughed some more. "I've already been there and back. Not once but a dozen times this summer already. Let's piggyback, Willie."

"Go to hell," I repeated.

"Go to heaven," Penny said. She liked that. "Go to heaven, Willie, go to heaven. Why don't people say that instead of go to hell all the time?"

"Puke," I said, but I guess I wasn't all that angry with her, because before I knew it, she had jumped on my back and I started running with her. I think I would have run forever if Aunt Addie had not spotted us.

"Penny!" Aunt Addie shouted.

"Always me, never you," Penny said. "That's the way with our world."

Maybe so, I was beginning to think. Maybe so.

CHAPTER TWENTY-ONE

BY NOONTIME, ROUTINE HAD ONCE AGAIN TAKEN CONTROL. EVEN Penny succumbed to it and permitted her conscience to humble her into a holding pattern. As if nothing at all had happened in the past days and weeks, she inveigled Aunt Addie to get her started on some knitting, and they made a pleasant, homely scene on the veranda.

Uncle Lambot came along to read the *Eastfield Observer*. After a while, Penny interrupted her needlework and massaged his forehead, rubbed some more, and kissed him again. Penny winked at me to let me know she was up to something. I crossed my fingers and searched for birds in the bushes.

Penny said, "Uncle Lambot, you're getting bald." That was bosh. Uncle Lambot had as much hair on his head as he had had when he was twenty-one. Aunt Addie said he was secretly proud of every thread of it, too proud for a Christian gentleman. "Your hair is grayer than last year, too," Penny said. That may have been true, but it was hard to tell. Uncle Lambot's hair had been salt-and-peppery as long as memory. If Uncle Lambot had suspected anything, he gave no sign that he did. As long as Penny kept on rubbing, the pleasure was all his.

Now Penny went into action. "Uncle Lambot, did you ever read *An American Tragedy*?" she asked. She knew as well as he that he had not. Besides his newspapers, and sometimes *Collier's* and the *Saturday Evening Post*, about the only reading material that attracted Uncle Lambot's attention was the church bulletin on Sunday and seed catalogs in the winter.

"Penny, let your uncle be. He's had a hard day," Aunt Addie ordered.

"I'll tell you, then, Willie, and no one else. Nobody else need listen," Penny said, massaging shoulders now, and being otherwise snotty. "It's about this girl who gets into trouble. Like Hilda. And the man responsible for her trouble lets her die when he could have saved her by not doing what he did. But he did what he did because the rest of the world gave him trouble instead of trying to help both of them."

"Penny, that is enough! What are you thinking of, talking about those matters in front of William? The very idea!" Aunt Addie snorted. I wanted to say it didn't matter, I knew everything anyway, and maybe more than she knew because of my teacher, Penny, but I didn't have to do so, because Penny defied Aunt Addie and forged onward. "So you want to know why it's called a tragedy, Willie?" Penny asked.

"Who cares?"

"The way I see it, maybe the tragedy was not that the mother had been done away with, that the father of her unborn child did the dirty deed. Maybe it was what caused him to do it."

"All right, Penny, all right! I said stop this conversation and I mean it." Aunt Addie looked to Uncle Lambot for help, but it was not forthcoming. Not yet. "What is it you want, child? You don't fool me one bit with all this chatter. What now?"

Aunt Addie should not have called her "child." Penny looked at her coldly. "Information, please."

"You seem to know all there is to know," Aunt Addie snapped.

"Willie, remember how we used to think if we couldn't find out something here, we could always find out from Aunt Harriet? Well, I discovered from Adam there were some things that Aunt Harriet never told us, some things she didn't want to tell, and that's why I think she made up stories. A clever cover-up," and before anyone could react to this, Penny asked, "Why didn't anyone ever tell us that Adam used to live at Aunt Harriet's?"

Aunt Addie shot a furtive glance at Uncle Lambot. He shot one back. "What difference does it make?" he asked.

"It was long ago, it never entered our minds," Aunt Addie said. "Penny, do you want to learn knitting or don't you? Adam's gone, and may he rest in peace."

Penny kept on rubbing Uncle Lambot's head. "Why didn't anyone ever tell us that Adam was Aunt Harriet's cousin?" she asked politely. "Nobody but nobody ever mentioned that, and I can't for the life of me understand why not. What's so bad about knowing that?"

Life on the veranda came to a halt for a brief moment with that pronouncement. Then Aunt Addie gasped, as if it were her last. Uncle Lambot shifted in his chair. He didn't even grunt. But he responded first. "What difference does it make?" he said again.

"Goodness, child, it was long ago," Aunt Addie managed to say.

"Please do not call me child. And it was not long ago."

"If Aunt Harriet wanted you to know, I guess she would have told you," Aunt Addie said. "Maybe she wanted it that way. Some things it's best not to know." She was not really upset now. You could tell she was trying to cope.

Penny's anger, however, was getting decontrolled. "Not, not, not, no, no, no, that's all we get. Damn it, why not?"

"Penny!" Aunt Addie shot back. A red flag warning.

"No need of that," grumbled Uncle Lambot. Another warning.

"Was it because Adam was kept in an institution all the time he was growing up down South and then there was not enough money for that, and he was shipped north where nobody would know? Was it because if he was Aunt Harriet's cousin, he would also have to be Aunt Lucretia's cousin, and, of course, that just would not do? How come no one ever talks about Aunt Harriet's family? Adam said Aunt Lucretia didn't talk to Aunt Harriet any more than you talked to our mother. What's so bad about Adam being the way he was?"

"What's past is past," Uncle Lambot claimed. "The less talk the better."

Aunt Addie agreed. "This is not the time," she said. She did not bother to explain why.

"I know, the time is never," Penny said scornfully. "It was not the time for Adam to die, either, because he was learning—he had a memory. Adam needed patience. He'd mention things, but he never seemed to be able to follow through. But he mentioned things. Why is it that Aunt Harriet never told us she'd been married?"

Aunt Addie was aghast. She and Uncle Lambot shot glances at each other again. "Never was married," Aunt Addie affirmed. "Adam didn't always tell it straight."

"She wasn't?" Penny asked.

"That's what I said."

"Then maybe some of the other things he said . . ."

"Aunt Harriet didn't always tell it straight, either," I reminded Penny.

"Could she have been married? Was she ever in love?" Penny asked. I think she was mindful of what we heard Elisha Woodbury say about her and Uncle Lambot.

"Penny, are you going to learn how to knit or not? I didn't ask you to do it. You were the one who asked to learn," Aunt Addie reminded her. She put her own knitting on the table, as if preparing to leave. "I have other things to do than sit and gab all afternoon."

"Sure, Aunt Addie. I don't have any more to say. I have to do a bit of thinking. Holmes is coming over this afternoon. He wants me to go swimming with him at the park in Westfield. I was thinking maybe he wants to rent a rowboat and take me out into the middle of the lake, just like in the book. Wouldn't that be neat?"

I thought Aunt Addie would swoon at that. She hadn't read the book, either, but she had had a lot of experience in putting two and two together. "You put my brain in a tizzy. I don't know what to say to you any more. If that's what you want to do, then do it." She began to sniffle, and I thought she might cry outright.

I wanted none of that. "I think I'll go mow the lawn," I said. "Now that Adam's gone, I suppose I'll have to do it."

"You're not old enough for that," Aunt Addie said, not meaning it at all, but it stopped the sniffles.

"I'm taller and stronger than Adam," I said and moved to leave. So did Aunt Addie, heading for the kitchen.

"Don't you want to know? Don't you want to help me?" Penny asked.

"I do the best I can for you. What is it now?" Addie said.

"I want to help Hilda," Penny blurted out, "and I'm going to do it one way or another. She is a human being. If we don't help her now, she won't be human much longer. Is that too much to ask? Jesus helped everybody, even those others wouldn't. Like Hilda. If he were here . . ."

Aunt Addie gave up and departed for the kitchen, shaking her head and hands. Penny stopped working on Uncle Lambot's head. "This place is hell!" She said it loud and clear. "You don't have to die to go to hell around here!"

"Penny!" It was not Aunt Addie, but Uncle Lambot. He turned in his chair and squared off at Penny. "You've said enough! Go help your aunt!" And when Penny didn't budge, Uncle Lambot said, "Did you hear me?"

His voice was loud and tough. Penny heard all right, but she was not ready for surrender. "You mean you don't want me to help another human being? Just as Jesus would have done?"

"You heard me. Go help your aunt. That's help enough."

The humor of the remark was lost on everybody. The drama wasn't. It crackled the air, and split Penny's cool right down the middle. She had tried to be nice; she had tried to explain. She got nowhere, except, Go help Aunt Addie, then get back into the old harness. Even from Uncle Lambot. Uncle Lambot, finally, was joining forces with Aunt Addie. She had suspected it for some time, but she hadn't really figured on it. She always figured that she was Uncle Lambot's favorite, which she was, and that she could keep it that way, by rubbing his head a bit, sweet-talking him on occasion, and doing as she pleased as far as he was concerned. Now she sensed she was losing, and you could almost see the hopelessness of the situation squeeze her face into the melancholy of surrender.

But that did not mean she was about to give up the good fight. Not yet. Instead of marching to the kitchen to aid Aunt Addie with her chores, she turned and marched off the porch. "Damn it! Damn it to hell!" she shouted. She pushed the screen door open with her foot, stumbled on the steps, and went sprawling into the grass. If she was hurt, she did not let it be known. She screwed up her face and thumbed her nose in the general direction of the house and shouted, "Kiss my razz!" The look on her face told you that she could have said a lot more and a lot worse, and nobody could do anything about it. Nobody. What I thought was going to be our own special password for the summer had gone completely sour.

CHAPTER TWENTY-TWO

THEY LEFT HER ALONE THEN, BECAUSE THEY DIDN'T KNOW WHAT else to do, I suppose. Penny picked herself up, went behind the barn, sat in the empty hen coop, and sulked. Aunt Addie went upstairs and I could hear her puttering and muttering. Uncle Lambot sneaked out to his Packard and drove off without a yes or no. I stood it as long as I could, then went to Penny. Another time she might have played the pixie and would have laughed everything away. Now she hardly noticed my coming. She was biting her nails and her face was drawn and sullen. Something was bothering her more than usual. That did not stop me, however, from venting my feelings.

"That was the dumbest. You could have picked something else to talk about besides that book. What did you say all that for? And talking about Hilda, you know they don't like that."

"And they didn't like my finding out about Adam being a cousin and living with Harriet, either. Can't see why not. Adam told me he liked living as he did. He was doing it all by himself, and he wasn't a burden to anybody. And don't tell me you weren't interested and didn't want to know. You should have seen your face. Your mouth opened so wide I could have pitched a baseball into it, and my aim is not that good."

"Yeah, well," I stammered, "you could do it differently, then. You scare them, if you want to know. You oughta hear how Aunt Addie talks about you on the phone when you're sneaking off somewhere."

"What, Willie, what?" Penny was interested.

"She says she doesn't know what's going to become of you. Says it all the time. She's afraid somebody'll take advantage of you, and she won't know how to cope with it."

"Like somebody took advantage of Hilda! Suppose they discover me to be pregnant, like Hilda, what then?"

"I wouldn't try to find out," I warned.

Penny smiled at me curiously. "Know what else I've been reading? Our conversation reminded me of it."

"No, and I don't care."

"*Measure for Measure*. Shakespeare. In Eastfield a prison is being made for Hilda because she got herself pregnant. In this story, the man gets tossed into prison for doing what somebody did to Hilda. What do you think about that little twist of life? The story is sexy. If it weren't Shakespeare, Aunt Addie would call it filth. Know where I got that nasty old book? From her elegant set in the parlor."

"Why don't you leave Aunt Addie alone?"

"Didn't you think that was interesting?"

"It's not fair."

"All is fair and fair is foul. Shakespeare. Something like that," Penny said. "I try to be reasonable."

"You gotta be kidding!"

"The moon shines in the day, and the sun is swallowed by the stars at night, but Aunt Addie never changes."

"That's dippy. Tell me one thing, Penny."

"What?"

"What's bugging you? You used to be fun, but you aren't any more. You get everybody edgy all the time. You homesick or something?" I asked.

Penny snuggled up to me. I moved away. "We never had a home, and yet we have one here. So maybe I'm homesick. You figure it out." She put her hand over mine. I pulled mine away. "Willie?"

"I don't want to hear."

"I suppose not. It's too bad the summer couldn't have been stretched out a bit, into nine summers, nine summers when there wouldn't be even one of Adam's cats to drown."

"Aw, crap, you make me sick."

Penny was hurt. "Doesn't drowning cats make you sick?" she asked, pleading for sympathy.

I got up and left her and told her not to follow.

I kept away from Penny the next couple of days. I don't think I said more than one or two words to her. When she tried talking with me, I went the other way. Sometimes I wanted to tell her things and I would go looking for her, but before I found her, I'd get angry all over again, and I wouldn't. Uncle Lambot and Aunt Addie dodged her whenever they could, for what reasons I didn't know. When Penny went outside, Aunt Addie didn't even bother to ask where she was going, she seemed that relieved. I supposed it had to do with Aunt Harriet, and fear that if they got friendly with Penny, she would deliver another barrage of questions they didn't want to answer. With no one saying anything, it was as quiet as a morgue about the place. It was a good thing we had a radio.

When I kept away from Penny, she developed a case of hurt feelings, and whenever she could, she whammied me, quite like Aunt Addie would do it. She did it until I couldn't take it any longer, and I asked, "What's bugging you?"

"That's what *you* asked the last time we talked, only you wouldn't let me answer."

"Nothing ever stopped you before," I said. That meant I would listen.

"Can't you guess? When is your birthday? Soon, isn't it?"

"September twenty-first. What's that got to do with it?"

"Well, then you will be older. A bona-fide teenager," Penny said, "and old enough to know many things."

"I've been old enough a long time. You said so. I know more things than I can handle and that's a fact."

"I don't doubt that. But just one more item," Penny said, as if what was bugging her was a minor matter after all.

"Well?"

"Hilda and me. We're birds of a feather, Willie."

I almost said, "Hilda can go to hell," but something—I don't know what it was—made me sense that she wasn't talking about Hilda. I looked straight at her, my face a question mark. Penny giggled nervously, and that irritated me. She noted it and sobered quickly. I walked away, and she came after me, squeezing my arm as if to plead with me. "I have to tell someone," she said.

"What now?" I said. I don't know how she did it, but sometimes she could say things in such a way as to make me feel older than she was. This was one of those times.

"How's your strength, Willie?"

"I can lift you any time," I said.

"Not that kind of strength."

"What kind?"

"The kind you need when you take a deep breath because you are

not sure you can handle what you are about to hear. When somebody tells you something you maybe don't want to hear. What I
have to say would shake Aunt Addie's teeth right out of her gums
if she knew."

"Oh, crap. I suppose you're going to tell me *you're* pregnant.
More of that I don't want to hear. You've said too much already,"
I said, and even without looking at her, as soon as I said it, I knew
that was it.

"That's my Willie. You do make things easier," Penny said, smiling, but soberly still. "That's what's wrong with me. Or what's
right. A half dozen times in the past two weeks, I thought you
would guess. I am honest to goodness making a baby inside of me.
Like I said I would. Isn't that great?"

I couldn't tell if it were just another of a thousand nutty ideas that
were yearly hatched in her head. In any case, I don't think she expected me to fall all over myself with joy.

"Come sit with me. I have to talk."

That was the last thing I wanted to do, but nevertheless I sat with
her on the forlorn steps at the other end of the veranda.

"I don't believe it. I won't believe it unless I see your belly swell,
and if it does, that's your problem, not mine," I said.

"Thanks, Willie, I needed that. We've been through so much together, I knew I could count on you when I needed you the most,"
Penny said. "It's not what I thought it would be like. Do you have
any notion how it feels to be pregnant for the first time in your life
when you are only almost seventeen and you can't tell anybody? Except you, Willie. Now that it is happening, I'm not certain how to
handle it. But you are old, Father William, my great and intelligent
brother, and you have more sanity than I am capable of showing at
this present time of my life. The only thing I can think of doing is
to make light of it, and I shall do that, but it is, nevertheless, a sub-
lime time of my life."

Now that she had mentioned it, she was not shy about talking, and
she talked in such a way as to make it sound no worse than a slight

itch. Obviously I didn't believe her at first, and asked her what she took me for for telling me such a dumb story.

"But I *am* pregnant," she insisted.

"Can't prove it by me," I said. I was positive she wasn't, but already I was wondering was Holmes, or Adam, or the Reverend James, or maybe even Mr. Nason responsible. Or that man in New York she said had invited her to his place. She never did make a clean accounting of that. The fact that she was there only a short time ago meant little to me. Despite what I had learned from Penny, I did not know all the ins and outs of baby-making. "How do you know?"

"The birds and the bees told me. A mother knows, Willie. That's how I know. Having a baby will make me a mother. What will you think of your kid sister then?" Before I could say anything, Penny bombarded me with some more questions. "Will having a baby make me poor white trash, like Hilda? Not our kind of people? One thing about having a baby, you can't forever hide the fact, can you? The time will come when Aunt Addie and Uncle Lambot and all of Eastfield will know about me as they do about Hilda. What do you think of that? I wonder what they will say then."

Penny kept on talking and my disbelief was changing into belief. "You really are going to have a baby?"

"Yes, and you will be an uncle. We'll all live through it, Willie, never worry about that. Even Aunt Addie will live through it, and she'll make an excellent nurse and trainer. A baby needs training, Willie. Routine. Don't do this, don't do that. Aunt Addie can supply the don't's, and I can supply the do's. We'll make a fabulous team, and she'll love it, because I can give her something she can't give herself."

"You really are pregnant." I made a statement instead of a question. That surprised me.

"You don't mind? I knew I could count on you, Willie, dear Willie. When the news is out, wouldn't you like to be at the next meeting of the Friday Club to hear how they handle it?"

"Kiss my razz."

"If it's a boy, I'll name it Williedearwillie. And if it's a girl, I'll call her Auntaddie."

"That's nutty."

"Willie, you're not angry with me, are you? It seems you've been angry with me quite a lot this summer. You never used to be."

"I'm mad, if you want to know. What you have done is not funny at all."

"Don't you believe me?"

"Maybe I do and maybe I don't. I'm beginning to think you're a phoney."

"I've been telling you all summer that I wanted a baby. I'm going to have a baby. I'll be a mother, soon, just like the woman on the train with the baby. In the parlor car. Remember?"

I remembered, and I remembered something else. "Maybe you went to New York to see a doctor about yourself," I said. "Why didn't you have him fix you?"

Penny was taken aback. "See! It's different, isn't it?"

"I never believed that junky story about a doctor anyway. But maybe he could have saved us a peck of trouble."

"You, too," Penny said sorrowfully. "It's not right for Hilda to get rid of her baby, but it's O.K. for me to do it. See what I mean? What's the difference, Willie?" Penny continued. "Want to know something? You know what Adam told me about Aunt Harriet, Willie? He told me she was pregnant, too, and she got rid of the baby. Aunt Harriet had an abortion way back when, Willie. What do you think of her now? It was all right for her to get rid of the baby because she was proper, and yet her baby could have been President some day, right? Something could have happened to her, right? I won't go to New York. You talked me out of doing that when you argued against my going for Hilda's sake. Suppose something happened to me like you said could happen to Hilda?"

Obviously, inasmuch as all this about Aunt Harriet was new to me, there was a certain inadequacy in my understanding of what she said. To say that my mind was in a jumble was to put it simply. There was hardly reason for me to respond other than how I did. "You're nuttier than a fruitcake," I said.

"It's different, isn't it?" Penny said. "But don't worry, Willie. I will have it. It will be more fun having the baby than not having it."

"If that's what fun is, you can have it. I don't want it. Ever. Stop playing games with me."

"This is not a game."

I looked at her squarely. "Bet it is. Know what I think? I think you're pretending with me to see if you can get away with it. All you ever do is pretend. You play dumb games, if you really want to know. Dumb, stupid games, and I think you're damn dumb to play them."

If you called Penny names, it was risky to do it other than with a smile. I didn't smile. "O.K., smart ass, a game, but not my game," Penny said with unusual severity. "Soon they will put me in quarantine along with Hilda, and then we'll see."

I got up and walked away from her. "Go to hell," I said.

"I've already been there," she shouted at me. "I'm not too young to be a mother, and that's what I'll be because that's heaven."

I don't know why, but that stopped me. Perhaps it was the determination with which she spoke. "You mean it. You really mean it," I said. "What do we do now?"

"That's my Willie," she said, coming to me. Penny could switch moods faster than light travels. In an instant, she was a sprite. She couldn't resist not being one. "Willie, remember the time I asked Aunt Addie where babies came from? Remember how she acted? Can't you imagine what will happen when I say ever so sweetly on some nice, quiet Indian summer afternoon in October, 'Aunt Addie, why is it that my stomach gets bigger and bigger even though I'm eating less and less?'"

I didn't think it was funny, but there was no point in talking further. I gave her a nasty look and ran off without even telling her to go to hell. I ran through the fields to the swimming hole, and only stopped when I saw that I had ditched her. I sat on a rock, took off my shoes, and dangled my feet in the water. I sat in a daze, nothing at all going in or out of my head for some time. Then I got to thinking about a new being, alive and growing in Penny, one that could eventually take my place, and that idea tampered with my streak of jealousy, and it hurt deeply. I tried to believe that maybe I had heard nothing about her having a baby at all, and I couldn't work it out in my head how Penny could get herself involved in the business of making a baby. I knew how it was done, but I could not picture Penny doing it. It occurred to me that I didn't even ask who the father was going to be. I remember thinking that as long as I didn't know who the father was, it would be easier to pretend that she was playing an ugly practical joke on me and that she was not really pregnant. If I didn't have to believe that, life would be bearable, despite the hurt for even joking about it. I decided I wouldn't ask her. I would let her keep her secret just as Hilda was keeping hers. For my sake.

For the first time ever, I think, I sensed keenly a weakening of the ties that bound me to Penny. I was being tilted toward Uncle Lambot and Aunt Addie. My sympathies on this matter were with them. Life had enough problems without Penny adding more.

After a while I moseyed over to Adam's. There wasn't much there, and it was sad in a way. We had had fun there, even if Penny and I felt that we never had much fun anywhere. I don't even remember what I saw of what was there. I felt something rubbing against my leg. I looked down. It was our favorite cat, Sheba. She had escaped Uncle Lambot's dragnet! I picked her up and cuddled her and decided that I would take her back home and keep her and not tell anyone. I could sneak food to her and keep her as all my own.

I took her to the chicken coop. I petted her for a long time, and I tried to figure out whether she was pregnant or not, as Penny did, but I couldn't. I left her, finally, and went to check out the barn.

I found Penny, swinging down from Olympus. She looked like a kid acrobat in a circus. In no way, I thought, could she be old enough to have a baby now.

When she saw me, she grounded herself. "I was thinking of New York," she said, as if it were any old summer day, and with no mind for discussion of recent events and our relationship. "What a place! I can't wait to go again. So you really think our guardian angels would let me go if I asked? Like hell they would!"

"Stop swearing. You sound like the boys in the locker room."

"What boys?"

"The boys in Des Moines."

Penny laughed at that as she used to laugh, and it was good to see and hear, and I laughed, too. "I forgot them," she said. "Maybe if we'd stayed at home, I could have got one of them to start my baby. Right there in the locker room, and if I did, I'd be having it about now. Why didn't I think of that before? I must have been awfully young then."

My laughter and moment of contentment disappeared. "That's not funny."

Penny took my hand. "Say something funny, Willie. For me."

Without thinking I said, "This morning I told Aunt Addie that you didn't speak for a whole week once."

"Funnee!"

"Well, I did."

Penny smiled and leaned warmly against me. "They don't really want me to stop talking," Penny said. "They wouldn't know what to do with me if I did."

"You been swearing a lot lately, and I know they don't like that," I said.

"My temper makes me. It gets quickly aggravated lately."

"All that tragedy crap. I don't get it. That aggravates me, though."

"You can get it if you try. The hip bone connected to the thigh bone. We've had enough death this summer to last us into the next century. Now they are killing Hilda and they don't know it."

"That's so much baloney and you know it."

"No, I don't know it. I don't know everything, Willie. I'm only almost seventeen, even though I sometimes feel prehistoric."

"What are you trying to prove?"

"I'm only trying to get them to think. And help," Penny said.

"Aunt Addie's always thinking. She just doesn't think the same way as you do. She thinks in circles. You zig and zag."

"How original," Penny said sarcastically. "I wish I'd thought of it."

"We've got to live here a long time. So leave her alone."

"A long time. Maybe, maybe not."

"It's not bad when you think of it."

"Not bad when you don't think about it. Do you like it here?"

"I'm getting used to it."

"Do you like them?"

"I never bothered to think about that," I said. "They are here. So I don't think about it. I like them."

"How about love?"

"I never thought about that either. Aren't you supposed to love relatives?"

"Willie, that's good. You always come through with something to ponder." Penny walked out of the barn. "Come on."

"Where?" I asked. "Most of the time you don't want me to go with you anymore."

"Willie, dear Willie, today I do. Come on. You can see what Mr. Nason is doing. I have to talk to Hilda."

"Like about going to New York?"

Penny didn't answer. "Coming?"

"Not until you tell me."

"O.K., O.K. How are your guts, Willie?"

"Not more baby crap," I said.

"Hilda and I are going to New York next week," Penny told me. "This time I'll not keep it a secret from you, but of course I'm depending on you at this end."

"You can go to hell. I'll tell so you can't go. I'll tell tonight."

"I knew you would cooperate."

"I'm warning you."

"Once more, and when I return, I'll place myself in a straight-jacket and give you the key. I'll be an angel and succumb to after-noon tea talk of nothing that a girl of six would not talk about. That will be the new game, Willie. I'll bore the starch out of Aunt Addie, and we'll see how she worries about that."

"You are something! Hilda's not your damn business, damn it."

"Hilda is my frend, and so are you. Willie, don't fail me," Penny begged. "She *is* my business. I can't not do it. Can't you understand this simple, little thing? I do not want to see Hilda die. It's as sim-ple as that."

"What's living? You having a baby?" I dared to mention. "What's the difference?"

Penny shrugged. "That's a good question, Willie. What's living? Good for you. I never thought of it quite like that. I always thought, what do we live for? Living is what we live for. Know what I mean?"

"Who cares?"

"Hilda not having a baby may be living. Hilda having a baby may be dying. Don't you see?"

Penny thought that an apt deduction of the situation. I didn't. "I don't see. What's the difference? You go to New York, suppose something happens to Hilda? You told me it could. Suppose she dies? Suppose you get caught? Suppose you are getting rid of a future President? What's it to you, anyway?"

Penny tried to make light of it. "Willie, I'm proud of you. I really am. Know why?" She answered her own question. "You're asking questions. You are asking just like I do. Questions are what make the world go round, questions are what swing the pendulum back and forth, I always say."

I did not take the compliment gracefully. I told her she was get-ting loony, and she'd better discover in a hurry she didn't have all the brains in the world.

"You're all heart, Willie," she said, and this time she walked away from me. I didn't follow but shuffled about here and there, ending up at the swimming hole again. I thought I might just as well go swimming and it didn't matter whether or not I went naked. But the water was icky, I knew it wouldn't be fun, and so I didn't bother.

I shuffled back home, to go to my room, and to sleep. I hoped for a long, long time.

When I got there Stan Wynewski's truck was in the yard, which was natural, because it was trash day. But it was unnatural to see Aunt Addie out there talking to him. It turned out that Stan's being there was a piece of luck that angered and relieved me, and was otherwise marvelously instructive.

"Willie, do you know where the plunger is?" Aunt Addie said in greeting. "I've hunted all over and I can't find hide nor hare of it. The toilet in yours and Penny's bathroom is plugged up. You haven't been throwing things down it, have you?"

"Nope."

"Well, somebody has," Aunt Addie fretted. Inasmuch as we both knew that only one other person besides myself used that bathroom, I knew whom she had in mind as the somebody.

"Come on, Willie, we'll see what we can do," Stan Wynewski said. "If you don't have a plunger, and you have to fix it, then you have to use something else."

Without bothering to think about it, and doing it as he had done it before, which may well have been because of his household situation, what with nine kids, Stan unceremoniously stuck his hand into the toilet bowl. "Sometimes in these old crappers, because of the bend at the bottom, stuff gets caught at the top, and if your fingers are long enough . . ." In seconds he caught something. "There," he said. "Willie, get me a wastebasket."

What he pulled out was mostly soaked and moldy toilet paper, but in the middle, something else. I saw it, and Stan noted that I did, and so there was not much point in ignoring it.

"Know what that is?" he asked.

"Kotex," I said. "Penny told me all about it a long time ago."

"That figures. I don't suppose there's nothing you kids don't know about what makes the world go around. That sister of yours is a pip. Tell her next time to put it in a bag and take it outside to the garbage."

Suddenly something occurred to me and I wasn't certain I knew the answer, and I decided to ask Stan about it. If anybody would know, he would. And he wouldn't mind telling. "Is it true that you can tell from this if somebody is going to have a baby or not?" I pointed to the stuff on the Kotex.

Stan looked at me and laughed. "So they say. As long as the spigot is running, all's clear. No baby. When you're older it's a good thing to know. When you're older, Willie."

"It's a good thing to know now."

Stan washed his hands. "You mean Penny?" He laughed. He had a deep, throaty laugh that pulled no punches, and it made for nice listening. "Tell you one thing, Willie, you have no cause to worry about Penny getting into trouble for a long time. That's not what happens in Penny's world, it just don't. Believe me, I know what's what with women. I oughta. I study them all the time. They never stay the same and they never change, and that's something I'll swear to on a stack of Bibles. Penny's going to do things her way, except for certain things, like having a baby before her time. She'll go by the book on that, you wait and see."

When Stan left, I took some milk and a piece of chicken out to Sheba in the hen coop, and I did some of my own figuring, even though I believed Stan. If Penny had dropped her Kotex into the toilet yesterday or the day before, it probably would have got stuck then, but it didn't. So I figured she must have dropped it in that day, and if she did, no baby was growing in her belly. To me it was that simple.

Being overjoyed and relieved with my findings, however, was not that simple. Inside me, positive emotions were getting whacked about by negative emotions, resentment, anguish, and anxiety among

them. I did not understand all the factors working to make a decision about what I should do. Perhaps they were not that important.
I know that I started on the run to find Penny and tell her I knew
what was what all the time and she was not that smart, but before I
found her, I slowed down, halted, and turned around. If I told her,
she'd deny it or find some way or other to confuse me further, and I
would get no relief from her at all. It was no longer like it used to
be, back in Des Moines, when whatever Penny did, she could do no
wrong. I was beginning to realize that I could not come to her with
everything that popped into my head, because there was no way of
knowing what she would do with what I told her.

So I began to play Penny's game of not telling all I knew. I would
not tell her what Stan Wynewski told. If she wanted to keep on
telling me she was going to have a baby, and if she wanted to tell
Aunt Addie and eventually fall on her face, that would be her business.

I had this thought in my head, that if I could keep quiet about it,
and if she kept talking long enough, one day around Thanksgiving,
I would ask her how come her belly wasn't getting any bigger, and
see what she would do about that.

CHAPTER TWENTY-THREE

UNCLE LAMBOT SPENT THE AFTERNOON AT THE MILL, AND WHEN HE
came home, he was in for a surprise. Aunt Addie had taken a
nap and hadn't bothered with supper. Uncle Lambot
checked on her. "A headache," he said. I worried. Aunt Addie never
got sick. And if she ever had anything wrong with her, she would

never tell. Once a window slammed down on her fingernail and blackened it, but she never said it hurt or anything. A mere headache would not keep Aunt Addie down. The only thing I could figure was that Penny finally got to her.

I worried enough to go to her bedroom, and you weren't supposed to go there, ever. But all was calm and peaceful, clean and spotless as you might suspect. Aunt Addie was not lying in her four poster as I thought she would be. She was sitting quietly by the window in her rocker, swaying gently. She looked real pretty with her hair riding neatly on her forehead, and shadows trimming her profile. Young looking, too, and that surprised me. And there was a nice resemblance to Penny. But it was a sad face, and I could tell she had been crying. Maybe a lot.

I couldn't think of anything to say at first, so I went to her and kissed her. It was unlikely for me to do a thing like that, but I did it, and Aunt Addie appreciated the gesture.

She held my hand.

I found my tongue. "You all right?"

"All right," she said.

"Can I get you anything?"

"I'm all right. Just resting. Uncle Lambot will fix supper."

"You hungry?"

"Nothing. Just resting. Taking a little vacation all by myself." She squeezed my hand. "Thank you, Willie, you're a good boy."

It sounded like a dismissal, but she held on to me. I sensed she wanted to talk. There could be only one subject. "I'm sorry about Penny," I said.

That pleased her. She gave my hand another squeeze.

"She likes you, she really does. I know that for a fact."

"Yes," Aunt Addie said. "That's nice."

"She gets all mixed up, that's all. For one thing, she can't stand not knowing."

"I know, and I'm not one for telling. That's the way I was brought up. Maybe it was wrong, but I'm used to it."

"She's been mixed up ever since we got here. She thinks someone set Aunt Harriet's fire, and she's got to find out."

"I know. She's asked enough times." Aunt Addie let go of my hand and rocked a bit. I had a feeling she wanted to say something else and I was right. Why she decided to try me on for size, I did not know then, nor do I know now. It could have been she was ready to talk to anyone who happened to have entered then. It could have been that she used me as a sounding board, knowing that there might be a few echoes bouncing off me, but not a lot of static. Aunt Addie could talk, all right, but not about herself. And she was not given to making speeches. Her words were sparse, and you had to fill in the gaps. But there was no hesitation once she got going.

"Lambot was on his way west and I was alone. Adam came eleven o'clock that night and told me that Harriet was sick and I should come. It was not the first time. When I had gone before, sometimes even later, Harriet wasn't sick, she was . . . Adam had been drinking and I thought maybe Harriet . . . When Lambot was home, I got up and went. I did not want to go that night. I did not want to get dressed and go out. I don't know why. Maybe I had it in mind that whoever tossed the rock through the window might still be lurking about, and I had no one to shout to on my way back, just in case. Maybe that was only an excuse. I gave Adam some aspirin. I told him to stay there all night, and if she got worse to use the phone. I asked why he didn't use it in the first place, and he said he forgot. He also forgot to go back to Harriet. I felt guilty about not going, and so I was awake when the fire . . . It lit up the sky, and I knew right away. On the way, I saw a light at Adam's. I don't know why, but I decided to look inside. Adam was there. I saw him through the window. He was naked, and he was wiping his head with a dirty towel. 'Adam!' I shouted. He took no note of me. I had to know what awful thing he had done, William, and I went inside. He didn't bother to cover himself. When he saw me, he stood there grinning. I asked him if he took the aspirin to Harriet's, and he didn't appear to know what I was talking about. His pants were on the bed and I remembered he put the aspirin in them. I found the aspirin. I asked him where he had been. He said it was such a nice night, he tried out the swimming hole."

Aunt Addie paused. She had a strange, faraway look on her face, and I couldn't tell if she thought maybe she had said too much.

"There were holes in his story. I wondered how he could not notice the fire as I had done, but I believe that he did not go to Harriet's, and her death was accidental. It's a wonder it had not happened before. But I could have prevented it, William. Yes, I could have. I left Adam. I didn't go to the fire. I went home. I remember laughing."

The way she told me, and the tone of her voice, with her quietness of manner, made me believe as she believed, that Aunt Harriet's fire was an accident and that it would not have happened, had she gone. She should have gone; it was her duty to go. She had not fulfilled her charitable obligation; thus she was responsible for the fire. But what really pricked her conscience after that night was the pleasure that came from having no sorrow in her heart for Aunt Harriet. That's what clamped her tongue. In my own way, I began to understand a bit about Aunt Addie, why it was that she was so jumpy that night when the Reverend James came to supper and Penny talked up a storm about heaven and hell, why she got so skittish whenever Adam was around Penny, and even why she did not want Penny to make a habit of associating with the Nasons.

She appeared to have finished, and I said, "I'll tell Penny." At the moment, I could think of no other reason for her telling me what she did.

"No, William. I'll tell her myself," Aunt Addie said, reasserting herself. "Thank you, William."

She waved me off, and I left, feeling sad, and yet not feeling too bad. Aunt Addie discovered she could talk to me. I was somebody she could like and trust, and I sensed something new developing in me that I could not describe. In that short interlude we had developed a new relationship and I rather liked it. Whatever it was, something happened that gave signals to me, however faint, that I would need Penny less because there were others, and there would be less loneliness. When I walked out of the room, I felt older than when I had entered. There was a new bond tying me to Aunt Addie. I wanted to keep it, and I was determined not to lose it by sharing it with Penny. Aunt Addie told me not to tell Penny and I wouldn't.

In the kitchen, Uncle Lambot was cooking up a storm. He was cutting onions, peppers, ham, and cheese, and he dumped all with a huge chunk of butter into the frying pan on the stove. "Make some toast, William," he said, as he beat up a batch of eggs. "We'll make Western sandwiches. Big ones. Get your sister."

"I don't know where she is," I said, but even as I said it Penny appeared. "Where have you been?" I asked.

"Around," she replied. "How come Uncle Lambot's cooking?"

"Uncle Lambot's night to cook. He cooks every Saturday."

"It's only Wednesday. Besides, he never cooks."

"I know that."

"I like it when he cooks. He's real good."

"I know that. He's a man."

"Thanks for everything," Penny said. "Willie, what gives?"

"Figure it out, you're so smart."

"William," Uncle Lambot admonished, and then he told Penny.

Penny doubted that Aunt Addie was immobilized because of a mere headache. "She's there because of me," she admitted. "I'm sorry, but I'm sixteen and I've been sixteen for a long time. I'm no baby, and I do not want to be babied except to be hugged and kissed. I want to be treated like an adult. If Aunt Addie's sick because of me, then I guess she has to be sick."

But before she had finished, Penny was crying. Tears first, then sobs, and she went running from the table to her room.

"Women," I grumbled.

Uncle Lambot seemed to like that, as if it were something a grownup would say. "Never did know what to do with them, William."

"Neither do I."

"Always had difficulty talking with them," Uncle Lambot confessed. "Never did know quite what to do. After supper, you go see Penny and you tell her . . ." but he didn't finish.

"Tell what?" I asked.

His answer was slow in coming. "Nothing," he mumbled and lapsed into silence.

When I went to my room that night, I found a note pinned to my pillow, "Come on down. Let's have a party. Love, Penny." The devil with that, I thought. But after about a half hour, I was there, sitting on her bed.

"Let's talk like we used to," Penny said.

"Talk is cheap." I didn't laugh, and neither did she. "Where did you go all afternoon?"

"Sounds like an accusation. To put you at ease, I didn't go to Hilda's. I didn't see Holmes or the Reverend James. Guess?"

"I wouldn't have asked if I knew."

"I walked down the road to see Seely Jones's cattle. Remember how we used to wonder what it would be like to be cows, doing nothing but eating and sleeping and being milked and going to the john whenever and wherever? Remember how we got to laughing ourselves silly about figuring a way to get cows to use toilet paper?" I remembered, but I didn't bother to give any indication that I did. "Then I visited with Mrs. Jones. She's sick, Willie, and I guess Mr. Jones is more likely to be a widower before she's a widow. She's as skinny as a pin and all shriveled. She wanted to know why we didn't visit her this summer, and I didn't know why. Do you?"

I merely shrugged.

"We talked about a lot of people, Adam, Aunt Harriet, the Nasons, Aunt Addie. She knew them all when she was young. She said Aunt Addie was pretty, but she didn't know it, and because she didn't, nobody paid much attention to her, but she didn't seem to care. Mrs. Jones said Mr. Jones knows a lot about her, because he and Aunt Addie used to walk home from school. In those days, they

walked all the way, can you believe it? Mrs. Jones said she thought
Aunt Addie had a schoolgirl crush on Mr. Nason, because he was
handsome and witty, but not too much of a crush, because he was
wild and never paid much attention to her. Mr. Nason had a crush
on Aunt Harriet, and she had a great big crush on Uncle Lambot.
It's all complicated. You look at Eastfield and you'd never think
anything happens. I guess more happens here than we thought. So
my head's been swimming. I doubt I'll ever sort out the pieces."

"Who cares? What you don't know won't hurt," I said.

"Thank you, Uncle Lambot. Don't you want to know?"

"No."

"Oh, well," Penny said as if she didn't mind. "Know what else
Mrs. Jones told me? She told me she hates cows. She has hated them
all her life. Every time she looks out a window she sees nothing but
cows all over the place. She's allergic to milk and butter and cheese,
she can't stand the sight of cows, and she breaks out all over because
of the smell. On top of that, she's got a husband who can't talk
about much else but cows. You know what I think, Willie, she
wants to die because that's the only way she can ever get away from
ever seeing a cow again. I wonder in her case if she were bad enough
to go to hell, would hell be nothing but a place for cows?"

"Who cares?"

"I do, Willie. She's sick and lonely and I may never see her again,
and that's sad."

"Yeah," I mumbled. I thought about telling her what Aunt Addie
said about the fire, but I didn't. "How come you think these things?"
I asked instead.

"That's the way I am, Willie, you know that. Just before you
came in, I was thinking about how life is one gigantic puzzle that
you never can finish, because as soon as you fit some pieces in, some
more are added."

"Yeah," I said. I guessed she was right about that, and there wasn't
much that I could say about it.

"After seeing Mrs. Jones, I went to Aunt Harriet's and sat on the steps. I just sat, trying to see how long I could sit without moving a muscle for the longest time. And I got this strange feeling that Aunt Harriet is still about, alive, and I will find her and discover that she is somebody I don't know. And you know why I thought that? Because we never really knew the real Aunt Harriet."

"We went to the grave, remember?" I meant the obvious.

"Maybe so, but that's what I thought. We didn't see her after death, Willie, and so maybe it's all a hoax. Once I thought she might be sitting with me, but I turned and there was nothing. Then I imagined her calling just as she used to call us when we got to the apple tree. I could have almost sworn I heard her."

"A ghost? That's nuts."

"Somebody was there with me. Really."

We heard the creaking of the floor boards in the hall outside the door. "And somebody is here," Penny whispered. "Aunt Addie. Under the bed, Willie. Quick."

If I'd have thought, I wouldn't have done it, but I didn't think and so I slipped under the bed, just as the door opened.

"Penny? Are you all right?" It was Uncle Lambot.

"Come in. Be my guest!" Penny greeted.

"I thought I heard you talking."

"To myself. I do that all the time. I recite poetry. Sometimes I just tell myself stories."

"You talk to yourself, it means you got money in the bank," Uncle Lambot said, a stab at levity.

"In that case, Aunt Addie must have lots. She talks to herself all the time."

Uncle Lambot ignored that. "Did I wake you up?" he asked. Obviously, if he had heard her talking, he knew he hadn't.

"No. I was reading."

His reply was slow in coming, as if he was not sure why he had come there.

"You're a great reader. Never did much when I was your age. Most kids don't," he said awkwardly.

"Aunt Addie doesn't think much of my reading."

"Think she does. My sister isn't given to expressing compliments. Or feelings."

"I wouldn't know."

"That's not nice. You can't find out if you don't try. You can't find out if you snip at everything she says."

"That's my problem," Penny replied. She paused longer than usual. "Sorry. I didn't mean it that way."

"You all right? You aren't sick or something?"

"I'm not sick. I'm something though. Something else."

He nervously shifted his feet, and I could hear him sit on the bed.

"There's no need to be nasty to your Aunt. She is doing the best she can. We have some problems and we have to work them out. For now, they weigh heavily on her, and I don't want to hear you swear or speak nasty to her again. At anybody. It's not right for a woman to talk the way you do."

"Uncle Lambot! You called me a woman! You are a dear!" Penny exclaimed.

"You will be a woman soon," Uncle Lambot answered with gravity. "But right now you're still a girl. I like to think of you as my girl. You know I do love you, Penny, even though I can't always show it. Maybe if I gave you a goodnight kiss, you'd believe it."

He got off the bed. His feet shifted again. It was absolutely quiet. Not even Penny talked. I figured Uncle Lambot was about to say something more, but if he had anything on his mind, he dropped it. "Don't wear out your eyes. Get some sleep. And in the morning you be nice to Aunt Addie," he said, and was gone.

"The coast is clear," Penny said.

I crawled out from under.

"You know what he did, Willie, know what he did? Uncle Lambot kissed me! He kissed me, Willie, what do you think of that? He looked at me as if he were going to say something else, but then he leaned over and kissed me, and he looked at me and smiled. He smiled at me, like I was some sort of angel. And do you know what else? Uncle Lambot patted me on the cheek." Penny showed me just how. "What do you think of that?"

"What are you crying for?" I asked.

Penny put her fingers to her cheeks and discovered tears. She tasted one. "I *am* crying, Willie, I'm crying! Real tears. Isn't it wonderful!"

"Puke!"

We heard the train whistle give a couple of toots. "It's still there," Penny said.

"Yeah."

For a second or two there was silence. For Penny, that was hard to take. I shrugged my shoulders and began to leave. "You sure do give your shoulders a lot of exercise," she said.

CHAPTER TWENTY-FOUR

THE NEXT MORNING, UNCLE LAMBOT SKIPPED BREAKFAST TO GO TO the mill. Aunt Addie gave us our breakfast call at the usual time. Penny came floating down the stairs on a pink cloud. I guessed that had something to do with Uncle Lambot kissing her. She was syrupy sweet to Aunt Addie during breakfast, but after, they were quarreling again in no time at all.

"Penny, after you do the dishes, would you sweep the back staircase, please," Aunt Addie said, politely enough, I thought.

"I just did it," Penny said matter-of-factly. That, of course, was not so.

"You just did it last week," Aunt Addie replied. "Makes no dif-

ference when you last did it. If the stairs need cleaning, that's when
you do it."

"Then they don't need it. The stairs were clean when I came down
this morning. I especially noticed because I am especially noticing
everything on this special morning. What a morning to notice
everything. Just everything! You'll never believe what I dreamed
last night."

"Tell me after you've done the stairs," Aunt Addie said.

Penny groaned. "You've spoiled my day already, just like that,"
she said with a shrewish snapping of her fingers. "Because of a speck
of dust a dream is lost."

No matter what they said, this was not to be one of those days in
which wavelengths could be synchronized. After supper that night,
Penny said, "Let's get out of here. And fast."

I was bored, so getting out was all right with me. We rambled
here and there for a while, perhaps giving Aunt Addie a chance to
call us for something if she wanted to, and when she didn't, we
headed for the Nason place. I didn't want to go there, but that is
where we went.

Hilda greeted us, and she and Penny sat on the dilapidated steps
at the side of the house. Hilda was wearing the red dress Penny
had given her.

"She likes it," Penny said proudly. "You don't have to stay with
us, Willie. Mr. Nason wants to see you."

I went, not believing, but not before I took a good look at Hilda.
She was pregnant all right. Her stomach was growing and the red
dress didn't hide that fact. She had not put on make-up and she almost looked like a kid again, and it was hard to believe that she
had the ability to make a real, live human being. "Where's your
father?" I asked, as if I didn't know.

"In the barn," Hilda said. "Ain't hardly left it all week. Ain't
feeling good."

"Go cheer him up, Willie," Penny prompted. "I want to gab with
Hilda. Women talk."

"Go ahead. He won't bite."

I found Mr. Nason easy. He was sitting outside the barn, sharpening a scythe. Like Adam, when we first saw him at his shack that summer. Mr. Nason was wearing overalls and an old khaki shirt that was tarnished green at the edges. He smelled, not a barny smell, but a dirty, pungent, sour human body smell. He looked about the same as last year.

Mr. Nason was long and skinny. He had a narrow nose and a narrow pointed, balding head. His face was smudged with beard, and his blue eyes were oddly framed in their sockets. I noticed his eyes this year more than last year. They were clean and clear, youngish looking, hardly the eyes of a man who drank a lot. His voice was not old and cracked, not sounding as you would expect it to sound when you noted his desiccated appearance. It was the voice of a young man, and I thought if you could only see his eyes and hear his voice, you might think he was about the same age as Holmes. But from afar, he looked more like a corpse with a couple of mechanical moving parts, and it was hard to believe that Aunt Addie or anyone else could ever have had a crush on him.

"Hi, kid," Mr. Nason said.

He was neither friendly nor unfriendly. "Hi," I said. He looked at me as if I was supposed to say something else, but I drew a blank.

"You got a question, kid, ask it," Mr. Nason said. "Questions is what keeps the earth from dying. You take your sister. She's already asked me enough questions to keep the earth alive for another ten thousand years to try to find the answers. You want to know what she asked?"

I mumbled something that was neither yes nor no.

"Say yes, kid. Ain't impolite to be curious. Otherwise there ain't much sense in talking, and you would only sit and watch me. Never watch people work unless you want to learn."

He beckoned me to drip some water from a can onto the scythe, and to sit down on a box opposite him. He continued honing.

"Even from me you can learn something. That's the beauty of

life. Everybody sees it different. Your sister makes me feel good. She wants to know what I know and that's the best thing you can do for anybody. And knowing is the best part of life. Your sister makes me feel special."

Mr. Nason reached behind him, fumbled with his fingers, and found a bottle. The bottle was amber-colored and half-filled with a brackish liquid. "You want some?"

I told him I didn't think so.

"Your sister had some."

I told him, then, I would try some. I took a swig, and it left a dry feeling in my mouth and a burning in my stomach. I didn't like it.

"Elderberry," Mr. Nason said. "Lotsa people drank it a few years back. Some still do. Think it's got sex power in it. Sam Brown used to think so. You knew him?"

"Yes."

Mr. Nason cleared his throat. He spat a chalky glob. It turned my stomach. "He used to come by and get some for his girl up on the hill. So he said. Didn't always go there, though. He had more than one iron in the fire, and some got bent. Have some more, kid."

I said no, and he told me Penny liked it, and then he asked, "She your twin? Don't look like you. You look older," he gurgled. I wished I hadn't come.

"She's not my twin. Sometimes she's older and sometimes she's younger," I said.

"Sounds like something she would say," Mr. Nason replied. "Know what she asked me?"

I shrugged again.

"She asked why I didn't talk to Mrs. Nason, why I didn't live in the house, did I like living in the barn, did I love Mrs. Nason, did I know who burned Harriet Stone's house, did Adam do it, was Adam smart, did Adam visit often, with me, or my daughter, or my wife, did I love Hilda, did I think I was crazy for living like I do, did I know where my life would take me, did I ever go to church or vote for Roosevelt, did I ever go to New York, did I know who loved who in this town? That's what she asked me this summer. Made me feel good. I been drinking most of the day, in case she asks. I drink most every day. Once in a great while only I don't drink. Don't know why I stop, but I do."

It was easy to believe that Penny asked those questions and more. I didn't have anything to say about them, and I poured some more water on the scythe, and waited.

"Some days I remember everything God ever put into my head. Some days I don't remember nothing, that's a fact," Mr. Nason said. "It's a game I play. Sometimes I win and sometimes I lose. I gave up on life a long time ago, so I play a game. I don't remember what I remembered when your sister asked me questions. I only remember the questions. I don't remember if she asked me yesterday or tomorrow. I don't know what I said. Maybe nothing. I remember questions, though. You got any questions, kid? Must have. More people been asking more damn questions lately. Mostly about the fire." He nodded toward Aunt Harriet's so I knew he meant her fire, and not Adam's.

"How did it start?" I asked abruptly.

"That's what they all ask and depending on what I say, they go away believing this or that person did it. They been asking lots of questions about me to see if I did it. Because they think I'm loose in the head, kid, like Adam, so I could do it, know what I mean? But I got no reason to burn. Even if I had reason, I wouldn't. So if they don't think me, they think Adam. Same reason. Like he was crazy. Maybe he did it. One thing, though, he ain't gonna tell. Another thing, neither is she going to tell. If somebody else tells, ain't nobody ever gonna know if it's true or not. So I say, no, Adam didn't do it, because you know it ain't gonna make any difference to him or to her. The world will survive without anybody knowing otherwise."

I figured later that maybe Aunt Addie was right about the fire, that maybe nobody set it, but I didn't have time to think then because Mr. Nason took another swig from his bottle and invited me into the barn. "I got lotsa books. Come and see."

Inside, first I saw the old cow stalls. He had patched walls together with odd pieces of wood, much as Adam had done with his shack. Two windows had sleazy, dirty curtains covering them like pieces of dead skin. On a cluttered table, a lighted kerosene lamp stood, and smoke funneled out of its blackened chimney. The room was not much bigger than Uncle Lambot's clubroom, and just like it, it had odds-and-ends furniture. There was a stale smell of urine about and it made me nauseous. I wanted to leave, but I stayed because I didn't know how to leave.

There were books all over the place, on shelves, on tables, on the floor in piles, all shabby and dust-laden, some looking as though they had been there for eons. Mr. Nason told me he got them out of garbage cans and at the town dump. He said you could get a lot out of the dump if you made a practice of looking. "Your sister asked if I read all of these books," Mr. Nason said. "I told her I read every one of them, and she said that if I did read them all, I read more than most people in Eastfield had read, and more than most who went to college. I told her this was my college. I lied. I don't read. I start to read, and when I do, I want to cry, so I don't read."

"I don't like to read," I said with some sympathy. "It gets Penny mad when I don't."

"She reads a lot."

"All the time."

"You can read and know a lot. You can read and know nothing. I gave her a book the other day."

"I know," I said. *"An American Tragedy."*

"Don't remember," Mr. Nason said. "You want one?"

"No," I answered.

"That's O.K.," he said. "I like you. I like your sister. She asked me how much courage I had, and I asked why, and she said she wanted to measure it because it must take a heap of it to live the way I did. I told her maybe it didn't take any, it all depended on how you looked at things. She liked that, and she said she wished could buy a couple of pounds of my courage. She asked me did I like living the way I did, and when I told her no, she asked why did I do it, and I asked why other people lived the way they did when they didn't like it. You get used to it, kid. You get in a rut, and after a while you don't know any better. I think about it every day. It ain't courage we got. Something, though, my wife and I. As long as we keep apart the way we do, we're somebody. Know what I mean?"

I was confused. I shook my head.

"Everybody's got to be somebody. We talk and live together like anybody else, and we're nobody. Even less than nobody because we ain't got nothing to be somebody. Except how we got Hilda. You know she's gonna have a baby?"

I nodded.

"You don't talk much, do you, kid?"

I nodded.

"Well, she is. She's gonna have a baby, and I know the father. All I gotta do is say so, and we'll have enough to fix up the house and everything. But you wanta know something? Money can't fix everything, and so maybe he ain't gonna know I know. Nobody ain't never gonna know. Right here in the barn when he thought I was elsewhere. I see him riding up and down the road, and one day I knew it was going to happen, only I didn't think it would, and then I was too late. But nobody ain't gonna know. Hilda ain't telling, and I ain't. Not even telling Pearl. I didn't even tell Adam." Mr. Nason looked at me as if searching for me through a haze. Then he grabbed my arm and shook me suddenly and fiercely. "I ain't telling anybody," he snarled. "And if you were your sister, you would ask me, 'Why?'"

"I'm not my sister," I somehow said.

Mr. Nason ignored that and answered as if I had asked. "That man was trying to steal my farm from me, and I let him know if he didn't stop bothering, I'd tell. And it ain't nobody else's damn business, that's why. We are going to keep the baby and the father ain't ever gonna have a look. It is going to be something we got that nobody else has got, and we are going to keep this place until hell freezes over. So that's what we got, right?"

I tried to slip from his grip, but he held on, his finger digging into my arm.

"We got a kid, a new kid coming, and it's gonna be all ours. Some people's gonna think it belongs to Adam. Some people's gonna think it's Sam Brown. Not so. Never had an affair with nobody, not even the woman up the road. Know for a fact. Your uncle did, though. Long time ago. He's the one. Knocked her up just like Hilda's got knocked up. A long time ago. Your Aunt Addie knows all about it and she ain't never said a word to nobody, but she knows. One night I see your uncle walking up the road, but he don't see nobody. Just as I was heading out to bring in our cow. And then I see your aunt traipsin' across the field and down the path with no never-mind for nobody. I don't know what happened, but after that I never saw your uncle go up there again for a long time. Harriet, she went away, and it was a long time before she came back. To work in New York, they said, but it's not so. Before that your uncle used to go there lotsa times. That's how come I know he liked to drink my elderberry. He used to take it with him, kid. When he was young. When we were all young and we didn't believe life had an ending. What do you think of that? It's a helluva world, I didn't tell you half of it, and I don't calculate anyone's ever gonna straighten it out, it don't make much difference what you do. Not a god-damned bit of difference. What do you think of that?"

The only thing I could think of was that I wanted to get away from there fast, but I was so frightened, I doubted I could have moved even if he let go of me.

"So maybe you don't think, kid. But you will. Even you will think these god-damned things some day. Everybody does sooner or later. So go, kid. Go tell Mrs. Nason you had a nice talk with her old man. Tell her that, kid, if you can find her. Tell her I'm a nice guy. If you can find her when she ain't layin' with someone. I'm going to bed now. I'm going to bed and cry. I cry every damned second of my life."

He pulled me close to him, and hugged me, and clung to me, as if he might fall. And he took my head in his hands, and pulled it toward him, and kissed me, and I was close enough so that my cheeks got wet from his tears. Then suddenly he shoved me, pushing me into a pile of books, which fell over and clouded the dust. "Get out, get the hell out of here, kid! Get out while you can!" Mr. Nason shouted at me. "Get out! Get out!"

I shot out of the barn and ran through the yard, past the house. I didn't even look for Penny. But she was waiting for me, sitting on the stone wall where Seely Jones had some of his cows.

"You look like you've seen a ghost," she said.

I sat next to her, all but collapsed.

"Did he try something funny?" Penny asked.

"He's drunk," I said, panting. "And crazy, real crazy. I never seen anybody like him, and I hope I never see him again. It's not like last year at all."

"Not at all," Penny agreed. "Everything is all messed up."

CHAPTER TWENTY-FIVE

"LEM'S BRIGHT, WILLIE, AND HE KNOWS A LOT. UNCLE LAMBOT OUGHT to invite him into his club."

"Uncle Lambot ain't that dumb," I said. "He's all messed up and I doubt he ever gets straightened out. I ain't going there again. It's spooky. Whew!"

"He's interesting," Penny insisted. "Get him talking and he's better than Aunt Charity."

"That's not hard to beat," I said. "Uncle Lambot and Aunt Addie are right. Nothing but trouble here. I think he's going to die. I thought he was going to die right in front of me."

"All have to die some time. After this summer we certainly ought to know that," Penny said matter-of-factly. "He says he's already dead."

I couldn't sit any longer and I started down the hill. Penny followed along. As we approached the bridge, Penny said, "It will please you to know that Hilda and I are not going to New York."

"Mr. Nason told me they are going to keep the baby. He told me he knows the father, but nobody is going to know, because they want the baby all to themselves, so the baby can help make them somebodies out of nobodies. Something like that."

"Something like that," Penny repeated. "Someone to love. Hilda doesn't care how much people will talk. Besides, it wouldn't be any different from now because everybody talks about her and her mother and father, and so what? She doesn't care if she's being selfish. She's never had a doll she can remember. She hopes it will be a girl, and if it is she is going to name it Penny, after guess who?"

"Bully for her."

"She wants to be a mother, the best mother anybody had, she told me. It's going to be her baby, hers alone and to hell and goddamn with everybody. Everybody except me, Hilda said. Mr. Nason didn't hint who the father might be?"

"He said it wasn't Sam Brown."

"Did he say who else it wasn't?"

"Nope, except maybe not Adam."

"That maybe eliminates two possibilities. We shall keep thinking until we can't eliminate any more."

"I don't care to know."

"I do. I think it has something to do with Hilda wanting to keep the baby."

"Maybe," I said, trying to make some sense out of what Mr. Nason had told me. "I'm glad you're not going to New York."

"Not with Hilda. With you, maybe. How about it? Let's just keep on walking to the train station now."

"Let's not," I said.

"You were right, my dear brother. About her not having an abortion. Hilda said a baby would give her a new life, and she thanked me for wanting to help. She said I was the first and only friend she ever had. Know what she did, Willie? She kissed me and ran inside the house. I think she went inside to cry. Her father cries a lot."

"I know. He told me."

We were at the bridge now.

We leaned against the bridge rail and watched the swirling water underneath.

"It's mad about something," Penny said. "Most summers it's lazy and non-committal. More or less like Adam, or Uncle Lambot. Remember the time he got mad about Aunt Addie cleaning the barn?"

I told her I remembered.

"When he got mad, he got mad. The river's beginning to get riled up over something. I wonder what's bothering it."

"Drowning in its own water," I said.

"Maybe it's mad at the world, and with good reason. Maybe it doesn't know what it's all about and has given up. Just like Mr. Nason. Or Mrs. Jones."

"Maybe," I said. "Let's go home."

"What's the matter?"

"I don't know. I feel kinda sick. You would, too, if you were with Mr. Nason when I was."

Penny wasn't ready to leave. "Know something, Willie?"

"What now?"

"I'm jealous of Hilda."

"That's crazy. Let's go."

"Well, I am. She knows what she wants, and she's not older than

I am. I don't know, and I've got to finish high school and go to some old woman's college, because that's what's got to happen to both you and me, except you can go somewhere like Yale or Harvard. We have to complicate our lives and that will produce discontent. She's got an uncomplicated future."

It was apparent to me that my sister had forgot that she herself was supposed to be pregnant, and I was tempted to call her attention to that oversight, but she kept on chatting as if she were delivering a lecture somewhere, and so I let her yak away.

"She doesn't know much, but she knows what she wants, and that's all anybody needs to know about one's life, I guess. I know everything except that one thing. I don't know what I want," Penny said. "Hilda does. You talk with her and you can feel it. All of a sudden she grew up. She's set for life. All she's got to worry about is three meals a day for herself and her baby, and staying warm in winter. And that's not much for worrying in Eastfield. You live here and you get fed somehow or other. Even Hilda. Not like New York. Everybody here somehow takes care of everybody."

I interrupted. "That's dumb, and that's a fact."

"Maybe so. Maybe it's dumb not to know what you want when you are as old as we are," Penny said. "Maybe I should be a man and join the army. That's what men can do when they don't know what they want, or when they want to escape from what they've already got. If I could, I would join the army on both counts."

"That's even dumber," I said. "Let's go."

She held on to my shirt sleeve. "One thing, if Hilda has a baby, she'll have money enough for it. Mine."

"Ours." I meant it was ours. Penny took it otherwise.

"Thank you, Willie, for your generosity. If it weren't for you, my favorite brother, I would have collapsed a dozen times this summer. Know something? I miss our parents this summer. Last year I didn't miss them at all. Good riddance. But I miss them now, and I don't miss Granny Winston as much as I thought I would. Or Aunt Harriet, if you really want to know, and I don't know why I am all mixed up this way. And you know something else, I keep making up speeches I want to give to Aunt Addie. She's on my mind all the time. And one thing else I know, I can't go much longer without crying me a great big river."

With that, Penny cried. She looked into the river below and cried, softly, but you could hear her, and you could see the tears roll off her face into the waters below.

I did not know what to do. Twenty minutes ago I was talking with Mr. Nason, and somehow he made me feel old, way beyond my years. Her crying made me all kid again, and it was all I could do to keep from crying. I guess I shed a few tears, and I guess maybe I put my arm around her.

We had not noticed the darkness creeping up on us until suddenly we were aware of the glare of headlights of an oncoming car. Lest it be by chance Uncle Lambot out looking for us, we ran off the bridge and hid behind a tree.

It wasn't Uncle Lambot. It wasn't so dark that we could not see that the car going up the hill was the bulky green Plymouth belonging to Holmes Woodbury.

"Like Mr. Nason said, the world is in a helluva mess," Penny said, trying to make light of it, and after a couple of curses, she asked, "Who do you suppose is with him?"

"Could care less. I couldn't tell if anyone was with him," I said. "It's late anyway and we better get moving. Aunt Addie's probably having a fit."

"To hell with her, pardon the expression. I bet they park at Aunt Harriet's, a nice, safe, secure place. Let's catch them," Penny said.

"Let's not," I said. "That's New England snooping. It's none of your business, and maybe he just kept on going."

"Maybe he didn't, and it is my business," Penny said. "We have to go to Aunt Harriet's almost, anyway, to go through the woods to go home. It's the shortest way."

Penny was right about that and so I followed her, her walk turning into a run. We wondered, when we came to the Nasons, if

Holmes might be there, but there was no car there, and we ran on.

Moments later, breathless, we saw Holmes's car, a darkened piece of sculpture, parked in Aunt Harriet's drive.

"The bastard," Penny swore. "Wonder who's with him?"

"Not Hilda this time. Who cares?" I whispered. "Let's go home."

"I care, that's who! I am jealous! I am furious!" Penny snapped, sotto voce. "He's my first boyfriend, Willie. A Harvard man, and I'm only sixteen even if he does believe I'm older. What a rotten, son-of-a-bitch trick, the son-of-a-bitch. Willie, you creep around to the other side."

"I will not. It's none of your business."

"Then we'll hoot like Indians. Just for fun."

"No."

"Where's your sporting blood?"

"That's not fair."

"You're damn tootin' it's not."

"Suppose he sees you, and he gets mad forever."

It was soon apparent that Penny had another idea. I heard her pawing the ground with her foot. Finally she found what she was looking for, a rock the size of a baseball.

"You're right, Willie. I really don't care, and it's not cricket to snoop. Besides, triangles make life interesting. More stories have triangles in them than no triangles. The Nasons have a million triangles. Aunt Harriet had them. Stan Wynewski. Now I got one. I think I'll tease him. Tomorrow I'll tell him I called him tonight, but that Aunt Lucretia said he had gone to church, to join the choir and choir practice, so I called the church and he wasn't there, and I'll ask him where he was." Penny stopped talking, wound up, and heaved the rock at the car.

There was a second or two of forest silence, and then a shattering of glass. Through no talent of her own, Penny had aimed at one of the car's window and scored a bull's-eye.

"There! That's one for the record book!" she exclaimed. "Let's beat it."

We ran at a gallop, running down the path past the apple tree, past Adam's place, stopping at the swimming pool to catch our breath.

"Hear the whippoorwill?" Penny asked. I listened. It sounded as thought it were miles away. "I wonder what he thinks as he whistles night after night."

"I wonder what she thinks," I said.

That pleased Penny. She told me I was a fast learner. Then she said, "Know what?"

"What?"

She didn't answer; instead she had a fit of the giggles.

"What's so funny?"

"What's funny is the rock, Willie. If I had tried a hundred years, I couldn't have done it better. It was a marvelous, devastating bit of luck. I'd give half my dowry to hear how he explains that broken window to Aunt Lucretia. I wish I had truly called him earlier, and I wish I could have said to him that if he ever went out with any other woman, I would bust a window in his car! And then I would have done it!"

"What does it matter? I never did like him."

"I did. Do. I told him I was crazy about him. I told him I loved him. What do you think of that?"

"I saw you kiss him," I said, as if that meant something.

"I'm glad that's all you saw," Penny said, and I wasn't certain what she wanted me to believe about that, but I didn't ask.

"I think the whippoorwill sings the world's saddest song," Penny said. "A sad, sad song, and right now, that one is singing for me." She said it, as if she were reading a line or two of poetry. Then she laughed again, and kept on laughing as if to keep from bursting into tears, I thought, but after a while, I laughed with her, thinking about Holmes Woodbury and the broken window and how lucky Penny was to have hit it.

"Willie?"

"What?"

"Let's skinny dip. It may be our last time ever."

"It's too late," I complained.

"Almost, but not quite. We are only young once. Another fifteen minutes from our beloved wardens will not matter a whit. They will groan and wail, but breakfast will be on the table in the morning, same as always." Penny took off her clothes and slid into the water, and so I did the same and followed after.

I could have stayed there all night. The cool of the clean water made you forget just about everything, and we had lots to forget.

CHAPTER TWENTY-SIX

AUNT ADDIE WAS OBVIOUSLY RELIEVED WHEN WE SHOWED UP, BUT she acted as though she were afflicted with the black plague when she saw our wet hair and divined where we had been. Penny said we had merely stuck our head in the pool to cool off, and we would have been home sooner but we went hunting for an elusive whippoorwill, none of which Aunt Addie took in good faith.

She bedded us down with a new edict, ordering us to remain at home every evening from then until school time. The next morning, she repeated the directive, in front of Uncle Lambot, including him in this matter of discipline whether he liked it or not. He was away now most of the time at the mill, and Penny said she had heard Aunt Addie tell him that it was because we were too much to take.

She had a point, but somebody had to take care of the mill. Uncle Lambot took a couple of mysterious trips out of town. Something about the mill, but he locked his lips and was grouchier and more somber than usual. Elisha Woodbury dropped by a couple of times and we guessed it was serious because they met in the parlor and Aunt Addie even served coffee and doughnuts. After Sam Brown did away with himself, the strikers mostly stopped striking because the mill had no more work and striking was useless. The mood in town was grim and Aunt Addie used it as an excuse to keep us safely down on the farm. Uncle Lambot did go ahead with the repainting of the church even though Adam's will was not closed, and we could go along sometimes to supervise. It seemed that was about all we could do.

It also seemed as if Penny had forgot about her pregnancy. I didn't say anything, and at times I wondered if I had been dreaming.

It appeared as if Penny was trying out for size every mood she could think of that summer. Myrtice Bean called one afternoon, and told Aunt Addie there was no accounting for teenagers. I figured Penny's moods had to do with Holmes, that she was stuck on him and he was not so stuck on her, and if so, maybe I ought to thank him. Whatever it was, at times she played Aunt Addie's game with grim determination, doing household chores as if they were not chores, reading in the house, and even taking naps in the afternoon.

Penny was not, however, suddenly graced with perfection, and she found ways to perform illegal acts. She skipped over to Hilda's when Aunt Addie did her weekly shopping with Myrtice Bean or went to some church affair during the week. Some nights, when snores assured Penny that her wardens were in deep sleep, she sneaked out of the house. She discovered a way out the window, down onto the veranda roof, down a post, and off. She wasn't the last bit frightened. She never asked me to go with her. She just went.

"Where do you go?" I asked one night.

"Just out. Hunting for whippoorwills."

"You must go somewhere."

"Maybe. I see people."

"Who?"

"Night people. And we sit in the pool when it's hot."

"Snotty."

"So I'm a snot. But maybe it's you, Willie. You never ask. Don't you care about me? Aren't you curious about it being a boy or a girl?"

She had not forgotten after all. "An ape," I said.

We got to arguing about my sense of humor. I got hot under the collar and changed the subject by telling what Aunt Addie told me about the fire, forgetting my resolve until it was too late. She left me abruptly and went off to sulk.

One night a thunderstorm rolled out of the hills and I knew Penny would not go prowling. Thunderstorms are more fun with some-body, so after Uncle Lambot and Aunt Addie had commenced their nightly snoring, I sneaked down to Penny's room. She was at the window, watching the lightning over toward Westfield.

"If you didn't know what it was, if you never read about it in a book, what would you think it was?" Penny asked. "Suppose you lived a thousand years ago, what would you think it was?"

"God, maybe."

"Willie!" Penny exclaimed, pleased. "What else?"

"Nothing?"

"Wouldn't you think it was a signal of something? Something good or bad?"

She sounded as though she had something else in mind. "What's up?" I asked.

"What do you mean?"

I couldn't explain. I said, "You ain't the same anymore."

"Ain't. Ain't is aren't," Penny said. "Aren't is plural and I am one, but you do not say, 'You isn't.' Neither do you say 'ain't.' It's con-fusing, isn't it?"

"And so are you."

"How do you like it, Willie, when it's quiet and peaceful, and no one disturbs anything, not even that little old church mouse? Would you like me to be a good girl until I get married or until Aunt Addie dies and I take her place, and then I'd be goodness forever? How would you like that?"

"A miracle," I said.

Penny threw herself on the bed. "I feel like I'm doing penance around here, and I don't know exactly why I should be doing it. To escape, I sneak out at night."

"You get caught, and you'll be doing something besides whatever you're doing," I said.

"So I get caught. You know where we are now? We live at the center of nothing. We live in *No Place*, U.S.A., smack in the middle of it. Nothing moves here. Nothing changes."

"The river moves," I said.

"That it does, and it remains the same."

I reminded her of the church being painted. She ignored that bit of evidence.

"This house. No joy. No excitement. No laughter," she said. "You'd think all that was indecent."

"Always complaining," I said.

"I've done my don't's to perfection for two weeks, and I'll go crazy with another day of it. Let's do something wild! Tonight!"

"It's raining," I said.

"That's my Willie, always playing it safe. O.K., not tonight, but tomorrow, watch tomorrow. I think I'll start the day off by asking if I can go to New York. Better, I'll simply say I'm going and ask Uncle Lambot for some money, and ask, incidentally, how much we have in the altogether. Then I'll tell them I'm sneaking out at nights, but I won't tell them how or where I go. And then, if that doesn't move them, I think I'll ask, if you fall in love, hopelessly, how do you keep from having babies? Not much, Willie. Little things, to get the ball rolling again."

"You're nuts," I said, and left without bothering with a goodnight.

But Penny did nothing the next day, except play the role of Miss Goodie Two Shoes. At supper, Aunt Addie and Uncle Lambot offered peace prizes. The day had been a sultry dog day, and we were having a veranda meal of peanut butter sandwiches and milk. All was serene. Uncle Lambot told me to get what was out in the barn.

I did as bid, and returned, beaming, with two gleaming bicycles, a red one for Penny and a blue one for me. I couldn't hide my pleasure. Penny smiled at first, then dabbed her face with suspicion when Aunt Addie wrote some more don'ts into the record.

"Be careful when you leave the yard. The way the cars whiz past here, I declare I won't have a moment's peace from now on," she said. "Ride in the yard, and up and down the road, but I don't want you to ride out of sight. Down to Seely Jones's farm is far enough." Aunt Addie ranted on, more than she needed to, and I suspect she thought, with the presents, that she could get away with it. She should have known better.

Penny should have kept still. She ought to have known that we would go so far one day, a bit farther the next, and before you knew it, almost anywhere. But the new don't's hit her alert button again, and she entered the battle arena, not even bothering with the amenities involved in gift-giving.

"Aunt Addie, it is my life," Penny said, measuring her words as did Uncle Lambot when he talked. "To do as I please with it. My life is a gift from God. If I want to toss it away, I can find a better way to do it than by letting someone run me down here in Eastfield, *No Place,* U.S.A. Why do you always worry about something happening that hasn't happened and isn't going to happen?"

Uncle Lambot offered a lame contribution on behalf of his sister. "Too many cars on the road," he grumbled.

I offered my bit. "You gotta be careful, Penny. You know how you fall over everything. You know when you start thinking about something you forget what you are doing."

"That's begging for trouble when there is none," Penny persisted. "I might not even bother to ride it."

"There's only one thing I ask," Aunt Addie said, ignoring Penny's nastiness and attempting to keep control. "When you go somewhere, you tell me where you are going. I'll worry enough as it is. I'd just like to know. That's not asking too much. And you needn't get snippy, young lady."

"Now who's getting snippy?" Penny asked.

If Aunt Addie had false teeth, she would have spit them out, I am sure. As it was, her teeth chattered, but they couldn't spill out a word.

"Penny!" Uncle Lambot warned.

"She's always at me, Uncle Lambot. Please tell her if something is going to happen, it is going to happen, and all her worrying won't stop it. Worrying does not stop the sun and the moon or anything else in orbit, or that damn pendulum that is always swinging back and forth in this house. As a matter of fact, it could happen that Uncle Lambot might accidentally run his Packard over me or Willie in our own backyard when we are not even on bicycles. Or we might accidentally . . ."

"Stop right there, young lady!" Aunt Addie yelped.

"If you don't want it, we'll return it," Uncle Lambot said. He pouted his lips, a clear sign of danger up front.

Aunt Addie had not surrendered. "I want to know, that's all. It's not too much to ask."

"And if I tell, the first thing you will say is no," Penny said. "You always say no, first, last and always. Why don't you tell me specifically where I can't go in the first place, and then I'll tell you what I will or will not do."

That got both Uncle Lambot and Aunt Addie real tensed-up, and if it had been me, I would have told her to go anywhere she damned pleased. Just go. But Aunt Addie was hesitant. The game required that she did not say what she could not control.

"Where?" Penny demanded to know. "I'd just like to know. To Hilda's maybe?"

Uncle Lambot came to life. "You are not to go to the Nason place, and that's that," he said.

"Why not?" Penny persisted. I shot her a dirty look. She'd been told why not a hundred times.

"Your Aunt Addie doesn't want you over there," Uncle Lambot groused. "That's reason enough."

"Maybe for her, but not for me. Why not?"

"Because I said so." Uncle Lambot didn't like to mess around.

That did not satisfy Penny. "Why not? I wish you would tell me why. I like Hilda. She likes me. I want to help her. I'm the only friend she has. Do you think being with her will make me bad? That's not what I learned in Sunday school."

"They're not our kind of people." Aunt Addie sought refuge in the familiar. As soon as she said it, she wished she hadn't.

"Then whose kind of people are they?" Penny demanded to know. "And what about my influence on Hilda? Don't you think I might be good for her? Forgive me if I sound ignorant, but I don't understand. Are you afraid I'll get a bad reputation and it will rub off on you, and someday we'll be like the Nasons, a fine old family, the salt of the earth, gone sour? Forgive me for asking, but how does one get a bad reputation by caring for another human being in trouble? Doing that is finding the keys to the kingdom, according to the Reverend James. How does it go, Aunt Addie? 'Let who casts the first stone . . .' How does it go?"

"We've had enough talk," Uncle Lambot said, his voice growing louder. "You'd best go to your room."

Not quite. Penny sallied forth one more time.

"Uncle Lambot, I'm Hilda's friend. What should I do then? Answer me that, and then I'll go. Should I suddenly ignore her? As it is, I am ashamed. What do you think she must think because I can't invite her here, never mind for lunch, I can't even invite her here to sit out under the trees. What do you suppose she will think if I never come to see her again? What do I do about that? Write a letter? 'Dear Hilda, I can't come to see you again, because it has been so ordained by my guardians, God bless them, who have brought me up in the Christian faith. Why? Because they said so.' How's that?"

"What did I just tell you to do?" Uncle Lambot asked as if Penny had not said a thing.

"O.K., O.K., I'll go, if that's what you want, Uncle Lambot,"

Penny said, without bothering to move. "Promise me one thing, Aunt Addie?"

Aunt Addie said nothing. You knew she was holding her breath.

"I'll go to my room, do penance, and pray, and when I go, promise you'll think about how it would be if I were in Hilda's shoes, if I were sweet sixteen, and suddenly I did something to get some money because you needed it, for whatever. And what I did . . ." Penny paused long enough to let that sink in, and it didn't take three guesses from anyone to know what was coming next. "And what I did for somebody else got me with a baby. It could happen. You don't mean it to happen, but it could happen. And you'd better think about it, because maybe, maybe . . ."

Penny let the rest dangle, and she clomped into the house, up the stairs, and into her room.

Uncle Lambot mumbled something and headed for the barn. Aunt Addie knocked Penny's unfinished milk to the floor, for which I was thankful, for that gave her something to sputter about, and something to do in cleaning up the mess. In a matter of seconds, it was as if nothing had happened. Nothing gained, nothing lost. But no peace.

I couldn't sleep that night. It was hot, and I wanted to talk to someone, even Penny, but I knew we'd fight. I went to the window and searched for stars through the sultry haze that had settled in with the night. Occasionally I heard the whippoorwill. I thought about its sadness, and I counted the number of times it could repeat its song without stopping. Once, twenty-six times. An awful lot, I thought.

I didn't hear Penny entering my room. I didn't even hear a step or her breathing until she sat beside me. I didn't say anything. I was determined I wasn't going to talk with her any more than I had to.

CHAPTER TWENTY-SEVEN

"ABOUT COWBIRDS," PENNY SAID.

I was supposed to say, "What about them?" but I didn't.

"Remember how they rode piggyback on Seely Jones's cows? Something else about them. Did you know they don't build nests? The mother cowbird lays her eggs in some other bird's nest, most likely a robin's, when the mother robin is out stretching her wings. And the cowbird is born and brought up by the robins, willy-nilly. I wonder about the mother instinct of the cowbird."

"How about the father instinct?" I asked.

"Both. Do cowbirds think they will botch the job, and so give their offspring the best deal possible by letting someone else do the work? Are they lazy? Is it for the best? Makes you wonder. You think about it, Willie, we're cowbirds. We've been dropped in someone else's nest whether or not anybody wanted it that way. Aunt Addie is like a mother robin, fussing and fretting all the time. Why I miss our mother is she didn't care what we did. Aunt Addie cares all the time, like mothers do. Funny, isn't it, how you have one thing and you don't want it until you get something else."

"That's for the birds," I said.

"Cowbirds. Oh, well. Only thought you would like to know what I was thinking. Know what else? Instead of saying what I did about having a baby, I wished I had said right out that I was *indeed* going to have one, and that it just happened. And after that shattered them, I would tell them I conceived without the help of anybody on earth.

And then I'd tell them I go out nights because I have conversations with the angel Gabriel."

"That's so much junk. You ain't going to have a baby." I didn't say I knew she wasn't. "You like to hurt."

"If they'd laugh, it wouldn't be cruel. Don't you think that's funny?"

"No."

"Well, it's fun thinking," Penny said. "It's that kind of funny. I asked myself how Jesus's mother, Mary, was picked for the job. Why not some other girl? Did she have to send in an application? What were her qualifications other than being a female? I wonder sometimes if I might have those qualifications. If I did, I could give birth to a girl Messiah and even things up. As they say on the old rancho, wouldn't that throw everybody for a loop!"

"Nuts," I said. "That's . . ."

"Dumb," Penny said. "I know, Willie. That's a great word you've discovered."

"If you're going to have a baby, why don't you tell them and be done with it?"

"I'm going to have a baby, Willie. Soon, even you will believe," Penny said, patting her stomach. "I'll then forever know what it is like for Hilda."

Again I didn't tell her I knew the score, but I hinted. "You're faking. You wouldn't know."

"Oh, yes, I would. Morning sickness for one thing, missing my period for another, and pickles and sauerkraut."

"Kiss my razz. I bet you never had it yet," I sneered. I meant going all the way.

Penny understood. "You'll have to talk to the angel Gabriel about that," she parried.

"Stupid."

"Not so. I've thought it all out this very minute. I'm going to have it, and so I might as well have it with hoopla and fanfare. But that's not what I came to talk about. I've been finding out things. At least I think I have. Want a couple of for instances?"

I nodded. The nod didn't say much.

"Mostly I've been talking to Mr. Nason. About the mill."

"And about what he said to me?" I was interested.

"Some weird things have been going on. Mr. Elisha Woodbury, no less, had been making visits to Aunt Harriet before she died."

"So what, they were relatives."

"Let me finish. Mr. Nason got it straight from the horse's mouth that Mr. Woodbury was trying to get Aunt Harriet to sell her share of the mill, but she wasn't budging without Uncle Lambot's say-so, because the agreement was when he sold it that he would have the right to buy it back. Mr. Woodbury told Mr. Nason that he wanted Aunt Harriet to sell so that he could force the sale of the mill so the money could be used to pay the bank back what the mill owed. Mr. Nason said he thought the real reason was that Mr. Woodbury likes to get his grubby greasy hands on anything he can, and that's one reason why he stopped by the farm, to buy the farm because it was next to Aunt Harriet's property, and he figured some day to own all of it, hook or crook. Mr. Nason didn't think much of him, but sometimes they would have some wine for old times' sake. And sometimes Mr. Woodbury would stop for something else. Know what for?"

"Nope."

"Well, he didn't exactly say, and so it's what you think. You know where Mr. Woodbury used to work when he was young?"

The general store. I remembered. I told her what I heard the men say in the clubroom when she went to New York. She didn't enjoy hearing it from me. She continued as if I had said nothing.

"Guess who else worked there, part-time, because she was related to Mr. Petersen, the owner? Mrs. Nason, when she was a girl. She dropped out of high school, and she worked there before she was married. There's a lot of story stuff there."

"So?"

"So I think Mr. Woodbury used to come to the Nason farm to see Mrs. Nason."

"So what?"

"Maybe nothing, maybe something. And I think he may have had his eye on Hilda. You think about it, and what Mr. Nason told you, and it all fits. Hilda said she did what she did for money."

"Mr. Woodbury's too old."

"Never too young or too old, according to the song. Mr. Nason said he told Mr. Woodbury if he pushed him too much to sell, he would let Mr. Woodbury know he wouldn't sell but just the same Mr. Woodbury would pay for it. So figure it out, Willie."

"I don't get it."

"It more or less fits. You know Mr. Nason. He's stubborn and he's not dumb. Can be drowning in his wine, but he'll not cross the borderline to complete mental collapse. But that's not all that fits. I took some flowers from the garden to Mrs. Jones and she told me I was beautiful inside and out to do that. She said she might think about living a bit longer because of me. What do you think of that?"

"What's that got to do with Mr. Woodbury?"

"I thought I'd toss that in. She told me Uncle Lambot found out about Sam Brown's dealing by going through his papers after his death. And it had something to do with Mr. Woodbury because Uncle Lambot came down to see her husband to help him borrow money from other sources, even Mr. Jones, so he wouldn't have to deal any more with Mr. Woodbury and the bank."

My mind was in a muddle, and I didn't really care to know more. "I'm tired, and I want to go to bed."

"Oh, but that's not all. I didn't tell Mrs. Jones that I already knew something about that because Uncle Lambot got to talk to my dear sweet rich Aunt Charity about a loan. It seems that Uncle Lambot has been all over the place. What do you think of that?"

"I told you I'm tired."

"And Aunt Addie's going to hold a meeting of the Friday Club to discuss the financial plight of the mill and see what the club members can do. Doesn't that beat all? Doesn't that intrigue you?"

"No."

"Willie, you don't watch it, you'll become another Mr. Nason."

"Leave me be."

"O.K., O.K., I'm beginning to put a puzzle together faster than somebody can add pieces to it, and some day I may finish it. If you don't want to help . . ." Penny went to the door, but before she left, she gave me something more to keep me from sleeping. "I have to tell them soon, Willie."

"See if I care."

"I think I'll tell Mrs. Jones first. She's sweet, but gullible and most susceptible to believing me. If I tell her I have conceived without the help of a male, she'll believe, and she will think it's fate that I told her first, and when she goes to heaven soon to meet God, she can tell Him I told her first. And then I'll tell Aunt Charity, as she will give me advice on how to handle the situation, and then . . ."

"Razzmatazz," I said.

The next morning I went wherever she wasn't. By ten I was out mowing the lawn. I wasn't keen about it, as it was hot and muggy, but at least when I was pushing the mower, Penny wasn't likely to bother me.

A kid on a bicycle stopped and asked for a drink of water. I took him into the kitchen and Aunt Addie recognized him as one of the Riley boys whose father had recently died from a heart attack. She fixed some lemonade and found some fresh cookies I didn't know she had, found out his name was Richard, said nice things about his father and mother, and Richard thanked Aunt Addie for all the food she had sent to the house, which made me remember what Sadie had said about clothes at Christmas. When Richard asked if I had a bicycle, I looked at Aunt Addie, and she said, "Be careful, Willie, and be home in time for lunch." She didn't say not to go here and not to go there, and so we up and went.

We rode all morning and it was great, and when we got back to the farm and Richard Riley was about to leave, Aunt Addie invited him to lunch, and she had enough food for an army. I don't know where it came from, but there it was.

After lunch, Aunt Addie said, "Why don't you two go for a swim? Not right away though. You have to wait an hour, so you won't get cramps." I could hardly believe it, and wondered how Penny would mess it up if she were there. Richard said no, that he had to peddle the weekly newspaper that afternoon, but how about tomorrow.

When Richard went, Aunt Addie said, "Would you like to help me polish the silver?" And before you knew it, we had it all from the dining room into the kitchen, both of us sitting on stools at the counter and polishing away. Yesterday I think I would have minded, but today I didn't at all.

"Don't you get tired of polishing?" I asked.

"Sometimes, but if I weren't doing this, I'd be doing something else. I play games. I like to see how much I can accomplish in a day. When I do the silver, I like to see how I can do it better and faster than I've done it before. See how I've laid it all out, and how I've got the extra cloths ready, and the hot water. You can't believe how long it took when I first did it." Then she changed the subject. "Did you have a nice time today?"

"Uh-huh. He wants me to come to his house."

"Richard Riley is a nice boy. I'm glad you've found someone your own age. It's not easy, living out in the country." She paused. "It's not been an easy summer. Maybe next week when school starts . . ."

I knew she meant Penny, and somehow she knew I knew without my saying it.

"Sometimes I don't know what to do, William. The Lord knows I've tried. It's not easy, when you don't start right from the beginning with children. Right from the day they are born."

"I'm not complaining."

"Thank you, William. I needed that."

"The thing you have to do with Penny is don't do anything," I said.

Aunt Addie smiled, raising an eyebrow at the same time, seemingly impressed that I was old enough to say something like that. "I suppose so," she said. "Your Uncle Lambot tells me we'll survive, but I wonder sometimes, what with the mill and all. Some days I question what God has us do, and I don't find many answers."

"That's what Penny keeps telling me. She doesn't find many answers, but she keeps trying," I said.

"Yes, how well I know," Aunt Addie said.

"I guess you can't ask Uncle Lambot for answers."

She smiled again, at my little joke. "During the winter sometimes I think he won't talk in order to punish me. He had rheumatic fever when he was a young man, and a doting older sister to take care of him, and maybe if it had been otherwise, he would be married and raising his own family and . . ." She stopped, as if maybe she was talking too much, and asked if I minded. I told her no, but she hardly heard because she had glanced out the window and saw Mr. Woodbury. "I wonder what he's up to now," she said, an unfriendly scowl crimping her forehead.

I looked out, too, and there was Mr. Woodbury getting out of his car and getting into Uncle Lambot's Packard, along with Uncle Lambot, who had suddenly appeared from nowhere. They sat for a moment or two and then drove off. Aunt Addie wearily shook her head. "I don't know," she said. "I don't know. Never lose trust, William, never give it up. There's not much left if you do." That's all she said about Mr. Woodbury, and she returned to Uncle Lambot. "He doesn't talk when he's got problems, and these days he has problems all the time. Right now he's got the mill and the mess Sam Brown left it in. But he is determined to keep it here and get it rolling again. A new man came today, a Mr. O'Connor, who managed a big mill in Fall River. Lambot had to pay him a bonus in advance, and your Uncle Lambot's had to go about borrowing for him, for everything, even postage stamps. It's not been easy. Lambot has been working like the devil himself all summer to swing an army contract for some blankets, and Mr. O'Connor says he'll all but guarantee we'll get it soon. We keep hoping. I know it's a sin to say it, but Sam Brown doing what he did to himself, maybe it was a blessing. He was deeper into the mill than any of us ever believed."

Aunt Addie picked up a silver bowl to polish. It was a heavy piece, a soup tureen, embellished with all kinds of curlicues, and it had a lid that was shaped like a helmet. "Look at the date, William, 1682. Made long before Paul Revere got started. It's extremely valuable, and I get a guilty conscience every time I look at it. We could sell it, I suppose, and the rest, but I can't bring myself to do it." She flicked some hair from her cheek and moved to another subject. Penny flipped from one thing to another in an instant, but unlike Penny, when Aunt Addie did it, she became embarrassed and insecure. "Don't gamble, Willie. Not even with two cents. Especially not with other people's money. That's what Sam Brown did over the years, and of course he lost. And all because of him a lot of people had to skate on thin ice for a long time. Your Uncle Lambot knows a lot about this, and it's making him real sick, and that's why he's not talking. I suspect he'll come around if the mill gets moving."

"We got money," I said.

"Thank you, William. You'll have to tell Uncle Lambot that. He's got some old-fashioned notions about using money belonging to the next generation. It may be he knows it is there as a last resort if all else fails. That's how I feel about the silverware. As long as you have something to hold to, however small, you survive. But your father didn't have so much as he was supposed to have. For one thing, the insurance. He had borrowed on it and he let his payments lapse. For another, he had debts, William, and I expect we'll have to pay them some day."

"I mean we've got money here, Penny and me. We brought it from home."

"I know, William. If you live like I do, you know what's been touched and not been touched, especially if Penny is doing the touching. It's in the Bible, and we shan't touch it. And you might tell your sister for me there's nothing in the attic. She must learn to put things back as they were."

"Are all girls like Penny?"

"In a way."

"Were you? Did you fight with your mother? Like Penny does with you?"

Aunt Addie didn't mind that at all. It was as if I were saying she was a mother and she had a daughter. Even Penny. I think she liked it. "I was very shy, William. There were things I wanted to say, too many things sometimes, but I couldn't find words. I was awfully shy with everybody."

"Did you like our mother? She said you didn't."

"Your mother was a spoiled child and wasn't accustomed to seeing another side of a question. Smart, though, she was a smart woman in her own way. Quick-witted . . ." She stopped, just as if someone had told her to shut up. I waited, but she went on to something else. "Your mother didn't think too much of me. Never did. Can't say I blame her much. I didn't think she was good for your father, and I didn't hide my feelings. Never knew how to do that. She was determined to marry him and show me a thing or two. Your grandmother, though, she got along with her. But they used to say your grandmother got along with anybody. To answer your question, did I fight with mother, I never much thought about it. You don't really remember as much as you think you do. I didn't know too much about mother, her family, what kind of a girl she was, or how she grew up. We didn't ask questions in those days. I didn't talk much with mother. I remember people saying I was not her favorite. It sometimes happens, I guess. Parents give birth sometimes to what they don't expect."

It was a lot she said, and I wondered what she'd think if Penny gave her the word about being pregnant. I also remembered what our mother said to our father during one of their arguments, and

I told Aunt Addie. "I heard mother tell father she didn't expect me, and he said not to blame him. And she told him she didn't expect she was supposed to have Penny forever. She said some funny things sometimes."

"We all do, William, and do . . . I do the best I can. It's not been easy, not easy. The Lord knows I made mistakes, but I don't know how else I would have done it," Aunt Addie confessed, and I didn't know what she was confessing. It didn't much matter as far as I was concerned. She talked with me, a whole act of a play, and I didn't mind listening at all.

When we finished with the silver, Aunt Addie said, "Thank you, William," and I think she meant for listening as well as for helping to clean the silver, which, truth to tell, I didn't do much. I sensed she wanted to be left alone, and I went outdoors. My first notion was to find Penny and tell her a few things, but she was a pain in the neck lately every time I tried to talk with her, and I thought, the hell with her. Besides Richard Riley was coming tomorrow, and with school next week, I had other things to think about. Aunt Addie, too, I had to think about her. I felt nice about her talking to me the way she did, even if I didn't understand all she was saying. She helped the Riley family and I was beginning to guess maybe others, too. I decided I'd go for a walk in the woods and square some of these matters away in my mind before I talked with Penny and let her interminable chatter mix me up all over again.

But that was not to be. Uncle Lambot drove into the yard with Mr. Woodbury, and as soon as he had stopped the Packard, Mr. Woodbury got out, got into his own car, and drove off, and Uncle Lambot headed for his clubroom. He had hardly disappeared from sight when Penny emerged from Aunt Addie's section of the Packard and came running toward me. Her face wore a smile that looked as if it had been snatched from a happy jack-o'-lantern, and she tingled all over with excitement.

"What a ride, what a ride, Willie! You wouldn't believe what I heard!" she squealed.

"That's a fact of life," I replied. "Why tell me if I won't believe?"

She told me anyway. She had been reading in the back seat of the Packard, and by the time she had found a comfortable position, she was sitting on the floor leaning against the seats. She heard Uncle Lambot and Mr. Woodbury coming to the car, and thinking they would pass, she sank to the floor so as not to be noticed. But they got into the car and Uncle Lambot zoomed the Packard out of the driveway before she could catch her breath. So she said.

"There was madness in the front seat, Willie. I could feel the heat. They got real emotional but when they finished, the world was the same as before. I guess. It would have made a great scene in a movie."

I was curious enough, now, to let her talk.

"Uncle Lambot never says much, and Mr. Woodbury talks all the time, but this time before they finished they sort of switched roles. Mr. Woodbury started right in on Uncle Lambot and said he just heard about a new man at the mill, and how come he wasn't informed."

"Mr. O'Connor," I said. "I think that's his name."

That stopped Penny. "How did you know? Why didn't you tell me?"

"Didn't." I let it go at that.

"Oh well, anyway," Penny continued with her own story. "Uncle Lambot told him he didn't see the necessity of telling, and that got Mr. Woodbury all wound up. He said, as a stockholder he ought to know, and the bank had a lot of money tied up in the mill, it needed it, and he guessed he'd have to call it in, with legal action, if necessary. That's when Uncle Lambot quietly blasted him. First he said, 'I found your letters to my brother when I was out in Des Moines, those offering to buy my brother's stock right after my mother died, upping the ante to three times what you claimed it would be worth even if we sold the mill. That's not like you, Elisha. Hard to believe you'd do that.' And just in case Mr. Woodbury was fixing something in his mind to answer that, Uncle Lambot whacked him with another revelation. I swear, Willie, I could feel the heat from Mr.

Woodbury's face when Uncle Lambot said, 'I've been talking with Lem Nason.' Uncle Lambot said Lem told him if he needed money, he'd sell the farm, all but the house and the barn, because Lem didn't need the rest, he'd sell it to most anybody except Elisha Woodbury, and when Uncle Lambot asked him why, Mr. Nason told him. What do you think of that?"

I think I knew what Mr. Nason told Uncle Lambot. "What else?" I asked. I didn't have to urge. Penny was full steam ahead.

"We guessed right, Willie! About it being Mr. Woodbury! In typical fashion, the way he talks sometime that drives you up a wall, Uncle Lambot just sort of let the words ooze out from him, as few as possible. 'He told me who the father was, Elisha,' Uncle Lambot said. He let that sink in and he said he guessed he needed a bit more time on the money deal, but he was sure that Mr. Woodbury wouldn't mind because he knew he would get it all back eventually. Mr. Woodbury's not that dumb that he felt it necessary to dispute Uncle Lambot. He didn't. I guess it comes with knowing one another a long time. Mr. Woodbury didn't come right out and say it, but he confessed. He told Uncle Lambot that if *he* had had to live with Aunt Lucretia, he'd be doing the same thing. 'Suspect so,' Uncle Lambot said, and Mr. Woodbury said, 'Something about the Stone family.' And then he told Uncle Lambot things maybe would have been different if he had married Aunt Harriet, but he wouldn't wish that onto anyone. It was marvelous. By the time they got back to the farm, it was as if nothing had been said. They said, goodbye and take care, like they always did. Smart if you think of it—they both have to go on living in Eastfield. Know what I mean?"

"You mean the Saturday club, the church, and things like that?"

"That's it, and you know what else I was thinking? If Uncle Lambot and Aunt Harriet had got married, they would have made the world's most unlikely, but possibly the world's most lovable couple. I'm going to press Aunt Addie about it until she spills a few beans. At least a bushel or two."

"Why don't you leave her alone?" I said protectively.

As if on cue, a yell shot forth from the veranda. "Penny!"

"Kiss my razz!" Penny hissed.

"I told you this morning I wanted your room picked up and cleaned today! I meant today! I do not want that mess there all year! You come in and stay in the house until it is done! Do you hear me?"

"That's why I don't leave her alone," Penny said. "I think I'll cozy up to her and try out a new whammy on her that I am about to invent. To see if I can't squeeze some information out of my dear Aunt Clammie, and to get her off my back. Tonight is Holmes's last night in Eastfield, and I think I'll just ask my beloved auntie what I should do in case he wants to go all the way. And I'll pause just two seconds and add 'again.' How's that, Willie? Want to come along and see what she says?"

"Aw, kiss my razz, right now," I said.

CHAPTER TWENTY-EIGHT

P ENNY DIDN'T WHAMMY AUNT ADDIE THAT DAY OR THE NEXT, AND when she did several days later toward the end of September, Aunt Addie received her whammy quite accidentally.

Before we knew it, we were in school, liking it and not liking it. I was an eighth-grader and Penny was a junior, and that meant we spent our days in different buildings. I could only imagine how Penny was already acting up all over the place, asking a thousand questions, establishing her own brand of superiority, and otherwise being obnoxious. The separation suited me fine.

At home, there was homework, which I didn't mind doing because

I could be by myself, and my bicycle and Richard Riley, and I pretty much escaped Penny on a day-to-day basis. She was involved in old and new problems of life and more or less ignored me. And I had to admit I missed her. At least I missed the way things were.

My thirteenth birthday arrived on schedule, on September twenty-first. On that day I added a century to my life, but for a few moments at the beginning, it was like old times, Penny being Penny. On that morning, she burst into my room at six-thirty and awoke me with a kiss and a hug, something she had not done for some time. "My truly miraculous brother! A proud, scrumptious happy birthday to you!" she proclaimed. She pulled the summer blanket off my bed, wrapped herself in it, and capered about, singing *Happy Birthday to You*. She pulled my sheet from me, unmindful that I slept in the nude. She mussed my hair. "I'll give you two bits to get your hair cut," she said, "and I'll scoop every lock into a silver box, mark it your thirteenth birthday, and treasure it forever." It was indeed like old times. I wondered, was I dreaming?

"For you today, Willie, dear Willie, I am your obedient servant, your slave, your genie. You may have your desires accomplished. Anything. Your pleasure is mine."

I got out of bed to dress. For the moment I succumbed to the immediate presence. "How about a statue of Ozymandias?" I asked.

"You remembered!" Penny exclaimed with delight. She nudged her nose into my cheek. "Kiss my razzmatazz! Kissing is the best. Kiss Aunt Addie, kiss Uncle Lambot, and most of all, kiss you, my crazy, hot-headed beautiful brother!" She bowed deeply before me. "Tell me your desires, O Aladdin. I shall be your magic lamp for the day."

"Tell the rain to stop," I said. It had been raining for three days, steadily, and all of Eastfield was sick and tired of it.

"Whoooosh! Abracadabra!" Penny sang out, rubbing an imaginary lamp. She went to the window and pulled the curtains. "There!" she said. I looked out and I could see the sun bubbling on the horizon. The skies were low and menacing, leaden in color. You could already feel the sultriness of the heavy weather. But the sun had found an opening, it had peeked at the world, and there was hope.

"What else, my Lord and Master? The lamp works well today. It is full of surprises. How would you like the answers to your math test for today? A new tongue with a motor in it to put into the mouth of Uncle Lambot? Or a box of thumb tacks for Holmes's Plymouth?"

"He's gone," I said.

"Don't I know it!"

"Did you?"

"What?"

"What you said you were going to do?"

Penny evaded a direct answer. "That's a long story. All I know is Holmes is gone, and we shall see what develops," she said, ambiguously, not to tease, but with some bitterness. And she added, "Aunt Charity has gone West for a month. And Aunt Harriet is gone, and Granny Winston, and our parents, Sam Brown, Adam, going, going, gone the way of our little friend Ozy Mandiass!" She tried to make light of it all, but it didn't work.

"Penny, please."

"How about one of Aunt Harriet's stories?"

"Stop."

"Not even from Aunt Harriet herself? All I have to do is rub the lamp."

"Damn it, stop it."

"Sorry, Willie, that wasn't funny, was it? What do you really want?"

"Tell me what I know," I said on impulse. "I want to hear you say it. Tell me it's one of your dizzy tricks. That's what I wish."

"What?"

"Are you pregnant or not?" The truth of the matter was that I no longer knew. Weeks had elapsed since Stan Wynewski un-plugged the toilet, and as far as I knew anything could have happened. Even last night with Holmes.

"Oh, that! It's no joke, Willie. Today is for real. Aunt Addie is real and Uncle Lambot is real and you are real, the wide world is real, but I am one colossal joke."

"Stop fooling. Are you or aren't you?"

"Oh, you mean . . ." Penny rubbed her stomach, finally grasping what was on my mind. "I had forgotten about that!" She rubbed her stomach again as if it were her imaginary lamp. "Whooosh! Abracadabra! No baby! That magic lamp never fails. It is foolproof birth control!"

"Think you're so smart," I said. "I found out right away. I found out you had your period after you told me." It came out at last. It did not surprise at all.

"I'm not kidding now. I'm not kidding myself, Willie."

Penny laughed. I didn't. I missed the pun entirely. "Honest to God, Penny! Are you or aren't you?"

"I thought you just told me you knew. I just said—no baby! So have a happy birthday. Join the mighty world of teenagers."

"You know something? I oughta punch you in the nose. That was a helluva thing to do to me. Suppose I had told Aunt Addie all about it?"

Penny giggled. "Wished you had! That was what I was hoping you would do. Wouldn't that have been something to behold! I think I'll tell her this morning. She's had it much too easy lately. Winter comes, and we'll be in the house even more. That spells trouble ahead, unless we take care of it now."

"How do you think up these things?" I asked with disgust.

"Comes naturally. Like sex, Willie. Would you like to feel my belly to make sure nothing's kicking?" Penny teased.

"I'd like to kick *you,*" I growled. "You think you're so damned smart. You think you're the first one! Well, you aren't. I know some things you don't. I know who had a baby and you don't know about that, and I'll be damned if I tell you."

That sobered Penny immediately. She pulled a bag of curiosity out of the air. "Who?"

"None of your business."

"I can make you tell."

"It's none of your business."

"All I have to do is rub the lamp, and you'll tell me what I want to know. The genie always grants wishes," Penny said, and immediately she whooshed and abracadabraed all over the place.

I suppose you could say it worked, because, after she kept bugging me for the next few minutes, I told her. "I remember what you told me what Adam said about Aunt Harriet having an abortion. That's not the way Mr. Nason told me. He told me all about Uncle Lambot and Aunt Harriet having a fling way back when, and how she got knocked up and went away and got rid of what she had, and all this had to do with Uncle Lambot and Aunt Addie not wanting to talk." I didn't expect it to come out that way, but it did. I hadn't wanted to tell her, because telling would be making it a reality, and it was the kind of reality that could dampen fond memories, but I blurted it out all the same. Maybe to hurt her, I don't know. Maybe to stop the nonsense about babies once and for all.

Penny was hurt. "You didn't tell me. Why?"

"Because you're such a . . . because I didn't, that's why."

"And Mr. Nason didn't tell me either. Why?"

"Why ask me? Ask him. Maybe he didn't remember. Maybe he didn't even remember you."

Penny dropped the subject of not knowing. "Uncle Lambot, of all people! And I had thought maybe it was a nobody who did it to Aunt Harriet. Not even Sam Brown. Just a mistake, and Aunt Harriet didn't want to pay for it all her life."

"Maybe it's not true. Maybe, if it is, it wasn't Uncle Lambot. Maybe Mr. Nason was making it up."

"Maybe—but I got a hunch . . . Did he say she had an abortion?"

"I don't think so. He said she went away and got rid of it."

Penny thought about it for a moment. "I asked Mr. Nason, after what Adam told me. He told me Aunt Harriet had a baby," Penny admitted, "but he didn't tell me about Uncle Lambot."

"How come you didn't tell *me* that?"

"Sorry. Chalk one up. Because it put my head into a whirl. Trying to fit some pieces together. Time to dream about it. Time to wonder, if she had a baby, how, who, what. And where that baby would be now. Suddenly Uncle Lambot enters the picture. Whew!"

"Suppose they didn't."

"Suppose they did. And suppose I might be that baby! Did you think of that, Willie? If she went away, like Mr. Nason said, she could have gone somewhere to have a baby just as easy as to have an abortion. The question is, *when* did she go away? It's been on my mind. You know how close and special I've always felt to Aunt Harriet. And I know I'm special to Uncle Lambot since that day he kissed me. Know something?" Penny said, as if to herself. "I always wanted Aunt Harriet to be my mother in the worst way, never mind who the father was. Another part of me didn't want to know ever. Know why?"

Penny sidled up to me and got cozy. "Because I love *you,* Willie, that's why. I love our relationship, you being, as we like to say, my older brother, and me, your kid sister. I think I could have filched an answer out of Uncle Lambot or Aunt Addie if I had put the question directly to them, for surely they must know one way or another, but I have not been able to do that. And the reason is simple. If I found out that's the way it was, then we would not be . . . know what I mean?"

Tears came.

"Cry me a river," Penny said. "We have had some elegantly beautiful tearful times this summer, and I don't suppose we'll have many more, because you are entering manhood," Penny said. "And that's sad. About not crying I mean." Our talk was getting heavy. Even Penny felt that, and she searched for some humor for relief. "I talk like Aunt Harriet. I do nutty things like she did. Do you think I look like her?"

"Like Uncle Lambot. You're like him, except for talking."

Penny thought that funny. I didn't. Aunt Addie called up the stairs from the kitchen. "I'm going to breakfast," I said.

"Wait. One more minute."

"What?"

"So Granny took me west to rear. At least to keep me until they decided what to do with me. That's why our mother didn't care two cents for me. Well, she did and she didn't, but not really. Know what I mean?"

"Mother didn't care two cents for me, either."

"I think maybe she did, Willie. As we grow older, we may have other thoughts about them."

"It is possible," I said, knowing I was already changing my mind about Aunt Addie.

"Get rid of a few secrets, and we'll change what we think even more. This family we have inherited doesn't talk about a lot of things, and money is not by any means the only thing. But speaking of money, know what I found after school the other day?"

"What now?"

"Aunt Harriet lied to us."

"So?" One more charge to demolish the goddess.

"She told us Aunt Addie had lots of money. She hasn't. Maybe she did once, but she hasn't got it now. I think it all went into the mill, along with Uncle Lambot's money. Uncle Lambot and Aunt Addie are fakes, Willie. They haven't any money, but they pretend they do, and everybody thinks they have lots of it. If they pretend one thing, I bet they pretend on others. The more you think, there's something peculiar here, something more than me. They may not even be brother and sister."

"Aw kiss my razz—OK? Just kiss my razz," I said, but I was curious about the money. "How did you find out?"

"Quite by accident. I was looking for the dust pan, and I discovered Aunt Addie's ledger under her mattress."

"Snooping again. That was no accident."

Penny stood corrected. "It was no accident. I snooped. I wish I had known. I wouldn't have said some of the things, had I known. I don't know how that fact of life could have escaped me."

"Easy. You overwork your brain. Doesn't make much difference if they have money or not," I said. "They'd never do anything with it if they had it."

Aunt Addie called again. "Penny, you'll be late for school!" This time her call was louder.

"It's still me, Willie, never you," Penny said. "Maybe I would not have said different things after all. Maybe I would have remained the same regardless of what she has done to save the mill, which we don't really know she did. I'm sorry that I did not confront Aunt Addie with news of a possible pregnancy in the family. Mine. I like drama. That would have been a marvelous moment to remember."

I didn't let her finish. "Crap!" I exploded.

"Crap," Penny repeated.

"You know, I'm beginning to think if you were pregnant, you wouldn't know you were. You're getting dumb enough. You used to be smart, but now you are just plain smart ass. You want to be pregnant, go ahead and be that way. Just don't tell me about it."

"I don't think you understand what I was saying. What I think I meant was . . ." She tossed her hands about, an unaccustomed gesture of indecision. "Hold on for a while longer, my dear brother, and . . ."

I had had enough. "Aw, go to hell, go straight to hell," I told her. Then I opened the door to go downstairs to breakfast.

On the other side was Aunt Addie. We had not been whispering exactly, and she had caught us, but good.

I never saw her looking so tall, so formidable, so forbiddingly starchy white, even though she was wearing her customary dark dress. But she was in command of herself, and there could be no doubt about that. She knew exactly what she would have us do.

"Willie, get your breakfast and get ready for school," she said with a calmness that was difficult to believe. "Penny, go to your room and remain there until I tell you otherwise." Penny stared in defiance, a reflex reaction she had perfected with much practice. Aunt Addie stared back and stared her down. She wasn't about to drop a pie or anything else this time. Penny went to her room.

CHAPTER TWENTY-NINE

N THE KITCHEN, UNCLE LAMBOT WAS DONNING HIS RUBBER RAINCOAT and hip boots. "River's rising from all the rain. Looks to spill over anytime. There's a warning of a hurricane on the radio," he said. "I'm going to the mill, Willie. Not much I can do if there's a flood, but I guess I better be there."

"Can I come?"

"You best stay here today and help your aunt. If the river over-flows into the field, move up into the barn. That's on high ground, and you will be safe there."

"Do I have to?" This was one day I didn't want to be about fending off two feuding woman for love nor money.

"One day out of school won't hurt," Uncle Lambot said. "Tell Aunt Addie I'll be home sometime."

I watched Uncle Lambot as he went to his Packard, moving for-ward as formidable as ever, and I thought if anyone could stop raging waters, he could. Outside, it began to look as though serious trouble was on its way in a hurry. The sun, which Penny had brought forth a few minutes ago with her magic lamp, had gone into hiding. The clouds hugged the earth as if they were towels to dry it, not to wet it. The wind was beginning to churn them as if they were being whipped by a gigantic egg beater. An eerie feeling caused me to shiver.

Aunt Addie came down the stairs in an agitated state. She was running all over the kitchen, picking up a dust cloth and dusting a mirror on the wall, stirring the oatmeal on the stove, kneading her hands, and looking uncertainly out the window. Muttering, "I don't know, I don't know. I just don't know."

Oddly, her actions did not give me discomfort. And I thought she might be asking for something, not just mumbling. "You have to tell her, Aunt Addie," I said.

Aunt Addie stopped whatever she was doing. She stared vacantly, her hands massaging her cheeks slightly. "Tell her?"

"About Aunt Harriet and Uncle Lambot. We both know. We found out. We're old enough."

"Yes," she said. "Yes." She straightened up and did a rare thing for Aunt Addie. She faced the small mirror she had just dusted. She smoothed her hair with her hands and fluffed her face a bit as if to remove wrinkles. She shook slightly and shivered as if to get control of herself. Taking a deep breath, but doing it calmly, she told me to get Penny.

Penny came down the stairs, not as a penitent, but nevertheless with some contriteness and some apprehension. She did not have to wait long to discover what Aunt Addie wanted her for. Aunt Addie was not one for wasting time for formalities or anything else. Assuming that Penny would know what it was all about soon enough, she made no introduction and waded into the heart of the matter, hesitantly at first, but once she got going, she ticked off parts of a speech as if she had rehearsed it all, and I suspect she might have done that a hundred times along the line. She sounded as she did when we were cleaning silver together.

"We did what we did because that's the way we are. Your Uncle and I are not inclined to spell out our troubles to others. We are inclined to take care of them ourselves as best we know how. It may not be the best way, but somehow we've managed. Everything we did at the time seemed for the best, and perhaps it was even the right thing to do. In time what we did became an inseparable part of our lives, and it is quite possible that we believed that we did right," Aunt Addie offered, more out of relief than as apology. I thought she was winding up a bit like Penny did sometimes, but she was not that experienced, and when she got going, you had to fill in gaps, the same as when she told me about the fire.

"It's the way we wanted it, the three of us. Harriet had a crush on Lambot as long as anyone's memory all through high school and beyond. There were no two ways about that. Lambot was not the marrying kind, any more than I was, or am. I suppose there's no accounting for it, but sometimes . . ." Here she groped for words, and one couldn't tell whether or not it was because of faulty memory, bitterness, or still that desire for privacy of the past. Then she seemed to forget what she was saying, and commenced anew. "Somehow we grew up with our notions, and time passed before we could change them. I guess you might say Aunt Harriet was stuck with her mother, and Lambot was stuck with the mill. And with me. They kept on seeing each other, but seemingly not doing anything with it, except tiring of a relationship they had both outgrown. Lambot may complain all he wants about the way I keep house, but he could not have stood Harriet's homemaking, and I think he knew and knows that.

"What other reasons of a personal nature?" Aunt Addie questioned as if talking to herself. "I don't know. I did not think it my place to ask. And then it happened. Aunt Harriet was going to have a baby, and nobody was pleased. Lambot had been very sick as a young man with the fever, and he thought of himself as partially an invalid, not ready to take on the responsibilities of marriage. Father was not a financial wizard, and—well, he was unstable, as you know. There were business entanglements that weighed heavily on Lambot. He was not in love; I knew he wasn't. He asked me for help. I gave it because I didn't want him to get married to Harriet, either. It is easy for me to say that now, because I knew it wouldn't work. But . . . other reasons . . . I knew what I would be. I was a Winston, born so, and so I would remain. When you get older, I hope you will understand."

"We're quite capable of that," Penny affirmed, but Aunt Addie was lost in her own reveries and did not seem to take notice.

"Turned out Lambot didn't need much help. I wasted no time in going to Harriet. She didn't want to marry Lambot. She out and out told me that Lambot was a true blue friend, and one she would need all her life, but he didn't know the first thing about being romantic, and I suspect she was right about that. Despite what happened, Lambot was very shy, so much so, I wondered sometimes if it did indeed happen with him or someone else. Harriet told me the traditional domestic scene was not her cup of tea. She said she'd make a lousy wife, a lousy homemaker, a lousy mother—lousy was *her* word, and I remember her saying it as clearly as if she just said it moments ago. She had just got rid of the burden of caring for her mother, she had to do something with Adam, she was in her mid-thirties, and she and Sam Brown—it was no secret that they had been seeing one another . . ."

Aunt Addie looked toward the window and noted the gloom as if for the first time that morning. The darkness caused by low-hanging clouds startled her, and so did the water. "Goodness, I hadn't realized. The Wampanaug is overflowing into the field, and it is still raining."

I went to the window to see. The field was already becoming a lake. I looked at the boat, and wondered, if the water got to it, whether it would float away. "Uncle Lambot went to the mill," I said. "He said there's going to be a hurricane, and I should stay home."

"Yes, yes," Aunt Addie said. She moved to the sink and puttered, acting again as if the outside did not exist.

"They were having an affair," Penny said. "Sam and Aunt Harriet. We found out. Maybe Sam Brown was my father."

"An affair with Sam Brown and the Lord only knows who else," Aunt Addie admitted, as way of explanation, but not as fault-finding. "Harriet was, well, she was a decent, concerned human being. She wouldn't hurt a flea if she could help it, and she was as honest as the day is long. I believed her, and so did Lambot. Harriet liked to make people happy, always. A bit lazy, but she liked happy people. Didn't much matter how she made them happy. About herself, I don't know—I couldn't be bothered. Sometimes I wished I could."

The main thrust of her speech was completed. Was she going to make a wish that she might have been more like Aunt Harriet? Or was she simply going to admit that she should have handled it differently, and that she could have done so? The possible answers were forever lost because Penny was putting herself into the story. "Where was I born?" she asked.

"New York. A private hospital. It was all done quietly. That's the way it was done then. Aunt Harriet liked the city."

"I knew it," Penny said. "I knew there was something other than just plain old New York that keeps pulling me toward it."

Aunt Addie smiled. "Possibly. But you didn't stay long. My mother took you to Des Moines. She had many reasons for wanting to go, not the least of which was Father, and Des Moines was a chance to escape the past, but I have no intention of reviving my memory of them. We did not intend that should be a permanent visit. We thought of adoption. We even thought Aunt Harriet might marry Sam and—Aunt Harriet had some bad habits, I need not tell you that—and there was my brother who would have to live next door all his life. Your grandmother fell in love with you as a baby and was quite content about the arrangement, and her other arrangement . . ."

"We know all about that one," Penny said. "We grew up with it, and it didn't bother us at all."

"Yes," Aunt Addie replied somewhat forlornly. "I often thought Mother might have figured you to be the daughter I wasn't. One that would grow to a beautiful woman, not a plain Jane."

Deep down Penny never considered herself a raving beauty, and that struck a note of sympathy in her. "I heard you were a beautiful girl. Mrs. Jones told me the other day," Penny said. "Willie and I think you still are."

Aunt Addie smiled wanly; otherwise she evaded the compliment. "How's the storm, William?"

"It's getting worse," I said. "The tree with the blue jay's nest is almost bent to the ground, and the water is almost up to the boat. Wow!"

Aunt Addie came to the window again. "May have to move to the barn. We better start getting things, just in case," She seemed relieved that the storm was getting big enough to force memory aside. Penny, however, was not ready to relinquish her hold.

"Granny Winston fell in love with someone else. I was then merely a convenient excuse for her to remain in Des Moines?"

"In our family, we are not inclined to conjecture, when it comes to sinning. Maybe it's not for the best, but we don't like to rock boats. That may have something to do with my reticence in telling. I should have told you sooner. I did not mean—I had to do what I did . . . because . . . that's the way I am."

"Speaking of boats, the water *is* up to our boat," I said. "I gotta go out."

"No, Willie," Aunt Addie said, and suddenly she was old Aunt Addie, all business. "We must get to work. I need your help. You and Penny." She turned toward Penny, but she was gone. Aunt Addie went to the stairs to call her, but she thought better of it.

"She has to think," I said.

"Yes. There are new relationships."

But Penny was back in a moment. She went directly to Aunt Addie and kissed her. For once, Penny didn't have a thing to say.

She might have said something if a flying branch hadn't slammed into the side of the house.

"Penny," Aunt Addie said, and that was all, for the outside was flinging itself upon us, but you knew she wanted that kiss, because even with an emergency pending, she took time to put her arm about Penny, shyly, and when Penny didn't move away, but leaned against Aunt Addie, I figured maybe Penny had been waiting for *that* for a long time.

"Uncle Lambot, then, is my father?" Penny asked plaintively. She looked at Aunt Addie, as if to ask, why didn't you tell?

Aunt Addie commenced to busy herself. "You learn to live with what you do. For their own reasons, all that knew, even if not satisfied, accepted the situation. After a while—to change that—you have to live with some things."

"You mean when people would find out. Like everybody in Eastfield?"

"Aunt Addie, it's getting worse," I said.

Aunt Addie nodded. She was already packing canned food and bread and butter and milk into cartons. Enough for all of Eastfield. "Penny, get the hamper from the bathroom and fill it with blankets from the linen closet. If we have to move in a hurry, I want to be ready. Hope and pray we don't have to leave the house, but just in case."

Penny started for the stairs, but she was in no hurry. "Uncle Lambot," she mused. "Guess what? When he comes back I can call him—I think I'll call him Father Uncle Lambot. Or should I call him Uncle Lambot Father? What do you think?"

"We can talk about that later. Right now, hurry," Aunt Addie prodded, and even with all that was going on, I couldn't help but notice that the edge had gone from Aunt Addie's voice, and she was asking, not demanding. I looked to Penny to see her reaction, but she was running to the window. I followed to see what for.

A truck drove into the yard. "Seely Jones," I said. "Somebody's with him."

"Mrs. Jones," Penny noted.

Seely Jones helped his wife from the truck, and brought her as quickly as he could up the veranda stairs where we had the door open for him. They were both soaked. Mrs. Jones looked hardly alive, and Seely Jones was breathless, but he wasted no time. "Addie, sorry to barge in on you, but I was to take my wife to the hospital for some tests, but the road is already washed out down by the bridge, and I have to leave Minnie here if you don't mind. I couldn't leave her alone. No tellin' what might happen, and I have to round up the dozen or so cows down in the Nason field. Got the others up into high ground last night and this morning, and it's a good thing I did." Seely Jones looked at me. "Willie, do you know the paths through the woods?"

I did, of course. He meant those going to Adam's and to Aunt Harriet's. I nodded yes.

"I haven't been there for so long, and I'm not sure I could find my way in this storm. Addie, could I use William? I'll need some help with the cows."

We were all now fully aware that it was not going to be any old rainy day, and Aunt Addie wasted no words. "There's some boots on the cellar stairs and a rain hat. Your raincoat's in the back hall," she said in reply.

"The Nasons," Penny said. "If the cows aren't safe across the road from their house, then the Nasons . . ."

"No, Penny, you stay here. Mrs. Jones may need a good nurse, and I'm not good at that sort of thing," Aunt Addie said. "Willie can find out about the Nasons."

Obviously that was meant as an invitation if it were needed. But Seely Jones said we had to get moving, and we moved. I didn't even have time to note Penny's reaction to what Aunt Addie said. It must have been something to behold!

It wasn't easy outside, with the high winds pushing us and the rains pounding. We couldn't go by way of the pool, or Adam's, for both were lost under water. But there was a path above the barn that curved until it hit into the path to Aunt Harriet's by the apple tree, and we took it.

Seely Jones carried a lot of beef on him, and once he had to stop and catch his breath.

"Suppose the cows won't come? Suppose they are scared?" I asked.

"You know how much a cow is worth? Ten cows are worth a lot! They'll come all right, whether they want to or not," and that got him going again.

We didn't have to go far, for just beyond the apple tree, we saw them coming toward us up the path. They were not alone. The Nasons—Pearl, Lem and Hilda—hardly clothed for the weather and soggy wet, were behind them, prodding them along.

Seely Jones ran to them. "Thanks, Lem, thanks," he shouted with relief.

"Not much else we could do," Lem Nason said, panting. "Other way, the bridge is out. Saw it go from the barn." He looked oddly at me for a second or two, just long enough for me to put a question in my head, and then he turned off. "Looks like our house is next, and so we had to come along. The cows got out of pasture and we only now got them together. Figured you'd want them, and figured maybe we could get to your place."

"Sure, sure, no trouble," Seely Jones invited.

And then Lem Nason said something that only Seely Jones could hear, and they both glanced at me, guilty-like, I thought, as if I'd done something.

We had not really stopped. There was no time to lose, and Seely Jones and I had already joined the Nasons and were moving the cows along. It was not easy work. "Doubt if we make it. It looks like it's going to get worse."

I remembered the invitation then. "Aunt Addie says for you to come with us. It will be safe in the barn," I said.

"The cows, too," Seely Jones said.

"Sure," I said. And despite all the commotion, and the turbulence that was already devastating the landscape, something was clicking in my head, something was putting bits of information together to give me a message other than what I had received.

I was walking between Mr. and Mrs. Nason, and for no reason that I can remember, I said, "The bridge. What happened?" Because of the howling winds, I had to shout, and so they both heard me. Mr. Nason went after a cow that didn't want to move, but the way he went, I knew he didn't want to answer. Mrs. Nason put her wet arm about me, in a motherly way, and it was not like her to do that, especially in the wind and the rain, and both of us dripping, and everybody wanting to move ahead.

Suddenly I knew. I don't what gave me the final clue, but I knew what it was.

I turned and started running the other way. I remember shouting, "Don't tell Penny," and I heard Seely Jones shout, "Willie! No, Willie!" but I don't remember anything else about my run, until I got to the Nasons, where I was stopped by rising and surging waters, and saw how the road beyond had been completely wiped out. Penny and I had talked about the rickety bridge, and I didn't need a search team to tell me what had happened to it. But I knew I had to see it for myself and there was no two ways about that.

Remembering that Mr. Nason had seen the bridge from the barn, I ran along the side of the house as best I could and up to the cement wall of the old manure pit. I could hardly see because of the rain and the mist, but every few seconds or so the wind would whoosh the rain aside as if it were opening curtains, and once it lasted long enough. One look was all I needed.

One end of the bridge was dangling into the water from its mooring on the bank. And, dangling off the bridge, caught and stuck, was the Packard. That car could have been covered with a ton of mud and I would recognize it. But even if I couldn't tell, I knew whose car it had to be. Its rear was sticking up into the storm, as if thumbing its nose, but at what I couldn't fathom, for its front was ducking its head and torso. Uncle Lambot's section was not to be seen.

I stood some moments in awe, looking out at what I could no longer see, and I was rooted to the earth as if I had grown there; no amount of hurricane could move me. I stayed, until a flying branch whacked my face and returned me to consciousness and sent me off and running. What I saw on the way home was a blur of rain and wind. Only later would I be able to recollect the concrete details of the experience. The gaping holes in the Nason roof, the timbers of the charred end being ripped apart, Aunt Harriet's place, the mist and the fallen branches covering it, even the stone steps, making it all look as if it never were, the dead apple tree that was the home of our beloved bluebirds, toppled finally, the field of grass now full of water, and Adam's place no more, and the boat which had been slowly sinking, now covered. And once, even though I was panting and hurting from the driving rain and flying debris, my energies drained, there flashed into my head, an image Penny had created, a picture of a monument to a great king, the mightiest of the mightiest. But I couldn't remember his name.

The world, however fast it was changing with the hurricane, came back into focus with sight of the house and barn, the floodwaters lapping the steps of the veranda, but the barn still high and out of harm's way. In front of it, I saw the cows—Mr. Nason and Seely Jones had partially opened the big barn door and were herding them inside. It must have taken them some time, and I must have remained staring at the bridge longer than I had realized.

"Willie?" Seely Jones asked.

I barely nodded. I knew the question and he knew my answer. He put his hand on my shoulder and that meant a lot. Penny poked her head out of the clubroom and we both saw her. "We'll work it out," Seely Jones said, and I told him, "Yeah."

There was a hurricane inside Uncle Lambot's clubroom that had no identity with the one outside. It was Aunt Addie. She was doing what she always wanted to do even if she didn't know it, managing as if she had prepared all her life for the event, with no never-mind for the outside.

When we got the cows in and the door closed, we went into the clubhouse, where there was a fire already going in the stove. Aunt Addie said. "William, you get into some dry clothes first, and then get some dry, clean hay, and bring it in for beds. Looks as though we'll be here for some time. And then you help Mr. Jones with the cows, milking, or whatever."

Aunt Addie had brought in a truckload of goods from the house, and how she did it and kept things dry, I'll never know. There were not only dry clothes for me, but for Seely Jones, the Nasons, and half of Eastfield if it decided to show. Penny working with Aunt Addie, and doing it as if she had been born to the practice, would have been, in a quieter time, a sight to behold. It was a kind of miracle, as were other happenings in the barn that day. A bed and other comforts had been prepared for Mrs. Jones, but instead of remaining an invalid, she decided to join the crew and took it upon herself to take care of all the wet clothing, and as the day wore on you could almost see life returning to her. I wondered about Mr. Nason, and if maybe I should tell Aunt Addie where Uncle Lambot kept some liquor just in case. But he didn't seem to need it, and every so often you could see him talking with his wife. Not much, but as much as they needed to talk, and a couple of times I noticed a smile hop from one face to another. It was nice to see and I could not bring myself to tell them what the wind was doing to their home, even though they asked. Aunt Addie talked with them and gave them things to do, and you would hardly believe she had ever had disdain for the way they lived. Hilda and Penny worked to-gether, sweeping and dusting, making beds, doing it all like a couple

of school kids on a lark. Or girl scouts at a camporee. Aunt Addie
didn't seem to mind Hilda's being there as far as I could see, and
once she even expressed concern about Hilda working too hard, and
you could tell that had something to do with what Hilda was carrying, because she was a lot bigger now than she had been in
August.

By noon Uncle Lambot's clubroom was unrecognizable, and sometimes we even forgot to note the outside. But the outside was there,
reshaping itself and producing new realities that were crowding into
that tight little isolated island of the barn, and we all knew in one
way or another that we would have to face up to a new world.
Sooner than later. Yet despite all the turmoil, I wondered about
myself, and how it would be when Penny and I came to realize that
we were not brother and sister, but cousins only. I had no cousins
that I knew of, and I didn't know people who had cousins, and so
I had no notion of what it would be like. I knew it would be different, and I did not want it to be. But I didn't think too much about
myself. Mostly I thought of Penny and how it would be when she
found out about Uncle Lambot. I didn't know how to face that, and
I found plenty to do so that I could avoid her.

Sometimes I couldn't keep out of her way. She liked to be in the
center of things, and she was in her glory in our little world. But as
the day wore on, a feeling that something was wrong took hold of
her. "I'm worried about Uncle Lambot. Really worried. I wish he
were here. I can't wait to tell him I know and then give him a huge
hug and a kiss that will land me sky high on cloud ninety-nine." In
the afternoon, when the hurricane was at its height, and we wondered if the barn would hold, and were worrying about Eastfield and
the Winston Mills at the side of the river, Penny began to ask questions in earnest. She asked Seely Jones what he thought was happening in Eastfield, if the mill would stand, and what Uncle Lambot
could be doing there. Seely Jones was not the most subtle creature
that ever lived, and when he hedged on his answers, and suddenly
decided that storm or no storm he'd better get moving to his own

place to see if it was still standing, Penny couldn't help but smell a mouse. Penny asked Mr. Nason questions about what it was like down his way, and he told Seely Jones he would go along and help him. Aunt Addie knew. Mr. Nason told her, and so did I. She said wait until the storm had calmed because it was easier on the nerves, but she was not good at hiding things. And Penny must have read her face.

Penny went to work on me. "The bridge, Willie. It's gone, and do you remember where we would say it might go some day—to the North Pole?"

I had already thought of that. I remembered.

"That means that Uncle Lambot won't be coming home tonight. Mr. Nason said that if it is as bad as it is here, then it must be worse in Eastfield."

"Yeah," I said.

Penny found a book and tried to get excited about it, but after a minute or two, she closed it and stared out the window.

"Willie?"

"Uh-huh."

"Tell me about the bridge."

"It's gone. I told you that."

"I know. I was thinking about it, and the things we said about it. We weren't so dumb. Makes you wonder."

"Uh-huh."

"Know what I was wondering? I was wondering about Uncle Lambot." Penny was not trying to trap me. I could tell by the way she talked. She was adding up the facts, the way she always did, the facts in the case of Uncle Lambot, the missing evidence.

I walked away. I dared not say anything, lest a tremor in my voice tell her the worst.

She followed me out to the barn. We scratched the noses of a couple of cows. "Maybe I ought to get some toilet paper for them." Neither of us bothered with a smile even.

But Penny didn't hear. "The silences, I have begun to feel them," she said. "Hilda mentioned the bridge, but then she sewed up her mouth. Hilda is not experienced in doing a cover-up. I heard Seely Jones tell Mrs. Jones that it was going to be hard on the kids, and when I asked what kids, they were both like kids themselves caught doing something they shouldn't. The silences are trying to tell me something. As for our dear Aunt Clammie . . ." She tried to laugh, but it didn't work.

"Penny," I started to tell, but I couldn't make it.

Penny took me by the shoulders and faced me about. "Willie, at least say Uncle Lambot will come when he can, or something like that. Say it, Willie. Say that much to me."

"I . . . I . . ." I stuttered to a halt.

"You have something to tell, I know you all too well."

I manufactured a tear or two. I bobbed my head.

"You know?"

I bobbed my head again.

"Then you have to tell me, Willie. You, and no one else. You have to tell me first just as I would have to tell you first. If there is nothing wrong, then look at me and tell me so. Remember crossing the Rubicon?"

"I remember." There were more tears.

"The bridge," Penny said. "Uncle Lambot didn't make it, did he? Tell me all you know, Willie. Don't make me ask the others. Chin up, now."

She raised my head gently. "Now tell me."

I told her then what I had seen, what I believed. Once I got going, it wasn't that bad, and I wished I could have done it earlier.

"Willie, dear Willie," Penny said softly. She held me tenderly, the big sister now with the kid brother, and kissed me. Then she went to Aunt Addie. The two of them nodded, and then the two of them came together and held each other for a moment of quiet affection.

Penny's mood did not last. She went to the window again. She looked as if she were quietly contemplating the storm outside, or perhaps reciting to herself one of her favorite pieces of poetry. But she was, in reality, revving up for an emotional flipflop. To hit us all with a brief, but stinging, Penny Winston whammy.

I could see her clenching her fists, and her shoulders twisted under her sweater. These were signals I had seen before, and I knew she must be biting her lip and smearing her face with a look of grim determination. I started toward her, to defuse her, but it was too late. Suddenly she turned and exploded.

"Damn it! Why wasn't I told? Why could not I have been told about my father? Why could not I have been told yesterday, the day before, or before that? *Why couldn't he have told me? Why did he forever disown me?*" She spit out the words as if each one was a bitter pill, and we were quick to note that she was venting her anger on the man responsible for her being. "What a dirty, rotten trick. I can't believe it. I cannot believe it. How could it happen?"

That was all. It was short, simple, and gripping. Then Penny marched, with that angry swagger of hers, out into the barn.

"Oh my God! The rope!" Aunt Addie exploded. She started after her.

I grabbed her arm. "I helped Uncle Lambot take it down, yesterday."

Aunt Addie paused.

"She'll be all right."

"Yes. Leave her be." Aunt Addie sounded dazed, but she was not. It was as if she had said, "Yes. She is a Winston. She'll make it." And in no time at all, Aunt Addie refurbished her self-control. She was not about to display one iota of weakness in front of our guests. "Take care of the fire, William," she said. "For supper, baked beans and sliced ham. I forgot to bring out the mustard. There's always something." Training took command, and I, for one, didn't mind.

I worried about Penny. She didn't come and she didn't come, and there was no telling what she might be doing. A couple of times I went out into the barn to look for her, but I couldn't find her. I thought maybe she had buried herself in some hay but if I went searching, and she discovered me, I thought that might make her angrier. The second time I looked, I saw that the back door to the barn was open, and it was being slammed by the wind. My first thought was that she had taken the path toward Aunt Harriet's and the Nasons', to see for herself. But when I went to close the door, and saw all the water less than a hundred yards away, my heart sank.

I returned to the clubroom, not knowing what to do. The storm outside abated, but the atmosphere inside was giving no relief. It was one of the bad times of my life.

I was about to tell Aunt Addie about the door, and tell her I was going searching, when suddenly there was a scream, and Penny burst into the clubroom. "Willie! Willie! Come quick!" There wasn't a trace of anger in her face. Her eyes were wide with excitement, and her lips had carved a message of joy.

Another flipflop, but this one I didn't mind. I didn't even wonder why, because I didn't have time. Penny grabbed me and pulled me out of the clubhouse, in and out of the cows in the barn, and to the back door.

"What?" I finally managed to say.

"Wait and see! You won't believe!"

I followed her to the chicken coop, and there inside, in an abandoned egg nest, lay Sheba, Adam's cat. And alongside her, feeding at her teats, were six kittens. In the storm, and all that happened, I had completely forgotten Sheba.

"It's like a miracle," Penny said softly. "Talk about nine lives."

I told her that I had found Sheba, that Uncle Lambot must have missed her, but that I was mad at Penny when I found her and decided to hide her and keep her for my own.

Penny didn't mind. Sheba was there. That's all that mattered. "I bet they are premature. I bet the hurricane did it. Willie, guess what?"

"What?"

"Sheba has a new family. You know what that means?"

"We've got to think up some new names."

"That, but something else. Someday Sheba's cats will grow up, and they will have babies, and the babies will grow up—the thigh bone connected to the hip bone. Know what I mean? Sheba will go on living in the other cats until there are no more. Cats, I mean. The end of time. What do you think of that?"

Now I knew what she was talking about, but I didn't really think too much of it. Penny was still Penny, that was what I was thinking, and it was beautiful. "We better get some food for Sheba," I said.

Penny agreed. "Guess we better go back. Aunt Addie will be worrying."

"Yeah," I said. "Maybe we can find a place for them in the house."

"We'll see to that," Penny said confidently.

When twilight came that night and no relief was forthcoming, we made preparations for a sleep-in. The ropes with the drying clothes on them were rearranged to give us all some privacy. The Nasons had one side of the room, Aunt Addie, Penny, and I another, and Mrs. Jones slept near the stove.

Hilda and her mother buzzed a bit, but not too much, and I wondered how they would make out tomorrow when they had to go home and there was no home.

Mrs. Jones and Aunt Addie had quite a chat about old times, and by bedtime Mrs. Jones was exhausted, and sleep came quickly.

Aunt Addie's corner was quiet. There was no snoring, and I guessed her mind must have been traveling ninety miles a minute, as Penny used to say, already deciding priorities for the hundred things she would have to do in the morning.

I smelled the cows and heard a quiet chewing of cud, and occasional mooing. I supposed we all did, but they could not be moved that night, and so nobody complained. I wondered about the milking, but Seely Jones had said nothing, and I guessed the cows must be betwixt and between something and were kept way down in the Nason pasture because they didn't need milking.

I was aware of Penny, and I was wondering how it would be when all the pieces were put in place and she came to know forever that we did not belong to the same set of parents. I guess I had a lot on my mind because I did not hear or notice her moving in on me, until she was close to me, and snuggling, so she could whisper into my ear.

It was like old times, but at first I was apprehensive. I hoped she wouldn't talk about Uncle Lambot.

After checking out the silence in the other corners of the room, Penny pulled a blanket over our heads and whispered, "About the man I met in New York."

I waited.

"He was for real. I didn't make him up. He wanted to fool around, and I asked him, 'Why?' and he said, 'Why not?,' and I gave him a whole mess of why not's. I was scared, Willie, scared skinny, but I didn't show it and I think he was impressed. We had a good discussion going, and all at once, he said, 'Damn it, I don't feel like it any more,' and so I went, telling him I was late for church and I would pray for him. Once outside I ran back to the hotel and locked myself in and read the Gideon Bible. I didn't pray for him so much as I prayed for myself. What do you think of that?"

I didn't say a thing.

"O.K. then. About Holmes?"

This time I talked. "What?"

"He's my cousin, Willie, and all the time I didn't know it. My mother is his aunt. Was. He didn't know it and I didn't. And Adam. If it's true he was a cousin of Aunt Harriet—my mother—then we are related somehow. And if he came from down South, maybe Holmes knows something about him that I can anticipate finding out. Willie?"

"Uh-huh."

"Holmes and I are only kissing cousins. Know what I mean?"

I guessed.

"And Adam, too. And the rest of them. And I'm not pregnant. Never was. And that's a fact. I'm sorry, Willie, truly I am. I got all mixed up on a lot of things."

I didn't say anything, but when Penny kissed me, and I didn't mind, she knew it was all right.

"The man on the train who wanted to see the sun rise before anybody else, remember?" Penny asked. "Maybe we could go there on the train and see the sun ourselves. With Aunt Addie. Like starting all over again. I guess I won't be calling her dear old Aunt Clammie anymore. She sure said a lot for Aunt Addie, didn't she?"

"A lot."

For a while, then, we said nothing. We listened to the cows and the dripping of rain water. I was thinking about Uncle Lambot, and praying, when Penny whispered, "Remember Pangloss? I read about him on the train. Remember how he said everything is for the best? I guess in the long run you have to make it that way yourself." She heard me crying in the dark. "Willie?"

"Uh-huh."

"I think it's way past nine o'clock, and we didn't hear the train clickety-clack and blow its whistle."

"Maybe it's late."

"No, I think not. We'll not hear it again, and tomorrow we'll find out what kind of people we are."

My nose was running. I sniffled.

"Willie, dear Willie," Penny said as she dried my damp cheeks with her fingers. "Life and all of its parts will never be the same again. Except one very precious thing."

I was supposed to say "What?" but I didn't. Penny responded as if I had.

"I'll always be your kid sister, Willie. Nothing can change that. If I had a thousand brothers, I could not have one better than you."

Penny could not have said a nicer thing at that moment. We put our arms around each other, and that's how we fell asleep, close, as we always were, as we always would be.